DIMMANGALI!
Speak My Name No More!

(A STORY OF THE UNDANBI PEOPLE OF SOUTH-EAST QUEENSLAND)

by

CLARENCE ALFRED DIEFENBACH

A catalogue record for this book is available from the National Library of Australia

Publisher:
ASPG (Australian Self-Publishing Group)
P.O. Box 159, Calwell, ACT Australia 2905
Email: publishaspg@gmail.com
http://www.inspiringpublishers.com

National Library of Australia Cataloguing-in-Publication entry

Author: **Clarence Alfred Diefenbach**

Title: **Dimmangali! Speak My Name No More!:**
(A Story of The Undanbi People of South-East Queensland)

ISBN : 978-1-922792-45-7 (Print)
ISBN : 978-1-922792-46-4 (Hardcover)
ISBN : 978-1-922792-47-1 (eBook)

Dedicated to the Gubbi Gubbi (Kabi Kabi) peoples, whose lands we occupy.

We acknowledge the traditional custodians of Country throughout Australia and their continuing connection to land, culture and community. We pay our respects to elders past, present and emerging.

About the Author

Clarrie Diefenbach was a senior lecturer at Brisbane College of Advanced Education until his retirement in 1987.

He has a Master of Education, the subject of his thesis being *"Student Teachers' Attitudes to Aboriginals"*. He had, for many years, been lecturing in Prejudice and Racism, and been appalled at some of the attitudes he had come across. This thesis was published in 2003 as a book titled *"Reflecting on Racial Attitudes"*.

His attempts to have Indigenous non-matriculated students admitted to Colleges of Advanced Education and Universities for training as primary school teachers was largely instrumental in the decision to admit such students into Townsville Advanced College of Education. He was initially disappointed that they had not been taken into Kelvin Grove campus of BCAE, but accepted the decision because of the greater number of possible students in the north.

Then, after further years of lobbying, he ultimately convinced the people who make such decisions to allow the Kelvin Grove Campus of BCAE to accept non-matriculated Aborigines to be trained as secondary teachers. He was overjoyed at this decision, for it was the first time in the whole of Australia that the powers that be were to admit that Indigenous non-matriculated students could perhaps become secondary school teachers, and he was determined that he would prove that he had been right in his long-held contention that they could.

The College's first intake in 1985 included Chris Sarra, who became NAIDOC's 2016 Person of the Year.

Clarrie dedicated his working life to the championing of Aboriginal causes, even visiting the Aurukun people in Cape York to better understand Aboriginal culture.

He has lived in South-East Queensland his entire life and is committed to both an accurate portrayal of the region's past and an enduring hope for its future.

Introduction

istory in Australia has been told mostly from the viewpoint of the "explorers" and "settlers" – the "pioneers" who "opened" up this vast continent for "civilisation". And, from the point of view of the white "settlers", this is undoubtedly a legitimate viewpoint. But it is important to remember that these histories stem from the philosophical premise that land should be "commercially productive". If a country is not producing "wealth", then it should be made to do so – and so on. In short, the histories have been told from an extremely materialistic point of view.

But there is a view of Australian history that does not stem from such a philosophical standpoint. It belongs to the indigenous people who have been here since the "dream-time" – or, as this story puts it, the "before-time". To these people, the land was not a cow to be milked of its goodness, but rather a spiritual entity that gave life to all – humans and animals and plants. Not only this, but the mighty beings of the time of creation had set down laws that must be obeyed at all times. And to break these laws could bring disaster as the spirits of the land took revenge.

The proponents of this philosophy could not help living each day in harmony with the natural rhythms of the earth. They could not help trying to ensure that the earth remained productive – but their definition of "productivity" was linked very much to the idea of spirituality. For if the spirits of the land were in tune with people and animals and plants, then it followed as a matter of course that all was right with the world.

Such people could not help being "religious". Their whole lives depended on their being in tune with the spirits that gave the land life.

Of course, they were human, and therefore were bound to fail in their efforts. And just as it is not reasonable to expect every materialistic person to be a millionaire, it is also unreasonable to expect that people who approached life from a spiritual standpoint were always obedient to the laws of the spirits. Above all, they were human.

They were highly civilised. Their civilisation might have been different from that of such places as England, but it was nevertheless as sophisticated. Their beliefs regarding the nature of illness and medicine might have been different from those we espouse today, but they were as legitimate.

And they were a proud people. They proclaimed their pride and freedom even in the way they walked. Mrs. Archer once drew the attention of her sons to a naked Aborigine who was walking past their house at Durundur, remarking that they would never see an Englishman hold himself with such pride!

The story told here is a work of fiction, woven round certain historical "facts". These "facts" have been taken mainly from white accounts of the period, but the attempt has been made to present them from the viewpoint of those who were already here when the first white explorers arrived. What is history like when viewed through their eyes? What would they have thought as they saw the "Endeavour" sailing past Fraser Island? How would they have reacted when they saw the first white people on

Bribie Island? How would they have attempted to come to grips with the earth-shattering events as these strange uncivilised beings arrived and destroyed life as they had known it since the beginning of time? What would they do as venereal disease and smallpox decimated their populations? What were their reactions to the massacres, the desecrations of their cemeteries and their sacred places?

Contrary to the opinion of many, there was much trade and social intercourse between the different Aboriginal nations. So Buruda, a "manngur" of the Undanbi, a nation of the area round Caloundra, knows what is going on in Redcliffe, Brisbane, Ipswich and Stradbroke Island. And throughout the story, it is the opinion of Buruda that moves our story along. For Buruda is not only a wise man, but also a mighty hunter and fighter, respected among the nations of south-east Queensland. He it is who first realises that these interlopers are not spirits of their dead returned to live with their old brothers and sisters. He it is who advocates driving these "makaron", these evil spirits, out of the sacred land of the nations.

There is no doubt that the Aborigines of South-East Queensland did all in their power to repel the invaders. Some history books tell us that Lieutenant Miller moved the first settlement from Red Cliff Point to Brisbane because of mosquito trouble. What those books don't tell us is that these mosquitoes carried spears, boomerangs and clubs! The Ningi were not an easy target for the "settlers".

It is the aim of this book to give people – both black and white – enjoyment. After all, that is what a novel should do, for people read to that end. And authors are like actors. They have no reason to exist if they are boring. After reading, the reader should be able to put a book down with a sense of satisfaction at having found something that was diverting.

But there are two other aims it is hoped the book will achieve.

The first is that Aboriginal readers will feel that the story has been told satisfactorily from their point of view. For if that occurs, there is no doubt that they will know that the dignity and integrity of their race have been affirmed, that an approach has been taken that will encourage their children to view their ancestors in a truly positive light. Their children may then learn to walk as proudly as the man pointed out to her children by Mrs. Archer of Durundur.

And the second is that white Australians will also see the original Australians as a people who have as legitimate a place in the scheme of things as whites. They will hopefully also realise that Australian history is full of lamentable events that need to be addressed if true reconciliation between black and white is ever to take place.

Chapter 1

1820: Memories of Flinders in the *Norfolk* in 1799 on Bribie Island, his brother Samuel, and the Sydney Aborigine Bongaree, who accompanied Flinders.

Buruda swung easily along and, as always, the familiarity of the pattern of the bush engendered a deep feeling of peace within him, a sense that all was as it should be and that it would remain so, as of course it must, because the unalterable laws of the Before-Time had to be obeyed. The warbling of kurumbul the magpie, the whispering of buran the wind through the kangaroo grass, the scent of the dibing blossoms in which the small black bees were at work, the whistling of wuruma the sea-eagle as he rose from feeding his young in his nest in a tall dead tree – all these were evidence of a oneness of spirit, a feeling that everything fitted perfectly into the land on which he left his tracks.

He could almost feel the throbbing heartbeat of the earth beneath his feet. His own heart swelled, a chant rising unbidden to his lips, and he sang quietly of the beauty of the spirit-land from which he and all beings in this Undanbi country had sprung.

Almost unconsciously he noted a number of kangaroo tracks on the ground, and recognised instantly that they were a family he knew well. A small new track among the more familiar ones caught his eye, and he saw that a new joey had made its appearance, so there were now the original two twos and another one in the little band. He took a little time to commit to memory some of the distinctive features of the small track, for, while the joey would grow and change, there were some things about the track that would remain with it while it lived. For Buruda knew that, while the earth had uncountable ways of showing the passage of creatures across its surface, to each creature it allotted a distinct and separate mark, so that all who knew the secret were able to read the story of animal movements over the land, even though these movements might have occurred many days before.

Once more he settled into the distance-eating stride that would bring him to the main camp of his people in plenty of time for the evening meal. Nor was he hampered by the paraphernalia he carried, though he was carrying more weapons than he would if he had been simply going on a hunting expedition. His fighting boomerang – the non-returning kind – hung suspended from his hair-belt. As a signal to the Nalbo, from whose land he was returning, he had painted it white as a sign of peace before leaving on his journey almost a moon ago. In his left hand he carried three heavy spears of ironbark, their sharp points blackened and hardened over the fire. In a possum-fur rug suspended from his shoulders reposed his heavy studded club which had often stood him in good stead in fights at close quarters. Close to it was the shield of soft wood which was used to parry blows from an opponent's club and which also served as a pillow at night. Also in the rug was the sharp-pointed throwing-club with which he could easily split an opponent's shield, and which he could throw with equal dexterity using either hand. And the narrow hardwood shield used to ward off spear and throwing club added its weight to the other weapons in the rug.

His knife of razor-sharp quartz attached to its handle by ironwood gum lay snugly in the dhilla which, suspended from his neck, nestled under his left arm. The knife was the slashing weapon used at the end of a fight, when opponents battled it out holding each other close with one arm, all other weapons having been discarded.

It did not strike him as incongruous that he was so heavily armed, even though he had been on a peaceful mission. No bu-ul in his right mind would ever travel out of his own country with less.

He smiled to himself as he felt the weight of the fur rug and recalled how hard he'd had to bargain for it. Normally a possum-fur rug could be got from the Nalbo people for a little white clay which could be found quite easily among the soft black rock on the shore opposite the northern end of Yarun, and he had therefore taken plenty with him. But for this rug he'd had to add some eagle feathers and two strings of shell beads before its owner would part with it. Not that he really blamed old Yerrawun, who had been loath to seal the bargain. It was one of the finest rugs he had ever seen, and the seams where she had sewn the skins together with kangaroo sinews were almost invisible.

His own possum rug he had left hanging up back at the home camp near the creek, and he knew it would still be in the same place when he reached there this afternoon. Nor was he worried about the other goods which he had left behind him. His two mula, the fishing nets so carefully worked so that no shame would attach to him if anyone cared to scrutinise them ever so carefully, would be exactly as he had left them. So would his beautifully-ground stone axe with which he could cut out possums from the hollows of the trees where they made their homes, or the hives of the little black bees that made such mouth-watering honey.

The rug on his shoulders was destined for Nerida's parents.

Nerida! Gogindi! He felt a quickening in his loins at the thought of her. She had been his promised wife for many summers. And he'd helped grow her up in the best human tradition, giving her father Wimbur, his mother's brother, the best fish from his catch and supplying him always with the choicest cut from any animal which he had himself killed.

And always Nerida had grown more beautiful. She had been ripe for marriage now for three whole summers, and Buruda had found it hard to curb his impatience. Three summers ago her mother Koppakkin had wound the hair and spider-web round the little finger of Nerida's left hand to ensure that the top two joints would drop off and mark her for all time as one of the coastal women.

Yes, it had been difficult to wait when there was no physical bar to his taking her.

The reason for waiting rested with old Gibberol. Indeed, Nerida's parents had given all sorts of reasons themselves, but somehow they didn't always ring true. No, it was Gibberol who had been working to thwart him.

Almost from the time when Bulangga, his father's brother and therefore one whom he also called father, had begun to teach him to throw a spear, Gibberol had singled out Buruda as a boy who would stand out from the rest of the group, and this despite a hot temper which seemed to land the boy in more fights than would normally be expected. And so it had happened. It was Buruda who had become the greatest hunter of his age cohort.

He it was who had excelled as a kivar, and by the time of the full dhur ceremony he had stood head and shoulders above all – even his teacher Bulangga. Nobody could make a straighter spear or throw it more accurately. He could hurl the boomerang and throwing club with deadly effect from either hand. And no man could use the light or heavy shields as skilfully as he.

So Gibberol had urged him to continue his education and learn more secrets even than had been unfolded to him since his kivar days. Gibberol himself had taken him in hand to teach him the art of healing and how to divine what spirits were to blame for certain conditions. It was Gibberol who had at last taken him to the forbidden place of still waters to discover whether or not the spirits would cause a rippling on the face of the still lagoon. And what elation Buruda had felt when, after only a very short time, he had seen the slightest movement on the surface, as the spirit had come to crown all the effort that had gone into his preparation. The signs had been so favourable that it had come as no surprise to Buruda when he had discovered the magic kundir stone left in the bottom of the pool by Dhakkin the rainbow. This was to be his personal healing-stone, and he always carried it on its string, carefully stowed in the dhilla hung round his neck.

By now Buruda was respected as a fully-fledged doctor – a manngur as powerful almost as Gibberol himself. And the discovery at the pool that he had his own special spirit to aid him in his work of healing had opened up a new era of learning for him. Gibberol had directed that he should travel to other places in order to serve a short apprenticeship with other manngur.

Two moons ago he had gone to the Dhundubari people to learn from old Bomarigo. Here he had also talked long with Nganku, another young doctor of the Dhundubari, and he had spent a whole moon with the two of them, fascinated by the old manngur who had such intimate knowledge of the spirit-land and the abode of the dead.

Of course, Buruda had known quite a lot about the spirit-world before he had visited Bomarigo. Indeed, even children were expected to know a lot about spirits from a very early age.

He had known, for example, that people's spirits sometimes returned after death to live in another guise with those still alive, without bothering to go through the process of rebirth through a woman's womb. Whenever the Dhundubari had met with the Undanbi at festivals, one of the dances often performed dealt with the visit many summers ago of a spirit canoe, and Buruda had always been intrigued by the fact that the Dhundubari had been the nation chosen by the spirits for this visitation, and that Bomarigo himself had been witness to the event.

But on this visit to Bomarigo, the old man had told him more about the visit than he had ever heard before.

"I was young then," Bomarigo had said. "They came in a huge canoe, and this canoe of theirs carried some white stuff on top that appeared as if it was woven from the bark of the dibing tree. This stuff was even whiter than the skin of the spirits. Their skin – as much of it as could be seen – was pale, like the flesh of the dead that has just been roasted. Only one of them was a proper black colour, and I would say he must have been only lately dead and had not been prepared properly for his journey to the spirit-land. All of them were covered up in strange wrappings that resembled the bark of no tree in which we wrap the bones of the dead, so it appears that in the spirit-land they exchange our bark for some other. Some of these wrappings were brightly coloured. Not one of them could speak the language of the living – not

Gubbi, not Wakka, not Dhandai, not Yugara, not Yugum. Instead, they jabbered away in their spirit tongue, seeming anxious that we should understand them."

The old man paused, and Buruda had asked if others still alive had seen them.

"Yes," Nganku had hastened to assure him, "there are lots of people alive who saw this. Yewoo was one, and my own father was there with Bomarigo when they met the spirits. I was only a toddler, and saw this meeting from the safety of the bush. But my own Dimmangali father was there."

Buruda knew that Nganku was referring to Yelyelbah, though of course he didn't say the name of his friend's dead father.

Bomarigo's eyes had appeared as if they were looking at some distant point in time. "Yes," he had continued, "they were strange, these spirits. They didn't seem evil, and yet they did." He had paused once again, and it was obvious to the two listeners that he was turning the contradictions over in his mind, as he had so many times before. "They had magic clubs that made a noise like Mumba the thunder when lightning strikes a nearby tree. And after the thunder, there was hurt. I was only a young manngur then, and I later sucked a stone out of one man's shoulder. And lots of strange things happened. Another of my friends fell down and broke his arm! He had never even looked like doing anything of the like before! Only a very clumsy fighting man would break his arm when he fell on the sand! He said it was as if the magic had thumped into his arm from behind as he was running away!"

The old man had stood up and walked about, remembering the fear and anger that had followed the thunder and the hurt. Once they had gained the shelter of the forest, how the fighting men had fumed, threatening revenge on these wicked spirits!

"Yet no-one knew how!" he had muttered sadly. "How do you fight the wind and the eternal?"

After a short silence, Bomarigo had continued.

Two days after the events he had just related the Ningi at Kuturrumba had found one of their nets missing. But in the place of the net the spirits had left a most marvellous axe of incredible design. The hard stone of which it was made had a hole through which the handle fitted so snugly that it was of unbelievable strength. And the stone itself was of a type never before seen on this earth. It had been ground down to an incredible sharpness, and the edge of it shone like the sun. It was so sharp and hard that it made light work of the hardest task of cutting possums out of their hiding places in the hollow branches, or of getting the sweet honey from the hives of the small black bees.

"Yes," Bomarigo had continued, "they were kind – and yet not kind."

Once again he had paused, and Buruda had asked, "Do the Ningi still have this axe?"

The old man had shaken his head. "I have not seen it for many summers. I think I heard from one of the Ningi that it was traded for a bride of the Yugumbir. But whether this is true or not, I do not know."

"They went into Nalbo land, too," Bomarigo had continued. "Durbai told me that they climbed Beerburrum, but he could never for the life of him work out the reason for this. After all, there was no special food there. And they walked to the bottom of Tibrogargan. Luckily they did not try to climb Beerwah, or they would have been blinded."

Buruda had nodded vehemently. All knew of the dangers of trying to climb the forbidden peak.

"There were other strange things they did on Ningi land," the old man had gone on. "They took one of their special axes and chopped down a pine tree and it fell with a great crash. The people around were more afraid than ever when they saw this. Never had they seen a tree chopped down so easily and quickly."

Again there had been a pause while the story-teller had collected his thoughts. Then he had half muttered, as if to himself, "Besides, it made no sense to the people that a good tree should be chopped down for no apparent reason."

The old man then had looked around him uncomfortably for a short time, his whole demeanour signifying that he himself found it hard to communicate the next bit of information, so outlandish it appeared to be. Then he had collected himself with a shudder, adding softly, "The thing that shocked the Ningi about this wanton act was that the visitors at no time tried to explain to the spirit of the tree why they needed to chop it down! At times these spirits seemed to have no consideration at all – neither for the people they were visiting nor for the spirits of the land upon which they trod!"

Buruda himself had shuddered at the very thought. Surely Bomarigo or the Ningi must have made a mistake! Surely not even returned spirits would act in this fashion! It was unthinkable that anybody would kill a tree without explaining the reason to its spirit!

Then, closing his eyes to regain the thread of his narrative, the old man had gone on. "For some time we wondered how to persuade these spirits to return to the spirit-land." He pointed to the south. "They went away down there for a few days and we thought they had gone. But, no – they came back. They pulled a canoe up on the sand at Taranggir, and we watched them from the safety of the trees. Then we saw them visit Undanbi land,

and they came back from there. We wondered and wondered how to get them to go. It was a puzzle, I can tell you. I am sure you will understand that we were very worried about the dangers of having these spirits around."

The two young manngur had nodded vigorously. They understood only too well the dangers of too close contact with spirits. Every human being was aware of these dangers.

"We were hampered somewhat by our inability to connect these spirits with any of our lately dead," Bomarigo had explained. "But none of our people recognised any of the spirits at all. If we had been able to make such a connection, it is possible that we would have been able to work out where we had gone wrong in the burial ceremonies that had allowed the spirits to return like this, and we might have been able to perform the ceremonies more properly and so get rid of them. But we could think of nothing. At last I composed a song – a spell – that I thought might work, and I taught it to the other men." He had pointed at Nganku. "Your father was one of the men I taught the song to. We bided out time until the chief spirits came ashore again near Taranggir, but before we could begin the song, a strange thing happened."

Once again a puzzled look had come across the face of the old manngur, and he had shaken his head. "The spirit who had not been dead long – the black one – gave us some spears. He also presented us with a curious notched stick into which he fitted a spear. The spear went a long way – much further than ours. Later, after they had all gone, we all tried to see if the stick made our own spears go further, but it was an awkward contraption and of no real use to us. Apparently spirits possess some kind of magic that makes such a stick work. We ended up giving it to the women to use as a fire-stick."

By this time the old man had been beginning to show signs that he was growing weary with remembering.

"But you will want to know about the chant," he had apologised. Gogindi! There was so much to tell, it was easy to leave things out! "We had practised it carefully. But the spirits weren't going to let us begin it too easily. They first performed a curious dance, which did not seem to us to contain any artistry or grace at all, and which was quite boring. But they finished at last, and at my signal each one of us attached himself to a single spirit, as we had planned earlier. We placed our mouths very close to their ears in order to ensure that they would have no difficulty hearing us, and we sang:

> *"The land you left is beautiful.*
> *It is the spirit-land where all must go.*
> *Go, my friends, go.*
> *Return whence you came.*
> *Take your canoes and go.*
> *If you are lonely, there are spirit friends for you in that place,*
> *And soon even we will join you.*
> *Go, my friends, go.*
> *Perhaps Dirai Yirki, the morning star, is your home.*
> *Perhaps it is in the rocks and trees of Undanbi land,*
> *Or even on our beautiful Yarun.*
> *But go, my friends, go.*
> *Soon we will join you."*

Bomarigo had sat staring into space for a long time after that, and neither of the young manngur had interrupted his reverie, content to sit there and let the import of his song sink in. There might come a time when they, too, would be called on to compose such a magic chant, and grant that Birral might send down the appropriate ideas from the stars!

The old man had at last stood up. "They went. I don't know whether it was the song, but they went. I think it might have been the song. We were pleased they had gone, and yet not pleased."

The visit of the spirits had been fraught with difficulties from beginning to end.

In the days following, Buruda had learned still more about the spirit visitors. But he had blanched when Bomarigo had made as if to tell him their names.

"Dimmangali!" he had protested weakly.

"Yes, Dimmangali!" the old man had agreed. "Sacred to the dead! Yet I do not believe that it applies to the spirit visitors. Who can tell about such beings? Are they dead? Are they reborn? Just where do they fit into the scheme of things? In any case, not long after they had gone a number of children saw a small cloud above the sea and thought they were returning in their big canoe, and yelled their names at the tops of their voices to alert us to the fact. We were worried for a long time after we saw it was only a cloud, for the children had put us all in danger by yelling the names. Or so we thought. But nothing happened. In fact, that was one of the best fish seasons we had ever had. So I do not believe that it is unlawful to mention their names. In any case, they would be spirit names, and would bear no resemblance to the names they had while living with men."

Buruda had been silenced. He could see that there were many mysteries still to be unravelled, and a whole lifetime might not be enough to do so, if Bomarigo's experience was anything to go by.

"I know the names of the chief two of the male spirits," Bomarigo had told him. "They were Midherplinda and Damwel. The name of the spirit who was still black was Bongari."

Yes, it would take a lifetime of thinking to digest the mysteries Bomarigo had unfolded to him.

After his return from Yarun, Gibberol had one morning brought two sticks to Buruda as he had sat outside the house of the bachelors mending a mula which had suffered from too heavy a catch of fish. Each of Gibberol's sticks had a large number of notches cut in it.

"Your education is all but complete," Gibberol had told him. "Already you have surpassed me. It is also high time that you and Nerida became husband and wife. It is not good in a group for a young woman of Nerida's beauty to be long promised but unwed."

Buruda had sputtered, the blood rushing to his face. He had already waited three summers longer than he had wanted to, and only the kindness of some of his Bunda visitors from other nations in lending him their wives on occasion had stopped him from tackling Gibberol before this. But he had stopped short of saying what was in his mind. In the first place, Gibberol was an old man and his mentor, and thus worthy of deep respect. And again, Buruda had early learned that he himself had a temper that had to be kept under control. Too often in the past it had landed him in trouble.

Gibberol had waited until Buruda's face had assumed its normal hue. Then – "I know that it is I who have kept you apart till now, but that is about to end. I only ask that you first spend as many days as there are notches on this stick with Durbai of the Nalbo. He may have something further to teach you."

Buruda had relaxed. He would certainly like to visit the Nalbo manngur, particularly since Durbai was Nerida's maternal grandfather. "I will do it, old man," he had agreed.

Gibberol had nodded approvingly, and had handed one of the sticks to Buruda. "Then you will from today start cutting across the notches on this stick. The other one I will give to Wimbur. He will expect you home the day the last notch is crossed."

So it had been. Today Buruda had crossed the last notch on his stick.

And the time with Durbai had passed interestingly enough. Not that he felt he had learned as much as he had from Bomarigo. But he had to acknowledge that Durbai was renowned throughout the whole of the Gubbi-speaking area, even as far north as K'gari, the big sandy island, as a foremost practitioner of divination. And during his time with the Nalbo, Buruda had witnessed for himself the great man in action. But Durbai had not been as helpful as Bomarigo in his explanations, and Buruda had been left with many unanswered questions.

Still, there was no doubt that Durbai knew what he was about. During Buruda's visit a man had suddenly fallen seriously ill, and no sucking of his breast had helped in any way. The kundir stone had also been of no avail. Just when Buruda had thought the old manngur must surely be defeated, Durbai had suddenly confronted the man's wife and accused her of stepping over her husband's shield when she had been placing the kangaroo sleeping-skin on the floor of the hut the night before he became ill.

Great consternation had ensued within the Nalbo camp. For a person to step over any possession of another was to ensure beyond a shadow of a doubt that an accident of some kind would befall that person. To step over a fighting man's shield was tantamount to removing the protection of that shield, and could easily result in his death.

This time the woman had been lucky. The sick man's kin had been content with beating her senseless. And it had not been long before the man had begun to get better, proving beyond any doubt that the culprit had been found.

Durbai had later explained to a puzzled Buruda that there were many signs that could point to the guilty person in these circumstances. Just as a man could tell what animal had made a particular track and how long ago it had passed, so it was with divination. Each person had a particular way of acting, and no two people were ever the same. When something happened that required divination, you had only to look at the way people were acting, Any change from the normal might easily point to the cause of any event, since those guilty tended to give themselves away by trying to change their particular way of behaving. The successful manngur, therefore, needed to know in great detail just what was usual in all people within the group – and even in people outside it.

"And the unusual often points the mind to the usual," Durbai had explained with a smile, knowing full well that Buruda would not understand. But that was Durbai's way. He liked to talk in conundrums before he explained.

"Take the case of the woman stepping over the shield," he had gone on. "Her behaviour was different from what I expected. Just what was different about it is hard to explain, but I knew it was different because I know my people so well. Then I remembered that she has always been careless in the way she sets the kangaroo skin down for sleeping, and it was this usual behaviour that cleared up the problem."

So as he strode onward toward the camp at the mouth of the creek flowing into Kaerwagum, Buruda reflected that his time with Durbai had been well spent. From now on he would be much more alert to human behaviour than he had been in the past. And if he performed this task well, he must become a more proficient manngur. When he had first become the possessor of a kundir stone he had felt pride in a task accomplished. Now he realised it had only just begun, and he felt excitement at the prospect of a lifetime delving into the deeper mysteries regarding the spirits of people and animals, and of the land from which all sprang.

Notes on Chapter 1

Most of the material in this chapter is taken from Steele's The Explorers of the Moreton Bay District 1770-1830. Thus Bomarigo, Yelyelbah and Yewoo are real historical characters who were there when Flinders visited the area in the "Norfolk" in 1799.

The pronunciation of "Mister Flinders" and his brother "Samuel" is also as Flinders noted it. Nor could it have been otherwise, considering the fact that Aboriginal languages have neither the "s" nor the "f" sound.

The account of what Flinders and his crew did is set down as one could expect an old man like Bomarigo to remember after the lapse of some twenty odd years. After all, it would be unreasonable to expect there to be no anomalies when compared with Flinders' interpretation of events when all history was transmitted orally. Besides, the reader must always bear in mind that the story is told from the perspective of a man whose perception of the universe differed greatly from that of the more materially-oriented European.

Bongaree, the Aborigine from Port Jackson who accompanied Flinders, did in fact show the locals how to use a woomera and presented them with one. The fact that his present was nowhere to be seen by the time of the next visit of the white man gives a pretty good indication of what the locals thought of its usefulness. Their method of spear-throwing was obviously sufficient for their needs, and the innovation must have been considered quite superfluous.

It was difficult to understand the incident (described by Flinders) of the singling out of individual sailors by the Dhundubari men who sang a song straight into the ear of the individual each had attached himself to. The explanation given for this event seems to be the only one that would fit neatly with Aboriginal beliefs and customs.

For ease of interpretation by the reader, the present spelling for individual peaks in the Glasshouse Mountains has been used. It is of interest also to note that Aborigines who were still in the region when Andrew Petrie later climbed Beerwah were in no way surprised when he became blind from cataracts in his later years. Aborigines knew that people who dared to climb this sacred peak would go blind!

Dhilla = Bag(s). Our word "dilly" is derived from this Gubbi word. (Note that in the Gubbi language the singular and plural were always the same.) The bags were made of hair, grass, or reeds, and many of them were beautifully patterned.

Dibing = Mosquito(es). (They also called tea-trees "dibing" because of the prevalence of these pests in ti-tree areas.)

"Manngur" needs perhaps a more detailed explanation. The word could be translated as "Doctor", and at times that word will be used. Gaiarbau (Willie Mackenzie) of the Dungidau people, whom the author once had the pleasure of meeting, said that the Gubbi word "manngur" meant "He's got something!" Thus the manngur was looked upon as a person who had far more knowledge than the ordinary man.

If one wanted to draw parallels between the Gubbi education system and the present-day white system, it would be legitimate to equate the teaching of the children up till the age of puberty as primary education. The boys then went through the "kivar-yangga", and became kivar or "young men". The time of learning up to the next stage (the "dhur" or "bu-ul") could be equated to a high-school education. The man who became a fully-fledged warrior ("bu-ul" or "dhan") at this last initiation ceremony could be thought of as having matriculated. It would be wrong to assume that a man's education stopped here, however. He could eventually become a wise enough man to be considered an elder. The elder could be thought of as having a degree.

The *manngur* was the Ph.D. of Gubbi society.

"Gubbi", "Wakka", "Yugar(a)", "Yugum", "Dhandai" were all languages one would expect the Undanbi to come in contact with. All these words mean "no, nothing, nowhere" in the particular area where they were used. All languages used the same word for "yes" – "yau" or "yau-ai". Gubbi was spoken from the southern end of Bribie Island (Yarun), the home of the Dhundubari, to the northern end of Fraser Island (K'gari). The Undanbi spoke Gubbi. The people to the west spoke Wakka. Yugar(a) was the language of the Turrbal who lived in the Brisbane and Caboolture River areas. Yugum was the language of the Yugumbir in the Logan and Albert River districts. The Dhandai language was spoken by the people of Cleveland and Stradbroke Island.

The name "Kaerwagum" has been used for Pumicestone Passage. This name was used for its southern part, and it has been used here for the whole length of the passage, though it is not certain this was so.

"Birral" means literally "Up in the sky", and is the name given by the Gubbi people to the supreme God. It undoubtedly has connections to their name for Beerwah, the highest of the Glasshouse Mts.

"Dimmangali" was the name given to all the dead. It was believed that to mention the name of a dead person would expose people to all sorts of harm from the spirit of that dead person.

$$\Large\diamond$$

Chapter 2

1820: Men of the Bunda skin dance the Fraser Island dance, commemorating the passing of Indian Head (Kow-Woi) by Cook in the year 1770.

The afternoon was wearing on by the time he emerged from the unmarked bush onto a well-worn track leading to the creek. His stride lengthened, and at the same time his quick ear caught a faint tapping sound that grew louder as the track approached a gap in the dense tangle of mangroves fringing the creek. Buruda's mouth watered as he thought of the succulent oysters that often clung to the finger roots of these trees. He was beginning to feel hungry, as he had not eaten all day. Besides, the tapping was growing louder every minute and it reminded Buruda that the women were preparing the bangwal, those wonderful fern roots which made such tasty cakes. And he knew, too, that there would be fish for him to eat as well, for nobody went hungry within the group.

And – gogindi! ariro! – tonight Nerida would prepare his meal!

Before he went further, he laid down his rug and weapons. Then, taking a ball made up of beeswax, goanna grease and charcoal from his dhilla, he carefully rubbed himself all over until his skin glistened with a jet-black sheen. He paid particular attention to the pubic area, where that morning he had carefully removed the hairs so that all would recognise his new marital status. He also knew that his bride would have had the hairs round her binang removed in like manner. Neither would from this day onward allow hair to show in that place, so that all who looked would know immediately that they were married people.

Finally, satisfied, he replaced the ball in his bag and took from that receptacle his finely-polished nose-bone. After he had put this in place, he adjusted the bands of spun possum-fur string round his head and arms. He had been away a long time, and the least he could do was arrive home properly dressed.

The incessant humming of the little salt-water mosquitoes that frequented the paper-bark forests, thus giving the dibing tree its name, was in his ears. They were now somewhat thwarted in their attempts to get at his blood. Not that it would have worried him greatly if they had been able to get at him, since he had long been accustomed to their stings. Still, he remembered fondly how as a boy he had always been pleased and relieved when his mother Ngita had made his skin shine with the black grease.

Taking up his burdens once more, he moved along the path to the gap in the mangroves. No sooner had he reached the creek than a joyous "Kui!" rang out from the opposite bank. Wungul, his father's brother's son and therefore one whom he called brother, had obviously been on the lookout for him. Soon a whole chorus of yells arose as all the bu-ul and the kivar raced into the creek to meet him as he crossed. A great deal of tearful hugging and hand-holding ensued, for it was only right and proper to show such delight at the homecoming of one already considered the greatest warrior in the whole of the Undanbi nation.

For his part, Buruda's eyes were also brimming with tears of pleasure as he returned their greetings. But, as was only right, it was the hand of Wungul, his favourite brother, that he held as he stepped from the water. And it was Wungul who took the lead in showing him the new hut that Nerida and the other women had prepared against this day. No longer would Buruda reside in the bachelor's quarters.

He carefully leaned his spear against a dibing tree near the hut opening and, having removed his weapons from the rug, placed it on the dibing bark which formed its roof. Wungul grinned broadly as he pointed to two fire-making sticks and the heap of firewood which had that day been placed in front of the hut opening. "You'll be making fire tonight!" he remarked, and the men who were gathered around guffawed loudly.

Buruda grinned in return as they all waited expectantly. What he was about to do was symbolic of what was to happen tonight. The fire sticks consisted of one male and one female part, and he knew they had been placed near his hut by Koppakkin, Nerida's mother, this being the closest she would come to having any contact at all with her son-in-law. Squatting down, he took the male stick between his hands, his right foot holding the grooved female stick firmly on top of some dibing bark. It seemed he had only begun to twirl the male stick, pressing firmly down as he did so and readjusting his hands upwards each time they approached the female stick, when a thin column of smoke arose from the bark. A soft breath was enough to coax a flame, and some judiciously-placed wood ensured that the fire remained alight.

He had his kira – his hearth fire. From now on it would fall mainly to Nerida to make sure it kept burning.

"E-e-e-e-e-e!" The assembled men's expression of admiration was polite, since there was not a bu-ul among them who could not have done it as quickly. A kivar might have taken fractionally longer.

But now it was time for them to disperse. Time enough tonight and tomorrow for exchanging news. From further down the camp Wimbur could be seen approaching, Nerida following behind him carrying all the paraphernalia needed by a wife.

Before he left, Wungul dropped four fat sea-mullet on a piece of dibing bark. Buruda's eyes gleamed with appreciation. He had never seen fatter fish.

Wimbur grinned as he reached the hut. "Welcome, Buruda!" he said. "I trust you had a profitable visit with my father-in-law?"

"Yes, indeed, Wimbur! But it's good to be back in Undanbi country." As he spoke, he lifted the possum-fur rug from the dibing-bark roof of the hut and handed it to Wimbur, who took it wordlessly.

Wimbur could tell from the feel of the rug that it was of excellent quality. It would certainly keep him and Koppakkin warm on the coldest of nights. But his eyes never left Buruda. Ariro! What a dhan this was!

Each time Buruda returned after an absence, the older man could not help feeling a new admiration for the young manngur. He knew some of Buruda's faults, not the least of which was a short temper. But what a bu-ul he was getting for a son-in-law! And what a husband for Nerida!

As Wimbur turned his attention at last to the rug, Nerida began to attend to her household establishment. First she carefully placed a pikki of water in the shade near the corner of the hut. Her many dhilla she hung on the branch of a bush nearby, and the stone and block of wood for pounding bangwal she placed just inside the hut opening, a little to one side. Her heavy digging-stick, tapering to a point at one end, she leant against a tree next to Buruda's spears. Next she placed the cakes of bangwal, which she had already prepared at her mother's hut that afternoon, near the fire to warm. Finally, selecting a part of the fire that had already burned down a little, she dropped the four fat mullet left by Wungul onto the red coals.

Wimbur, satisfied with his inspection of the rug, turned back to his own dwelling.

The two young people looked at each other and touched.

"Welcome to our house," Buruda breathed.

"My own dhan! My husband!" she smiled, her dark eyes dancing. "At last you are my husband! At last!"

They sat in front of the fire. The busy noises of the camp around them faded from consciousness. Their eyes devoured each other.

The tribal markings that declared him a bu-ul of the Undanbi, perfect in their symmetry, stood out boldly on his chest and shoulders. What a dhan I have! Nerida thought. How the blackness of his beard contrasted sharply with the white flashing teeth! How neatly he had wound his long hair up on the top of his head! What strength there was in those arms! How handsome he was!

Buruda, for his part, wondered how he had ever been so foolish as to let Gibberol talk him into delaying taking his bride. How had he ever thought that the women lent him by other Bunda on his visits lately could compensate for waiting for this woman of his own? How had he ever thought that becoming a better manngur was important enough to justify waiting to possess this vision of loveliness? Her short hair and necklace framed a face that was so beautiful it almost robbed him of his breath. Her firm breasts swelled under his gaze. His eyes darted to her pubic region and with a surge of joy he saw what he had known he would see – the hairless sign of marriage that proclaimed to all the world that she was his.

"My woman! My wife!" he breathed, reminding himself at the same time that he should never allow that short temper of his or his penchant for looking at other women bring any sorrow to those eyes that were admiring him so openly right at that moment.

The appetising smells of the roasting fish and the warming bangwal brought them both back to earth.

"We eat, my husband!" Nerida laughed. Taking the fish from the fire, she deftly removed the scales with a yugari shell before placing them on a piece of dibing bark, ready for Buruda to remove head and guts neatly with one quick movement.

All over the camp other families were also beginning the evening meal. Two foraging dogs belonging to members of the group slunk up to grab the head and guts that Buruda had cast aside. A third dog joined them and tried to steal portion of the prize, but a low growl from the original claimant was enough to warn it off. It went elsewhere to seek food.

The mullet were large, and Buruda's beard showed traces of their fatness as he satisfied his hunger. And never could he remember bangwal as tasty as Nerida's! Soon only the backbones remained of three of the fish, and the waiting dogs, turning up their noses at these meagre remnants, moved off in search of richer pickings elsewhere.

Buruda sighed heavily, replete. "I have not eaten so well for many moons!" he said, drinking deeply from a shell dipped into the pikki.

Nerida's teeth flashed in an appreciative smile. "Perhaps you have not been so hungry for many moons!" she reminded him. Taking the remaining mullet, she wrapped it carefully in dibing bark before placing it in one of the hanging dhilla out of reach of any ranging dog. This would be reheated and eaten at daybreak before the next day's work began.

By now the sun had sunk behind Tibrogargan, visible up the creek in Nalbo country to the west. The mountain was standing tall and looking out to sea, as always. And as the shadows deepened, in that sacred time between light and dark, when the glow of the small fires in front of each hut began to pick out the whiteness of the bark of the dibing trees scattered thickly throughout the camp, a voice rose from a hut further up the creek, lamenting the dead. High and clear came the wail, taken up almost immediately by others.

"Ai-i! Ai-i! Ai-i!"

And even the dogs joined in. "Ai-i! Ai-i! Ai-i! Idh! Idh! Idh!"

"Ai-i! Ai-i! Ai-i!" Buruda and Nerida cried, clasping each other for comfort as they did so. For this was the time of the day when sadness always enveloped the camp. This was the time when in each mind's eye there arose the image of some lost loved one. This was the time when the mind might even recall in secret the name of some departed relative or friend, but the only name that would pass the lips of the living would be "Dimmangali!"

So the camp lamented. Here and there, as grief became unbearable to someone whose loss at that moment was being strongly relived, the general lament would be punctuated by curses and threats, particularly if the death still remained unavenged, and a spear would be flung savagely into the ground. But gradually the wailing lessened, and by the time it was fully dark it had ceased altogether. This group of the Undanbi nation had fulfilled its mourning obligations as the law said must be done, and the spirits would be satisfied. No harm would come to the people of the camp this night.

Buruda and Nerida released each other and wiped away their tears. Here and there a laugh could be heard as somebody talked of the day's happenings. Children ran in and out among the huts, shrieking their delight at being alive.

Suddenly from the open space in the centre of the camp a tongue of flame shot up toward the starlit sky. This was the signal that the night's entertainment was about to begin, and within a very short time the whole camp began to drift toward the large campfire that was brightening the area. Buruda and Nerida parted as they reached the place, Buruda to take his place among the men, and Nerida to sit with the women.

Once again Buruda found himself the centre of attention as those who had not greeted him that afternoon now took the opportunity of doing so. Old Gibberol's tears of joy were enough to gladden Buruda's heart, and the old man made him promise to talk to him on the coming day about what he had learned from Durbai. But even in his happiness at once more seeing the old man, the young manngur could not help feeling worried at his apparent frailty. Certainly he looked thinner than when they had parted only a moon ago.

"Are they feeding you enough, old man?" he asked concernedly.

Gibberol chuckled. "Yes, my son," he assured him. "It is just that I am not young, you understand."

Then others came to claim Buruda's attention.

At last the greetings were all over and some semblance of order began to appear among the assembled throng. People arranged themselves on three sides of the fire and back from it. Children – boys and girls mixed – were seated on the opposite side of the fire to the women, while the men were seated on the side of the fire opposite the vacant space reserved for performances.

As if on cue, the men seated themselves according to the skin to which they belonged - Bunda, Balkuin, Barang or Dhuroin. The women also were arranged according to skin, but the apparently careless arrangement of the groups was such as to ensure that no woman was forced to look straight at any man of the skin which made it possible for him to be a son-in-law, for son-in-law and mother-in-law must forever shun close contact with each other.

Even the children, random though the arrangement might appear to the observer, were seated in such a way as to take note of this law of skins. Not a single girl or boy was in close contact with an incompatible member of the opposite sex. From the toddler stage, the law of skins was always drummed into children.

"You should not talk to that girl!" a mother would admonish her little boy. And when he was old enough to understand, he would be told, "She could some day be your mother-in-law if she has a little girl of her own."

Not a single person was thinking of this pattern of skins, yet if the pattern were to be disturbed in any way, there would be an instant reaction of shock. All in the group were aware of the law regarding the fitness of things, and it was as natural as breathing for their minds to register the slightest infringement.

A hush settled on the gathering as five kivar danced in from the darkness, accompanied by the clicking of two boomerangs. One kivar was meant to portray an inept hunter, another his dog, while the other three were kangaroos – an old man, a doe and a joey. They were consummate actors. Every time it looked as if the hunter would be in a position to spear one of his unsuspecting quarry, the dog would run in front of him, tripping him up. The angrier the hunter became and the more he thrashed his poor unfortunate dog, the more frequently the dog would appear in the wrong place at the wrong time. Apparently there was something amiss, to say the least, in the way the hunter had trained his dog. And all the time, the three kangaroos cropped unsuspectingly at the grass, moving without concern from one juicy tuft to another. The finale came as the old man kangaroo serviced his doe, quite unaware of the fact that the hunter had once more taken aim with his spear. Not that it mattered, for the dog had again tripped him up and the heavy spear had transfixed the foot of the hunter, who left the scene hopping in agony, his dog racing happily round him wagging his tail.

The appreciative audience guffawed from end to end, and the finale saw them rolling on the ground convulsed with laughter, tears streaming from their eyes.

It was some time before they could sit up again, and the grinning kivar had well and truly regained their places before the last remark had been made.

Wungul slapped Buruda on the shoulder. "Have you ever seen anything like that?" he gasped weakly.

But Buruda was still spluttering too much to reply.

When all had settled down, it was the turn of the women. The Baranggan group drew aside and carefully painted up for the dance of the bangwal-digging, always a favourite. Their white markings looked impressive as they came dancing in from the darkness, their heavy digging-sticks held in front of them, while the seated women of the other skins sang and pounded rolled-up possum skin rugs and the unmarried girls slapped their thighs.

Buruda's chest swelled with pride as Nerida danced into the light. She was without doubt the most beautiful, the most graceful of them all. And he knew she was dancing only for him. Peering out of the corners of her eyes as she danced, she saw him watching her, and his attention drove her to excel herself. Despite the growing coolness of the night, she was glistening with sweat when the dance ended.

"A-a-a-a-a-a-a! E-e-e-e-e-e-e!" The cry of approval rang out from the audience as the women returned to their places, still painted for the dance.

During the ripple of conversation that followed the women's dance, Buruda turned to Wungul. "Bomarigo told me something new about the spirit's canoe on my last visit," he said. "He said that the children had thought the canoe was returning when they saw a small cloud down low near the sea. It has given me an idea for adding a little to the K'gari spirit canoe song. Do the Bunda want to dance while I sing?"

Of course they did, the Bunda assured him! They were most eager to perform with their skin-brother who was becoming recognised as one of the most important bu-ul in the Undanbi nation. Indeed, all those gathered tonight believed that Buruda was one of the most important bu-ul among the whole of the Gubbi-speaking people, from the Ningi in the south to the people of K'gari in the north. And since by definition outsiders were inferior, that meant he was one of the foremost men in the whole of creation.

Of course they wanted to dance!

There was a murmur of expectation as the Bunda bu-ul rose and left the circle of light. The people knew it would be quite a while before the performers had readied themselves for whatever it was they were presenting. The same had applied to the Baranggan women who had just danced. The time of preparation for a worthwhile dance was always long drawn out, for no dancer, man or woman, would want to appear before an audience without very careful preparation. In the first place, there was always the return to the performers' individual huts to procure the necessary accoutrements, and then there was the needful careful delineation of the white clay on the torso, so that the lines were as symmetrical as human art could make them.

So the audience had plenty of time while they waited to discuss the quality of performance of those who had gone before and to ponder upon the possibilities inherent in any coming act. They could even gossip with one another about what they had heard about individuals within the group or outside it, if they so desired. Sometimes one of the assembled would even tell a story.

Tonight the talk revolved round what the Bunda men were about to do. Word soon got round that it was the K'gari spirit canoe dance that was to be performed. This too was an old favourite, and was extremely complicated, since some participants had to take the part of a big canoe with white trees growing out of it, while others had to be spirits who moved around on the canoe as it glided through the water.

This was not a sacred dance. Nor was it a story of the Before-Time. Instead, it was the story of how, long ago, a big canoe with something white above like thick white bushes had drifted past K'gari while spirits walked about within it. It had eventually disappeared over the edge of the sea, as if it had buried itself in the sands of Thurvur, just as yingu-yingu the soldier crab buried itself in those same sands when the tide came in each time.

It had been many moons since this dance had been performed within the group, and a murmur of approval greeted the news that this was to be the subject of the next performance. It was important that these songs be kept fresh in the minds of the people, for they told of momentous happenings that affected the very fabric of society. And it must always be borne in mind that what had happened once could happen again.

Since that time, for example, spirits had come even closer in their canoe to the Dhundubari of Yarun, almost within touching distance of the people at that moment sitting round the fire, waiting for the Bunda to perform!

It was good that Buruda had chosen this theme, they remarked.

It was what was to be expected from a manngur like Buruda, others added.

But suddenly the buzz of conversation ceased. From the darkness could be heard the rhythmic clicking of approaching boomerangs. Buruda was concealing his approach by holding a bush before him, while at the same time he was clicking his two boomerangs only softly, and the impression that their clicking was coming from far away in the darkness was so effective that it was almost uncanny.

Suddenly he discarded the bush and there was a gasp of amazement as he seemed to materialise out of nothing in the full light of the fire. He was in full regalia, his nose-bone gleaming whitely against the blackness of his beard, the white paint standing out boldly on his torso. In his hair the white breast-feathers of wuruma the sea-eagle fluttered as he danced.

The beat of his boomerangs grew more insistent as he raised them in his right hand high above his head. And still he danced.

"E-e-e-e-e-e-e-e!" the audience breathed.

And just as it seemed he would drive them mad with the wildness of his dancing, he suddenly paused. The clicking ceased abruptly. Then, as he stared back into the darkness from which he had emerged, there came the faint ghostly clicking of more boomerangs.

Then Buruda began to sing.

"I stand on Kow-woi," he intoned gravely.
"I stand on the heights of Kow-Woi,
And I look down and see –
What is it I see?
Is it a cloud?
Yes, it must be a cloud,
And the cloud is low to the sea
Like something that is not a cloud.
It is like a smoke-signal,
But one that keeps together in the wind.
It is a smoke-signal,
And yet it is not a smoke-signal."

As he sang, painted dancers appeared just beyond the full light, their movements making them look like shimmering smoke, just as the song said.

Buruda sang again.
"It is clearer now,
And it is a big canoe
With white on top like clouds –
And yet not clouds."

"E-e-e-e-e-e-e-e-e-e!" the audience breathed. These words were new, and the dancers were breathing life into the words, for they were now closer to the fire, and their mingled bodies looked just like a canoe, while in their arms they held dibing bark so white that it looked like clouds, and yet not clouds –

"There are strangers in the canoe,
And they walk around as if on land."

Behind the dancing canoe with its clouds appeared three dancing figures that in the half-light appeared to be within the canoe.

"E-e-e-e-e-e-e-e-e-e!" all the people breathed.
"These strangers – where are they going?
Where do they come from?
Why do they pass Kow-Woi?
Where are they trying to steer?
They are going to Thurvur.
These strangers will bury themselves.
On Thurvur will they bury themselves."
The canoe and the dancing figures were falling back into the
darkness, the hands of the dancers making scrabbling motions
at the ground.
"Like yingu-yingu they disappear.
They bury themselves in the sand like yingu-yingu.
They are like smoke as they disappear –
Like a cloud,
And yet not like a cloud."

The dancing canoe had by this time gone from sight, and the boomerangs were hushed. Only then did Buruda's boomerangs again begin their clicking, as he began to dance once more. Slowly, like a ghost, he danced backward into the darkness until the blackness swallowed him.

And his boomerangs fell silent.

" A - a - a - a - a - a - a - a - a - a - a - a - a - a - a - a ! E-e-e-e-e-e-e-e-e-e-e-e-e-e-e-e-e-e!"

Then a torrent of conversation burst forth as all persons present tried to show that nobody had appreciated the performance quite as much as they had.

"Buruda has given a new meaning to the dance!" one exclaimed.

"Yes. We used to sing of trees with white leaves on the canoe. The clouds give a different sense altogether!"

There was much speculation as to where the new interpretation sprang from, but none doubted that it added a new dimension to an old story.

It was the last performance for the night, no-one attempting to present another piece after the efforts of the Bunda men. Besides, it was growing late. And as the people were returning to their shelters they were still discussing just how a cloud could accompany a canoe on its journey past K'gari.

Buruda and Nerida walked silently to their hut. Upon reaching it, Nerida spread the kangaroo skins out on the dibing bark which protected them from the dirt floor, and then placed Buruda's shield in position to serve as his pillow, carefully padding it with dibing bark. This done, she arranged a small heap of the same bark next to the shield to serve as her own pillow. Since the season of wallaidhau was almost fully on them and the nights were beginning to cool off, she laid a possum-fur rug over the kangaroo skins to serve as their cover.

In the meantime Buruda had strategically placed a few more sticks on the fire, which had died down to a smouldering mass of embers during the night's entertainment. The fire would help to keep the air within the hut warm, and either one of them would add a little fuel at intervals during the night. Had there been a breeze blowing into the opening, a small windbreak would have been quickly erected to protect the hut from the fire, but there was no need of it tonight.

Nerida was already lying under the rug when Buruda stooped to enter the hut. Before he joined her, he replaced his nose-bone in his small dhilla, which he put within reach at the rear of the hut where it was out of harm's way.

How beautiful she is! he thought once more, as he felt the warmth of her body. His greedy hands explored her contours, and as he felt the white clay which had been painted on her for the dance, he once more remembered how graceful she had been.

And he was amazed to find that his hands in their explorations were uncovering within him sensations that he had never before experienced. This was quite different from any encounter he had previously had with the women lent him by his Bunda friends.

What a woman he had!

And Nerida's heart fluttered, keeping time with the movement of her hands upon his chest. How the cicatrices from the kivar and the dhur ceremonies stood out! She, too, could feel the clay still on his body, and she remembered with pride his triumph of so short a time ago. What a husband she had! How envious the other women would be!

She could feel her firm breasts swelling as his hands moved on her, and then her own hands went in search of his dhun.

Gogindi! Ariro!

But he could wait no longer. His dhun was not to be denied. And he could tell from the way Nerida's hands were guiding him that her need was as great as his own.

Then unexpectedly he found that nothing he had ever known before could ever parallel the ecstasy his body was experiencing, for all at once it seemed to him as if he possessed a strength that no bu-ul could possibly have! And how enchanting and tantalising it was to to feel Nerida's lips exploring his face and chest, while all the time moaning to the cadence of his rhythm!

Then it was over, and at last they both found release with great shuddering breaths.

It was some time before their bodies parted, so content were they to remain locked together, basking in the warm afterglow of their passion.

And when they once more lay under the rug, it all began again.

Twice more they made love before Buruda's deep breathing told her he had fallen asleep. For her part, reluctant to let go of the moment too soon, she lay there savouring the scent of his breath, the warmth of his body, the feeling of deep security engendered by his enveloping arms.

Somewhere in the camp she heard a man's voice raised in anger. That would be Ngandun. He was always chastising poor Buldarin. Nerida's arms tightened round her husband. She was sure he would never speak harshly to her like that.

From the bush over the creek came the mournful cry of kuwir the curlew, identifying himself to his mate. "Kuwir! Kuwir!"

But the sounds were beginning to fade from her consciousness. From the ocean side of Yarun, so near across the narrow stretch of water called Kaerwagum, the muted roar of the waves was a lullaby.

"What a dhan I have!" was her last conscious thought as she drifted off to sleep.

Notes on Chapter 2

The Fraser Island (K'gari) song has been adapted from a translation by Edward Armitage of Maryborough, 1923. The song describes Cook passing Indian Head in 1770.

Thurvur is the name for Breaksea Spit.

Much of the material relating to marriage and songs and myths has been taken from descriptions by Berndt and Berndt (1977).

The Undanbi were so called because they called their fully initiated men "dhan". The Gubbi word for such a man was "bu-ul". The Undanbi used both terms.

"Pikki" was the flower-sheath of the palm-tree, used by the Aborigines to carry water. The name "Piccabeen" is still used for the palm-tree in question.

The four skins mentioned were the male names of the skins. The suffix "-gan" must be attached to signify the female equivalent. Thus Buruda's sister, if he had possessed one, would have been Bundagan, and a brother to Nerida would have been Barang. The marriage laws of the Gubbi people were very strict, as in all Aboriginal societies. The ideal marriage partners would be what has been referred to as "cross-cousins".

"Gogindi!" "Ariro!" were expressions of surprise or anticipation.

"Kira" was the word for "fire". The camp was "Kiraba" or "Kirami" i.e. "Place of the fire".

The Gubbi expressed their appreciation by a long-drawn out "E-e-e-e-e-e!" It was the equivalent of our applause.

$$\diamond$$

Chapter 3

1821: Life with the Undanbi

Wallaidhau, the time of cold, was upon them once more, and Buruda shivered in anticipation as he emerged from under the possum-skin rug. Nerida was already up and, having coaxed some flames from the fire, was warming herself before it while a stingray left over from the previous evening's meal was heating.

After greeting his wife with a smile, Buruda's first task was to insulate himself somewhat against the cold by rubbing his body with his ball of charcoal, goanna grease and beeswax. This done, he turned his attention once more to Nerida. Strange how he never seemed to be able to get too much of her. He still looked at other women, certainly, as all dhan did, and wondered about the possibility of taking them. But it had not been the same since he had taken Nerida to wife. Somehow he seemed to get more excitement from looking at her than he did with others.

He smiled to himself. On the hunting trip a few days ago she had confided to him that she had felt a spirit take up its abode in her that day. So it would not be too many moons before a baby appeared.

He gave his attention to his mula, the deep scoop nets whose mouths were held open by two light cotton-tree branches sprung to form arches, one of these projecting to form a handle. As he inspected them, his mind pondered on the deep mysteries of life. The spirit residing in Nerida's womb at this very moment had sprung from a black rock close to the trading track that led past the foot of Tibrogargan, very near Nalbo country. Nerida had shown him the rock, and he had given his opinion that a boy would be the result, since there was a definite male configuration to the outcrop.

Still, you could never really tell about spirit homes. His own spirit home, secretly shown him by his mother Ngita so many years before, was a rock split by a pandanus palm on the headland past the dhur ring at Caloundra, and the split rock looked for all the world like a woman's binang.

No, you never could tell.

But one thing was sure. Only his father Dhubal, his mother Ngita and Buruda himself knew the location of Buruda's spirit home, for to give others this knowledge was to give them unlimited power over his destiny, the power even to destroy him. For any damage done to the spirit birthplace was also done to the spirit within a person.

So nobody but himself, Nerida and the son or daughter born to them would ever know the exact spot from which the spirit had sprung to take up its home in Nerida's womb.

The mysteries were deep, Buruda reflected. The spirits within the land waited patiently for a suitable woman's body to come within reach, but they could only enter a woman whose body had been properly prepared for them. It was this preparation that was the task of the husband. Thus it was

Buruda's penetration of Nerida that had prepared her womb for the spirit, and Nerida had known exactly when the spirit had entered her body by the tiny movement within her that always accompanied such entry.

Nerida smiled as she looked at the way his hands had become still on the net he was holding. His eyes had that distant look in them that showed he was deep in thought. How different he was from the other dhan, who talked a lot more and thought a lot less! She reflected on the way the two of them fitted so well together, for she too was a dreamer, and she could often tell what he was thinking by just looking at him.

"Are you thinking of our coming babe – of whether it will be a boy or a girl?"

Her voice jolted him out of his reverie. He drew closer to the fire, suddenly becoming more aware of the bite in the air as Bigi the sun rose over Yarun to the east. "Yes," he admitted, "but I was thinking of much more than that. Mostly I was thinking of how beautiful you are, and of how fortunate the spirit is to have chosen you for its home." He smiled tenderly as she handed him some dibing bark with warm stingray on it. "And I was thinking of the mysteries of birth."

"Mysteries! Mysteries!" she teased him. "My husband must always think of mysteries!"

But, despite the bantering tone in her voice, he could hear also the pride she had in his power. And he knew that she herself often pondered on the deeper things of life. There were of course many forbidden topics that he could not discuss with her, simply because she was a woman. But often, after their nightly ritual of giving and receiving bodily pleasure, they had lain awake talking of the meaning of life, and the importance of ensuring that all the necessary rites were performed, so that there might be no block to the continuance of the provision of all good things by a bountiful nature. It had been borne in on Buruda very quickly after their marriage that Nerida possessed a mind that was in many ways more profound than those of some of the manngur he knew, and he unashamedly sharpened his own ideas on the grinding-stone of her logic. There had even been times when he had wished she had been a man instead of a woman, so that he would be able to share all his thoughts with her, even those relating to the dhur. But these wishes had been only fleeting, forgotten quickly in the renewed pleasure of her body.

The stingray was good.

"I put the barb in your dhilla in case you need it for a spear-point," Nerida told him.

But the camp was stirring. Standing up, Nerida took her digging-stick and two dhilla, preparing to join the chattering women and children who were approaching from the main camp near the creek. She would refill the pikki, which was below half full, when she returned from her bangwal-digging later in the day.

Ngita and her sister Mundul, whom he also called mother, called out "N'gara!" to him as they passed, and he replied, "Nara!" Many others also greeted him, but his warmest rejoinder was to those two who had been the main ones he had relied on for suck until he had been weaned. Both of them had little ones belonging to other women on their shoulders, the tiny hands clutching tightly to the hair of their human carriers. And he knew that the now pendulous breasts of the two would still be called upon to nourish one or the other of the little ones before the foraging party returned to the camp round midday.

Nerida took her place between these two and Koppakkin, who quite properly was holding two dhilla in front of her to hide herself from Buruda as she passed his hut.

But now it was time for Buruda to prepare himself for the day's labour. Slinging his two mula over his shoulders, he joined Wungul, who was leading a group of men. Talobilla, the son of Buruda's elder brother Tarrum and therefore one whom he also called son, was with the men today.

"N'gara, father!" he said.

"N'gara, son!" Buruda replied.

He looked at Talobilla. Yes, there was more than a hint of fuzz beginning to show on the lad's face, as well as in the pubic area round his dhun. It was time he became a kivar. Buruda noted with approval that the hole he himself had pinched in Talobilla's septum to receive the nose-bone had healed, and that the lad had dutifully kept it open by keeping a small stick in it.

Talobilla was a son to be proud of. He had practised his hunting skills assiduously, taking every opportunity of going with the men whenever he had been allowed. He could already make a straight spear, meticulously shaping it over the fire and forcing the hot wood into shape by holding it between his strong teeth while using his arms to force it straight. He was a good boy.

But there would need to be a new name conferred upon him at the ceremony. Talobilla – dolphin – was a good name for a little boy. But a kivar always had a more adult name bestowed on him, and this, in addition to the secrets of the ceremony itself and the tribal marks he would receive, would set him apart for all time from the women and children he had been wont to mix with before.

Still, enough of that till later. A suitable name would suggest itself.

Wungul remarked to Buruda, "I think the mullet will be gathering on the sand-banks opposite the bar today."

Others in the group echoed this opinion.

"Yesterday I saw a big shoal just outside in the surf opposite Woorim!" Ngandun remarked. "They ought to have come in last night."

"It won't take us long to get them today," one of the kivar suggested.

"The tide will be full soon," Buruda agreed, "so they ought to be there. Still ..."

Yes, you could never really tell about mullet, or any other fish for that matter. But they all knew they would get a good meal of some sort, for they were all intimately acquainted with the ways of the sea. As they approached the shallow sand-banks where they expected to find the fish, they split into three separate groups, six dhan and two kivar in each group. These groups would act independently of one another, and if even one of the groups succeeded, there would be plenty for all.

Each group had a young lad as helper. The job of each lad would be to try to lure the fish in closer to the shore if they happened to be too far out. Talobilla was the lad attached to Buruda's group.

While the three groups quietly took their places, a kivar climbed a casuarina tree on the water's edge.

It was not long before the cry came. "Over there!" They all looked up at the kivar to find he was pointing down to the left.

"How close?" Wungul wanted to know.

"Not far out!"

Retreating behind the cover of the bushes that lined the shore, the men quickly made their way down to the place indicated. Peering out from behind their shelter, they were confronted with a shoal of mullet that made the water black with their numbers.

"They're a bit far out!" Bulangga muttered.

"But what a shoal!" another breathed.

Each group now took up position. In Buruda's group, Talobilla took up his place in the centre, with four men on either side of him, Buruda being the lead man on the lad's left and Wungul the lead man on his right. They always partnered each other in this way whenever they could.

The kivar in the tree was becoming slightly frantic. "They're moving up this way!" he yelled urgently. "You'll have to hurry!"

Keeping low, the groups moved swiftly to the water's edge. Surely enough, the mullet had moved upstream, so that only Buruda's group still had the blackness of the school in front of them. But it was too late for the other groups to re-deploy, as the fish were moving further out. They'd have to act now.

Talobilla carefully threw a small stone out beyond the school, and then another. The two boys with the other groups did the same. The fish reacted by coming in just a little closer. Again Talobilla threw a stone beyond the black mass, but this time there was no reaction. So he took a little ball of wet sand and threw it into the water on the near side of the school, causing the inquisitive fish to come in to investigate the swishing sound.

All this time the men had remained absolutely motionless, each man with his two mula in readiness on either side. The thongs loosely laced round their wrists held the handles of the mula firmly in place. It was the pressure of these handles against them that caused calluses to grow on the outer parts of each man's wrists. These calluses, gained from continuous use of the nets, thus served as one of the ways in which the coastal men could be distinguished from those of the inland, since these did not use the nets to such an extent in providing for their daily needs.

Once more Talobilla threw a ball of sand into the shallow water near the shore. This time only a few fish reacted.

A swift glance passed between Buruda and Wungul. As one they raced into the water, their mula held high. The others in their team ran after them, the group thus forming two lines in the water some four strides apart. The fish could be seen darting hither and thither, panicked by the noise. Then, as Buruda and Wungul met so that a semicircular line of eight men blocked the escape of the imprisoned mullet, they all dropped their mula into the water, one on each side of their bodies, and then brought them together in front, this final action ensuring that the mouths of the two mula met, thus preventing the escape of any fish caught in the scoops.

The other two groups of men had simultaneously performed the same manoeuvre.

Now the only task remaining was to bring the captured fish to shore and examine the results of their labours. The two groups which had overshot the school found no difficulty in doing this, since each man had at most four fish. Indeed, two men had missed out altogether. But for those who had been right in amongst the shoal it was a different story. Buruda, Wungul and two others in the team were finding it hard to bring in their catch, so heavy were the loads within the mula. They yelled for help, and soon willing hands were assisting them.

There was much laughter and back-slapping when the job was finally done, though there had been a nasty moment or two when it had appeared as if both Wungul's and Buruda's mula would break under the weight. Still, they had held and, helped by much advice from those who could not get close enough to lend a hand, they had at last managed to bring the fish to shore.

"There's enough for two days here!" Wungul enthused, puffing from his exertion. And all agreed.

Suddenly they heard a hail from across the water and, looking in the direction of Woorim, they noticed a number of men waving branches to attract their attention.

"Hullo! The Dhundubari want a share!" Bulangga chuckled. "Well, there's enough for all!"

But that apparently wasn't the case. The men on Yarun were yelling out that the dolphins had responded to their calls and had brought the tailer into the surf, and that there were great heaps of fish there for the spearing. Did the Undanbi want to come over and share in the fun?

"Not today!" Bulangga shouted back, holding up a fat mullet in each hand to show that they had enough and to spare. "Maybe another time!"

The Dhundubari bu-ul waved in reply and disappeared round the point to get on with their fish spearing.

Someone cut two fire-sticks and started a fire. Soon a number of fish were roasting, the men relaxing on the sand behind the shelter of some low wattles. Here, in the warm sun out of the wind, they talked of the coming bunyi festival. It had been three summers since the last one, so they could expect a message from the Dallambara as soon as nguruingan, the time of heat, had made itself fully felt. There was much boasting about the feats that would be performed at the feast, and one or two mentioned old scores they intended to settle.

"Before the bunyi feast we'll have to make some more kivar," Buruda reminded them. "Talobilla here is ready, and I have heard that the Tumbra, the Ningi and the Dhundubari all have some lads who should be put to the test."

Talobilla's heart swelled, his eyes gleaming. If he were made a kivar before the bunyi time, he'd be able to show all who would be gathered at Baroon how well his father Buruda had prepared him for manhood. Meantime he'd practise all his hunting skills so that no shame would come to the Undanbi nation through him.

But the fish were ready, and soon all were feasting. The boys and kivar were careful to select only male mullet, for the roe was forbidden to them until such time as they had undergone the full dhur ceremony. While they ate, the dhan talked of where and when the ceremony should be held. Some argued for the Ningi kivar ring, since there were plenty of oysters to be had in the vicinity, Others suggested Yarun, since the tailer would be plentiful on the ocean beach. Some wanted it held in the ring near Coochin, because there were plenty of kangaroos and emus there.

But Buruda wanted the ceremony held in the ring at Caloundra, near the bar dividing Yarun from the mainland. His reason for this preference was simply that he wanted his and Tarrum's son inducted into manhood at a spot that was close to his own beginnings, but of course he was careful not to suggest this as a reason.

So he simply said, "If we hold it right here before the moon is half spent, there will still be plenty of mullet and tailer to make it easy to supply our visitors with food."

Not surprisingly, Buruda's opinion carried the day. More and more the Undanbi were becoming used to agreeing with most suggestions of their young manngur, nor was this because of their knowledge of his short temper. The talent that old Gibberol had discerned in the young lad even before his kivar days had become obvious to all.

It was agreed that tomorrow a messenger would be sent north to the Tumbra, while another would go in the other direction to the Dhundubari and the Ningi. And during the coming days they would need to ensure that the ring was fully prepared.

By now Bigi was ready to begin his downward path in the sky. Dividing the fish so that all would have an equal load, they made their way back to the camp, the fish heavy in the mula over their shoulders.

The women had returned from their bangwal-digging, and Nerida was sitting near the fire weaving a beautifully-patterned dhilla of coloured reeds. She had already prepared a number of these, as had all the women. At the coming bunyi festival they would be in great demand, for these reeds did not grow in the country of the "Wapa", as they scornfully called the slow-speaking inland people.

Her eyes widened as Buruda unceremoniously dumped his mula containing their loads of fish on the ground before the hut. "Arum!" she gasped. "We'll be eating well for a couple of days!"

Buruda laughed. Selecting four of the fattest fish, he said, "I've already eaten, so I'll take these to old Gibberol. He's been looking quite ill lately."

Today Gibberol was looking weaker than ever. He seemed hardly able to lift himself into a sitting position to greet Buruda. "Ah, the bones are getting old!" he complained, as his wife Garwidha took the fish and placed them on the fire.

"These mullet will make you feel better, old man," Buruda assured him. "And when you have eaten them, I'll bring more."

Gibberol smiled. "These will be plenty. I don't need much now to keep me going, and Garwidha won't eat more than these in the next two days."

"But you need to get your strength up, my old friend!" Buruda protested. "How will you ever get strong enough to take part in the next dhur if you don't eat?"

"My next dhur, Buruda?" The old man chuckled. "You and I know that my next dhur will be in the spirit-land. To every dhan, even to a manngur, must come the time of letting go." He sighed. "And Garwidha – she is too young to have to put up with an old man like me. Already I see her looking at some of the young bu-ul --"

"You hold your peace, my husband!" Garwidha broke in fiercely. "You know I've never even glanced at another dhan!"

"Now, now!" Gibberol placated her. "Now, now! It's just that I would not blame you if you did." He turned once more to Buruda. "You will make sure she is looked after?" he insisted.

"I will, my friend," Buruda assured him. "She will not want for anything."

"Good! Good!" Gibberol seemed satisfied. Then he went on, as if the thought had only that moment occurred to him. "You are Bunda, like me," he pointed out, "and Garwidha is Baranggan. Perhaps..."

Out of the corner of his eye Buruda could see that Garwidha had stiffened with interest at her husband's suggestion. Nor, he realised, was he really opposed to the idea. Garwidha, though a good deal older than Nerida, was still handsome enough. She was not quarrelsome, and therefore would not spoil the harmony of his household. No, he was not against the suggestion. He was also aware that, if he were simply to take her when the time came, not one person in the whole camp – man or woman – would think he had acted wrongly.

Nevertheless, such decisions should not be made quickly, but only after weighing all the possibilities. There were other men whose needs would have to be considered.

At last he said, "Old man, if that is the best thing to do, then I will do it. But I cannot say right now that that is the best thing. I have not thought about it enough. There may be other ways that are better, and I will need to ask the other dhan. But whatever happens, Garwidha will be with a husband who will be kind to her, I can promise you that. Even if I do not take her myself, I will look after her as you have done."

There were tears in Gibberol's eyes as he squeezed Buruda's hands between his own. And tears also stung Buruda's eyes as the realisation came to him that the pressure exerted on his hands was so pitiably weak.

Gibberol turned to Garwidha. "I want to talk man-talk with Buruda," he told her. "Go, woman, and find something else to do."

"I will try to hold my spirit within this old body as long as I can," Gibberol explained, after Garwidha had left. "But it is a comfort to know that you will be there to make certain that all the rites are correctly performed when the time comes for me to let go." He chuckled to himself. "It may seem ridiculous for an old fool like me to be giving advice to a greater manngur than I have ever been. But as one who has often performed the same task in the past, could I ask you to be careful when apportioning blame for my death?"

Buruda knew what the old man meant. There always had to be blame for any death, even that of an old man. And there had been isolated cases in the past where an unscrupulous manngur had taken the opportunity to apportion blame in such a way as to allow him to settle an old score. Yet all manngur knew that there was very little blame to attach to anyone, and very little recompense required, for the death of any person who had been allowed to live out a long and fruitful life.

"I will not name an unlikely culprit," Buruda promised. "Nor will I require a death for a death. But the loss will be heavily felt, as you know, and a culprit will be named."

Gibberol was satisfied with the reply. It was a wise one, no less than he would have expected from Buruda. For quite a while the two sat together, hand in hand, content with each other's company.

At last Buruda stood to go. "Hold on to your spirit as long as you can!" he urged the old man. "We need you here! And eat up your fish to keep your strength up!"

Nerida was still at work on her dhilla when he arrived back at the hut. The fish had been roasted, cleaned and wrapped in dibing bark, and were hanging up in two big dhilla. The fact that she did not look up at him struck him as strange.

"Did you enjoy the fish?" he asked her.

Still she did not look at him. "Well enough," she answered shortly. "And how is Gibberol?"

The tone of her voice alerted him. So Garwidha had been here already!

He chose his words carefully. "His spirit will soon leave him. Just how soon, it is impossible to say, but it is certain he will die soon. I think he will last until after the kivar-yangga, which we will be holding in another half-moon."

He paused, certain that he had added no fuel to whatever was smouldering inside her. He had not mentioned the name of Gibberol's wife.

But she was determined to have it out in the open. "And Garwidha?" she snapped, concentrating her gaze upon the dhilla in her lap.

Buruda sighed, only too aware of the feelings sometimes engendered in a first wife by the taking of a second. How to ensure that, if he were forced to add Garwidha to his family, the action would not be a cause of disharmony?

In any case, he had not yet thought enough about the problem to be sure that he would not have to take Garwidha.

He reflected that it might help if he used Nerida's own quick mind to help him come to a conclusion. "I haven't really thought about it," he answered her. "What do you think?"

Nerida was not to be hoodwinked. "It doesn't matter what I think, does it?" she ground out between clenched teeth. "It all comes down to what the men think, particularly what you think!" Her eyes were still bent on her work. There was more then a trace of venom in her voice.

Buruda's temper threatened to surface. He opened his mouth to reply in kind, to let this cheeky woman know that she was dealing with a man of importance among the Undanbi! Blood rushed to his face.

But something about the tilt to her head told him of the hurt she was feeling, and he remembered how he had promised himself on the night of their marriage that he would try never to do anything to hurt her. Besides, she was carrying a child, and all dhan knew that women were a bit harder to get along with at such times.

Besides, what she was saying had some basis in fact.

He took a deep breath. The wish to strike back had passed.

This wasn't going to be easy, he reflected. Nonetheless, he must persevere. "Yes, that's so," he admitted. "But at the moment I don't know what to think. I thought you might help me to form some opinion as to which would be the best family for her to join."

"You could take her!"

But there was no anger left within him, and the bluntness of her statement failed to rouse him. He sat down beside the fire to warm himself before he replied.

"I could - yes. She is Baranggan, like you. And she wouldn't quarrel with you the way some would. She would be able to help you dig the bangwal, and when our little baby arrives she could help give him suck and lighten your load. She could be a great help to you if I were to take her."

"I am strong and don't need any help!" Nerida rejoined sharply. "And I can get plenty of women to give our little one suck if I can't manage it myself!"

Buruda sighed. This was the first time that they'd come close to quarrelling. Yet still he refused to be drawn. He felt he knew some of what she was going through. "So where else could she go?" he asked gently.

"There are other Bunda in this camp."

"True. So let us think of the other Bunda, and consider each one in turn. Wungul, for instance?"

"Yes, Wungul! He is like you, with only one wife!" For the first time she looked him directly in the eye, and he recoiled before the hurt he saw there. "But I suppose you'll tell me that Baldhin won't have it – is that it?"

He nodded slowly. "You are right. We both know that Baldhin would make Wungul's life a misery. She is so jealous that she scolds him unmercifully every time another pretty Baranggan comes within spitting distance. Haven't you seen the way Baldhin reacts sometimes when you pass their hut? And you are her friend!"

The fire started to go out of Nerida's eyes. "Yes, that's true," she admitted, her shoulders slumping. Then she looked appealingly at him. "But don't you think I'm just a little bit jealous, too?" she pleaded.

"Yes, my wife. I know." He smiled. "But you would always realise that, no matter how many wives I take, you are the one I love. In that way you are different from Baldhin."

The dhilla lay forgotten in her lap. "Then you will take Garwidha?"

"If I have to," he admitted. "You already know that. Still, you haven't finished going through all the Bunda yet. There are lots more."

But all the fight appeared to have gone out of her. She had already performed the very same exercise before he had returned. Indeed, her mind had been looking for alternatives from the very instant Garwidha had apprised her of the fact that Gibberol had started to discuss the subject with Buruda. Every name that had occurred to her had brought with it its own objection. This one already had two wives. That other was such a poor hunter that he would find it hard to provide for two wives in difficult times. This was too old. That was only a kivar, and therefore not eligible.

"There are none."

But Buruda himself had had time to think, and was fast coming to another conclusion. "Are you really sure?" he pressed her. "What about Naruman? He has no wife yet."

"But he ..."

"Yes, I know he is aptly named '*Kick*'. He is the dhan with the name of a boy. And he sometimes acts as a boy still, even though he has passed the test of the dhur. He is very young and foolish, always ranting and raving when others are quiet. But he is a qualified bu-ul, and he has no wife."

"But he is already promised!" Nerida protested.

He smiled at her sudden lack of logic. "And am I not? Besides, his promised bride is yet young – only four summers old. He has to grow her up yet."

A glimmer of hope appeared in Nerida's eyes. Perhaps Buruda was not set on having Garwidha after all! But then another thought occurred to her, and her face fell. "Poor Garwidha! You wouldn't do that to her, would you? I'd almost sooner have her here as my sister!"

Buruda chuckled. "Are you sure it's *poor* Garwidha?" he asked. After all, she loses an old man and gains a young one. And who can tell – perhaps she is still young enough for Naruman to prepare her binang well enough for a spirit to choose her as its home."

"Then -?"

"Yes. I am decided."

"Garwidha will be disappointed," she murmured.

"Will you be disappointed?"

"Of course not! But – poor Garwidha!"

"Then it is settled, my wife. I will talk it over with the dhan as soon as we have an opportunity. But don't feel sorry for Garwidha. With us she would have needed to learn to fit in as sister and second wife. She has become used to telling Gibberol what to do, and he has more and more got used to letting her have her own way. Now with Naruman she will not be short of excuses for trying to change him, and who knows – she may even succeed!" He laughed. "And if she does succeed, then his poor little promised bride will get a far better bargain than she would have if we were to let Naruman go on kicking and squealing like a boy until he marries her! No, I think the dhan will all see that this is an ideal solution to a difficult problem."

Nerida laughed light-heartedly as she turned once more to her dhilla. She felt as if a great weight had been removed from her spirit. For a short time there she had been convinced that Buruda had become anxious for variety in his marriage. She decided she had a little more time to spare before she would need to start pounding the bangwal in preparation for the evening meal, so settled herself to her task. This was going to be the prettiest reed dhilla at the bunyi festival.

For his part, Buruda stretched. His two mula and all his weapons were in good order, and he was beginning to feel lethargic. Laying himself down beside the warm coals, he was soon fast asleep. It had been a late night last night round the communal fire.

But the dreams that came to him were neither pleasant nor easily understood.

They started ordinarily enough. He found himself standing on the shores of Kaerwagum looking at Yarun. The sky was blue, and he could hear the mullet jumping, so it must be high tide.

But when he looked at his feet he found to his utter dismay that he was making no tracks on the sand! No matter how hard he tried, he could make no impression! It was as if he no longer existed!

Then the dream progressed in some confusing manner so that he heard the death-wail of the Undanbi somewhere in the distance. And when he looked again at the sand, the tracks were so alien that he could feel the hair rise on the back of his neck! Some were like human tracks, well-defined, but without toes! Some were of animals that were obviously four-footed, but the feet were so hard that they sank deep into the hard wet sand! Some of these were two-toed, and some were of animals with no toes at all, these last reminding him more of a crescent moon than of anything else he had ever seen!

And then the nightmare progressed till he saw some dead people. He knew they were Undanbi, though the faces were indistinct, so that he could not put a name to them. Their bodies were covered with sores and spots, the like of which he had never seen! There were even sores on their private parts! And the stench of corruption was everywhere!

And then he found himself looking at a landscape inexplicably devoid of trees and animals!

He tried to scream, but no sound came from his mouth.

The sound of the bondaban could be heard in the distance, telling the world that what was being seen was for the eyes of bu-ul alone.

And the death-wail came once more, but more distant than ever.

And then he mercifully found himself awake with sweat streaming from every pore of his body.

"Are you all right, my husband?" he heard Nerida inquire anxiously.

Her hands had lain idle on her work for some time now, disturbed as she had been by the groaning coming from Buruda, his sleeping body contorting unnaturally. Since everyone knew it was dangerous to disturb a person so obviously struggling with some spirit in the land of dreams, she had waited until now to speak.

He passed a hand over his eyes and smiled at her, albeit rather weakly. "Yes," he assured her, "I'm all right."

But he knew he'd have to think long and hard about the desolate land he had just visited and the strange scenes he had witnessed. And he sensed that the knowledge that had been vouchsafed him during his sleep had been too sacred to share lightly with those who were not ready to receive it. He would not be able to share it with Nerida. The noise of the bondaban had been enough to tell him that.

"I'm all right, my wife," he assured Nerida once more.

And with that she had to be content.

Notes on Chapter 3

The Gubbi word for mother-in-law was "ngulungan", which was derived from the name for a female bat. This was because the mother-in-law often had to adopt the position of having two dhilla held up in front of her to avoid eye-contact with her son-in-law. This gave her the appearance of a bat.

"Woorim" was the name given by Aborigines to the northern tip of Bribie – not the south, as at present.

The name "tailer" probably derives from the Gubbi name for the fish – "dai-arli" – not, as has often been argued, because these fighting fish take bait from the tail.

The ability of the Aborigines of the region to work in co-operation with dolphins is well documented.

"Baroon" was the name given to the whole of the Blackall Range, not just the pocket containing the present dam.

The place-name "Caloundra" has been used, but this was probably a name given by the Aborigines to the place only after the coming of the white man, when logs were floated down the Passage. It means "Place of the beech log".

The Gubbi word for a lad who had undergone the first stages of initiation was "kivar" or "kippa". The Ningi kivar ring mentioned is at present-day Kippa Ring. The Caloundra kivar ring was visible up till about 60 years ago in the yard of a house in Leeding Terrace. With one development following another, it has disappeared, and is probably under part of the present Centrepoint building.

Chapter 4

1821: The Kivar-Yangga

The kivar-yangga, the making of young men, was here. For days the dhan of the Undanbi had laboured long and hard to ensure that the kivar ring at Caloundra was ready. A wattle tree had been carefully dug out by the roots, stripped of its bark, and then cut off at about the height of a man and a boy above the ground. After the roots had been trimmed to form a circle with a diameter equal to the height of a man and the bark interlaced among the roots to form a flat surface, the tree had been firmly rammed into place upside down in a deep hole in the centre of the kivar ring.

"E-e-e-e-e-e-e-e!" the men had all exclaimed proudly when it was all finished. Their visitors would not be able to criticise their kakka!

Even Buruda was satisfied. The fact that the wattle tree had been covered with a profusion of fluffy yellow flower balls when they had taken it from the ground had been an extremely good omen.

But since his dream he had remained troubled, convinced that whatever disaster the dream had foretold could be prevented only by very careful attention to every detail in the sacred rites.

Since that day he had made two secret journeys to the forbidden place known only to him and Gibberol, and there, having passed the marked trees that declared to all who came near that trespassers would die instantly, he had uncovered the special stones and carefully rubbed them while chanting the sacred songs that had always ensured the increase of the animals and plants in the past.

He hoped that these ceremonies would continue to bring blessings on the people, and that the evil spirits would also be appeased. More he could not do.

Even old Gibberol had not been able to shed any light on the meaning of the dream. "It is beyond me, my son," he had said wearily, as if the action of thought was becoming too much for him. "I may know more soon, when I reach the land of the spirits."

The kakka's perfection therefore pleased Buruda, and so did the rest of the work done in preparation for the ceremony. The figures of clay and grass set by the dhan beside the road connecting the two circles were just right. By daylight they were shapeless, mere suggestions of what they were to represent. But by torchlight they assumed the aspect of powerful mystical beings whose expressions changed as the light fell on them from different angles.

No, there was nothing here that could give any vengeful spirit a reason for seeking retribution against the people.

Only Gibberol, too weak by now to participate in the ceremony, had been left at the camp at the mouth of the creek. A young girl had also remained there with Garwidha to assist her in procuring food while the rest of the people were absent.

The rest had vacated the camp so as to be nearer the place of ceremony. Huts had been set up on the banks of the Creek of the Wood Duck, ensuring plentiful fresh water and bangwal. There the women would stay throughout the half-moon of the ceremony. Although the men would also remain with them until the rites began, they had constructed other shelters for the dhan and the kivar on the headland at the bar, right beside the kivar ring. At this place another fresh water stream tumbled down through a small patch of scrub toward Kaerwagum. Here they would remain aloof from the women until all rites had been completed.

A place had been appointed near the women's camp for exchange of food between the two parties. Here the men would leave meat and fish, while the women could leave bangwal as well as the tasty seeds and bulbs of magum, the blue water lily. In this way there would need to be no contact between the two, yet at the same time nobody would need to forgo part of their natural diet.

The baiyaba, the fighting ground where trials of strength were to be engaged in at the close of the ceremonies, was cleared of some low bushes that had grown up since these grounds had last been used for a full dhur.

Nothing else remained to be done by the time the first visitors were heard coming from the south. It was the Ningi who were the first to arrive, and they politely sat down within sight of the women's camp, talking excitedly as they waited. After a suitable interval had elapsed, some of the Undanbi dhan sauntered over, and soon there were enthusiastic cries of delight as friends were reunited after such a long time apart. Then when Bulangga, who had been appointed spokesman, had pointed out exactly where the Ningi were to make camp, their women set to with a will, bending saplings to form the domes of their huts and fixing dibing bark over the interlaced framework. Assisted by friendly Undanbi women, they had their huts ready in no time.

By this time the Tumbra, those of the red noses from Maroochy, had arrived and were sitting down nearby waiting patiently to be recognised and invited to join the throng. While members of other nations would paint their noses only when the ceremonies began, the Tumbra habitually kept theirs covered with kutjin, that beautiful red clay, to signify their close affiliation with the black swans that were so plentiful in these parts.

Soon they too were being greeted and embraced by Undanbi and Ningi friends, and the building of their huts was proceeding apace in the area set aside for them. And hardly had they begun work than the Dhundubari sat down nearby, having walked along the ocean beach of Yarun and crossed Kaerwagum in their bark canoes, which they had pulled ashore at the Undanbi village back near the creek.

As smoke began to rise from all the fires, Buruda took Nganku and Bomarigo aside. Later he would also consult with the Ningi and Tumbra manngur, but first he wished to speak with Bomarigo about his disturbing dream.

"Ah!" Bomarigo remarked interestedly when he had heard the details. "Did I ever tell you about the tracks left by Midherplinda and Damwel?"

"No."

Bomarigo's voice took on an excited tone. He handed Buruda a stick. "Then draw for me one of the tracks that were like those of a man without toes!" he urged him.

Carefully Buruda traced out one of the tracks he had seen in his dream. Finally, after he had drawn the outline, he took a small stone and carefully pressed down the area within the outline, so that the edge took on the harsh definiteness that he recalled so clearly. At last he was satisfied that he had a good likeness. "That was one of the tracks," he told Bomarigo.

The old man's mouth hung agape. "Impossible!" he muttered. "It is very much like the track of Midherplinda! Not exactly, mind you – but very similar!" He turned to Buruda once more, poking him in the chest at each word to emphasise what he was saying. "Are you sure I did not tell you of these tracks?"

"I can answer for Buruda," Nganku broke in. "You haven't even told me about them. And I was there all the time you were talking to Buruda about Midherplinda."

A look of great respect came into Bomarigo's eyes. "In your dream you have been visited by Midherplinda, or some spirit very much like him. And secrets have been revealed to you that have been hidden even from me, who met him face to face! You must therefore be able to interpret what they told you. What meaning do you give to the dream?"

"I was hoping you could help me," Buruda replied. "After all, you are the only manngur I know who has come into close contact with the spirits."

"And learnt nothing, except possibly how to make them go away," Bomarigo admitted ruefully.

"Surely there was something in the dream that gave you a clue as to its meaning!" Nganku broke in. "Did it show you something that has already happened, or something that will happen? Or did it show something that is happening in the spirit-world?"

Buruda shook his head, and suggested that they should first consult with Girrimar of the Tumbra and Kamkuri of the Ningi before he ventured an opinion. "It will be better to get their views first, before any idea of mine drives out any new thought they might have," he explained.

So it was done. But even though they talked together until sundown, the other two manngur could add nothing to what had already been said.

"All I can say is that, since the dream tracks and the spirit visitors' tracks are very similar, it is indeed a very big thing!" Kamkuri remarked, shaking his grizzled head. "A big thing indeed!"

"And a big thing deserves to be given a lot of thought," Buruda told them. "I have already thought about it a long time, but I think we should all consider it more deeply until the end of the kivar-yangga. By then we may have some greater knowledge. Perhaps – who knows – a spirit may visit one of us in a dream and make it clearer."

And there they had had to leave it, returning to camp in time for the evening meal and the mourning cry for the dead, which that evening was extremely impressive with so many voices, each group trying to outdo the others in the public expression of their pious grief.

That night the festivities continued until the early hours as new dances and songs were presented, together with old favourites. They would probably have continued till daylight if Bomarigo had not drawn their attention to the serious business they would be engaged in for the next half-moon.

"Friends," he reminded them during a break in the presentations, "if you look at the sky you will see the two dark circles where the spirits perform their own dhur, and these remind us that we too will be expecting much from those about to become kivar. They need some sleep first, and so do the bu-ul who will be conducting the ceremony."

"Bomarigo wants to get to his woman!" some wag yelled, and they all laughed as they made their way back to their own hearth-fires.

As she lay wakeful listening to Buruda's heavy breathing beside her, Nerida started suddenly as a stream of invective followed by the heavy thud of a club against flesh signalled Ngandun's displeasure at something Buldarin had done. The noise disturbed Buruda, as it did many others in the camp.

"Keep the noise down!" Buruda called out, his temper getting the better of him for moment. Then – "I wish Buldarin had built their hut further away!" he muttered testily. "And I don't know why Ngandun can't treat his wife better!"

Nerida snuggled closer to him as the disturbance settled. She knew Buldarin would have a great swelling on her head tomorrow. She also knew that the poor woman had built her hut close to Nerida's in the hope that Ngandun would try to keep his temper more under control in a place so close to the manngur. Obviously it hadn't worked.

She sighed as she pulled her husband's protecting arms more tightly around her. She could feel him becoming aroused at the close contact, and soon she felt herself being transported as he lifted her onto his thighs and entered her.

But even as she reached her climax, a small part of her hoped that Buldarin couldn't hear them. The poor woman had enough to put up with without having to listen to the happiness of other couples.

The whole camp was astir at daybreak, despite the late hour of their retirement the night before. A hurried meal was followed by a noisy general exodus as men, women and children made their way to the large ring where the first part of the ceremony was to take place.

Talobilla was the only boy of the Undanbi who was to pass through the kivar-yangga, but there were three lads from each of the other nations who were to take the tests. Each of the aspirants kept very close to his mother, since the mothers would be important participants at the initial stage.

Upon arrival at the ring, the boys were ordered to sit on the ground facing the centre, with their mothers directly behind them. Then all fell silent as the dhan left the ring and quietly melted into the surrounding bush. For what seemed an interminable time, even to those who had seen it all before, there was silence. Then a quiet whistle from one of the invisible men set all the women slapping their thighs as the mothers sang the song of parting. Their mournful voices bewailed the passing of time, since those they loved would now die to them and reappear as kivar who would no longer owe them obedience. And then, very gradually, the song changed to one of triumph, and the slapping became more urgent as the mothers gave praise to Birral for such strong boys who would always feed and protect them in time of danger.

At the same time the waiting dhan joined in the chant, their boomerangs clicking as they advanced from the surrounding bush toward the circle. As they came into view, the watchers saw for the first time which bu-ul had been chosen to wrest the waiting boys from the clutches of their mothers. Those so chosen were in the forefront of the advance.

Talobilla felt a surge of pride as he saw Buruda stamping toward one of the Dhundubari lads, his two clicking boomerangs held high. Talobilla knew that his father Buruda would play a large part in his initiation into manhood in the rites to follow. He also knew that, at this early stage, no close relative was allowed to take him from his mother. It was Nganku who stamped fiercely up to Talobilla, chanting in time to the clicking of his boomerangs.

All at once the chanting, slapping and clicking stopped. As one, the bu-ul facing the candidates held out their boomerangs, and the boys grasped them. At the same time the mothers let out a long-drawn wail as they grasped the hair of their children from behind. Then, as the boys were raised to their feet by the bu-ul pulling on their boomerangs and their mothers pulling on their hair, there began a ceremonial tug-of-war for possession.

The remaining men began to chant once again, clicking their boomerangs and ordering the mothers to let go. Simultaneously the surrounding women began slapping their thighs, imploring the mothers not to surrender their charges. And as each side became more insistent, the mothers and those trying to take their children away gave the appearance of struggling mightily to prevail.

With a final wail of despair the mothers released the boys, and the chanting stopped once more.

To Bomarigo fell the task of ordering the women to leave the vicinity and not return. Pointing his boomerangs for emphasis, he reminded them that there were sacred things beyond their ken that were about to be done. The boys would be returned to them at the end of the ceremony, but they would not be the same as they were now. The women no longer had a part to play in their upbringing. During the ceremony all women and children were to stay clear of certain boundaries, which he carefully specified.

"If a woman, for whatever reason, oversteps any of these boundaries," he told them flatly, "she will die! If a child, for whatever reason, oversteps any of these boundaries, that child will die, and also the mother of that child! There can be no exceptions, for the ground is sacred while the kivar-yangga continues!"

Nerida felt her skin crawl while she listened, and she knew that the other women would be feeling the same, even though they had heard it all before. Each time they were uttered, the words of warning brought home to the women the extreme holiness of the ceremony, and each time it was as if they were hearing the words for the first time. She knew that the mothers would be feeling tremendous pride in their sons, as would all who had ever given suck to these boys. And she also knew that the warning just given had made them all reflect on the seriousness of the rituals, and the necessity to obey the law so that people could continue to live in harmony with the forces that allowed their existence.

Bomarigo had finished and, as he turned away to face the pathway that led to the smaller circle, all the bu-ul raised their hands and shouted, "Go! Go now, and do not look back!"

The women and children did not look back as they left.

Talobilla sat in the shade of the shelter which had been prepared for the candidates and looked at the ground. He had been ordered not to look at the sky, for Birral would strike him dead if he did so. He did not quite understand why Birral would do such a thing to him now, when he had never struck him dead for looking at the sky before. Nevertheless, he did not doubt the consequences of disobedience, for questioning had no part to play in the rites to which the boys had been subjected.

While he sat there with his fellow candidates, he mulled over in his mind the events of the last half-moon.

After the women and children had left, the bu-ul who had wrested them from the control of their mothers had painted them and applied feathers, so that now they too were in full ceremonial dress. Those who had not yet had a hole pinched in the septum now had it done, and small sticks had been inserted. Talobilla had been thankful that Buruda had already taken care of his nose, as he knew how uncomfortable the others would feel for a while with the small plug keeping the hole open. The stick in his own nose felt quite natural by now.

After that, all bu-ul had painted themselves, carefully applying the paint and ceremonial feathers, and finally inserting the white nose-bones in noses which had been painted red with red clay. When this had been done, each candidate had been presented with a small dhilla to hang over his shoulder.

It had been his favourite father Buruda who had given him his beautifully decorated dhilla. "Nerida made it for you," he was told. "And I made what is inside."

Talobilla had made as if to explore the contents of the dhilla, but Buruda had held up a warning hand. "Later!" he had admonished him. "First you must listen!"

Bomarigo, the leader of the rituals at this stage, had begun by telling the boys that, just because they had been taken from their mothers for the purpose of being made men, there was no guarantee that they would emerge as such. There had been cases in the past – few, admittedly, but cases nevertheless – where candidates had failed the tests and had had to remain boys all their lives, laughed at by the women and taunted by the children. There was much proving and much learning to be done before the decision would be made to place upon them the marks that were the badge of manhood.

Then a fearful thing had happened as the tests had begun. The boys had been instructed to close their eyes and not to open them on pain of death until they were told. And Talobilla had felt the hair rising on the back of his neck as the silence had suddenly been shattered by the sound of what he knew were the bondaban, the bu-ul roarers. He had heard them before, but always from a distance, and always the noise had engendered fear and unease. But here, close up, the sound had been positively nerve-shattering.

Like nothing on earth, the pulsing, throbbing roar, rising and falling like the chant of some huge ghostly multitude, had filled his ears until they had hurt. And underneath the roaring throb of the bondaban had been heard the stamping and singing of the bu-ul.

"Look now!" had at last come the stentorian command, and this time Talobilla had recognised Buruda's voice. His eyes had snapped open obediently, and the sight had almost taken his breath away. Never in his life had he seen anything so awe-inspiring, as the imposing forms of the bu-ul in full ceremonial dress, led by his father, the most majestic figure of them all, had danced the dance of the spirits to the roar of the bondaban whirled by two men from each of the four nations.

Never before had he seen a bondaban, and Talobilla had strained his eyes, trying to catch a glimpse of these instruments that made such magical sounds. But they had seemed only a sort of blur as the bu-ul had whirled them round and round on their heavy strings.

Then the dance and the chant had stopped, and the bondaban had fallen silent near the feet of those who had been using them. And it had been their very simplicity that had made his eyes pop. Each was just a flat stick with a hole in the end. How could such a small thing make such an unearthly noise? Maybe it was the magical painting that did it, he had reflected in the short space of time following the dance. His quick eye had noticed that each of the bondaban had different markings on it from that of its neighbour.

But he had had to take his mind off them quickly and listen, for Buruda had begun to speak again. And as he had spoken, he had paced back and forth, leaping into the air every now and again to give added emphasis to his words.

"You have heard the bondaban before," he had told them. "Now you have seen them. They are used to warn off evil spirits from the ceremonial grounds, and to bring closer those spirits who will guard you during your trials. Each bondaban brings different spirits, and that is why they are painted differently. You will not learn the meaning of these patterns until you are made bu-ul at the full dhur. It is enough for now that you know you will not be alone in the tests. The spirits will be around you at all times, and we bu-ul will ensure this is so by whirling the bondaban and dancing the spirit dance at the appropriate times."

Then had followed a magical moment which Talobilla was sure he would remember all his life. Buruda had told them to look inside their dhilla and take out what was inside.

The first thing Talobilla had taken out had been a knife, fashioned of quartz chipped to extreme sharpness and embedded in ironwood gum which attached it firmly to a beautifully decorated wooden handle. With such a knife Talobilla had been sure he would be able to skin a kangaroo in the blink of an eye, or bring an enemy to his knees long before his own back had been lacerated to any great extent.

He could have looked at the knife for hours, but he had become aware that other lads were standing and swinging small copies of the bondaban. He looked. Yes, there nestling inside his own dhilla had been a small roarer covered with delicate patterning in white and red clay, attached by a string to a smaller stick which was obviously to be held in the hand.

Standing up, he had joined the other lads in lustily swinging his instrument. The resulting roar had not been as deep as that of the bondaban, but to Talobilla's ear it had seemed as if the tone of his was just that little bit deeper than that of the others. His excitement had given him the feeling that his whole body was vibrating in harmony with the throb of the roarers.

"Gubbi! Gubbi!"

The peremptory command had come from Girrimar of the Tumbra, and the boys had instantly stopped their whirling.

"No!" Girrimar had said yet a third time in the silence that had followed. "Now is not the time to make your wabbalkan roar! You will be told when to swing them, and when you are not told to swing, they must remain still!"

He had then taken one of the wabbalkan from a Tumbra lad and, after swinging it round his head a couple of times, had deftly flicked his wrist. The sharp crack had made every boy jump, so unexpected had been the sound.

Then Kamkuri of the Ningi had leapt forward, turning as he spoke to ensure that every candidate could get a view of his fierce countenance.

"That snap," he had told them, "is made to frighten the makaron, the evil spirits who themselves use Mumba the thunder to terrify people! But you must not snap your wabbalkan often, or these evil spirits will get used to it and come to trouble you!"

At that point Nganku, brandishing his spear, had sternly admonished them, "No woman or child must ever see a wabbalkan! When the kivar-yangga is finished, you will burn them, just as we bu-ul will burn our bondaban! You will never talk of the secrets of the kivar-yangga! Not a word will ever pass your lips regarding the sacred things that will happen to you as you go through the rites that make you young men!"

Then, as one, the bu-ul had leapt in the air, slapping clubs against spears, and had shouted, "Death by the spear! Death by the club! Death to him who breaks this law!"

The nose-bones gleaming white beneath their red noses had seemed to Tallobilla to symbolise the bones that would be broken by the heavy war-clubs and the blood that would flow from a spear-thrust if anybody ever broke the covenant of silence.

There had followed many days of seeing wonders, of having secrets revealed, of learning discipline. They had seen the glorious kakka and learnt its significance in the making of men, and then had been ordered to sit with closed eyes while the bu-ul destroyed it with sharp blows of their axes. They had been taught the sacred chants that they would need to know in order to participate as kivar in the rites of increase.

And they had been forced to sit with stony faces while several bu-ul had acted in such a comical way that it had been agony not to be permitted to roll on the ground and laugh. They had had to endure gross insults in silence, while at the same time their very natures had cried out for the opportunity to fling the insults back in the faces of their tormentors.

"You must learn discipline!" their teachers had kept impressing on them. "Discipline! All emotions must be banished! To lose your temper may leave you open to destruction by an enemy! That same enemy might trick you by making you laugh when you should be vigilant! Nobody with the rank of kivar should ever allow his feelings to betray him when he should be wary!"

And in the midst of the insults and ribaldry, a bu-ul would suddenly thrust his face close to that of one of the candidates and ask a question about some sacred law, or order him to repeat a chant that had already been taught. Or he might use ordinary words in a new way that was known only to men, and expect instant understanding and coherent replies, since the secret new meaning had already been revealed earlier.

"You dullard!" they would thunder if there was any hesitation. "How do you expect to be able to speak men's language in front of women? By your stupidity you will make every secret known to the whole camp!"

So they had concentrated, and gradually the new learning had become second nature. And at the same time they had been able to discern within themselves a gradual growing, a burgeoning of new creatures protected from evil by sacred ritual. And they had felt that these new persons within were also being nurtured by the enormous strength of the forces of good, the power of those creatures of the Before-Time, whose presence could be sensed in the mystical figures lining the pathway joining the two sacred rings.

Along this path they had been guided every night by the light of flickering torches, to the pulsating sound of the bondaban and the chanting of the bu-ul, and each night some different aspect had been pointed out to them.

All these things Talobilla remembered as he sat with the other candidates staring at the ground. They had been sitting like this all morning, without food or drink of any kind, and his back was aching. But despite his hunger and thirst, he felt a strange contentment, for he knew that he had performed creditably throughout the testing. Most of the time Buruda had taken a leading part in the rituals. And, while he had been careful to present the same countenance to Talobilla as he had to the rest of the lads, Talobilla thought he had detected a fierce pride in the eyes of his favourite father whenever they turned in his direction.

I will never shame him! Talobilla thought fiercely. I will always –

But his reverie was interrupted by a sudden loud command from Bomarigo. "No longer must you look down to avoid the wrath of Birral! Stand up and behold Birra, the sky!"

Talobilla stood, and instantly felt himself being grabbed from behind by two bu-ul, one on either side. Unceremoniously a leg kicked from behind, so that he buckled at the knees. To his surprise, however, he did not fall to the ground, but landed on the backs of two other bu-ul who were waiting behind him on hands and knees.

He managed to cast a swift glance around him, and noticed that all the other lads were being dealt with in similar fashion. Like him, they ended up stretched out face upward on the backs of two bu-ul, held firmly at the same time by two others. None of the four bu-ul belonged to the same nation as the lad they supported. Talobilla found himself lying on the backs of two Ningi dhan, while a dhan from the Tumbra held his left arm and another from the Dhundubari held his right.

At that moment, when all the boys were ready, the bondaban began to whirr and pulsate. At the same time, all bu-ul began the chant of the kivar-yangga, and those not occupied with holding boys or whirling bondaban began to dance on the ground in the centre of the ring.

Only the five manngur remained aloof.

A savage joy lifted Talobilla's heart as he knew that at last the time had come for him to receive the marks that would show to all who looked that he was considered worthy of becoming a kivar of the Undanbi. The sun burned down on his outstretched body, still aching from the enforced inactivity of the morning, and the dust raised by the stamping feet filled his nostrils. But his mind registered none of these things. He heard only the sacred sounds of the chant and the bondaban, saw only Buruda as he danced up to him, coming to a stop in a kneeling position in the dust between his legs.

He felt Buruda's questing hand reach into the dhilla nestled below his left armpit and withdraw the knife that rested there. Then, as Buruda raised the knife for all to see, another dhan who had been kneeling behind him began to beat Talobilla's ears with open hands, while the roar of the bondaban and the chant of the bu-ul swelled even louder.

Talobilla guessed that these actions were meant to dull the pain of the marking, but as Buruda cut the pattern of the Undanbi on his chest, he found himself welcoming the pain, which served only to increase the intensity of his elation. Even when the powdered charcoal was rubbed into the copiously bleeding wounds to ensure that the cicatrices would stand out boldly when they had healed, Talobilla felt little pain, so transported was he by the sensation of power engendered by the transition into manhood.

When it was over, Buruda leaned forward and whispered into his ear just loudly enough for Talobilla, and nobody else, to hear above the throbbing and the chanting, "Turugun!"

And tears of joy cascaded down the kivar Turugun's face as, having received the name that he would bear until his death, he stood to face the world.

The noise continued for some time, since the other manngur each had more than one candidate to mark and name. But eventually it was over, and all newly-made kivar were standing facing the centre of the ring.

As quiet descended, Buruda was the first to step forward, leading his son by the hand.

"Turugun!" his voice rang out, and the assembled multitude welcomed the new kivar into the fuller life of young manhood, booming out his new name, "Turugun!"

One by one the other kivar were introduced by name, and each time the name was echoed by the bu-ul.

Then followed the ceremonial burning of the bondaban and wabbalkan on a great bonfire in the centre of the ring. They then returned to the larger circle, the bu-ul systematically smashing the grass and clay figures as they went. No trace of the sacred figures must remain, since disaster would surely fall upon the people if the figures were to be profaned by the eyes of the uninitiated.

The kivar-yangga was over for this season.

Only the fighting remained to be accomplished.

Before the triumphant procession made its way back to camp, the five manngur withdrew from the rest of the dhan to discuss once more Buruda's dream.

But no matter which way they looked at it, there was no answer.

The only explanation they had been able to come up with that made any sense was that Buruda had journeyed to the land of the dead. But if that was the case, then it must be a fearsome place indeed. But Midherplinda's footprints were there, so it just had to be the land of the dead.

And maybe Buruda had not been able to make any footprints because he was not yet a spirit.

But the strange animal tracks, with none of the familiar animals around? Well, maybe that is what happened in the spirit-land. Maybe animals took on strange forms, too.

And the death-wail, with the people dead in horrifyingly strange ways? And the emptiness of the land?

"That could never happen!" Girrimar stated emphatically. "There will always be the dhundharin, the helpful spirits who will ensure the increase of the animals and trees and people."

Buruda nodded. "Yet we should not forget what the old ones have taught us, that the increase depends on how well we perform the ceremonies," he admonished them. "Perhaps, then, the last part of the dream was meant to show us that we will have to pay more attention to the way we perform the rituals of increase. Maybe the dream is showing us that, if the birds and animals and trees are kept healthy, the other things cannot happen!"

So it was agreed. They would learn from the dream.

"And we must be very careful indeed if Midherplinda or anyone like him returns!" Bomarigo warned.

But the time had come to show the newly-made kivar to the women, so they rejoined the rest of the dhan.

Notes on Chapter 4

"Bondaban" was the Gubbi name for the so-called "bull roarer". Indeed, the name "bull roarer" still owes its origin to the Gubbi language, since it refers to the noise made at the making of "bu-ul" or men. It certainly had nothing to do with the sound made by a bull!

The Tumbra of the Maroochy River area painted their noses red to show their relationship to the black swan. The word "maroochy" was used by the Gubbi people for the black swan, but they also used "kuluin". "Maroochy" is a loose form of the Yugara word "muru-kutji", literally "nose-red".

"Makaron" were evil spirits. This word was later used for the white people.

"Dhundharin" were good spirits.

Chapter 5

1821: The Baiyaba

Throughout the kivar-yangga Nerida had felt a vague unease. This had been the first time since she had come to Buruda that she had had to sleep without his comforting presence beside her, and her spirit had not rested well. Always in the past, before her marriage, the time of ceremonies had made her fearful, but at least she had then had the company of her mother Koppakkin in the hut. This time she had only herself to rely on, and the long nights had been filled with foreboding.

One night had stood out as particularly terrifying. That evening, as usual, after the cry for the dead, the women and children had assembled round the camp-fire, blazing high to keep makaron at a distance, to tell stories and sing songs before settling down to sleep. Suddenly from the direction of the headland had come the distant droning of the bondaban, and they had all huddled together, fearful of they knew not what.

The sound awakened fears enough during the full light of day. By night it had the power to conjure up nameless terrors, while imagination added shape and substance to the shadows cast by the flames of the camp-fire.

When the magic throbbing had at last died away into blessed silence, someone had giggled nervously, and then they had all joined in, laughing uproariously, thankful for any little incident that would allow some easing of the tension. Then, while all the women had slapped their thighs in time, Mundul had sung them the story of the mountains of the Nalbo. She had sung of how the eldest son Coonowrin had refused his father Tibrogargan's order to assist his pregnant mother Beerwah in her attempt to escape the waters rushing in from the ocean outside Yarun, and of how Tibrogargan had consequently brought his eldest son a great blow to the side of his head with his club, bending his neck forever.

The familiar favourite had helped them relax, and they had all chattered afterwards about the consequences of these actions in the Before-Time. The tears that formed streams flowing from the crooked-necked Coonowrin were living proof, for example, of the deep contrition felt by the eldest son for his cowardly actions. And likewise the refusal of Tibrogargan to forgive his son was still there for all to witness, as he continued to stand looking vigilantly out to sea, his back to Coonowrin.

The Tumbra women had then danced the story of Maroochy, that beautiful young wife of the powerful manngur Ninderry. The dance told of how Coolum, bewitched by Maroochy's grace and charm, had descended on the camp one night while the bu-ul were all away at the dhur, and dragged her screaming into the night. A long chase by Ninderry had ended with his hurling his boomerang and decapitating Coolum. But, before he had been able to take his wife triumphantly home, Coolum's vengeful spirit had spitefully turned Ninderry to stone.

The women from all four nations had slapped their thighs enthusiastically as the dancers had stamped to the ageless rhythm of the story, and those children who had not already dozed off on their mothers' possum skins had listened open-mouthed to the tale. Again, when it was all over, there had been endless observations about the visible results of these happenings. For instance, you had only to stand on any reasonable eminence in Undanbi territory to view Ninderry standing up tall, having released his boomerang at Coolum, whose squat body still stood headless near the sea. As usual, the women had wondered long and hard why Coolum's head had ended up so far away from the body. And, as usual, they had reached the conclusion that Ninderry had been a mighty warrior indeed, able to hurl the boomerang well with either hand. For it was obvious that it was a left-handed throw that had caused the head – now known as Buderim – to land where it had.

And what of Maroochy, Ninderry's beautiful wife? Her tears were still visible in the river flowing so close to her husband, and then curving away to avoid the body of the hated Coolum.

And anyone could see, in the ocean near the scene of the story, how old Mudjimba, Maroochy's mother, had hurled herself into the ocean when she had learnt the fate of her beloved daughter. And if you looked carefully, you could see that Mudjimba still had her back turned to her son-in-law Ninderry, obeying the law of skins even in death.

After the discussion had ended, a Dhundubari lad, due to pass through the kivar-yangga next time it was held, had grated savagely, "If a bu-ul from another nation were to come and take one of our women while our dhan were away, I'd split his head with a club!"

"Indeed, my boy!" his mother had remarked. "And tell me, pray, where you'd get this imaginary club! Would you use my digging-stick?"

The idea of a boy chasing a fully-armed marauding warrior with a digging-stick had led to a great roar of laughter at his expense, and he had hung his head, muttering to himself that they would see next season, after he had become a kivar!

Afterwards, Nerida had slept soundly, her earlier fears forgotten. Indeed, with so many women round about, it had been impossible to remain fearful for long. But some time in the early hours she had awakened with a jerk, having been alerted by the sound of a strange footfall. There – it had come again! And, her senses heightened by abject fear, she had listened to the stealthy approach of some unknown person or thing to the back of her hut. While she had lain there, her mouth wide open to cover the sound of her own breathing, her imagination had run riot. Was this a bu-ul of another nation coming to take a woman – perhaps even her? Was he from the Dallambara? Perhaps he could even be from the Badtjala on far K'gari!

Was the story of Maroochy about to be re-enacted?

She had been able to feel her heart pounding frantically in her breast. For what had seemed like an eternity she had held her breath, wondering whether she should lie still, or scream and rouse the camp. There seemed to be only one person, and she did not doubt that she would be able to give a good account of herself if she were only given the chance of reaching her digging-stick in time. And if she could rouse one or two others, it would be a doughty bu-ul indeed who would be able to stand against them!

Then, just as she had decided to make a dash for her stick, she had heard the footsteps go back past the back of her hut.

Apparently whoever it was had not been interested in her. In fact, it could easily be just one of the women answering the call of nature. Still, it was not likely, for no such woman would feel the need to tread so stealthily.

Despite her attempts to reassure herself, she had slept no more that night. Instead, she had quietly brought her digging-stick inside the hut, ready to rouse the sleeping camp at the first sign of trouble. Only when the first bird calls had heralded the approach of daylight had she been able to relax her vigilance.

As soon as her eyes had been able to pick out the shapes of the trees beyond the smoke of her hearth-fire, she had quietly gone round to the rear of her hut and bent down to study the tracks on the ground. Patiently she had waited for the light to grow stronger, squatting motionless, anxious to examine the tracks before any other person chanced along to obliterate them.

But before the light had grown strong enough to clearly distinguish the characteristics of the tracks, Buldarin had quietly joined her. "What are you looking for?" she had asked, as the camp was beginning to stir around them. "Is something wrong?"

"I don't know. It's just that somebody came by last night."

Then they had both seen it at once, and both had gasped. There before them the light had at last revealed a clear footprint of Ngandun.

Buldarin had begun to tremble. She had thought she was safe from her husband for the duration of the kivar-yangga. "What could he have been doing last night? Why -?"

But Nerida had had no answer. The only thing they had both been able to see was that the tracks had skirted both their huts and seemed to be headed in the direction of a dense clump of bushes near the creek.

"Maybe he was sent back on man's business connected with the kivar-yangga," Buldarin suggested hopefully. But even as she had spoken the words she had known that such an explanation would be highly unlikely. Dhan remained with dhan for the whole time of the ceremony, and there were established procedures to be followed if, by any chance, messages needed to be carried back to the women's camp.

They had made their way hurriedly to the clump of bushes, worried that the tracks would be overlaid by others as the camp awoke. They could already hear some children playing a skipping game near the middle of the camp, and some of the mothers appeared to have joined in, judging by the shrieks of laughter.

As it was, they had been too late. Just as they had reached the bushes, Yerakun had emerged to confront them, carrying sticks for her mother's fire.

"N'gara!" she had greeted them.

They had returned her greeting, and had been able to see from the state of the ground that they had missed their chance. Yerakun's tracks appeared to be everywhere.

"What are you doing here?" Buldarin had demanded.

"Getting sticks for our fire. I didn't get enough yesterday."

"Then your mother ought to give you a good taste of the digging-stick!" Buldarin had gritted, piqued at having been thwarted.

The girl had tossed her head and left.

"Pity she hasn't been given a husband to keep her in order!" Buldarin had muttered to Nerida as they had retraced their steps. "She's been old enough these last three summers to have the hair round her binang taken off!"

Nerida had tried to calm her. "She has to wait yet. Her promised husband is only a kivar."

But Buldarin had refused to be mollified. "She's always struck me as the type to cause trouble!" she had grumbled. "She's got too fine an eye for the bu-ul, if you ask me! At least she can't cast her net at Ngandun, since she is Dhuroingan!"

But as Buldarin's words had sunk in, Nerida had felt the blood drain from her face. What if -? She had dared not pursue the thought further, it had been so unthinkable.

Yet, try as she might to forget it, the thought had kept intruding. Later that day, when they had left the bangwal in the appointed place, her head had been full of it. And later still, when they had returned to pick up the luscious fruit-bats left there by the dhan, who had that day hunted at Currimundi - the place of the flying-fox - the thought had still persisted.

That night, as the distant throbbing of the bondaban had reminded her of the sacred ceremonies being performed not far away, it had conveyed another message as well to Nerida – a message of death to all breakers of the law. She had found her mind to be only half on the night's entertainment and later, as she had again lain wakeful, the thought that she had tried so hard to smother had surfaced once more in all its horror.

What if Ngandun, a Barang, were associated with Yerakun, a Dhuroingan, and therefore one who should be avoided by him as he would avoid a mother-in-law?

The idea was so preposterous that Nerida had at last been forced to admit its impossibility. It would be tantamount to imagining that someone could eat his own dung!

No. Ngandun was a bad-tempered dhan who treated his wife shamefully, that was true. But he could not do what she had been imagining. Nobody could do that!

Having dismissed the thought as ridiculous, she had at last fallen asleep, but her sleep had been disturbed by vague dreams that she had been unable to recall in the morning. All she remembered was that they had not been pleasant.

And despite her determination to cast the idea out of her mind, she had found herself watching Yerakun more closely. That morning, after collecting water-lily bulbs from the creek, the women had wandered toward the hill in search of bangwal, only to retreat hastily as they had heard the yells of bu-ul in that direction herding kangaroos into their kangaroo-catching nets which they had stretched between trees.

Had Yerakun not lingered longer than the other women before she had turned away?

I am being silly! Nerida told herself. Of course Yerakun likes men – everyone knows that! But I must stop seeing something where nothing is!

Gradually, as the kivar-yangga drew to a close and the thought of Buruda's return had begun to occupy her mind, she had been able to forget her suspicions. But she could not drive from her mind the thought that Ngandun had visited the camp at a time when she would have expected him to be totally engrossed in the sacred rites being performed at the Caloundra rings. She would be able to tell Buruda about that and let him work out what the problem was, if any. Perhaps there was a very simple explanation, after all.

The women and children were all gathered facing the direction of the sacred rings. They stood in order of geographical origin, with the Tumbra closest to their land to the north and then the Undanbi, Dhundubari and Ningi. As they waited, the women clapped their hands and sang the song that told of their boys returning as kivar from the land of the dead. It was a song of triumph, and even the children joined in the chant as they stamped so that the dust rose from round their feet.

Then the horde of bu-ul and kivar appeared, the Undanbi in the van, this being their land. The women let out one great shout of welcome and then fell silent, waiting expectantly.

They did not have long to wait.

First came Buruda, striding forward holding the hand of his son who had left as Talobilla only a short half-moon before. But this was no Talobilla Buruda was about to present to the people. Here was a young man, holding himself proudly, still bloodied from his new birth, the marks of manhood standing out boldly for all to see, his dhilla nestled beneath his left arm.

Buruda and the newly-made kivar halted. Then, holding up the hand of his son, Buruda shouted, "Turugun!"

The response was instantaneous. In recognition of the fact that a new young man had been added to the ranks of the Undanbi warriors, a resounding shout rose from the assembled women of all four nations.

"Turugun!"

Then came the turn of the Tumbra to present their graduates, followed by the Dhundubari and the Ningi. And each time the forest echoed as the women shouted the names by which the new kivar were to be addressed.

The formalities over, the bu-ul came forward to greet their wives and rest while the evening meal was being prepared. The new kivar, however, only too aware of their status, ignoring the women and children, repaired with their fellow kivar to the special shelter set apart from the rest. They would keep themselves separate in this way until the time of their full dhur in a few seasons' time, accepting bangwal from the women, but cooking their own meat and fish, and abstaining from all forbidden things such as fish roe.

That night the festivities were kept short, for husbands and wives had been apart for a long time, and there was much to make up for. Besides, tomorrow they would be at the baiyaba, and all dhan would need to be fresh in case a challenge was mounted against them.

Next day all repaired to the fighting-ground, the bu-ul fully painted and armed, nose-bones gleaming, the swan's down on their bodies fluttering in the morning breeze. The women took their place according to their nation on either side of the ground, their digging-sticks stuck in the ground in front of them, children behind them out of harm's way.

First the newly-made kivar took their places on the baiyaba. Two opposing sides had been agreed upon – Undanbi and Tumbra against Ningi and Dhundubari. To make the sides even in number, two kivar of the Undanbi who had been inducted only last season joined Turugun in the field. All kivar wore the headband with the long tail dangling behind which distinguished them, even at a distance, from bu-ul. They were fully painted and feathered.

Their weapons today were two spears and a shield.

Despite the fact that their cuts were now painful, it did not take them long to prepare. Anxious to show their mettle, the two lines drew up at either end of the ground and, at a signal from

Bomarigo, advanced towards each other, making fearful threats as they came. They stopped when they had reached a spear's throw apart, each planting a spear upright in the earth beside him. Then, carefully grasping the shields by the handles so that their left arms were invisible, they hefted their spears, arms poised for the throw.

This was the time of proving. The spectators – men, women, and children – held their breath, all watching their favourites closely, willing them to show superiority in the battle about to begin. Though confident of Turugun's ability, Buruda still felt a quickening of the pulse. He was aware that, even with the greatest warriors, something could go wrong.

Then the first spear arced through the air. It was Turugun who had thrown it, and Buruda watched intently as it sped straight and true to its target. His opponent, a Ningi kivar standing opposite him, had all his work cut out to take the spear on his shield so that it was deflected and sped by, missing him by the narrowest of margins.

"E-e-e-e-e-e-e-e-e-e-e!" came the appreciative exclamation at throw and parry. Both kivar had performed creditably.

A flurry of spears followed as the rest of the kivar got into the fray. The spectators, finding it hard to keep up with all the action, had to confine themselves to following the fortunes of their own particular heroes. Buruda saw Turugun easily take the spear thrown at him on his shield and then, treating it with contempt, reach for his second spear as it flashed past him.

"E-e-e-e-e-e-e-e-e-e!" Turugun's action had been noted by many, and even the Ningi spectators appreciated the skill shown. It was obvious that this young warrior would be one to watch in the future.

But all the kivar were performing well, and as the fight proceeded, some began to show the results of much practice as they waited until the last moment before dodging or turning a spear aside. Again and again spears were retrieved and thrown with neither side gaining the advantage. But at last they began to tire, and some began to take slight wounds as they left it too late to parry or dodge. Finally, one of Turugun's spears found the thigh of his opponent, and Bomarigo called a halt.

"Gubbi! Gubbi!"

Buruda was well pleased, and even more so when he saw Turugun walk up to his fallen adversary, remove the spear, and then present his own thigh to his opponent, having first helped him to his feet.

The Ningi kivar was well aware that to refuse the offer would go against custom. The law demanded that thrust be returned for thrust. Without hesitation he transfixed Turugun's thigh.

And then a great "E-e-e-e-e-e-e-e-e!" burst from the throats of the assembly when Turugun, as soon as the spear had been withdrawn, picked up his weapons and strode toward the waiting Undanbi bu-ul, refusing to recognise the pain that all knew he must be feeling.

Tears of pride streamed down Buruda's face. This was the son he had trained!

A short interval followed before the next contest. Then suddenly a Tumbra bu-ul led a team of eight onto the field and defied all and sundry to match them man for man. It was Wungul who led the Undanbi team to take up the challenge, and soon a battle royal was in progress between the two sides, heavy spears flying through the air as insults were traded for insults. But these were seasoned warriors who knew how to conserve energy as they fought, highly skilled in the use of spear and shield.

The spectators looked on critically, savouring the skill at verbal abuse as much as the fighting ability of the participants.

At last Bomarigo called a halt, both sides satisfied that they had shown the newly-made kivar how bu-ul ought to fight.

All day challenges were made and accepted. Now and again a wound severe enough to require urgent attention would necessitate the immediate cessation of hostilities, but most contests continued until Bomarigo decided that the kivar had learnt enough from that particular battle. For it was the teaching of skills of war that was the main object of the fights.

By late in the afternoon all bu-ul except the very old had participated. Buruda had led an Undanbi team against one from the Dhundubari led by Nganku. Twice the force of the impact of Buruda's spear on shield had almost knocked his opponent from his feet.

The day was fast drawing to a close and the crowd were beginning to think that it was time to return to camp and partake of the food they had left there. Besides, after a while you could get tired of these shows of strength.

Then a single Tumbra warrior, Yelabon by name, strode out onto one end of the baiyaba. He carried two spears, a boomerang and two clubs – the throwing-club as well as the one used at close quarters. He carried both types of shields also.

His weapons left no doubt that what was to follow was to be no mere exhibition for the benefit of the kivar.

Placing both spears upright in the ground and laying his clubs and light shield beside them, he yelled, "There is amongst the Undanbi a cowardly hater of dogs!"

The words drew a sharp intake of breath from the spectators. This was a serious matter. A dog was a member of the family, so any insult to a man's dog could easily result in a struggle to the death, unless others intervened.

Yelabon sprang into the air and yelled the name they were waiting to hear. "Come out and face me, Piringa! Or do you fight only defenceless dogs?"

Nothing loath, Piringa stepped out from the ranks of the Undanbi, armed in a similar fashion to his opponent. He knew the incident Yelabon was referring to. It had all stemmed from the fact that Piringa's wife was a Tumbra. Last summer, while they were paying a visit to her relatives, Yelabon's dog had attacked their little four-summers-old boy, inflicting a nasty bite. Yelabon had seen the incident, but had only half-heartedly called his dog off, so that Piringa had felt impelled to hurl a stick at the still-snarling dog, hitting it a resounding blow on the back. The incident had threatened to develop into a fight at that very instant, and would certainly have done so had Yelabon not been restrained by friends standing nearby.

No, Piringa was not surprised that the man's smouldering resentment had at last burst into flame. Taking up a position facing his opponent, he arranged his weapons as Yelabon had done. Then, leaping high in the air, he shouted for all to hear, "What you see opposite me is not a man, but a turd that has no words to stop a dog attacking a little boy! I can even smell him at this distance!"

There followed a time of deadly insults, each man trying hard to unsettle his opponent before the fight began. At last, impatient of any more delay, Yelabon hurled his heavy hunting boomerang at Piringa and, even while it was still a swishing blur in the air, followed it immediately with a spear, obviously hoping that one of the weapons would find its target while his enemy was occupied dodging the other.

But Piringa was no novice. Stepping nimbly aside so as to be out of the way of the trajectory of the boomerang, he replied by releasing his own boomerang and spear at his adversary. Then, even as both men caught the first spears on their shields, they plucked the others from the ground and sent them whistling through the air. These too were deftly turned aside by both men.

Again there was that sharp intake of breath from the onlookers as they saw Yelabon pick up the throwing-club with his toes and transfer it quickly to his throwing hand, Piringa matching him movement for movement.

Since neither man had bothered to retrieve his opponent's spears, it became obvious to the crowd that both were eager to get to close quarters. This was a grudge fight indeed!

But the throwing-clubs would not be effective at this distance, so both scooped up their remaining weapons, hurrying forward until they had reached club-throwing distance. Then, dropping the broad shields and heavy clubs to the ground once more, each flung his sharp-pointed club with all his might. With dull thuds, both were taken squarely on the hardwood shields, to fall harmlessly to the ground.

Once more that sharp intake of breath as both, discarding the heavy shields and scooping up club and light shields, raced forward. And as they ran, both plucked knives from their dhilla and placed them between their teeth.

No hesitation. The instant they reached striking distance, each swung his club at his opponent's head, at the same time raising the shield to protect his own. Again and again the heavy clubs thudded against shields, denting the soft wood as they absorbed the shuddering shock of the blows.

But neither seemed able to gain the advantage, so they began to direct their blows at shoulders and legs, hoping to outwit each other by guile. But their clubs continued to meet nothing but shields.

The crowd scarcely seemed to breathe. Gogindi! Ariro! These bu-ul were bu-ul indeed!

But the two were beginning to feel the effects of the long struggle. Their grunts became more audible each time they swung the heavy clubs, and the hissing of breath between teeth tightly clenched on their knives told the story of endurance reaching its limits.

Then at last Yelabon's club grazed Piringa's shoulder. Almost at the same instant, Yelabon received a blow on the thigh.

"E-e-e-e-e-e-e-e!" from the crowd.

With howls of rage, the combatants sprang apart to discard clubs and shields. Then, taking the knives from between their teeth, they grappled, each grasping his opponent round the neck with his left arm to prevent accidental disengagement.

The slashing that followed was watched even more intently by the spectators, for under no circumstances could the marks of the dhur be defaced. The law stated that cutting had to be confined to the back and thighs. Any infringement could mean instant death, for no person had the right to disfigure the sacred marks on chest and shoulders that distinguished the dhan of one nation from those of another. At times a bu-ul might receive a spear wound on chest or shoulder, and even the heavy blow of a club could cause disfigurement of the marks. But these were something caused by chance, since nobody could be expected to foresee where a spear might hit, or the point to which a club might be deflected by a shield. The marks made by a knife, however, were marks made when men were holding each other in the manner laid down since the Before-Time, and it was only by deliberate action that shoulder or chest marks could be defaced from this position.

But there was no need to worry about these two. Soon their backs were a mass of blood as both men slashed away with a will, their knives working energetically.

Then, as it became obvious that neither would yield and that a great amount of blood had been spilt, Bomarigo's voice rang out, "Wa! Enough!"

Knives stopped in mid-air, and both men released their hold to stand panting with exhaustion. Then they grinned at each other.

The crowd appreciated it. "E-e-e-e-e-e-e-e-e-e-e!"

So all the fighting came to an end. After Buruda and Girrimar had applied powdered charcoal, eaglehawk down and white clay to the gaping wounds, the two former combatants collected their weapons, albeit using toes rather than hands to pick them up from the ground, since to bend over was extremely painful. They would sleep on their bellies for a half-moon or so until the wounds healed.

That night there was much exchanging of gifts among friends of the various nations. In the morning they would be going back to their own countries.

Piringa and Yelabon exchanged clubs.

Notes on Chapter 5

The place-name "Currimundi" means "place of the flying-fox". It should more correctly be "Girramandha", named after "girraman", the flying-fox or fruit-bat.

"Baiyaba" was the name given to the fighting-ground.

✦

Chapter 6

1821: Death of a Manngur

Shortly after the first bird call, the Tumbra set out to retrace their steps northward. Before they left, they asked for and were given permission to hunt flying-foxes at Currimundi, since these animals had been scarce lately in the dibing forests near Ninderry, and they wished to have one more feast of this delicacy while they had the chance.

The remainder of the group left for the south soon afterwards. They kept together till later in the morning, when the Undanbi camp at the mouth of the creek was reached. The canoes of the Dhundubari had been left at that spot at the beginning of the kivar-yangga, and it did not take them long to launch them ready for the crossing of Kaerwagum. After the smouldering fire-sticks had been carefully laid on clay and sand in the centre of the canoes, the heavily-laden craft nosed their way out of the mouth of the creek.

Much good-natured advice was yelled at the departing people as they left for, despite the fact that the visitors were taking the loan of some of the Undanbi canoes as well, the frail craft were carrying almost double the number they had carried earlier on the crossing to the mainland. The reason for this was that the Ningi had also decided to make their way home along the ocean beach of Yarun, for there would be plenty of tailer to spear on the way, and the Dhundubari had generously granted them leave to collect yugari at the same time. The Ningi would recross Kaerwagum at the southern end of Yarun to reach their own country.

The north wind, which would pick up later in the afternoon, was still only a gentle breeze, so most of the canoes managed to negotiate the narrow crossing without too much trouble. To the intense delight of the Undanbi people, however, one of the canoes turned over when an argument broke out between two bu-ul over which pole should be used to execute a turn to keep them off a sandbank.

The cursing, yelling and screaming that ensued were enough to ensure that all the Undanbi watchers – men, women and children – went into paroxysms of laughter, rolling on the ground for a full ten minutes. This was better entertainment even than the cursing and threats at the baiyaba! A fitting ending indeed to a time of friendly intercourse!

But order returned after the canoe was righted and continued on its way, albeit without the smoke of a fire coming from its centre.

The Undanbi waved their last farewells as their friends disappeared over the narrow sandhills of Yarun to the ocean side, and the camp settled down to its daily routine. Women took their dhilla and digging-sticks and, accompanied by the children, left to dig bangwal. The men moved down to the sandbank where the creek entered Kaerwagum, carrying their mula.

But Buruda was anxious to see how Gibberol had fared during their absence. A dhan had been sent from the ceremonial ground each day with food for the old man and Garwidha, and every day the courier had returned to Buruda with the report that the old man was well. Still, Buruda wanted to find out the state of Gibberol's health for himself.

Turugun, despite the tenderness of his cuts and spear-wound, jumped at the chance when Buruda handed over his mula and suggested he take his place for the morning. Buruda knew that the young kivar would serve the fishing team well.

As soon as he saw Garwidha, Buruda saw there was no need to inquire about her husband. Her brimming eyes told the story.

The old man made a weak attempt to smile as he opened his eyes and looked up from underneath the possum-fur rug. "So you are not yet the only manngur of the Undanbi!" he said, with a poor attempt at a chuckle. "There is still life in the old man!"

The voice shocked Buruda. It was no more than a whisper.

"You have not been eating the meat and fish I sent you!" he chided the old man. His sharp eyes had not missed the fact that Gibberol's dog was fatter than usual.

"No matter!" Gibberol whispered. "I am not hungry."

Sitting down, Buruda took his old friend's hand. It seemed cold to the touch, as if life had already begun to ebb.

For a long, long time he sat near the man who had loved him so well and taught him so much, never relinquishing his hold on the hand for a moment, as if that slender contact with the living might be enough to keep death at bay. Meanwhile Gibberol dozed, his breathing shallow, only a slight twitching of his limbs every now and again signifying that his spirit was still there within the wasted body.

Once he roused himself enough to whisper, "I told you I would not die while the kivar-yangga was being celebrated!" Again that ghost of a smile.

A little later he stirred once more and said something so softly that Buruda could not catch it.

"What did you say, old man?" he asked gently. Then, placing his ear low against Gibberol's lips, he heard him say, "It's cold!"

It was quite hot inside the hut, as Bigi had hardly begun his downward journey in the sky. But Garwidha, in response to Buruda's shout, obediently brought in the skin of a kangaroo and gently placed it over the possum-fur rug to give some added warmth.

Time passed. The women returned from their digging and the men from their fishing, and Buruda still sat there, holding Gibberol's hand. There was about the camp the silence of expectation of death.

Even the children's games were uncharacteristically hushed.

Again the old man tried to speak, and Buruda bent low to listen. He could not make out what the old manngur was saying, but a few words came through to him.

"------------ dream -----------care ------------- makaron!"

Then, with a supreme effort, the old man tried to sit up, and gasped, "Buruda! Take care! The dream!"

At that, falling back, his eyes rolled, and he moved no more.

Buruda, still holding the old man's lifeless hand, began the death-wail of the Undanbi, and Garwidha joined in. Soon the cry was taken up all over the camp. High and shrill it rose, berating the old man for leaving the people so desolate. Why, they chided him, had he left so soon? Was the hunting better in that other country? Was not the land of the Undanbi beautiful – more beautiful than the land of the spirits? Return before it is too late! Return to your loved ones!

And Garwidha, tears coursing down her cheeks, tore at her face with her nails to gouge out the marks of sorrow. Then, dissatisfied with the amount of pain she was inflicting upon herself, she took a sharp shell from the ground and scored her face until it streamed blood.

When Buruda was satisfied she had done herself enough damage, he firmly took her hand and removed the shell.

Wungul arrived at the hut opening, and together the two men carried the almost weightless body to a spot beyond the confines of the camp. Here, hidden from prying eyes, they would be able to prepare it in the manner laid down by the law. Garwidha, the blood clotted upon her face, accompanied them, still wailing piteously.

Leaving her and Wungul to watch over the old man, Buruda returned to the hut. The possum-fur rug and the kangaroo skin, since they had been in contact with the body at the moment of death, must be destroyed, as must the hut where he had breathed his last. His weapons and nets, too, must be burnt. By consigning all these items to the flames, two purposes would be fulfilled. The old man's spirit would not only have shelter, warmth, and the means to hunt and survive in the spirit-world, but also it would not feel the need to return to familiar possessions lying about the camp, where it might inadvertently cause trouble.

So he removed Garwidha's dhilla and digging-stick to a safe distance, and then he and the other dhan who had gathered round draped the rug and skin over the hut roof. Then, after leaning the old man's weapons against it, he applied the torch. As he turned to make his way back to the body where he had still much to do, he knew he did not need to remind the dhan to make sure nothing but ashes remained. They knew the law as well as he.

Garwidha had already started a fire, and Wungul had made the first incisions preparatory to flaying the body. Painstakingly the two men worked, carefully separating skin from wasted flesh, until at last the body lay divested of its earthly covering. Then, with great tenderness, Buruda took the skin, complete with hair and nails, and placed it over three spears which Wungul had set upright in the ground near the fire. The smoke from the fire would not only drive the old man's spirit away, but would also cure the skin, preserving it for all time, so that it could be cherished by those who had loved its owner during life.

Thus did the people honour their dead.

And all the while the three of them sang the chant of the dead, Garwidha rocking back and forth in her sorrow. And from the camp nearby the people also sang, tears running down their cheeks, even as they got ready for the evening meal.

Buruda examined the wasted flesh left on the bones. The law demanded that, unless there was a very good reason, the flesh of one newly dead should be consumed by the people, particularly close relatives, so that the strength and characteristics of the dead person should not be altogether lost to the nation. But where was the strength here? The old man had used it all up in life, so that there was none left.

Yet he was determined that the spiritual power that had been encompassed in the body of his old friend should not be lost. He knew that, if he had been able to speak, the old man would have told him that he wished that power to be conferred on Buruda alone.

So let it be! The power of the old manngur would be added to the young manngur. Taking his knife, he sliced a piece of tough old meat from the thigh and placed it gently on the fire.

Garwidha went to fetch dibing bark, while he and Wungul carefully stripped the flesh from the bones until they lay white and bare on the bark by the fire. Having done that, they wrapped the flesh and waste parts ready for burial.

After that, Buruda took the piece of flesh from the fire and bore it to his mouth. It was so tough that he found it hard to chew but, after he had succeeded in swallowing it all, he felt a deep sense of accomplishment. He was sure the old man's spirit would be smiling approvingly.

Trusting nobody but himself, he returned to the camp for Garwidha's digging-stick. Then, taking the bark containing the flesh and the waste parts, he walked away from the camp. Bigi was already sinking below the trees. Choosing a secluded spot, he dug a hole almost as deep as the digging-stick itself, chanting all the while. When he was at last satisfied, he placed his precious bundle at the bottom of the hole and replaced the soil on top, finally rolling a log over the place to thwart any inquisitive dog.

It was almost dark by the time he returned to the fire. Wungul had already left, and Garwidha had the old man's bones decently wrapped in bark and deposited in a dhilla, which she had hung in the smoke near the skin.

"Do you want help to build a shelter here?" Buruda asked her.

She shook her head. "No. It will not be too cold tonight, and I will be all right here by the fire."

"Nerida will give Naruman bangwal to bring you, and he will bring you fish as well," he told her. "And I'll tell him to bring a skin to cover you." He placed a kindly hand on her shoulder. "The old man would want you to rest well tonight."

She nodded silently, and he left to search out Naruman.

After he had spoken to Naruman about tending Garwidha, he added, "After four days, when the time of deep mourning is over, you will remove the hair from round your dhun and Garwidha will come to you."

He was pleased to see that Naruman accepted his responsibilities with an appropriately grave countenance. Perhaps this dhan with the name of a boy would yet mature sufficiently to make Garwidha a worthy husband.

There were no singing and dancing that night in the camp. Green bushes were placed on all hearth-fires, for all dwellings had to be cleansed and purified with great clouds of smoke. This smoke would serve also to guide the old man's spirit toward the sky, where it would reside and hunt for a time before returning to a spirit-place on earth.

In the morning the camp was astir early. For four days from the time of death there would be a period of deep mourning, and only upon the night of the fourth day would the people return to the already purified camp. In the meantime they would go south to the creek called Coochin to hunt and fish there. And Buruda had given instructions that nobody was to hunt or eat goannas during that time.

"You all know that the old man was a goanna," he had told them. "And he left no sons or daughters within the Undanbi. As a mark of respect for Dimmangali, our old friend, we will all be goannas during the four days of weeping. Therefore the goanna will be forbidden to us for that time."

So even those who did not have the spirit of the goanna within them – but rather swans, sea-eagles, kangaroos and such – also became goannas for the time of mourning.

And before they set out across the creek towards Coochin, all men and women covered themselves with kutjin, the red clay that would serve as a sign to all creatures of the deep reverence they felt for the one whose spirit had left them. Men and women took separate paths, for the dhan would hunt on the way and the women would dig bangwal. It was not a very long journey, and they would all reach the camp by mid-afternoon.

Buruda and Garwidha took a more roundabout route, Buruda carrying the old man's skin and Garwidha the dhilla containing the bones. At this early stage of the separation of the spirit from its earthly body, there was every probability that Dimmangali would tend to want to remain near the familiar frame that had so lately housed his spirit. That was as it should be. That was why it was so important to ensure that nothing but love and respect should be felt in the immediate vicinity of the bodily remains, so that the spirit would feel more secure in its new surroundings. Then it could happily prepare to jump off into the sky, if it had not already done so, from the headland near where so lately the dhan of the four nations had conducted the kivar-yangga. This was the place from which all Undanbi spirits jumped up into the sky.

So Buruda and Garwidha, the two who had loved Dimmangali most, walked separately from the others, their very presence enveloping the earthly remains in an aura of love.

In the midst of his deep feeling of loss, Buruda's thoughts returned to the death scene of – how long ago was it? Surely not just yesterday afternoon! It seemed like longer than the whole half-moon of the kivar-yangga! Once again he heard Dimmangali's gasp. "Buruda! Take care! The dream!"

In that moment of death, had the old man been able to understand the meaning of Buruda's dream? Or had he had another dream that he wanted to tell Buruda about?

What a pity the wise old manngur had not lived long enough to explain the meaning of his last words!

But there was no escaping the fact that the old man had either had a dream, or had had a vision about Buruda's dream. And whichever way it had been, Dimmangali had seen great danger for Buruda, or for the Undanbi, so that his last breath had been used to call a warning.

And the warning had also been concerned with makaron, those evil spirits against which every person needed protection!

Buruda had faced danger many times in his life, and had not quailed. But always he had been able to assess the danger, which had been real and visible, generally taking the form of an ambitious bu-ul of another nation wanting to measure his strength against that of the Undanbi manngur. The marks of the wounds he had sustained in these encounters were there to prove that he had always been facing the danger that threatened.

But how did you face dangers when you didn't know where they were coming from? he asked himself. How did you fight makaron?

And in his mind he once more heard the voice of Bomarigo. "How do you fight the wind and the eternal?"

What could you do to fight the evil spirits, other than perform all the necessary ceremonies? And he had fulfilled all his obligations in this area, as well as impressing on the dhan that they should do their part conscientiously.

As far as Buruda could see, nothing more could be done to "take care", as the old man had warned.

Suddenly he and Garwidha stopped short, and his mind jerked back to the here and now. There in front of them was a goanna, its head held high, its gaze directed at them.

Garwidha addressed the reptile. "Ah!" she said. "You are sorry you left, are you? Why did you have to go and leave me?"

At the sound of her voice, the goanna scuttled away into the long grass, and they continued looking after it until the rustling sound of its passage had died away.

Buruda remarked that the appearance of the goanna was a good sign. The reptile had not been frightened of them, and had left with a minimum of fuss. He felt that this showed that Dimmangali was happy in his new form, and that his spirit would jump off within a day or so from the headland opposite Woorim.

They reached the camp at Coochin well before the others, and he selected a place for Garwidha a little distance away from the other shelters. The camp was still in good order, having been used recently.

First Garwidha collected sticks and, using the smouldering fire-stick she had carried from the other camp, soon had a fire going. While Buruda carefully draped the skin over three spears which he set upright in the ground in the path of the smoke, she began stripping bark from nearby dibing trees. Then, taking his sharp axe, he quickly cut some small springy saplings for her to use as the framework of her hut.

Satisfied that she was well taken care of, he walked over to the main camp, where the women could now be heard arriving. He had hardly reached his hut, where Nerida was already busying herself pounding bangwal, when the dhan arrived with some stingray and mullet. A couple were also carrying some mullu, the beautiful black snakes with red bellies. There would be no shortage of food tonight.

But, Buruda mused, that was usual for the Undanbi. At rare times the Nalbo, Dallambara or Dungidau would ask permission to come and hunt within Undanbi land, since in those countries, particularly in times of drought, there was sometimes a shortage of food. Such requests were never refused, for the law stated that, provided the proper forms were followed, people must be sustained, even though they might be strangers from another land.

But Undanbi land always seemed to be able to provide its people with adequate nourishment. If the land itself was sometimes deficient in food, it was often at that time that the sea proved most bountiful. Never within living memory had the Undanbi been forced to ask another nation for permission to hunt within its boundaries because of a shortage of food in their own country.

And as these thoughts crowded in on him in the midst of the noise of wood on stone as women pounded the bangwal, it seemed to him as if he could once more feel the comforting throbbing heartbeat of the very earth.

Surely it was strange that his old friend had warned him to take care! The earth itself was taking care of him and his people!

A string of abuse suddenly shattered the peaceful sounds of meal preparation. Buldarin was once more being blamed for something she may or may not have done.

Dhubal strode purposefully over to Ngandun, and the whole camp was pleased to hear the old man's words as he shook his finger threateningly in the face of the ill-tempered husband.

"Surely you can show more respect for Dimmangali!" he berated him. "His spirit, which could be nearby, will be outraged by your lack of consideration! Any more of this in the next four days, and the bu-ul will meet to consider a just punishment for you! Be silent, man!"

Ngandun was silent before the old man's anger, knowing the threat to be no idle one. Buldarin would at least be guaranteed a measure of peace for the period of mourning.

But the disturbance had jogged Nerida's memory, and she told Buruda of the visit to the camp during the kivar-yangga.

"Why should he do that?" he wondered. "Surely he seems to dislike Buldarin enough to be able to keep himself away from her for a half-moon!"

"But he didn't visit Buldarin," Nerida told him.

"Then who -----?"

"I don't know. Yerakun had covered all the tracks by the time Buldarin and I had followed them in the morning."

"Yerakun?" He looked up sharply, his voice heavy with suspicion. "Why should she -----?"

"She was getting wood. Before sun-up. Her mother had sent her."

"A likely tale!" he muttered. "But let us leave it all until we are back at the old camp. Our old Dimmangali deserves a time of peace and quiet from us."

"But maybe Ngandun will get his meeting of the council of the bu-ul yet!" he added savagely to himself.

Naruman passed as he made his way to Garwidha's hut, a juicy piece of black snake wrapped in dibing bark in his hand. Remembering his promise to the old man that Garwidha would be well looked after, Buruda was content. He would keep a fatherly eye on that union after it was consummated at the end of four days.

Notes on Chapter 6

When moving from place to place, it was usual for the women to carry a smouldering fire-stick to save having to make a new fire in the new camp. The Undanbi name for a camp was "kirami" or "kiraba" – literally "place of the fire". Considering how easily they could make fire, the custom of carrying fire probably served as a reminder of the continuation of the thread of life.

The people of south-east Queensland did eat part of their dead, but they were not cannibals in the usual sense of the word. Meat was plentiful, so the eating of human flesh was not necessary for their existence. The eating of their dead had a deep religious significance.

The present-day spelling of the place-name "Coochin" has been used. It is the same word as "kutjin", the red clay of mourning.

It was normal for people to be given a "totem". Thus Gibberol was a "gutji" or goanna. It was the task of people of a specific totem to ensure the well-being of that particular animal

"Yugari" was the name given by South-East Queensland Aborigines to the mussel which buries itself in the sand on the beaches. We still use this word.

Chapter 7

1821: Mourning

Never before had goannas been so plentiful as they were during that short stay at Coochin. Every day they saw many scurrying away to the safety of tall trees. The children would stand at the bottom of a tree in which one of the creatures had taken refuge, and then slowly circle the trunk to see how well it could match their movements, and so keep itself hidden from them. When they tired of the game, they would spread out on all sides of the tree so that the goanna no longer had any chance of hiding. Then they would squeal with delight as it scuttled further up the tree, obviously unaware that for these days it was safer than it had ever been before.

All agreed that the presence of the reptiles was a good omen, a sign that the weeping time for one of the greatest of their number involved the animals as well as their brothers and sisters of the Undanbi.

Despite the deep sense of loss felt by the people, however, all knew that the old manngur who had helped so many during his time among them had merely entered another stage of his existence. In between bouts of weeping, therefore, life went on much as usual. They hunted, they fished, and they dug bangwal and water-lily bulbs.

There was even some time for laughing, particularly when Naruman managed to follow a little black bee to its home in the hollow of a dead gum-tree. As the hunting for the day had finished and there was plenty of daylight left for pounding bangwal, they had all gathered to watch the fun.

For his part, Naruman was out to show his new maturity, keeping a grave countenance as he uncoiled his yurru, the strong vine tree-climbing rope with a loop in the end. Tucking his rag-like gimpi into his hair-belt, he placed the rope round the trunk and ran the free end through the loop. After he had ensured that there was just enough slack in his rope to allow him to lean back into it with his buttocks, he wrapped the free end twice round his right leg and grasped it tightly between the first and second toes. With his axe he quickly chopped a toe-hold about chest high, and then swiftly jerked the rope upwards and leaned back into it, walking up the trunk at the same time. Fitting his left big toe neatly into the cut in the tree, he balanced himself with both feet against the tree and made a second cut at just the right height above him to allow him to repeat the manoeuvre.

Naruman might be a dhan with the name of a boy, but there was nothing lacking in his hunting skills. So expertly did he make his toeholds and so smoothly did he jerk the rope upwards, that a watcher from a distance could have been excused for thinking that a huge goanna was slithering up the tree. Only the redness of the clay on his body would have revealed him as a man rather than an animal.

He had to negotiate two branches before he reached the site of the hive, but there was hardly a pause each time as he disengaged the rope from his foot, climbed onto the offending branch, and then readjusted the rope to allow him to resume his upward motion.

Then he was there. In front of his face was the hole in the trunk where he had that morning observed the little bees disappearing and reappearing.

"How many?" someone called from below him.

Naruman's sense of mischief asserted itself for a moment. "Bulla kalim!" he yelled down, grinning broadly. He knew the answer would be a disappointment to those below, their mouths already watering at the thought of the sweet gilla. A hive with only three bees visible at the entrance would probably mean a very small amount of honey indeed.

But his happy nature couldn't leave them disappointed for long, so he gave them the good news, "Gubbi! Gurwindha!" And the way he elongated the word signifying a number greater than four left them in no doubt that there would be at least a taste for all.

"G-u-u-u-u-u-u-urwindha!"

"E-e-e-e-e-e-e-e!" came from his appreciative audience, and the women began to pull their own gimpi from their dhilla in eager anticipation of the rain of plenty expected from above.

Skilfully he began widening the small entrance hole with his axe. Bees came swarming out to crawl into his hair and beard, but the only way he acknowledged their presence was to poke his bottom lip out and blow them away from his eyes. Later he had to leave off chopping at intervals to brush them away from his ears. On the whole, however, the defenceless creatures could do nothing to prevent the invasion of their home.

Soon the entrance was wide enough to allow him to insert an arm. Leaning back against the rope, he felt inside, and his eyes gleamed as his fingers came into contact with the honeycomb full of the beautiful sticky honey.

"Ready!" he called down, and dropped a handful into a gimpi held by one of the women. Again and again he inserted his arm and brought it out with honeycomb to drop to the waiting women. And at intervals he licked the honey from his fingers for, as the discoverer of the hive, it was his privilege to partake of the bounty in this fashion. Finally, when there was no more comb left in the hive, he took his own gimpi out of his belt and pushed it into the hole, wiping it round and round till all the honey that had run out of the broken honeycomb had been mopped up. Then, after dropping his gimpi to be caught by someone below, he brushed the bees from his hair and body and descended the tree as he had climbed it, leaving the little creatures in peace, to find some other home and make some more sweet honey.

The people returned to the camp amid a great deal of laughter and excitement. Most were chewing on a piece of honeycomb, and those who had none had already begun to suck the gimpi that had lately held the honeycomb dropped from above. These gimpi would be shared again and again. And even when there appeared to be no sweetness left in them, they would be soaked in pikki of water to yield a sweet drink.

Naruman took his gimpi to Garwidha and allowed her to suck her fill before he took his turn. He explained to her that he had already had a large share while up the tree.

And as he left her to return to his bachelor hut, Garwidha reflected that she was probably getting a better husband than she had anticipated. Naruman appeared to have hidden depths to his nature that she had never before noticed as he had clowned and yelled around the camp. The sweet taste of the gilla in her mouth attested to the fact that he had let her have more than a fair share of the bounty.

The stay at Coochin also yielded other delicacies. At their main creek camp the teredo had been scarce for some time, and it would still be quite a while before more would have burrowed deep into the logs which the dhan had placed in the water above the small island near the mouth of the creek. At Coochin, however, there was a superabundance of these delicious long worms that were so easily obtained by breaking apart the waterlogged wood made rotten by the creatures' bore-holes.

On the second day the whole camp had gorged on them, so that not even bangwal had been required to supplement the meal. After other logs had been rolled into the water to allow the teredo to replenish themselves for future use, the rest of that day had been spent in performing various tasks about the camp. Some dhan had nets to mend where the mesh had broken from too much use or too great a weight of fish. Others fashioned spears or boomerangs to replace weapons that were splitting. Soft and hard shields needed to be redecorated with new red and white clay, since many patterns were showing deterioration where the paint was flaking away from recent use on the baiyaba.

Some women busied themselves repairing dhilla or making new ones. Others shredded bark and rolled the inner fibre on their thighs to ensure a plentiful supply of string for dhilla or rug-making. Reed dhilla and shell necklaces were needed for the coming exchange at the bunyi festival.

The new kivar Turugun was the busiest of all. He carefully selected two ironbark saplings just a little thicker than the diameter of a spear after the bark had been removed. He then spent all day carefully preparing four long pieces of straight wood, and then gradually shaving them down with his knife to spear size. For the next two days he would let them season in the smoke of his fire, straightening them at times with strong teeth and arms if they showed signs of warping. The points he would harden in the fire itself, and finally he would make the shafts perfectly smooth by sand-papering them with sharkskin.

And children continued to run and skip and jump and play, sometimes even forgetting themselves enough to get in the road of the adults, who generally were indulgent enough to say nothing or very little about being interrupted in their tasks.

But with all the business of life going on, nobody forgot the time of weeping. If any red clay was lost from their bodies in their daily tasks, it was immediately replaced. At varying intervals someone or other would begin the death wail, and then others would join in. After the evening meal the lament for the dead would go on for twice as long as usual out of respect for their departed friend. There was no way that daily tasks and pleasures could be allowed to blot out from their minds the loss the nation had so recently suffered.

Towards the end of the fourth day, since by now it was certain that the spirit of Dimmangali had jumped off into the sky from the headland opposite Woorim, Buruda called the people together. Solemnly they sat, waiting for their manngur to determine just who had been responsible for the death of their old friend. Would it turn out to be someone from their own nation? And if so, what would be the penalty exacted for the death?

Each of them could not help feeling a certain amount of trepidation as Buruda stood facing Garwidha, since there was never really any way of telling what judgement might be passed by a dead man's bones.

Buruda addressed the assembled throng, pacing back and forth as he did so. "Our Dimmangali has gone," he began, "and his bones will now tell us who or what caused him to leave us for the spirit- world. And when we know the culprit, it will remain for me to decide the penalty."

"Yau-ai!" they all agreed.

"Then let us begin!"

"Yau!"

Sitting opposite the manngur, Garwidha took the pelvic bones of her late husband from her dhilla. Placing them tenderly on the ground before her, she laid the dhilla containing the remainder of the bones aside. Then she took a block of wood and held it poised in the air above the bones, waiting for the first name to be called.

The people held their breath.

"Wungul!"

At the sound of the name shouted by Buruda, Garwidha brought the block of wood down hard on the bones. Nothing happened.

"Bulangga!"

Again the block of wood came down. Again nothing.

Systematically Buruda worked his way through the names of the Undanbi, with periodic interpolations of names of people from neighbouring nations. Still the bones said nothing. Gradually more and more people began to relax, as it appeared that this time the bones would point to no culprit, although that hardly seemed possible.

The sound of his own voice calling out names and the sound of the block of wood as it descended on the pelvic bones began to exert an hypnotic effect on Buruda, so that it appeared to him as if he was calling out names in a dream. And suddenly, in this trance-like state, there arose before him a picture of a being so horrifying that it could only be an evil spirit, so alien was its appearance. Involuntarily he called out its name.

"Makaron!"

It may have been the sharp tone of Buruda's voice, or perhaps the unexpectedness of the name that caused Garwidha to strike harder. Or it may simply have been time for the bones to talk. Whatever the cause, the bones broke with a resounding crack.

The people looked about them in fear. If a makaron, an evil spirit, had caused the death of the old manngur, might it not be still about, looking to cause others mischief?

Buruda shook his head to clear his brain of the image that had so startled him. He had identified the cause of the old manngur's death – there could be no doubt about that. But what to do now? He could see the fear on their faces as the people looked to him for guidance. He would have to choose his words carefully.

"We know now what caused Dimmangali to leave us," he told them. "But there is no way that a penalty can be set for a makaron."

He heard the sharp intake of breath as he once more pronounced the dreaded name, so he hurried on.

"But there is also nothing to fear from a makaron if all obey the law. If one of our number is harmed by a makaron, it shows that someone within our group has broken the law. Therefore, someone must have done something wrong to allow a makaron to take our old friend from us. Since he was so old, it would need to be only a little thing. Therefore we must all take care in future that, even in the smallest matters, we obey the laws set down in the Before-Time. We bu-ul will speak more particularly about this, but even our women and children need to take care that their actions are always blameless."

"Yau-ai!" The agreement was emphatic and unanimous.

"For this time," he told them finally, "the bones have spoken. And since they have not named a culprit from within the nation, it must indeed have been a small matter that allowed the makaron to work its mischief. Otherwise the bones would have cried out for punishment of the law-breaker himself. Our old Dimmangali is not holding anyone responsible for his death."

With that they were satisfied.

Now that the bones had spoken, only one ceremony remained. Reverently they watched as Garwidha and Buruda took the broken pelvic bones, together with the others from the dhilla, and carefully wrapped and tied them so that they were encased in a cylinder of bark.

It was Buruda who carried the casket, leading them to the sacred tree some distance away. They visited this tree only to bury one of their number. At all other times they kept their distance, for the site itself was sacred, as unmistakable markings on trees round about signified.

Buruda took his rope, adjusted it, and quickly carried the casket up to a hole high in the tree trunk, the others standing silently by. There was no need for him to cut toeholds with his axe, for that had been done long, long ago – long before any of them had been born, when the first burial had taken place at this spot.

The casket fitted easily into the hole, and the people listened intently as Buruda released it and it landed with a dull thud on other cylinders inside. And at the moment of impact, they began the death-wail, lamenting not only the loss of the old manngur, but also the loss of all whose bones lay within the tree trunk.

The death wail continued until they were outside the marked boundaries of the sacred ground, and then it ceased as abruptly as it had begun.

The time of deep mourning was at an end. The red clay of mourning could be washed off. The normal flow of life could now resume. Husbands and wives could once more find pleasure in each other's bodies.

For his part, Naruman tried to look nonchalant as he waited beside his hearth-fire for his new wife to arrive.

But he would have to wait. Garwidha had something to do before she would make her way to her new husband's hut. Lovingly she folded the skin of her old husband and placed it in one of her dhilla. Then, carrying all her goods, she first made her way to Buruda's hut.

"You were the one he loved most, even more than he loved me," she explained to the manngur. "I want you to have a piece of his skin to keep beside you so that you will never forget him."

Wordlessly Buruda took the skin from the dhilla and cut a small square off, deeply aware of the honour this woman was according him. The marks of grief standing out starkly on her face were mute testimony to the depth of her love for her old husband, and he knew she would cherish the skin for many, many seasons to come, before she would at last suffer it to be placed in the tree trunk with the bones. To be offered a piece of such a memento was the highest tribute that could be paid him.

Tears coursed down his face as he reverently placed the piece of skin in the dhilla nestling beneath his left arm. He would never let it go.

Then at last Naruman saw her coming, and his face lit up. He had begun to believe that he had removed the hair from round his dhun in vain. But now he was about to have a wife in very truth.

Notes on Chapter 7

The gimpi (gympie) is the Queensland stinging tree. The Aborigines used the inner bark of these trees as rags to wrap things in and to soak up such things as honey.

The Gubbi word for the black native bee was "gilla". Since the honey came from the native bee, it was also called "gilla". It is interesting to note that the Aborigines of south-east Queensland used words differently from Europeans. Provided the material did not change, the word for that material remained the same. Thus the name for the stringy-bark tree was "dhura". A hut made from the bark of this tree was also called "dhura", since the material had not changed. A canoe made from the "kundu" tree was still a "kundu". A rag from the "gimpi" tree was still a "gimpi", and so on.

The Gubbi people, like all other Australian Aborigines, found that a simple numbering system fulfilled all their needs. They did not have a system using the base ten, as we do. Their base was two, and they usually found that to count up to five was enough. Beyond that, it was sufficient to use the word for "lots". "Kalim" was the word for "one", and "bulla" was the word for "two". Their word for "lots" was "gurwindha". They would count to five by saying, "Kalim, bulla, bulla kalim, bulla bulla, bulla bulla kalim." If they wanted to signify a number greater than five, they simply said, "Gurwindha." Strangely, the listener would have an excellent idea of the number this word signified by the way the speaker used it. The more drawn out it was, the more it stood for.

✦

Chapter 8

1821: The Storm

Next day, having washed off the red of mourning, they rubbed themselves and the children with their balls of charcoal and goanna grease before setting out on the return journey to the camp at the mouth of the creek. The day was a strange one for the time of the year. Nguruingan, the season of heat, had not yet arrived in its entirety, but even so early in the morning the heat was oppressive. Had it not been for their protective black layer, the babies carried on their mothers' backs would have been severely plagued by the hordes of mosquitoes that rose in clouds as they moved through the grass.

The heat told them that the great shoals of mullet would soon give way to smaller catches. Not that that mattered. There would always be plenty. Besides, there would soon be juicy whiting to be speared. And the stingrays never left, and these and whiting could be trapped in the permanent fish-traps that the dhan would begin to repair and restore to full efficiency in the coming days.

Every now and again a small party of dhan would disengage itself from the main group to hunt for animals to augment the meal that evening. Strangely, only three goannas were speared, though they took a number of delicious kakkar, those spiny creatures that lived on ants. The women kept together as a group, chattering good-naturedly and stopping periodically to dig bangwal and yams as the roots presented themselves. Of course, each time a yam was dug, half of it was returned to the ground to ensure a plentiful supply of this tasty root at all times in the future. There were severe penalties for not doing so, and besides, it made good sense to look after the plants in this way.

At intervals, adults and children would jump into the water, splashing each other with squeals of laughter, making the fish shoot out into the comparative safety of deeper water.

At last, as Bigi reached his highest point in the sky, the sea breeze began to ruffle the surface of the water, bringing some relief from the stifling heat. It quickly strengthened, so that within a very short time there were white caps on the normally placid waters of Kaerwagum.

Bulangga looked to the south-west, where a faint line of clouds could be seen building up on the horizon. "The wind is blowing into a storm," he remarked. "I think it will be a big one."

All agreed that it would be a good idea to have the meal over before the storm struck, as it was always a nuisance when the bangwal cakes could not be properly cooked because of the sudden onset of rain. And the sobering thought of the flashing might of Bulla-Bira the forked lightning which sometimes accompanied the terrifying roar of Mumba the thunder caused them to quicken their pace somewhat in order to be certain of reaching the camp before the storm broke.

But Buruda could not shake off a nagging sense of foreboding that had nothing to do with the storm. Some nameless disaster seemed to be hovering just beyond the limits of consciousness. Maybe, he reflected, it was caused by the knowledge that the bu-ul would soon have to tackle Ngandun regarding his unauthorised visit to the camp of the women during the kivar-yangga. And, if Ngandun could not satisfactorily explain it, what then? The council would have to decide what penalty should be imposed for daring to break the bond of brotherhood during the sacred time of the making of kivar.

Still, since he was their manngur, they would expect Buruda to have greater knowledge of the event than they themselves had, and even the old men would look to him to supply them with this knowledge. All morning, therefore, he had kept near Ngandun so that he could make a close study of his every action. But nothing had seemed untoward. As usual, Ngandun showed the skills of a seasoned hunter as he accompanied other dhan in their short forays afield. As usual, he shot a malevolent glance in Buldarin's direction every time her voice rose over those of the other women. As usual, his conversation with the other dhan was congenial. And as usual, his glances were inviting as he looked toward the young women, particularly those who already had the joints of their little left fingers removed and were not yet married.

No, there appeared to be nothing strange about Ngandun that would allow Buruda to impart greater knowledge to the council when it met, as it would have to. Yet a little thing kept pulling at his mind, reminding him of something that was small, and yet not small. In his ears came again the voice of Durbai of the Nalbo, urging him to get to know in great detail what was usual in all people.

Once again he heard the words of the wise old manngur. "The unusual often points the way to the usual."

But there was nothing unusual in Ngandun's behaviour – that was the trouble. Everything he was doing, at least upon this particular occasion, was everyday in the extreme. And how could this everyday behaviour help to account for the fact that a bu-ul of the Undanbi had deserted for a time his place at the making of young men?

Then at last his perseverance paid off, and he wished it had not. His heart missed a beat as the enormity of what he had just seen hit him like a heavy blow from a club. For one brief moment he had caught a look that passed between Ngandun and Yerakun – a look that lasted only for the blink of an eye. But it had flashed between them like the chain lightning that always preceded the heavy crack of thunder close at hand.

And such a look was profane, and strictly forbidden by sacred law to pass between the skins of Barang and Dhuroingan!

For what seemed to Buruda like an age, but which in fact was as much time as it took to take four breaths, a red haze passed in front of his eyes, and for that brief time he experienced once more that almost uncontrollable rage that had been the main cause of trouble in his youth, and that he had tried so hard to eradicate since his kivar-yangga. Unconsciously his right hand brought a spear up to throwing position, and his body automatically tensed to hurl the weapon at the law-breaker.

Then he managed to control himself, though the effort left him weak and shaking. He could feel the blood drain from his face as he deliberately turned away from the perpetrator of this heinous crime. The very idea made him ill.

They had been quiet about it, to be sure, but there was no doubt about what he had seen! Durbai had been right. The unusual did point to the usual. And the opposite applied, too. Ngandun, with his dislike for Buldarin, would naturally have an eye for the women. And as he pondered the matter, apparently unimportant incidents from the past assumed much greater importance in the light of his new knowledge. He could now see, for instance, that Ngandun had often meddled with the wives of other dhan without invitation, particularly at times when the nations had gathered. But so circumspect had the man been that no bu-ul had ever called upon him to face them on the baiyaba. That was the strange thing about it all – the way he had managed to hide his actions from everybody!

So it wasn't really strange that Ngandun had left the kivar camp to dally with yet another woman. But why not a woman of the Tumbra or some other nation? Or even a Bundagan of the Undanbi? Why this disgusting liaison between a Barang and a Dhuroingan?

But there was no doubt about that liaison. The forbidden look that Buruda had caught left room for no other interpretation.

Buruda caught Ngandun's eye and motioned for him to walk aside with him away from the main group. When they were out of earshot, he told him, "The bu-ul will meet to decide your fate as soon as we reach camp!"

Ngandun's mouth fell open foolishly. "But what ---?" he spluttered, and then stopped suddenly before the look he saw in the manngur's eyes. He paled as Buruda turned away to join the rest.

How much did they know? Ngandun wondered. He had always known the dangers inherent in this particular liaison, but had relied on his own cleverness to keep him out of trouble. He had never had any woman trouble in the past. But the manngur had been far too clever for him! He knew what the sentence would be. Listlessly, eyes downcast, he accompanied the others, replying in monosyllables when addressed. Soon they left him to his thoughts, wondering why his mood had changed so suddenly.

Meanwhile, Yerakun had not missed the byplay, and was also walking on legs that suddenly felt too weak to hold her. Sightlessly she stumbled on, automatically keeping up with the women as she pondered her inescapable fate.

For his part, Buruda was wondering how the Undanbi had so far managed to escape the wrath of the great spirits of the Before-Time. Surely he must have been remiss in the way he had divined the cause of the death of old Dimmangali! But the bones had spoken, and had not placed the blame on this unspeakable creature in dhan form! And the bones could not lie. Relieved, he realised that this vile being could not have been the cause of the old manngur's death, which would, as he had told the people earlier, have resulted from a small thing, his being so old. No, the bones had not made a mistake. Whatever disaster befell the people from this infraction of the law would be vastly more catastrophic than the death of an old man! The people must act quickly to avoid such a disaster!

Calling some of the elders aside, he informed them of what he had discovered.

"Impossible!" Bulangga gasped. "Nobody could do that!"

Buruda understood the scepticism of the older man. "But he has done it, nevertheless!" he told the men flatly. "And it is up to the bu-ul to meet as soon as possible to decide what ought to happen to him! And the women will have to deal with the other one!"

"There is only one penalty!" Dhubal reminded them, and they nodded.

The news spread like wildfire, and the band of people that waded across the creek to reach the camp and rekindle their fires was a very different band from the one that had set out so lightheartedly from Coochin that morning. There was no laughter, and any talk was in hushed tones.

The heat was becoming even more oppressive. And the north wind, which was blowing against the outgoing tide, was lifting the waters of Kaerwagum into even more savage waves. But their minds were on neither the heat nor the wind. Even the ominous sound of thunder, rumbling closer now, was lost to them for the moment. Nothing could drive from their minds the dreadful tidings that had been communicated softly from mouth to mouth during the last part of the journey.

The fish-traps were forgotten.

Barang and Dhuroingan! Unthinkable!

Automatically the women began to pound the bangwal, but there was an alien sound to it, as if they had no heart in their task. Buldarin sat listlessly before her hut, her hands idle, her dhilla of bangwal lying untouched. Beside her sat Ngandun, waiting motionless, unmindful of his detested wife nearby. Yerakun, with her mother Karum and her father Barga ashen-faced nearby, sat before their hut. They too were motionless, eyes staring into the distance at nothing.

Dhuroingan and Barang! Profanity of profanities!

Somewhere a child began to cry, unnerved by the unnatural silence of the camp, and soon others joined in. Mothers tried in vain to comfort them. There was about the people a more profound sense of mourning than had been evident even in the death of the old manngur, and this feeling was being communicated even to those too young to understand. The wailing of the children was a true reflection of the loss felt by a nation which had been betrayed beyond belief by those it had nurtured and loved.

Barang and Dhuroingan! Seeds of destruction!

For no incompatible skins could even talk without some dire consequence. Therefore, when two such skins had entered the final intimacy, the consequences did not bear thinking about!

Dhuroingan and Barang! The ultimate treachery!

So engrossed were the bu-ul and the women in their own thoughts as the elders moved amongst them that they failed to take note of the rapidly approaching storm, despite the increasingly harsh claps of thunder. It was Buruda who first drew their attention to it, as he ran down to the bank of the creek to implore the storm to bypass their camp.

"Go!" he yelled at the billowing thunderheads towering high above the greenish-black clouds below. "There is no need for you to punish all the people! Let us punish the offenders in the manner laid down by the law! Go! Leave us alone!"

The other bu-ul also rushed down to face the storm, the elders adding their entreaties to those of their manngur. The only dhan who did not move were Ngandun and Barga, both of them motionless, hoping that the storm would somehow put an end to their misery.

But the tempest was not to be denied. Like billowing smoke from a raging bushfire, the thunderhead writhed and twisted, and beneath it, in the depths of those green-black clouds, the forked lightning flashed continuously, the thunder roaring like the crack of a gigantic wabbalkan.

In the sudden calm before the onslaught, all the dhan scattered like leaves before the wind to race for the shelter of their huts, where the women and children had already taken refuge, the half-pounded bangwal forgotten near their fires. Even the dogs showed an unwonted lack of interest in any food left lying about, intent only on finding shelter with their human families.

Then it struck.

Within an instant, despite the curved nature of the roofs, designed to withstand the severe winds of the coast, the writhing gale ripped the bark away as easily as if it had never been tied to the framework. Here and there, where roofs clung obstinately for an instant longer, it lifted the frameworks themselves from the ground, tumbling them over and over through the camp, the terrified screams of the occupants drowned in the never-ending ear-splitting roar of the thunder. Trees crashed to the ground, while families cowered under rugs and skins, held desperately over their bodies by hands that clutched their covering as tightly as the talons of wuruma the sea-eagle clutches the fish he has captured. Then came the hail. Driven by the gale, large as the eggs of nguruin the emu, it lashed at the frantically-held coverings, until it seemed to those holding the skins that their bruised hands could hold on no longer. But they did hold on. To hold the skins was hurtful. To let go could mean death. They held on grimly.

And even in the total darkness under the coverings, the blinding light of the forked lightning sought them out, just as it sought out trees to shatter in its anger. And even though the howling wind and thudding hail drowned out all other sounds, there was always the sickening sensation of the sudden shocking inward pressure on their ear-drums, followed by a popping release, to signal the roar of the thunder.

On and on it went – interminably, inexorably. In the midst of it all, his hands tightly clutching the rug sheltering him and Nerida, Buruda wondered if this was the end of the earth. Was this what his dream had meant? Would the birds and animals all be killed, the trees be stripped of their leaves, the ground be pounded into a mass of nothingness beneath the bodies of lifeless people?

Maybe. But he hung on stubbornly, nevertheless.

Then, after an eternity, the hail gave way to rain.

And after another eternity, the gale howled less, so that it was almost a relief to be able to hear at last the distinct sickening thunder-claps.

Then, at last, comparative silence. Even the children had become too terrified to continue screaming and crying.

Gradually the rugs were laid back, and the bruised camp began to come alive. People emerged, still too dazed to inquire about the welfare of others, simply astounded to find that they themselves appeared to be alive.

The scene etched itself on Buruda's mind. Trees were down. Hardly a leaf remained on those still standing. The ground was covered thickly with a white layer of ice. Those dhilla which had not been blown away had been shredded by the hail. Many spears and boomerangs were broken. Nets had had holes punched in them by the hail or by flying branches.

Devastation! And all because a Barang had mixed with a Dhuroingan!

Friends began to call to friends and, now that the danger appeared to be over, they took stock. Strangely, all had survived, with the exception of Yerakun, whose breast had been transfixed by the sharp end of a shattered branch as she had sat unmoving where the storm had found her. Her parents, although they too had not moved to shelter, were alive, though badly slashed and battered by the hail. Ngandun and Buldarin were also alive, having been protected from the worst of the battering by the trunk of a huge gum tree which had missed them by a hand's breadth as it had crashed to the ground in the first fury of the storm.

Some hut frames were still standing, and women lost no time in clearing the thick hail from those sites and stripping bark to get a cover for these for the night. Families could share till tomorrow, when more permanent arrangements could be made. Piringa, his lacerated back bleeding anew from the effects of the hail, found some dry bark on the underside of a fallen dibing tree and, after some difficulty with damp sticks, was able to start a fire. Soon each standing hut had its fire smoking before it. A semblance of order was beginning to emerge from the chaos.

Bulangga, as one of the highly-respected elders, began the proceedings they had all been dreading.

"Bring the unspeakable creature!" he grated to two of the younger bu-ul, and they hurried off to fetch Ngandun.

A woman elder came across and, indicating the body of Yerakun, said to Bulangga, "Will you dispose of that?"

Bulangga nodded. It was rightly the business of the women to deal with the Dhuroingan law-breaker, but the storm had already taken care of that. He said to two other bu-ul, "Fetch the body of that foul woman!"

After the shivering Ngandun had been brought and the woman's body had been dumped unceremoniously in their midst, Dhubal addressed the bu-ul. "It is not necessary for us to draw aside from the women at this time," he reminded them, "for the matter in question affects them as well as us. But they will remember to keep silent while the council is meeting here, for it is only bu-ul who have the right to speak on matters concerning one of their own. It would be different if the woman were not dead, for the women would have to speak for her."

Wimbur spoke up. "There is a decision to be made about this foul piece of dung who stands in our midst! But first let our manngur speak, for it was he who found out about this disgusting act!"

Buruda stepped forward. "You know that the kivar-yangga demands the presence of all bu-ul and kivar, who keep themselves aloof from camp matters unless they are sent on business from officials at the ceremony," he began.

"Yau-ai!" they agreed.

"Ngandun" – and in Buruda's mouth the name became a vile curse – "came back to the women's camp under cover of night and had congress with a woman of incompatible skin!"

The thought made most of those present hawk and spit on the ground, as if some rotten decaying flesh had been forced between their teeth.

"We know that this act has already been judged by the great spirits of the Before-Time!" Buruda continued after a pause. "The Undanbi have been punished by the spirits living in the storm! They have wrecked our camp! And they have shown their wrath unmistakably by killing the woman involved! No more proof of guilt is needed than this, surely!"

"Yau-ai!"

Buruda looked around him. "The spirits were right to punish us!" he went on. "No nation should allow such people as these to exist! We should have found out sooner, and eradicated this weeping sore from our midst!"

"Yau-ai!" Those whose weapons were still whole rattled them together to show their rage.

"The spirits themselves have condemned this foul deed!" Buruda said. "But the law states that the bu-ul accused of an offence has the right to defend himself before we pass judgement!"

Bulangga stepped forward. "True! So let us hear what this thing has to say for itself!" He turned to Ngandun. "Tell us you are innocent!" he taunted him.

Ngandun looked at the ground. He said nothing.

"Then your name is Dimmangali!" Wimbur shouted, leaping high into the air. "Just as this thing lying near you is Dimmangali!"

"Dimmangali!" the whole camp shouted.

Piringa and Wungul stepped forward. Taking white clay from their dhilla, they smeared it over the condemned man until he was white from head to toe. Then, painting two spears white and placing them on the ground before him, they stepped back.

"There are your weapons!" Bulangga shouted at him. "Defend yourself if you dare!"

But Ngandun knew he did not dare. White was the symbol of peace as far as weapons were concerned, so he dared not use them in battle. Besides, he was already quaking in anticipation of whatever punishment would be his when he entered the spirit-land for the crime he had already committed. He had no wish to add to this punishment by committing another crime.

So he stood unmoving, the paint of shame stark on his body. He saw Buruda balance himself preparatory to casting his spear, and involuntarily braced himself to meet the shock of impact. The spear flew straight and true. Like the forked lightning itself it came at him. But his last thought as he was hurled into eternity was not of fear but of shame, as he saw on the face of the manngur the revulsion and contempt he felt for this member of the Undanbi who had betrayed them.

He was dead as the other bu-ul flung their weapons.

The guilt of the nation had been expunged.

Without ceremony the bu-ul gathered up the two bodies and carried them with difficulty through the fallen trees. The ice numbed their feet, but they hardly noticed. At last they reached a spot which they considered a decent distance from the camp, and here they dumped their burdens.

For these there would be no death-wail, no flaying, no preservation of power by eating flesh, no waiting for bones to talk. What was needed was to get rid of the bodies as soon as they could, and in such a way, if possible, as to prevent their spirits exacting vengeance on the living.

It did not take them long to dig two deep holes in the sandy soil. While the digging was in progress, a number of bu-ul gathered bark to line the holes. Then the two were placed separately in the holes, their backs turned towards each other, obeying the law of skins in death as they had not done in life. Then, after covering the bodies with bark, they pushed the soil back into the holes on top of them.

It was done. Thus those condemned to death by the law were buried. Thus the Undanbi protected themselves against the spirits of the condemned.

They turned to go back to the women, but Buruda held them there. He had already shared his dream with the manngur who had attended the kivar-yangga, but now he felt a strong compulsion to tell his brother bu-ul. He had a feeling that the devastation wrought by the storm could have been prevented if only he had acted in time. A council meeting could have been held early in the afternoon on the way back from Coochin, and punishment carried out then and there. That is what should have been done. In that way suffering could have been avoided.

This time he intended to delay no longer. So he talked earnestly for a long time, while they stood shuffling on the ice-covered ground. Eagerly they questioned him, and when he made the footprint of Midherplinda, they studied it with care. When he at last finished, he had awakened in all a fierce determination to do everything in their power to ensure that all ceremonies were meticulously observed.

"There is no room for slackness!" Bulangga urged them all. "Our manngur's dream has shown what can happen when we do not fulfil our obligations! No bu-ul must shirk his tasks!"

"And not only bu-ul!" Wimbur reminded them. "We must also make sure our women and children make no slips!"

"And kivar, too!" another added.

Darkness had fallen by the time the sombre group of men finally picked their way through the blighted bush back to their makeshift camp.

Perhaps even this storm, sent to punish them for this heinous crime, was after all a very small warning of what could happen in the future if they became lax in their observance of the law.

Notes on Chapter 8

The four male moieties in Gubbi were: Dhuroin, Bunda, Barang and Balkuin.

Female moieties were distinguished from the male by the addition of "-gan".

Legal marriages and their offspring were:

HUSBAND		WIFE	BOY CHILD	GIRL CHILD
BALKUIN	m.	DHUROINGAN	Bunda	Bundagan
BARANG	m.	BUNDAGAN	Dhuroin	Dhuroingan
DHUROIN	m.	BALKUINGAN	Barang	Baranggan
BUNDA	m.	BARANGGAN	Balkuin	Balkuingan

✦

Chapter 9

1821-22: The Bunyi Festival

Slowly the Undanbi people made their way up the steep track that wound its way from the well-defined trading track at the foot of the mountains. The Dallambara had at last sent word to all the nations round about that the bunyi were ripe and plentiful. From all directions, therefore, people were making their way to the that beautiful forested valley nestling in the scrub-covered Baroon Mountains. From as far south as the people of the Turrbal and the Garumngar they were coming, and from as far north as that great sandy Island K'gari – the Ngulungbara, the Badtjala and the Dulingbara.

The bu-ul led the way, followed by the kivar. All were heavily armed with full fighting gear, since no dhan would think of attending a bunyi festival with less than a full complement of weapons. A time of feasting and friendly rivalry the festival might be, but it was also a time when national feelings could suddenly surge in passionate breasts, or personal rivalries erupt in the time it took to draw a breath.

Therefore the dhan, though joking freely, were on the alert. It would be unthinkable for any untoward event to occur on the way to the festival, since the law stated that a nation invited to attend such a feast was immune from attack. Nevertheless, they were on foreign territory, and it was incumbent on them to be in a position to defend their women and children if any danger presented itself on the way.

The women, burdened heavily with articles of exchange as well as their usual dhilla and digging-sticks, brought up the rear, following with the children the leisurely pace of the dhan. Here and there they paused to use their strong white teeth to crack those tasty barpul nuts that grew on spiky-leaved bushes in the scrub. Nobody was in a hurry, for they would reach the clearing in plenty of time before dark, having camped on the road near the mountains of the Nalbo the night before. Besides, the food to be gathered from the scrub on the way always proved a welcome change of diet, and it would be a pity to forgo these delicacies, even though there was a natural eagerness on their part to get to the Baroon meeting-place where they would be able to greet old friends.

For Buldarin, the memory of the nightmare of that stormy afternoon three moons ago was beginning to fade. Karum fell back to walk beside her, and the two exchanged happy smiles. Since Buldarin had joined Barga as his second wife, Karum had taken the younger woman to her heart, loving her more as a daughter than as a sister. Indeed, Buldarin had proved far more dutiful and helpful than the Dimmangali daughter who had brought such shame to her family. And the two women had been able to console each other and Barga in the difficult time following the storm.

"Here, eat this!" Karum urged Buldarin, holding out a nut. And as Buldarin savoured the succulent kernel, she reflected fondly on the many kindnesses shown her by the older woman. For instance, as soon as Barga had recovered sufficiently from that horrifying time to begin to show interest in women once more, more often than not Karum would urge him to pleasure himself with Buldarin rather than herself.

"She is young enough for you to prepare her binang for a baby spirit!" she would say to him. "Go to her and enjoy yourself!" And since Barga was never loath to follow Karum's advice, Buldarin gradually began to see that marriage in this family entailed pleasure rather than blows and bruises. For her part, Karum could not help feeling a warm glow every time she witnessed Buldarin's delight whenever Barga satisfied himself with his younger wife.

And Buldarin could not do enough for her elder sister. The pikki was always full of water, there was always plenty of firewood, and Buldarin dug enough bangwal to satisfy their needs. Indeed, if Karum hadn't protested that she needed something to do, Buldarin would have been happy to pound all the bangwal herself as well.

So the evil that had brought on the savage storm appeared to have been properly eradicated. The death of a cruel husband and a faithless young woman had left a happier nation. True, a full half-moon had passed before some semblance of order had been restored to the former camp, which had been moved a short distance up the creek to an area less cluttered with fallen trees and debris. New weapons had had to be fashioned and mula repaired. All the canoes, even those borrowed earlier by the Dhundubari, had been smashed beyond repair, beaten into shapeless strips by the lashing hail. The dhan had laboured long and hard preparing new bark strips from suitable trees, joining the ends together, carefully drying and shaping the craft in the smoke, and finally waterproofing the joints.

The women too had been hard put to it to repair the damage. Dhilla had been blown away or shredded. Pikki had disappeared altogether. The reed dhilla they had prepared so carefully for exchange at the bunyi festival had been ruined, as had most of the shell necklaces.

And in the midst of all these repairs, food still had to be procured. The fish-traps at the mouth of the creek had been the first priority for the dhan, and afterwards they had occupied themselves with other urgent tasks. Both men and women had found themselves sitting round their hearth fires at night fashioning dhilla and mula, instead of singing and dancing round the communal camp-fire.

Still, the time of rebuilding had at least helped to take their minds off the cataclysmic horror of the storm and its immediate aftermath. By the time they had begun to resume a normal lifestyle, even the trees had begun to send out fresh shoots. The earth was once more bountiful.

The lesson of the storm had been learnt by all. Dhan were even more assiduous than usual in their vigil over those animals they called brothers. Those of the goanna totem were quicker to warn the others if numbers of goannas appeared to be falling off in any area. Those of the wood-duck totem were equally vigilant in doing the same as far as those birds were concerned. For Buruda's dream stood as a warning to all – each member of the nation must work to avert disaster, and they could do this only by ensuring that the balance in all areas of nature remained undisturbed.

But now, as they at last reached the top of the range and began to follow the crest of the long ridge that would eventually lead them to the Obi Obi valley on Baroon, there was a feeling of well-being in all of them. They had plenty of goods for trading. They were going to meet old friends. The fact that some of these friends would speak strange tongues, saying "wakka" and "yugar" for "no" instead of "Gubbi", worried them not at all. Most of them were proficient enough linguists to make themselves understood in these other languages. Indeed, there were some like Buruda who spoke four languages as if they had been born to them. But even for those who did not, there were always plenty of friends to interpret.

And in all minds was the thought of the bunyi nuts. It was as if they could already hear the thud of the cones hitting the ground, smell the delightful aroma of the nuts roasting on the fire. Some of their mouths were already watering as they remembered the glorious taste of the chewy kernels.

The bu-ul in the van quickened the pace on the more level ground as they followed the well-marked track through the scrub, and those behind altered their speed to match, all now eager to reach the camp-site as soon as possible. But Bigi was half-way down to his home below the mountains before they at last sat down in view of the Dallambara camp.

After a suitable time had elapsed, Ngalumun, the Dallambara manngur, came across to welcome them and point out to Buruda where the Undanbi camp would be. Ngalumun would look after them during the whole of their stay, detailing which bu-ul of the Dallambara were to supply them with nuts. For none but the Dallambara were allowed to climb the bunyi trees. And all who came were also aware that no axe must deface the trunk of a bunyi tree, on pain of death. The trunks were rough enough to give sufficient purchase to the feet of the Dallambara men as they used their ropes.

This was the first time that Ngalumun had taken it upon himself to be the official guardian of the Undanbi during the festival. Last time he had attached himself to Yuonmandi, the manngur of the Kombobura. Everyone knew that this time Ngalumun had attached himself to them because of the acknowledged power of Buruda, and they basked in the reflected glory of their famous manngur as they set up camp.

Here at Baroon there were no dibing trees, whose paper bark lent itself so admirably for roofing the huts. There were, however, large stands of stringy bark, and in no time at all the huts were ready, their hearth-fires smoking before the openings which, as custom decreed, faced the east, the direction from which they had come to attend the festival.

Within the next two days many other nations arrived and set up camp in the areas set aside for them. The Dhundubari were allotted a spot close to the Undanbi, and the huts of these two peoples were the only ones facing to the east, whence they had come. Those of the Dungidau and Garumngar faced south-west, the Nalbo and Turrbal south, the Ningi south-east, and the Tumbra north-east. The hut openings of the Kombobura, Dhungwubera, Dulingbara, Carburrah, Badtjala and Ngulungbara all faced north, those of the Baiyambora north-west.

And in this veritable city there followed almost a moon of unbridled merry-making, as the Dallambara kept them all supplied with bunyi nuts. The only task to be performed was to carry the nuts dropped by the guardians of the trees to those people below who had been assigned to the particular Dallambara bu-ul. At any time of the day, it seemed, the smell of roasting nuts permeated the air, as one family or another decided that the time had come for yet another taste. Bellies became rounded from the surfeit.

Every night the dancing and singing continued almost until Bigi began to lighten the sky in the east. There were old songs to sing, new dances to perform and, with so many nations gathered together, stories to tell of events that had occurred since the last festival three summers before.

There was also the serious business of letting all people know of those who had left for the spirit-world, for accidental use of their names, even innocently, could have dire consequences. Thus very little time elapsed before the Undanbi let others know that their old manngur had died, and that the husband of Buldarin and the daughter of Barga and Karum had met an untimely end because of their transgressions. And in turn they learnt of the deaths of those from other nations, whose names were therefore Dimmangali. This information was even passed on to the children, so that they too might remain safe from the wrath of any spirit whose earthly name was now sacred.

The days were spent in dozing, eating and playing. Children fascinated one another for hours with wara wara, that game where string stretched on fingers was displayed in a host of interesting designs, which the watchers were supposed to predict. At other times they would splash round in the cool waters of the Obi Obi. The older children even dared to venture into the turbulent cascades where the creek, roaring through the narrow gorge at the northern end of the valley, drowned out their shrieks of delight as they vied with one another in demonstrating their boldness. No amount of warning by their mothers could stop the older boys from indulging in this dangerous pastime.

Meanwhile, teams of bu-ul and kivar strove with one another in various ways, always playing to an admiring audience of women.

One of the most popular competitions involved wrestling.

Daily, teams wrestled mightily for possession of a beautifully-decorated spear, which was lost to a team as soon as the leading man in the team was pushed over the marked line by one of his opponents. The trophy could thus change sides a number of times during any given contest. Each nation had only one team of six players, and all had practised hard before meeting at Baroon. Day after day the teams struggled for supremacy.

At last, after days of effort, the only teams still in the event were the Kombobura and the Undanbi. The trophy was stuck upright in the ground behind Buruda, for the Undanbi had been the last to gain possession, having previously wrested it from the Dulingbara and defended it against four other teams in succession. Now the two final teams stood facing each other, a line behind each team, bu-ul opposing bu-ul.

Wungul made short work of his opponent, muscles bulging as he forced the man backward over the line. Piringa, too, managed to gain the upper hand over his opponent. But two other Undanbi bu-ul, although they strained until their eyes bulged and their bodies became slippery with sweat, were slowly forced back over their line.

Each of the victorious Kombobura men then tried in turn to force Buruda over the line to allow them to get at the trophy. And he forced each of them over their own line with an ease that brought a gasp of disbelief from the on-lookers.

The fifth Kombobura bu-ul also was forced back by his Undanbi opponent.

Only Yuonmandi remained on the Kombobura side, facing his three opponents.

Would Buruda be forced back, so that it would be left to Wungul and Piringa to try to wrest the trophy back from Yuonmandi?

Silence had descended over the valley as the contest raged. Here at last was the contest they had all awaited since the wrestling had begun. It was the two bu-ul facing each other in the middle of the marked-out area that riveted their attention. But what bu-ul these were! Both were manngur, and both famous throughout the nations. Who would prove supreme this time? The onlookers held their breath.

For a short breathing-space Yuonmandi and Buruda eyed each other. Then they came together, the muscles of their necks bulging, their legs straining, arms clasping each other as tightly as an old man kangaroo grasps the dog that has stupidly followed him into a deep waterhole. Grunting, panting, each struggled to gain the ascendancy. But neither would give way, and it appeared that they would remain forever in one place, locked in combat as if their feet had been glued to the ground with iron-wood gum. Then, at last, after what seemed an eternity, a look of consternation began to spread over the face of the Kombobura manngur, and those who were watching most closely noticed that his feet had been forced back ever so slightly, that there was a very small skid mark in the dust beneath his feet.

The end came quickly. Suddenly, the muscles on Buruda's back bunched even more tightly and, with a despairing groan, Yuonmandi knew that his feet had been driven back over his line.

"E-e-e-e-e-e-e-e-e-e-e!"

The Undanbi had taken the trophy for this year. Yelling excitedly, Wungul flourished the painted and feathered spear in the air as they walked triumphantly back to their camp.

But there were other games as well. One of the favourites was purru purru, played with a piece of kangaroo skin stuffed with grass and sewn into the shape of a ball. Teams ran to a pole stuck in the ground, the person with the ball having to get rid of it as soon as he was touched by an opposing team member. Unlike wrestling, this was an extremely noisy game, always accompanied by much yelling and shrieking. The kivar particularly liked this game, and even women and children played their own versions of it.

Then there was murun murun, where teams of many players tried to bounce a club-like stick along the ground further than anyone else could. Astute exponents of this game would try to get the stick to shoot the greatest distance by aiming it at a clump of grass, which tended to make it take off with great speed. Turugun excelled at this game, earning more points, scored by notches cut in a scoring stick, than any other member of his team. He was the main reason why the Undanbi team was eventually declared the winner.

Every now and again, in any part of the huge encampment, somebody would start up a game of skipping. Two people would begin swinging a yurru, and very soon a great number would be involved, trying to outdo one another in and out of the swinging rope, or seeing how long they could skip before being caught a sharp blow on the ankles. Men, women and children all participated in this game, which was at times even noisier than purru purru.

And when these games palled, there was always boomerang throwing. Three concentric circles had been marked out, the smallest one having a diameter equal to a little more than the height of a man. The centre of these circles was marked with a peg, and it was at this peg that each man stood as he hurled his boomerang. Each had to throw a right-hand and a left-hand boomerang. The accuracy of the throw was measured by the distance a man had to move to catch the returning boomerang. The further out from the peg, the worse the throw.

During the festival there were many bu-ul and kivar from all nations who never had to move outside the circumference of the innermost circle to retrieve their boomerangs. But as the days passed, more and more people began to notice that Buruda never seemed to have to move his feet from their original throwing position to catch the return, no matter whether he had thrown with the right or left hand. Thus there was always a highly appreciative set of spectators whenever he took up his position at the peg.

Meanwhile much bartering went on. Nerida managed to get a beautiful possum rug of the much-prized black fur from a Dungidau woman, in exchange for four of her beautiful reed dhilla and three shell necklaces, although she had to ask Buruda for some white clay to help seal the bargain. Naruman was delighted when he found himself presented with a young pup, lately captured in the bush near Yabba by a Baiyambora kivar, and which Garwidha had received in exchange for her dhilla and shells.

Towards the end of the festival, all visiting bu-ul pitched in to help the Dallambara fill huge cane baskets with nuts. These heavily-laden baskets were then buried in mud near the banks of the Obi Obi, where the nuts would remain perfectly preserved for future use. This work was designed to repay in part the hospitality shown them by the Dallambara.

The day before the end of the festival Buruda arranged with the other manngur to have a meeting of the bu-ul apart from the women. At this council of the nations, they heard of his dream and of the deathbed warning of the old manngur Dimmangali. There was much consternation among them, particularly when Buruda came to the part about the lack of plant and animal life in the land.

All were quick to see the connection between Midherplinda's footprint and the devastation in the dream.

Yuonmandi summed up the feeling of the council. "We must beware of these makaron!" he shouted for all to hear. "If any spirits visit us, we must be sure beyond doubt that they are indeed spirits of our dead brothers!"

"If not, they must be done to death!" a bu-ul of the Dulingbara yelled.

"Death!" shouted the throng.

But Bomarigo wasn't so sure. "How do you kill a spirit that uses Mumba the thunder?" he muttered to himself as the meeting broke up.

At any meeting of the nations, there was always much exchanging of women for the night, since the law decreed that, provided bu-ul of the same skin were agreed, it was right and fitting to show friendliness by allowing such a brother access to one's wife, particularly if that brother's wife happened to be unapproachable because of her time of the moon. Indeed, despite the fact that Buruda had had no need of such a service because of Nerida's pregnancy, he had accepted the offers of two Badtjala bu-ul and enjoyed their wives on two separate nights. To refuse would have been ill-mannered. And Nerida had found herself giving comfort to those same two bu-ul when it came time for Buruda to reply in kind.

Sometimes, however, it could happen that a man and woman might neglect to obtain the permission of the woman's husband before sneaking off to a rendezvous in the dark. And, although in such a vast concourse of people many such liaisons might go unnoticed, there were always times when an irate husband would discover the deception. If an agreed and ample recompense was not immediately negotiated, the result would be a kin-bumbe.

On the last day, therefore, they all assembled at the baiyaba. There were five kin-bumbe to be fought this day, and the people waited with eager anticipation for them to begin. There was always a great slanging match under these circumstances, and the insults traded were often more interesting than the duel itself. Nor were they disappointed this time. The fact that two of the kin-bumbe involved people speaking different languages only added spice to the spectacle. There was something quite diverting when a Turrbal man used Yugara insults to a Dhundubari, who naturally replied in Gubbi. But it was even more exciting to listen to Wimbur, Nerida's father, cursing in the quick Gubbi tongue, while his opponent, a Dungidau man, replied in the slower inland Wakka language.

And there was also an added attraction this time. At the close of the kin-bumbe two women of the Turrbal people decided that the time had come at last to settle a long-standing feud that had been festering since the time of cold. The fact that the cause of the feud was not apparent to most of the onlookers did not detract in any way from the spectacle, as they laid into each other with a will, using their digging-sticks as both weapons of offence and defence, their screams of rage adding to the enjoyment of the spectators. Long and hard they went about their bludgeoning, and they stopped only after the Turrbal manngur stepped in and separated them, both bloodied and sore from the encounter.

But Wimbur, sore from his own encounter, did not appreciate it as much as usual. And as Buruda later tended the groaning man's wounds, he chided the older man. "You should know better, father-in-law!" he chuckled.

"Ah, but she was beautiful!" Wimbur protested.

"I think you will remember her beauty less when Koppakkin sees you tonight!" Buruda warned him, and Wimbur was silent at last, dreading the tongue-lashing that he knew would be his as soon as Koppakkin could get to him. Indeed, he reflected ruefully as Buruda applied more clay and down to his wounds, he'd be lucky not to get a clout or two over the head from her digging-stick!

"Let me stay in your hut tonight!" he pleaded.

But Nerida would have none of it, so he at last reluctantly picked his painful way to his own hut and the waiting Koppakkin.

Next morning, with tears and laughter, the festival broke up. That day the Undanbi travelled down the mountain with the Ningi, Dhundubari, Turrbal and Nalbo, camping on the great trading track below. The following afternoon they arrived back at their camp by the creek.

The festival had been a joyous time. They had obtained many valuable articles from their trading, and the bunyi nuts had been delicious. But it felt good to be back again in Undanbi land, and they looked forward once more to meals of fish and bangwal.

Even the cry for the dead that night sounded better, though not as loud or prolonged as it had been at the festival. But somehow, among their own familiar trees, it felt more genuine, as if the Undanbi spirits of the dead could hear and appreciate it more fully than they could on foreign soil.

There was something right about being once more in their own country.

Notes on Chapter 9

"Barpul" was one of the names given to the so-called "macadamia" nut. It is a pity that this colourless botanical name has superseded

names that would more readily show the origin of the nut. The previous name "Queensland" nut would more readily show its origins. But the Aboriginal word is surely the most apt name of all. Thankfully, the name "Bauple" nut, which is a corruption of "barpul", is still used by the inhabitants of the Queensland town of Maryborough. Other Aboriginal names were "burrum" and "kindel-kindel".

The town of Eumundi is named after Yuonmandi.

Wara Wara was a game like cat's cradle.

Purru Purru: Perhaps this was the real Australian Rules game?

Murun Murun probably got its name from its resemblance to a species of lizard. The stick often looked like one of these lizards as it slid along the ground.

The South-East Queensland Aboriginal system of law has been called the "pay-back" system, but this is probably an over-simplification of the way it worked. It is true that recompense needed to be made before a wrong could be seen as having been righted. It is also true that even the person wronged had to keep the peace once restitution had been made. But there was much more to their social system than this. It was more a system of "balance" they were interested in – balance in Nature as well as in every dealing anybody had with their fellow human-beings. For instance, even in pitched battles between neighbouring peoples, they would ensure that the numbers on both sides were relatively even before hostilities began. Sadly, this was not the way the white man made war.

Kin-bumbe = A fight over a woman.

✦

Chapter 10

1822: A Baby for Nerida

Nerida's time had come. The Undanbi were camped near Currimundi, enjoying the change of diet, for it was time when fish were not quite so plentiful, and the succulent flying-foxes were always there.

As soon as she had felt the first pain, Nerida had gone aside in the company of Koppakkin and Ngita to a shelter earlier erected in readiness out of sight of the main camp. She knew that the coming birth would be painful, for everyone knew that the spirit-child waxed large within the woman's body during the time of waiting, and sometimes fought its way into the world only with difficulty. But she had no fear, for she had strictly obeyed all the laws of the waiting time during her pregnancy, abstaining from all types of food which were forbidden to women whose bellies held spirit-children. Thus no crab or crayfish had entered her mouth for the whole time, although she had often been envious of Buruda when he had smacked his lips with relish as he had eaten one of those glorious mud-crabs that could be hooked out of their holes in the oozing black mud in certain parts of the creek, or speared in the light of a blazing torch at night.

So, even as the pains came more frequently, she reflected happily that she would soon be able to enjoy again the taste of crabs, which were full of meat just now, and could be found in the waters of Currimundi as well.

Nevertheless, she was not sorry that she had obeyed the law. There were many cases that all women knew about, where babies had been born malformed in some way, and all because the mother had been careless about the rules that traced their origin back to the Before-Time. In such cases, there was only one thing to be done, and that was to destroy the offending spirit-thing with all dispatch, burying the body in the sand as quickly as possible to ensure that no harm would befall the people.

No, it did not pay to treat the laws relating to childbirth lightly. Even the positioning of the birth shelter had to be attended to with great care, so that it faced directly away from the camp situated on the banks of Currimundi. This ensured that the secrets of birth would remain locked away from the men and children. Had the opening faced toward the camp, even though it was well away and out of sight, some knowledge of the secret happenings could accidentally make their way in that direction, with dire consequences.

The two older women massaged Nerida's back as she squatted, legs wide apart, over the shallow hole dug earlier in the soft earth. The movement of their hands served somehow to dull the sharpness of the pain of each contraction. And since the breaking of the waters a short time before, they had been singing the birth song, their voices keeping time to the movement of their hands.

Then Nerida's breath drew in sharply as the pains suddenly became more urgent, more excruciating. At the same time Koppakkin and Ngita's hands became more insistent, their voices louder, as they implored the spirits of the land to assist the emergence of the spirit-child into the world of people. One last mind-searing pain in the region of her binang drew an involuntary gasp from Nerida, despite her earlier determination to allow no cry to escape her during her ordeal.

Then blessed relief, as the spirit-child slid softly onto the dibing bark lining the shallow hole.

The song of the two women ceased as they quickly took the child up and cleared the remnants of the caul from its head. Although she had been told often enough what to expect, Nerida's first reaction was one of amazement at the extreme lightness of the skin. How could any land creature be so pale? But it was always so with creatures who emerged from the spirit-world. Even the tiny joey in the kangaroo mother's pouch was pale and hairless, quite unlike the buck kangaroo it would eventually become. And helpless pups were always lighter in skin than the mother.

But Nerida's mind quickly moved from contemplation of the skin. This little being had the tiniest dhun, so it was a man-child. And as Nerida took in this fact, Koppakkin twisted the umbilical cord and cut it with a sharp shell.

Ngita's hands meanwhile were once more insistently kneading Nerida's back and stomach, and soon the afterbirth fell into the hole, to be quickly covered up, thus ensuring that no trace of the material remained that had so recently housed the spirit-child. Such precautions against disaster were always taken, and these two women, very knowledgeable in the laws relating to childbirth, would see that all procedures were carried out correctly.

Despite the discomfort she could still feel in her binang, Nerida observed very closely all that was being done. From now on she herself could be called upon to assist other mothers giving birth, and it was only by observing others skilled in the art that such knowledge could be perfected. No amount of telling could impart knowledge as well as direct observation.

The removal of the caul, the expulsion and burial of the afterbirth – all had taken place within a short space of time. But the tiny babe had begun to cry, bewailing the loss of its comfortable home in its mother's belly. All this was as it should be, and there was a broad smile on Koppakkin's face as she allowed the child's lips to seek her sagging breast.

"Ah!" she murmured as its cries suddenly ceased. "He has a strong suck! He will grow into a strong man!"

"Suck! That's what we'll call him!" Ngita chuckled. "Bunbithin!"

So it was that Buruda's son was given his child name.

Koppakkin removed the baby's lips from her breast and handed him to Nerida, who by now had taken her place in the shelter's opening. A further wail was quickly smothered as the questing lips once more found a breast to suck.

"Bunbithin!" Nerida laughed. Then once more she murmured, "Bunbithin!"

But how could such a pale babe be called a boy? The word for boy was "nguin", and it was also the word for charcoal, and a less charcoal-like creature could not be imagined in the whole of creation. Rather did his skin have the appearance of a log which had lain long in the sun without ever feeling the touch of fire.

Still, that was about to be remedied. Unceremoniously, Koppakkin retrieved Bunbithin from his mother and, ignoring his wails of disappointment at again being thwarted in his quest for sustenance, carefully rubbed his whole body with her ball of goanna grease, beeswax and charcoal. This done, she dusted this glistening coating with a covering of finely-powdered charcoal.

Bunbithin's lusty howls brought chuckles from the three women. "You wouldn't like it, my little fellow, if you were to stay pale as you grew up!" Koppakkin told him, shaking an admonitory finger in the little face. "One of these days you will be pleased we helped you get your proper colour!"

He certainly looked more like a proper nguin as his mother proudly took possession of him once more and tenderly guided his mouth to her breast.

Nerida marvelled at herself as she gazed down at this new person sucking at her nipple. How was it, she wondered, that she could feel so calm and quiet after the agonising pain of only a very short time ago? How was it, indeed, that she seemed to be forgetting even the discomfort in her binang as each moment passed? And how was it that she could feel such a deep sense of protectiveness and love in so short a space of time for this beautiful babe whose lips were already beginning to suck less vigorously as sleep overtook him, exhausted from the battle he had fought to gain his place in the fresh air?

Both Koppakkin and Ngita knew, as they pounded the bangwal to make cakes for the meal that evening, just how she felt. Each remembered the occasions, years before, when they had had similar feelings for a newly-arrived child. And each remembered many women who had looked at their babes in the same way as Nerida was now looking at hers.

"He's perfect!" Nerida murmured, as she laid him gently down on a clean piece of soft dibing bark.

The two older women could find nothing wrong with that statement.

Nerida brushed a fly from round Bunbithin's lips, where traces of milk still lurked, and wondered aloud how it was that her baby could look so much like Buruda. "It is almost as if Buruda himself has been to the spirit world and returned!" she said.

Ngita agreed. "That is certainly just what Buruda looked like when he was born!" she marvelled. "It is as if he were my little nguin again!"

Koppakkin smiled as she pounded away at the bangwal. "That is surely not surprising!" she told them. "That son-in-law of mine is a famous bu-ul! If any bu-ul was going to prepare his wife's binang properly to receive a spirit-child, it would have to be Buruda! No wonder the spirit took on his form when it entered my daughter! It could hardly be otherwise! When a woman's binang has been prepared by someone as strong as my son-in-law, it is only natural that it would try to take on his form!"

So there it was. The likeness of the tiny babe to his father was simply another proof of the might of the Undanbi manngur.

Nerida smiled again as she stroked the tiny charcoal-covered body, her fingers beginning at the head and ending at the toes. She wanted to commit to memory every little part of him, for she knew that all too soon this little spirit-child would be taken from her. In her mind's eye she saw again the mixture of pride and anguish in the face of Talobilla's mother as Nganku had taken the child from her, to be reborn a kivar and become Turugun.

So Nerida devoured her baby with her eyes, hoping always to be able to recall these sacred moments of birth.

Ngita went off toward the camp and returned shortly with five flying-foxes, which were soon sizzling on the fire while the bangwal cakes baked in the ashes on the fringe.

"Buruda asked about you," she told Nerida. "And Wungul was there, too. It's hard to tell who is happier. Wungul can't wait to start teaching this little baby who looks just like his father! He reckons he'll soon have him throwing tiny spears and boomerangs!"

Nerida smiled. "He'll have to wait a few moons, at least until our little Bunbithin can walk!" she remonstrated, and they all laughed.

The two women would stay with Nerida for the whole five days of seclusion, making sure that everybody, including the children, stayed clear. For this was the sacred time for women in childbirth, when the new babe was re-accustoming itself to life among people. Nobody but the mother and tending-women must glimpse the baby until this period was over.

As Nerida composed herself for sleep that night, Bunbithin's body curled in the curve of her own, her last thoughts were of Buruda. For one fleeting moment she surprised herself by feeling a slight twinge of jealousy at the thought that some other Baranggan might this night be sharing his bed. But then she told herself not to be silly, that it was only natural that some Bunda brothers would offer him the comfort of their wives while she was absent. In the same way she would in the future find Buruda offering her to a brother in a similar situation. Everybody knew that it was nothing to create a great fuss about.

Besides, she had a new baby. She could feel the whisper of his breath on her breasts as he slept. Her lips curved in a soft smile as she dropped off.

Buruda was glad that the time of waiting was over. For the five nights that Nerida had been away, his Bunda brothers had overwhelmed him with offers of their wives for the night. Even

Wungul, who had only one wife, had insisted that Baldhin keep him company the first night.

Strangely, though Buruda had always in the past looked forward to the variety that these encounters offered, this time he felt little heart for them. He could not understand his reluctance, but felt obliged to acquiesce, having no desire to hurt his brothers' feelings. Generosity was something you could not ignore. To hurl back a proffered gift into the face of the open-hearted giver would be churlish in the extreme. He also knew that there was no doubt in the minds of many of those who offered him such hospitality that they already owed their manngur for favours already received. It was only just that he should give them this opportunity to pay measure for measure.

So he accepted as many of the offers as he could, and once each encounter had begun he had found himself entering into it with his usual gusto. And those wives who comforted him found that they themselves received comfort in full measure.

Then, at long last, came the day for Nerida's return. And, although he would have to hold himself aloof from her for two whole moons, he knew his brothers would not feel the same compulsion to offer him solace while Nerida was in the hut. Under such circumstances, it would be up to Buruda himself to ask a brother if such comfort was needed.

Waiting for Nerida's return, Buruda smiled as he thought of how thankful he was that tonight he would have Nerida at his side once more. There was something about her very presence that was better than the most enjoyable sexual experience with other women. He was sure he would not have to ask any of his brothers for help in the next two moons!

The sky was overcast, and a sharp shower had just passed over when the first smoke was seen rising from the direction of the birthing-place. Ngita and Koppakkin had set fire to the temporary shelter, thus ensuring that all signs relating to the birth would be obliterated forever, and therefore nobody could inadvertently fall into error by stumbling across some forbidden aspect of this period sacred to women.

As the smoke rose into the air, the people assembled to await the arrival of the new member of the nation. Some of the more curious women hurried off toward the smoke, for they knew that Nerida and her two attendants were already approaching, and were anxious to be amongst the first to see Nerida's son. The men stood waiting, talking excitedly, but taking no step down that faint track that led to the place that only a few short days before had been the scene of an event that was sacred to women and which, until the time when the smoke had begun to rise, had been forbidden to all but the three participants.

From now on women might ignore the fact that a birth had taken place in that area, but the dhan would stay clear of it until next time they camped at Currimundi.

A chattering crowd of women appeared, and it was Mundul, Buruda's mother's sister and therefore one whom he called mother, who was carrying the child cradled in her arms. Grinning broadly, she first brought it to Buruda, and a great shout arose from all the dhan as he took it from her and held it up for all to see.

"Another Buruda!" one called out, and all laughed with delight as they saw the uncanny resemblance of the newborn child to its father.

Next Wungul took the boy and looked long and hard at him. As Buruda's favourite brother, he would be responsible more than anyone else for the education of this child. It would be Wungul who would teach him how to make and handle weapons. Wungul would teach him how to unravel the secrets of animal tracks, and how to decipher messages carried to his nostrils on the wind. From Wungul he would learn how to fashion mula and use them in the daily search for food. It would be Wungul who would reveal the first piece of sacred knowledge at this boy's kivar-yangga.

Suddenly the baby's eyes fluttered open and its tiny hands began to grope. At the same time its face turned in towards Wungul's chest and the lips searched for a nipple.

A great shout of laughter went up from women and men alike. "Bunbithin!" they roared.

The noise startled the young child, and its face puckered as Wungul shamefacedly returned the tiny form to Nerida, where the questing lips at last found the softness they were searching for.

That evening was showery, and Buruda was thankful for that. There would be no gathering round the communal campfire for dancing and singing, so he could savour Nerida's return to his hut. True, there now was another little being there as well. But Buruda already felt a great tenderness in his heart for his tiny son, particularly whenever he noticed the softness in his wife's eyes as she nursed her tiny babe.

And Nerida smiled secretly as she saw the contentment on her husband's face as he sat in the hut opening looking into the flames which, though protected from the main force of the showers, sputtered now and again as raindrops hit them. She knew without being told that he was thinking of the bounty of the earth, which had so generously presented them with the spirit of this helpless babe she was holding to her breast. She knew he would be thinking with satisfaction that once more all the necessary rites had been performed correctly to ensure the ongoing prosperity of the Undanbi.

Suddenly into her mind came the memory of the fear that had been evident that day he had awakened from his bad dream. What a contrast the peace in his face at this moment represented!

She had never been told what the dream was about, nor did she want to know. But as she recalled the effect it had had on her husband, her skin seemed to crawl, and she clasped Bunbithin more tightly to her breast. Birral grant that whatever Buruda had seen had nothing to do with her little one!

Then her fears were forgotten as the tiny lips once more sought her ever-willing breast.

✦

Chapter 11

March, 1822: Bingle explores Pumicestone Passage in the _Sally_.

The Undanbi men were shouldering their merbung, those huge kangaroo nets, preparatory to setting out on a hunt, when the young Dhundubari kivar arrived, somewhat out of breath after an all-night journey along the ocean beach of Yarun. So anxious had he been to arrive in time to catch the men that he had not even bothered to launch a canoe, but had elected instead to take the swifter course of wading and swimming over Kaerwagum at the northern end.

His message was so urgent that he did not stand on ceremony. Between gulps of water offered him to assuage his burning thirst, he blurted out the news that the spirit canoe had returned, and had been entering the wide southern part of Kaerwagum even as he had left the afternoon before.

"Bomarigo wants Buruda and some Undanbi warriors to come as quickly as you can!" he said.

Preparations for the move were made in great haste. Three teams of four men each, having collected their weapons, dragged the canoes into the water. By the time all this had taken place,

Buruda had charged the remainder with the care of the women, who had earlier left with their dhilla to dig bangwal.

"Forget about the kangaroo hunt!" he told them. "Take your weapons and find the women! Do not leave them under any circumstances until we return!"

"Yau-ai!" And the bu-ul set out at a trot to guard the women.

The Undanbi warriors who were to accompany Buruda and the Dhundubari kivar were soon swiftly poling the canoes over to Woorim, and on the way Buruda closely questioned the news-bringer. It seemed that this spirit canoe did not have quite the same look as the one used by Midherplinda so many summers ago. But it still used the clouds or whatever they were to move along, and Bomarigo was convinced that the spirits would once more land on Yarun. He only hoped that this time there would be no use of the magic thunder-sticks to bring hurt to the people.

"Our spears and throwing-clubs may be useless against spirits!" Wungul grated, as he felt the canoe move ahead under the pressure of water against his strongly-pulled pole. "But that won't stop us throwing them if these spirits use magic!"

There was a grunt of agreement from as many as were close enough to hear.

Then the canoes grounded against the sands of Yarun and, having dragged them safely above high water mark, they gathered their weapons and quickly covered the short distance over the sand-hills to the ocean beach.

The tide was out as they turned south, and the sand was hard, ideal for allowing great distances to be covered in a short time. They used the long, loping stride that would least sap their energy, their weapons held loosely, now over one shoulder, now over the other, now trailing low in the hand. And always with them was the sense of urgency, the feeling of the need to arrive in time for whatever was about to befall the Dhundubari, be it good or evil.

Buruda glanced sideways at the kivar who had brought the message. He knew that the lad would be very tired from his night-long journey, but he could see no sign of flagging as the kivar kept pace with the Undanbi bu-ul.

"Why don't you rest and follow us later?" he suggested.

But the kivar only shook his head determinedly. He had no intention of missing out on the events about to happen. Besides, what kivar within the surrounding nations would not happily endure all sorts of privations for the honour of accompanying the great manngur Buruda?

"No!" he answered shortly. And that was all.

Buruda nodded, satisfied. Such a kivar as this would bear watching. He must keep an eye on him to see how he performed at his dhur. But Buruda did not doubt that the lad would play his part with distinction.

All day they drove south, pausing only once to turn aside to a patch of scrub containing a pool of fresh water, where they drank deep to quench their thirst. They also gathered some of the pale, green-spotted midyim fruit to stow in their dhilla under their left arms. These they would later put in their mouths to suck. They would not only allay their hunger but also help to keep their mouths moist.

Then they resumed their journey.

But despite their rapid progress, Bigi was low in the sky when they eventually turned their faces towards the west away from the seashore, and set their feet on the track that led across the southern end of Yarun to Kaerwagum. It was dusk by the time they reached the Dhundubari camp.

Again there was no sitting down and waiting on ceremony. Bomarigo, Nganku and a host of bu-ul rushed out from the camp as soon as the Undanbi bu-ul appeared. At first Buruda and his friends could not make out what had happened, so great was the desire of all to give their individual versions. But then Bomarigo held up his hand, and the chattering died down.

"You have come in time, my friends," Bomarigo told the relieved Undanbi warriors. "The spirit canoe is sitting out in Kaerwagum, and no spirit has yet set foot on Yarun. If they do so tomorrow, or on some other day, we will be ready for them."

It was Buruda who asked the question hovering on all their lips. "Where is the canoe?"

The Dhundubari led them quickly to the shores of Kaerwagum, where the spirit canoe could still be dimly seen. Fires were twinkling from holes in the side, and some shapes could be observed moving about among the big sticks that projected from its centre.

Buruda gasped. Its immensity was something he had not been prepared for. Somehow the descriptions he had heard of the canoe that had passed K'gari and the one that had earlier visited Yarun had not conveyed to him how huge they were. He had of course envisaged a much longer canoe than the ones the people used, and even a wider one. But this – this was beyond belief!

"How many spirits in the canoe?" he wanted to know.

But Bomarigo could only spread his hands. "Gurwindha!"

The length of the word in Bomarigo's mouth gave Buruda the impression that there were not too many, but at the same time Bomarigo had shrugged his shoulders, indicating that he did not really know the exact number of spirits involved. So it was really hard to say.

"It doesn't matter!" Buruda assured his old friend. "If it comes to a fight, we'll match their numbers with our bu-ul!"

Long after the stars had appeared they continued to squat, peering intently into the darkness to see if the spirit canoe would divulge any of its secrets. Strange sounds came to their ears. Now and again a spirit would laugh. Again, another would shout, for no apparent reason. Then suddenly there arose an eerie wailing sound, and voices could be heard in what appeared to be extremely unmelodious singing. Or was it perhaps their peculiar cry for the dead? And, at any rate, would the already dead cry for themselves? Who could tell?

The sound raised the hair on the back of the watchers' necks.

They gave up their vigil when the last fire had been extinguished on the canoe, and it had become only a blurred shape in the night. Then, returning to the camp, they talked and planned as they ate a late meal of bangwal and goanna prepared by the women. By the time they at last turned in to sleep, all dhan had been briefed on their role in the next day's events.

The camp was astir before daybreak. As the light strengthened and they watched the spirit canoe from behind the cover of the dibing trees on the shore, Buruda noticed that the young man who had brought the news to the Undanbi had taken his place somewhat in advance of the other kivar.

"A good lad, that!" he remarked to Nganku.

And Nganku smiled, gratified. "I taught him myself!" he said. "He is the son of Bomarigo and his youngest wife. He will become a bu-ul at the next dhur."

Seeing the pride in the face of the Dhundubari manngur, Buruda once again experienced the feeling that all was right with the earth. How could anything go wrong when young men were being taught by those who took their responsibilities so seriously? He thought of his own pride in the accomplishments of Turugun. How could any spirits have power to harm any nation that had such kivar?

But here before them on the face of Kaerwagum was the unknown. How would the day turn out? Would they be mourning their dead at its end? Would the spirits land? Would they destroy, or would they do good? Or would they not care, and do neither?

The spirits began to stir on the big canoe. A rattling sound was heard, like the noise made by a stick dragged quickly over a rough rock. Then from the watching host came a quick indrawn breath of wonder as clouds started to billow above the canoe and it began to move.

Yet they weren't clouds, Buruda said to himself. They had none of the indistinctness which the edges of clouds sometimes exhibited. Rather did they look like giant wings. Still, whatever they were, they seemed to possess some magic, for the canoe was travelling along much faster than the speed reached by their own pole-propelled craft.

At first, as they had planned, the dhan kept behind the cover of the trees as they kept pace with the spirit canoe. Many times they were sure it was coming to shore to allow the spirits to land, but every time it looked as if it would run aground, it would suddenly turn and move away toward Ningi country. It was almost as though the spirits were aware of the watchers behind the trees and were tantalising them. But what would be the purpose of such a game? Truly the ways of spirits were different from the ways of men!

As the morning wore on and the canoe made its way further up Kaerwagum, the second part of their plan was put into action. It had been decided that, if the spirits did not land, they were to be invited to do so by a number of the bu-ul, while the main group remained hidden behind the trees, ready to respond to any sign of treachery.

Nganku led the contingent whose task it was to extend the invitation. Breaking off bushes, they went down to the water's edge, waving the branches at arms' length, touching the water first at one side and then at the other. Such signs, they knew, were a universal sign of welcome, and ought to be understood even by spirits. At the same time they called out loudly, "Come in, friends! We want to meet with you and talk of the wonders you have seen in the land of the spirits!"

For a time it appeared as if the spirits would completely ignore the invitation. Now they approached, now they turned away. They came to Taranggir, and for a short time it seemed almost as if they would repeat the visit of Midherplinda at that point. But they passed it. Still Nganku and the bu-ul with him continued to keep pace with the canoe, calling out their welcome. And still the remainder of the dhan kept out of sight in the trees, keeping up with Nganku.

Bigi was at his highest point when it happened. The clouds, or wings, or whatever they were over the canoe, appeared to fold up, and it came to rest. Shortly afterwards, a smaller canoe was let down into the water, and a number of spirits, wrapped in strange-looking trappings, descended into it.

Then – wonder of wonders – the small canoe seemed to grow legs from its sides, and began to walk over the water toward Nganku and his bu-ul!

Up to now Nganku and his men had held their ground, but this was too much for them. With one accord they hastily retreated to the safety of the trees. By the time the spirit canoe had reached the sandy shore just opposite Daki-Bomon, the excitement and fright of the bu-ul had increased to such a pitch that they were shouting at the tops of their voices, begging the spirits to take their walking canoe and leave.

But Bomarigo and some of the older men stood silent. They were frightened as well, but these older men remembered the earlier visit of Midherplinda when the canoe had also looked as if it were walking to the shore. Bomarigo tried to calm those nearest him, telling them that in reality the legs were only poles. Gradually some of the panic subsided.

As far as Buruda was concerned, terror was a luxury he felt he could not afford at the moment. He had a feeling that there was much to be learned if only he could keep his wits about him. Those around him were looking to him and the other manngur for wisdom, and he knew that fright often drove wisdom away. He might die today, but before he died he should learn something. Perhaps this was the beginning of the fulfilment of his dream, but even so, he could do nothing to try to avert disaster if he did not control his passions.

So, as the canoe came to rest on the sand and the spirits sprang out, Buruda held up his hand for silence.

"Gubbi!" he commanded them. "Enough! You all learned, even as early as your kivar-yangga, that you should not give way to fear or anger, for in that case any enemy, no matter how weak, can overcome you! Do you not remember those lessons now?" He pointed to one of the lately-initiated Dhundubari kivar. "This kivar and others who were with him were taught this only a few short moons ago, and you bu-ul were the ones who taught them! How could you teach them things you do not know yourselves?"

There was a shamefaced murmur of agreement from all. But one of the bu-ul answered quietly, "Yes, Buruda, you are right. We should not give way to fear. But how do we not become afraid when we see the strange power of the spirits?"

Buruda smiled at the man. "I am afraid as well!" he told him, and paused to allow the men to recover their self-respect. "But we must not let fear cloud our wits! We are bu-ul and kivar, and to bu-ul and kivar falls the task of protecting our women! Only with cool heads can we do this!"

Again there was a murmur of agreement.

"So let us leave the trees and show these spirits that we are not afraid of them! We can learn nothing further from the shelter of trees! And – who knows – these may be good spirits, sent to bring us valuable knowledge!"

The place where they emerged was over a spear's throw from the spirit landing-place. This was only sensible, for no reasonable fighting man would give an advantage to a possible enemy.

The crowd of dhan stood silently facing the spirits, and the spirits stared back at them. For a long time neither side appeared to move a muscle, each waiting for the opposite party to make the first move.

Again it was Buruda who stirred the dhan into action.

"I will go forward to meet them," he told his companions. "I will take no weapons, for it is important that they know we intend them no harm. But it is a foolish bu-ul who puts himself into danger with no hope of retreat. Therefore, I will expect you to follow me, fully armed but far enough back to let them feel secure, yet at the same time close enough to allow you to attack if they make any obviously hostile move."

Bomarigo demurred. "Your plan is good, but it is I and not you who will go!" he told Buruda. When he saw that Buruda wanted to interrupt, he hastened to go on. "I know that it is always the boldest warrior who takes his place in the van on the battleground. So it has always been from the Before-Time. Therefore you ought to be the one in the lead. But this is Dhundubari land – not Undanbi. Besides, I have some experience with spirits, and it does not make sense to deprive our strongest fighting man of weapons and then place him in the area of greatest danger. These spirits will use Mumba the thunder and not spears! If you look, you will see the thunder-sticks in their hands!"

They looked, and saw that it was so.

"I am old," Bomarigo continued, "and the wisdom of my age tells me that I must be the one to meet the spirits first." He smiled at Buruda. "Your wisdom, great though it is, has time to grow even greater. It must be given that chance! Mine has reached its peak and, if it is time for it to vanish into the land of spirits, so be it! I will lead you to meet the spirits, my son! You will remain armed and lead the bu-ul if I die!"

Buruda had to agree with the old man's reasoning.

Carefully Bomarigo held his spears aloft for all to see, and then thrust them into the sand one by one, so that the spirits could see he had none left. He did not, however, turn his back to them. Had he done so, they could have seen the throwing-club which he had earlier placed in his belt in line with his backbone. He had no intention of making himself completely helpless.

He began to move in the direction of the spirits.

At the same time one of the spirits laid down his thunder-stick, stepped out from among the group round the canoe, and began to walk toward Bomarigo.

There was no doubting the courage of the old manngur, but the sight of the spirit coming toward him made him stop in his tracks, and he began to tremble. In the long time since he had had to deal with spirits, he had remembered nothing but his fear, and it was this memory of the fear of ages ago that he now had to learn to conquer. Buruda, seeing him stop, motioned for the dhan to stop also. They needed no urging to do so, poised as they were for fight or flight.

The spirit also halted.

For a long time nobody moved. Bomarigo shook with fear, but stood his ground. The men, well behind him, needed not to be told how much courage it took for him to remain where he was. The old man might have some experience with spirits, but these particular spirits might indeed be quite different from those of a generation ago.

Buruda's heart filled with admiration for the old man as he remembered his words, *"How do you fight the wind and the eternal?"* Yet here he was, demonstrating once more his preparedness to face the unknown for the good of his people.

At last the spirit held out an axe, and Bomarigo, interpreting this as a sign that no harm would come to him, once more began his slow journey forward. This time the spirit stood still, waiting. Almost imperceptibly, trembling but determined, Bomarigo closed the gap.

The last few paces' distance was covered at less than a snail's pace. The spirit continued to hold out the axe. The other spirits stayed near their canoe, holding what Bomarigo had called their thunder-sticks. Buruda held his place behind the old man, well within a spear's throw of the spirits, the dhan behind him, all ready to release a shower of weapons at the first sign of treachery.

Then, after a painfully long time, the fingers of Bomarigo's outstretched hand brushed the fingers of the spirit, and the dhan held their breath. But nothing untoward happened. Instead, the spirit placed the axe on the sand before the old man's feet, and then, after placing a knife beside it, retreated to his canoe.

So obvious was the goodwill of the spirit that Buruda planted his spears upright in the sand and ran forward to join Bomarigo. All the dhan did likewise, yelling for the spirit to return, pointing to their spears in the sand behind them.

At that instant a number of ducks, disturbed by the sudden shouting, rose from a marsh behind the tree line and flew overhead. Buruda saw the spirit who had met Bomarigo pick up his stick and put it to his shoulder. And then they heard the noise that could only be described as Mumba, though it was not the same. Some smoke came from the stick, too, as though there had been a little fire there.

All this, despite the fact that Bomarigo and the older Dhundubari men had prepared them for it, was utterly astounding. But nobody was hurt by the thunder, nor indeed did they expect harm. The spirit had been too friendly for that.

And, wonder of wonders, a duck fell at their feet, quite dead! Buruda picked it up, amazed. There was blood on it, but how it came to be dead was beyond comprehension. Only a few short breaths ago it had been flying with its brothers in the direction of Ningi country. Now it was ready to be roasted on the coals! But, while it was plain that this was yet another gift from the spirit, how this gift had been presented was a mystery.

Still, there was yet another mystery that was occupying Buruda's mind more thoroughly than the mystery of a dead duck. There before him on the sand were the imprints of the spirit's feet, and he felt the hair rise on the back of his neck as he realised that they bore a startling resemblance to the imprints he had seen in his dream. Squatting down, he began to study them carefully.

At the same time, other bu-ul bent to study the prints leading to and from the landing-place of the canoe, which was now making its way back to the large one. Buruda placed his right foot beside one of the prints, and found it not much different in size from his own. Other bu-ul made the same comparison.

"But where are the toes?" Nganku called out.

No-one could answer the question since, of course, there were no toes to the print. And no matter how many times they looked away and back again, the fact remained that the spirit's feet were toeless. Even the prints of the other spirits where they had stood round the beached canoe showed the same strange characteristic.

There was a sudden shouting from the trees behind them, and they turned to see Kamkuri leading a contingent of Ningi bu-ul toward them. Again the customary ceremony was dispensed with as the new arrivals were quickly apprised of the day's events. Kamkuri told them that the Ningi had waited on the mainland side of Kaerwagum until the spirit canoe had moved north that morning, after which they had crossed to Yarun.

"At first we thought the spirits might land in Ningi country," Kamkuri told them. "But as soon as we saw they were keeping much closer to Yarun, we launched our canoes in case the Dhundubari might need help."

All that afternoon they examined the prints, and at the same time the strange axe and knife were passed around from hand to hand, to enable all to examine them closely. The edge of the axe was obviously much sharper than they could ever hope to make one of their own stone tools, grind them as they might. The knife, while no sharper than the quartz edges of their own, nevertheless appeared strange, in that its face presented one straight edge. Their own knives were often a little jagged and uneven. The handle, too, was strange, in that it was beautifully fitted to the blade, and felt much better to the hand than those of their own knives. The handle of the axe, also, was much stronger than their own.

But the thing that caused them the greatest wonder was the fact that the stone out of which the axe-head was ground appeared to have come with a smooth hole in it, into which the handle had been fitted. What kind of land must the land of the spirits be to have these sorts of stones lying round ready to be picked up! Or did the spirits, indeed, have some magical means of making smooth holes in solid rock?

Buruda's mind, however, was occupied with the mystery of the footprints. He had hoped that a more careful examination might reveal to him whether or not these particular spirits had any connection with his dream. But, try as he might, he could come to no firm conclusion, even by the time Bigi had dropped below the horizon and they had made their way back to where the Dhundubari women had erected shelters for the night.

That night, after they had eaten sparingly of bangwal, for the dhan had been too busy to hunt and the women had been too interested in the events to do much digging, Buruda presented his findings to a special council of the bu-ul of the three nations.

"The tracks resemble the tracks of my dream," he told them, "but there is not one that is the exact track that I saw. We have to remember, too, that these spirits have presented Bomarigo with gifts of an axe and a knife, and even gave us a little food by killing a duck as it flew over our heads with its brothers. These actions are not the actions of those who would do us great harm. In my dream it seemed that the track I saw would bring a great disaster, at least to the Undanbi. So it does not seem that these spirits out on Kaerwagum have anything to do with these terrible happenings."

Nganku agreed. "I would say that these gifts demand repayment," he stated. "We should supply these spirit visitors with food during their stay."

An approving "Yau-ai!" came from the assembled bu-ul.

Kamkuri went even further. "These spirits may decide to stay and teach us how we can make such weapons ourselves," he said.

Others remarked that even the secrets of the sticks of thunder might be imparted to them in due course, and this would make hunting so much easier.

But Buruda injected a note of caution. "These are spirits," he reminded them, "and the ways of spirits are not the ways of men! From the Before-Time, dhan have used spears, boomerangs, mula and kangaroo-nets to hunt. The earth has supplied food in great plenty to the people of our nations. Why should we wish it to be different? Our laws teach us how to ensure the increase of all creatures that spring from the earth. Why should we desire the thunder-sticks to make it easier to kill food? These animals are our brothers, and they know that we need them for food. They respect our boomerangs and spears. Leave the use of thunder to the spirits! We have no need of it!"

Kamkuri added his support. "Buruda is right. Our women use their digging-sticks every day, and the earth gives them bangwal. Would it be better if bangwal appeared by magic instead of by digging? Would it be better for us if our food dropped dead at the sound of thunder rather than by hurling our spears?"

"Leave spirit things to spirits!" Bomarigo warned them all.

Next morning they were early at the scene of the previous day's events. Spirits were moving on the canoe, but there was no sign of the white wings on the sticks projecting from it, so perhaps they did not intend to move. Buruda was relieved to find that the high tide of the night had obliterated all tracks up to high water mark. He had half expected that the water might not have the same effect on spirit tracks as it had on the tracks of men, and it was a great relief to find that at least in this respect they were the same.

Once more they broke off bushes and made the sign of welcome, and after a while the small canoe began to make its way to shore. The spirit who had presented Bomarigo with the axe and knife was standing up in it. This time there was not the same panic as on the day before, for they had all been able to see that the legs of the canoe were in fact only specially shaped poles.

As the canoe grounded, the spirit who had been standing jumped ashore. Bomarigo immediately held out four fat mullet, and the spirit smiled as he took them, handing them to one of the other spirits, who threw them into the canoe.

A great shout went up from the assembled people, and the women, up till then timidly staying within the cover of the trees, joined in. It was a good sign that the gift of fish had been accepted so readily. Those who intended harm could be expected to act differently.

The spirit then took the dhilla that covered its head and handed it to Bomarigo, showing by signs that he should put it on his own head. Bomarigo was somewhat reluctant to accept the gift, for he had suddenly remembered that the hurt from Midherplinda's thunder-sticks had come after one of the bu-ul had tried to take the dhilla from Midherplinda's head. Besides, he felt rather foolish about the thing. Nevertheless he complied, for to refuse would be ill-mannered. Obviously these spirits carried their dhilla on their heads, rather than under their left arms.

Still, as he looked at the dhilla being put on Bomarigo's head, Buruda was puzzled. There would not be enough room left between a person's hair and the dhilla to carry anything like a knife or a ball of wax or white clay. Besides, since the opening faced downwards, would not all these things fall out? In any case, there had been nothing in the dhilla when the spirit had taken it off his head, so of what use was it? Truly the ways of the spirits were strange! Perhaps, after all, it was just an ornament. Yes – that at least made some sort of sense. It made a good ornament.

But, as they had yesterday, the tracks left by the spirits were occupying the attention of all the men who could crowd in close enough to get a glimpse of them. Buruda looked instead at the spirits' feet, and experienced a sudden feeling of revulsion at the sight of the toeless things that met his eyes. How could any creature, even a spirit, manage to move itself around on such monstrous feet?

Then the spirit laughed and, to a gasp of disbelief from the assembled throng, appeared to remove the outer part of its foot. This done, he peeled off a thick sort of brownish skin, revealing a foot complete with toes. True, it was paler than if it had just been roasted on the fire, and therefore looked quite unnatural. But it was indeed a foot, nevertheless!

"Toes! Toes!" The call went up from those who were close enough to see. The spirit had toes!

Gleefully the people began to dance. In their relieved exuberance, Nganku and Wungul embraced the spirit, ignoring the foreign feel of the loose pieces of bark enclosing the body and the strange smell that emanated therefrom. Kamkuri and Bulangga each presented the spirit with a spear. Buruda added a shield, for if a warrior used spears in a fight, he also needed a shield to deflect those of the enemy.

Nganku signified an interest in the thunder-stick, and the spirit allowed him to handle it. Buruda also touched its smooth surface, surprised to see it had a big hole in one end. But both were very tentative in their approach to the strange weapon. Strange things should be handled with great care.

The spirit smiled as he took it back from Buruda. There were three pelicans swimming close to the shore about a spear-throw's distance from them, their huge bills probing the shallows for any unsuspecting fish they could find. Drawing Buruda's attention to the birds by pointing in that direction, the spirit lifted the stick to his shoulder.

It was all Buruda could do not to run, so great was the noise of the thunder at this close range. As it was, it seemed to him that his feet lifted off the ground. And, to add to his dismay, the strange smell of the smoke made his nose wrinkle. But his fright left him in an instant, for there, for all to see, was one of the pelicans floating lifeless, while the others took off, their huge wings struggling for lift as their feet beat frantically at the water.

It was Turugun who retrieved the bird and brought it back, its pendulous under-bill flapping grotesquely in death.

Once more the spirit offered the thunder-stick for the inspection of any who desired to handle it, but this time not even Buruda would touch it. "Gubbi!" he muttered shortly, signing for the spirit to take it away. Then, to emphasise the point, he repeated the word more loudly. "Gubbi!"

The spirit laughed. It seemed to Buruda that it was a companionable laugh, and not one of scorn for a bu-ul afraid to touch a weapon offered in such a friendly fashion. Somehow, for all his strange appearance and smell, Buruda found himself conceiving a liking for this spirit man. A man he must be, for there was the stubble of a beard on his face. Besides, his hair was too long for a woman. And surely, even in the spirit world, the hunting would be done by the men. So, even though he could not see his dhun because of the queer outer covering, Buruda was fairly certain it was the spirit of a man.

The time had come, Buruda thought, to introduce himself to the spirit. Pointing to himself and looking the spirit full in the face, he said carefully, "Bu-ru-da!" Once more he said it, thumping himself in the chest so that there could be no mistake. "Bu-ru-da!"

Once again the spirit laughed. "Buruda!" he repeated gleefully, poking Buruda in the chest. "Buruda!" Then he thumped himself in the same region and said something that must have been his own name, but that was so strange-sounding that Buruda knew he could never hope to repeat it, for in the middle of the name was a strange hissing sound like the sound of dibing bark being ripped from a tree. But he had to try, and the spirit laughed and said it more carefully the second time.

Buruda's tongue did its best. "Midherbingul!"

And the spirit smiled, satisfied.

So they learnt his name. Round the campfire that night they discussed at length why it was that the first part of the name should begin with the same strange sound as the name of Midherplinda, the earlier visitor of so long ago. A suggestion that all spirit names began like that was soon set aside, for there had been other names on that first canoe – Damwel and Bongari – that did not have that sound. Perhaps Midherplinda and Midherbingul were relatives.

There was also much discussion about the relationship of the spirits to those still alive. This was very important to know, for how else could the appropriate skin be assigned to the individual spirits? One woman thought that Midherbingul bore some slight resemblance to Dimmangali, a son of hers, who had been killed in a kin-bumbe three seasons ago. But of course, it was fruitless to pursue such conjectures, since they could really only be verified by referring to tribal markings and other bodily scars. And since the spirits kept their bodies covered at all times, it seemed unlikely that anyone would ever know just who the spirits had been in real life.

The spirit canoe stayed in the same place in Kaerwagum, opposite Daki-Bomon, for four more days. Each morning the bu-ul presented Midherbingul with as many mullet as were needed for those on the canoe.

On the morning of the fifth day they saw the wings on the canoe unfurl. The great crowd of people assembled to watch, and then kept pace with the canoe as it returned down Kaerwagum toward the open sea. They were genuinely sorry to see it go, for Midherbingul had found a place in their hearts with his gifts and friendly attitude.

"Come back! Come back!" they called, waving green branches. But the spirits, although they waved their hands in reply, maintained their course back toward the land of the spirits. All the people had tears in their eyes as the canoe disappeared round the southern point of Yarun. Indeed, the cry of sorrow that rose from men and women alike was almost as great as the evening cry for the dead.

The Undanbi wasted no time in leaving. There was nothing more to hold them in the land of the Dhundubari, and they were anxious to return to their own people with the story of the strange happenings they had witnessed. Many a long hour would be spent describing the weird strangers, and many a long hour would be spent in composing new dances and songs to bring these descriptions to life.

Midherbingul had gone, but he would be remembered in the songs of the Undanbi.

✧

Chapter 12

June, 1822: Edwardson in Pumicestone Passage in the *Snapper*.

Nerida's heart was singing. It was a glorious day. The crisp air of the morning in this cool time of wallaidhau made the blood sing in her veins. She luxuriated in the feel of the cool play of her muscles as she dug, her digging-stick loosening the soil round the roots of the bangwal. In the branches overhead sang kurumbul the magpie, secure in the knowledge that some juicy titbits would be unearthed for him by the women toiling below. Truly it was a wonderful day.

And what could be more wonderful than feeling the weight of her little Bunbithin on her shoulders as she worked? Young as he was, he had already learnt to grasp her hair to make his position less precarious. All the women remarked that he had a stronger grip than most babies twice his age. So advanced was he that it would not be long, she was sure, before he would be able to ride on her shoulders without the help of a rug or dhilla, secure enough in the grip on her hair, even when asleep.

She smiled to herself as she worked. How well-named he was! His lips possessed much power – so much so that, even though Nerida herself had plenty of milk to satisfy his needs, many women often begged to be allowed to have a short turn at feeding him, just for the satisfaction of feeling his tremendous suck.

While she was thinking, the happy chatter of the women as they worked and the shrieks of the children as they chased one another back and forth round the trees receded into the background. But a sudden burst of laughter from both Garwidha and Buldarin, who were working close beside her, disturbed her reverie. She looked up quickly, only to find that their laughter had been directed at her.

"You are a dreamer!" Garwidha teased. "You didn't hear a word we said! Don't tell me you were thinking of that husband of yours again!"

"Or your baby!" Buldarin chimed in, and both women laughed again.

Nerida grinned shamefacedly as she met the eyes of her two friends. "I was just thinking of how happy I am," she confessed. "And, yes, Bunbithin was part of it."

"No wonder!" Garwidha remarked. "He is a strong boy! I only hope my little boy, when he comes, will be as strong!"

"Boy! Always a boy!" Buldarin chided her. "How do you know it will be a boy?" Her eyes softened as she added, "I won't mind if mine is a girl."

"Well, boy or girl, it is all one to me," Garwidha laughed. "I'm just pleased that that husband of mine prepared my binang properly so that a spirit child could come in!"

Buldarin smiled as she bent once more to her digging. She felt just as pleased that Barga had done the same for her. What a different life she now led! No more knocks and curses! Even now, without looking over toward the spot where Karum was at work, she knew that the older woman would every now and again be casting a solicitous glance in her direction. It was marvellous to live in Barga's hut with such a caring sister and husband. Life was good.

And Garwidha also daydreamed as she worked. How Naruman had changed from the petulant, immature dhan they had all known! Now, he was one of the most responsible of the bu-ul. No longer did his name fit his personality in any way.

The dhilla of all the women were now getting full. It was time to start making a leisurely return to camp, which at this time was situated south of Coochin. This was the area where Kaerwagum entered a maze of channels, so shallow that it was possible at low tide to wade easily across to Yarun. It was here that the outgoing tide often could not make up its mind which way to run, whether south past Daki-Bomon to Ningi country, or north toward Woorim. So shallow was the water, that this was the place where the father emu often crossed when he felt the need, coaxing his half-grown chicks to follow, their long necks stretched high with anxiety.

The waterways at the mouth of Coochin were also ideal for the use of fish-traps, and it was at one of these that the dhan were busy today with their fish-spears, tipped with the barbs of stingrays. Only yesterday they had repaired the grass and brush walls of the traps. Today they would expect many sorts of fish, especially whiting and bream, to be trapped on the sandbanks behind the walls, where they would come at high tide to feed on the plentiful yabbies and soldier crabs which made their homes there.

The tide had been out early this morning, so it was possible that the dhan would even now be back at the camp. The water would by now have risen over the top of the grass walls, and the fish would therefore no longer fall such easy prey to their spears.

The thought of the fish was beginning to make old Ngita's mouth water. She was in the lead of the chattering procession of women as they passed the last clump of casuarinas hiding the camp from view. But at the very moment when she was about to open her mouth to remark on her mounting hunger, the sight that met her eyes brought her to an abrupt halt. So quickly did she stop that an unwary boy cannoned into her, almost knocking her over.

Her feeling of astonishment and fear communicated itself to the group as if by magic, and a sudden silence fell. For there in a narrow channel, clearly visible through a break in the mangroves, was a spirit canoe. This was one of the smaller canoes which, as the men had described to them, was propelled by the use of their specially shaped poles – not the other one with the wings above it.

But what were the spirits doing here so far up Kaerwagum? Never before had they been in this place! Fearfully the women shrank back into the shelter of the trees, and the children hardly breathed. One thought was uppermost in all their minds – had the spirits seen them? And another thought followed swiftly on the heels of the first – would the spirits come ashore and harm them?

Each woman grasped her digging-stick more fiercely.

It was Ngita who sent one of the older boys to fetch the men. "Hurry!" she whispered. "Tell them that we are in danger!" And the boy needed no second telling, making a beeline through the trees to the camp, keeping well out of sight of the spirits in their canoe.

Of course, Bunbithin would choose that instant to wake and vigorously demand to be fed! In one smooth motion, Nerida dropped her stick and used both hands to swing him from her back to her breast, where his yells ceased as his questing lips found what they were after.

Silently they watched the canoe edge its way slowly along the narrow channel. Every now and again the spirits would get out and wade as they pulled it from a sandbank. They gave no sign that they had seen the watching women, but were apparently interested only in seeing how far the channel would take them before it petered out.

So intent were the women on the scene before them that they were startled to hear Buruda's voice, so noiselessly had the dhan come up behind them.

"So they have returned!" he said quietly, and then added, "But no spirit in that canoe has the look of Midherbingul!"

And truly it was so. The one who appeared to be the main spirit was much stockier than Midherbingul.

"These are different!" Wungul stated flatly.

Dhubal echoed all their feelings as he asked, "What is their purpose, then? Are they here for good, or for evil?"

As he spoke, all the men grasped their heavy spears more firmly. They had discarded their light fish-spears as soon as the boy had arrived with the news of the spirits.

"Let some of us invite them in and find out," Buruda suggested. "But while we do so, let the rest keep hidden. I do not trust their thunder-sticks!"

Buruda, Turugun, Wungul and Dhubal broke off some bushes and ran down to a place where a break in the mangroves gave access to the water. Then, as they waved their branches in the universal signal of welcome that even talobilla the dolphin understood, they called out, inviting the spirits to land and exchange gifts. But the only answer from the spirits was to move their canoe further away, the tide having by now risen sufficiently to allow the canoe to float over all the sandbanks.

"How ill-mannered!" Naruman muttered. "Don't they understand even the simplest things?"

But Bulangga was more tolerant. "They may forget a lot of things in the spirit-land," he said. "You should remember that a newborn baby has forgotten how to live with people. Maybe the same thing applies to these spirits."

"But why are they here at all?" Wimbur wanted to know. "Why can't they stay in the spirit-land until the proper time comes for them to return as babies? Have we broken some laws? Have we forgotten to perform some of the death rites, that these spirits are so restless?"

Still, whatever the cause, the fact remained that they were here, and were not responding to the invitation being extended by the four on the bank. Instead, they were obviously making sure that the canoe stayed safely more than a spear's throw away. Disappointed, the watchers saw the canoe point once more in the direction from which it had come – back toward Daki-Bomon. Soon it had disappeared, hidden by the thick growth of mangroves.

Buruda was not willing to give up so easily. From here almost as far south as Daki-Bomon there were so many mangroves clustered on the banks of Kaerwagum that no man could hope to keep up with the canoe by travelling along the shore. "But we should not let them vanish without trying to make closer contact!" he urged the dhan. "If spirits continue to visit us, we must do our best to find out why!"

They all agreed. "Yau-ai!"

"We need to know if there is a larger canoe with wings!" Buruda went on. "Maybe Midherbingul will be on that canoe, or even Midherplinda. So let us take some fish for the journey and make straight across country to Daki-Bomon as fast as we can. Maybe the Ningi will be gathered there, and it is possible that they have already contacted the spirits."

Preparations were quickly made. Leaving half the men to protect the camp, the others, fully armed, were soon trotting through the dibing forest toward Daki-Bomon. They crossed Tibrogargan Creek by means of the canoes which were always kept on the banks in readiness, and Bigi had just reached his highest point when they broke out of the bush onto the shore where Daki-Bomon entered Kaerwagum.

Sure enough, a large canoe was resting almost at the same spot where Midherbingul's had been only a few short moons before. "But it is not quite as big as Midherbingul's canoe," Dhubal pointed out. "This is another one."

A loud hail from the southern bank of Daki-Bomon drew their attention. There, at the northernmost boundary of their land, the Ningi people were gathered – men, women and children – and it was obvious from the green branches in their hands that many of them had been engaged in inviting the spirits to come ashore and meet the people.

Buruda cupped his hands round his mouth to make his voice travel further. "Have they come in to meet you?" he yelled across the water.

It seemed as if the throats of all on the southern bank contributed to the answer. "Gubbi! Gubbi!" The tone of the reply had an element of disgust, and Barga hawked loudly and spat on the ground to show his displeasure.

"Naruman was right!" he growled. "These spirits have no manners!"

The Ningi immediately launched a number of canoes, and soon Kamkuri and some Ningi bu-ul had joined the Undanbi on the northern bank.

They listened as Kamkuri related what had happened. Indeed, it had been very little. The large canoe had entered Kaerwagum the evening before last, and the Ningi had immediately given the sign of welcome. The canoe had rested opposite the mouth of Ningi Creek that first night, only to spread its wings early next morning to make its way up to where it was now sitting. All the way up, the Ningi had waved branches, and they had also noticed the Dhundubari doing the same on Yarun. And when it had reached its present position, some time had elapsed with no indication that the spirits would respond to their greeting. They had been visible walking around on the canoe, but not one had even raised a hand to show they had seen the people on either side of Kaerwagum.

"Are they deaf, then, and blind?" Buruda wanted to know.

"It is almost as if they are in another country," Kamkuri admitted. "They do not seem to see us, even though they look in our direction."

"But that is ridiculous!" Dhubal spluttered, his grey beard quivering with anger. "Midherbingul could see and hear – and so could Midherplinda, as some of you Ningi saw for yourselves all those seasons ago!"

They all agreed that it was probably plain bad manners or ignorance, rather than any other cause, that made these spirits ignore them.

Kamkuri went on to explain further. The spirits had eventually launched their small canoe the afternoon before, and the people from both sides of Kaerwagum had waved their branches even more frantically, vying with each other in their attempts to lure the visitors to their nation.

"But they came to neither of us!" Kamkuri told them, and his expression once more showed disbelief at the recollection. "They went up towards Coochin instead! And even though the Dhundubari kept up with them and continued their waving, they ignored them! At dusk the small canoe had returned, and still they had not given one sign that they know we exist!"

Kamkuri's words made Buruda more fearful. In his dream he had not been able to make any foot-prints on the sand, and had not seemed to exist! Was it just possible that this canoe, whose spirits did not recognise the existence of those on the bank, could be the forerunner of the disaster his dream had seemed to foretell?

But Kamkuri was continuing. Today, he said, the same thing had happened. The small canoe had been launched, and again the invitations had been ignored. The Dhundubari had given up waving their branches halfway through the morning, and the Ningi shortly after that.

But the Undanbi men were beginning to feel hungry. A couple of them started a fire, and soon the aroma of roasting fish met their nostrils. While they ate, they considered what might be the best course of action.

Dhubal, still angry over the ignorance of the spirits, was all for waiting until dark and then poling out to the canoe. "If we do it quietly," he urged, "we could have them all speared before they even know what is happening!"

But he found few to support him. Not many were keen to find out what it was like on a spirit canoe. For all they knew, Kamkuri pointed out, that was just what the spirits wanted them to do. Perhaps, once they had the men on their canoe, they would unfurl their wings and carry them all away to the land of the spirits.

And Buruda kept hearing the words of Bomarigo. *"How do you fight the wind and the eternal?"* No, he was not eager to test the power of the spirits, certainly not while they might use their thunder-sticks. Midherbingul had been friendly, certainly, but he had also shown them what he could do with the use of Mumba. A duck had died in mid-flight, and a pelican had expired as he was unwarily gulping down a fish. A man might die just as easily, and it seemed to take only one crack of thunder to do it. The two birds had died with no spear flying through the air from the thunder-stick. All it seemed to take was for the spirit to wish them dead and then point his stick, for whatever had killed the birds was as invisible as the wind.

How *could* you fight the wind and the eternal?

Buruda looked across at Yarun, where the Dhundubari were sitting round on the sandy beach, giving the appearance of being just as dispirited as the group on this side of Kaerwagum. Like the Undanbi and the Ningi, they obviously found it impossible to understand how any visitors, men or spirits, could enter the country of any nation without recognising that certain proprieties must be observed.

As he looked, the Dhundubari suddenly rose to their feet and pointed excitedly up to the north. The cause of their interest was soon obvious. Round a bend in the channel came a small canoe. It was the one the Undanbi had seen up at Coochin.

Once more the Dhundubari waved their branches. But the Undanbi and the Ningi looked on silently from the mainland side. They had had enough already.

Once more the spirits ignored the Dhundubari's invitation.

The small canoe reached the larger one, and they saw it being hoisted up from the water until it sat on the bigger one. Then, before their eyes, the wings unfurled, and the canoe began to move down Kaerwagum toward the open sea.

The Dhundubari kept up their waving as they ran along the bank toward the south. But Kamkuri spat, and a low growl escaped the throats of the group on the Undanbi bank of Daki-Bomon as they watched the canoe grow smaller and smaller.

Bigi was only a hand's breadth above the horizon and the chill of the late afternoon was making itself felt when Buruda and his dhan turned their faces once more toward their camp near Coochin. They and the Ningi bu-ul had wrestled with puzzles all afternoon, and they still knew no more than they had known when the discussion began.

All they knew was that these spirit visitors had been made welcome, and in return they had been treated like dung, which was best buried in the earth and hidden from sight.

They hoped fervently that this was the last visit the spirits would pay them.

Chapter 13

1823: Three Cedar-Getters – Pamphlet, Finnegan, and Parsons – are wrecked on Moreton Island in April. They reach Redcliffe by June. They are on Bribie Island by September.

The season of wallaidhau was here once more, and the Undanbi were waxing fat from the mullet that filled their mula. Even the dogs were finding it unnecessary to look for extra food, sated as they were by the continual supply of fish. And following the mullet were huge shoals of tailer which made the waves of the ocean beaches black with their numbers, so that even the smallest boys could be sure of hitting a target with their undersized fish-spears.

There was now plenty of time for the bu-ul to lie around in the warm sunshine and talk.

But even times of plenty bring their problems, and the over-supply of leisure meant that there was also plenty of time to cause trouble. One day Piringa took exception to the way Karperi was eyeing Piringa's wife as the women were returning with their dhilla full of bangwal, and hardly enough time had elapsed to draw three breaths before the two were dodging each other's spears on the creek bank.

Later Buruda had to dress a deep spear wound on the upper part of Karperi's thigh. The patient was quiet enough while the powdered charcoal, eagle's down and first layer of white clay were being applied. But when it came time to apply the clay that had been heated in the coals until it steamed, it took four bu-ul to hold him down.

Buruda had little sympathy for him. "If you want to look at another dhan's wife," he growled, "you can expect to take the consequences! As it is, you can consider yourself lucky that you will still be able to service your own wife! This wound is very close to your wundu and dhun! Now lie still while I finish!"

The four bu-ul were able to relax their hold somewhat after the last layer of clay had been properly baked by applying a glowing stick to the poultice. Karperi was greatly relieved when the final bark covering was put on and held firmly in place with possum-fur string.

"I'll have a look at it in three days' time," Buruda told him. "You will have to lie down in the meantime to make sure that the dressing stays in place." And he smiled to himself as he noticed the look that Karperi's wife shot at her husband. The next three days would not be comfortable ones for the man.

Karperi wasn't the only one to get the sharp end of Buruda's tongue regarding the incident. "Fights such as these should be conducted properly at the baiyaba!" he told Piringa. "The camp is not the place for a kin-bumbe!"

And the older bu-ul in particular were even more critical of Piringa, reminding him in no uncertain terms that spears flung round a camp could very easily find an innocent mark – even a small child!

So Piringa's satisfaction at having shown Karperi that he should leave his wife alone was tempered somewhat by the knowledge that his summary action had attracted much disapproval.

The dressing was removed from Karperi's thigh after the passage of three days, and the wound was found to be completely healed.

Buruda then decided to take the opportunity of making a leisurely trip with his family to Warudhra near the trading track at the foot of Baroon. There he hoped to find a new axe-head, for he had ground the chips out of his present axe so often that it was becoming too light to be of much use.

Turugun accompanied him, for this would be an ideal opportunity for him to further refine his skills in the presence of his mentor. The young kivar never lost sight of the fact that within three or four seasons he would be called upon to pass through the dhur, and he therefore let no chance slip that would allow him to become more skilful in all the manly arts.

It was a contented little group that occupied the shelter Nerida erected on the creek bank. It did not take Buruda long to find a suitable black stone that was hard enough for his purpose, and which at the same time was close enough to the shape of an axe so that he would not have to spend more than four days of unremitting toil to grind it to the desired edge. And having found it, he wasted no time moving to the rocks nearby where deep grooves bore mute testimony to the fact that the Undanbi had long used these rocks to sharpen their axes.

Turugun also found a beautiful stone, and proceeded to make an axe as well, despite the fact that his own was still in prime condition. It never hurt to have another tool in case one broke. Besides, such tools were always useful in trading.

So the two squatted side by side, intent on their task. Every now and again Buruda would begin the age-old chant that appropriately accompanied the grinding of axes, and Turugun would chime in.

By the morning of the fourth day they were satisfied. On each axe-head was a beautifully-ground edge that could be guaranteed to cut even the hardest wood. On the upper part of both faces of each blade were two grooves, perfectly sited to accept the pliable stick that would be bent round it and tied firmly to form a solid handle. This handle would be held in place with strong twine and ironwood gum.

"They may not be as sharp or as strong as the axe that Midherbingul gave to Bomarigo," Buruda grunted, "nor do they have any hole to put the handle through. But they are sharp enough and strong enough to perform every task we will ask of them, and our handles won't release the heads until they are too worn to be of any use. Why should we want different axes?"

Turugun agreed. He was proud of the fine finish he had got on his axe-head, and he knew without being told that Buruda found his work faultless.

And as the two fitted the handles that afternoon, heating the ironwood gum so that it was easily moulded into the grooves, Buruda was once more reminded of the bounty of the earth. In the last four days they had easily picked up all they needed to fashion two beautiful tools. Each night they had feasted on goanna and bangwal. Today an unwary echidna had fallen easy prey to Nerida's digging-stick, so that the two men had not needed to disturb themselves to hunt for food. Tomorrow night they would be back at the creek flowing into Kaerwagum, and once more would be able to fill their bellies with tailer or mullet.

Truly the earth was a wonderful provider.

Hardly had they finished fitting the handles when they became aware of a bu-ul approaching along the trading track from the south. Stuck in his possum-fur waistband, his white boomerang proclaimed his peaceful intentions. He sat down a spear's throw away, signifying his willingness to visit if the small group by the creek wished it.

Buruda recognised the bu-ul as a Badtjala man named Darvoi who had performed well at the last bunyi festival. After a short interval he went over and invited the man to join them.

It appeared that Darvoi was returning home after a visit to his mother's brother, who was a bu-ul of the Ningi. After the necessary preliminary greetings were over and he had admired the two finished axes, he launched into an account of the spirits who were visiting the Ningi people.

"Spirits?" Buruda asked, flabbergasted. "Are there more?"

"There are three of them," Darvoi assured him. "And the Ningi tell me they are different from the others."

"Different? How are they different?"

"Well, in the first place they are not covered with special bark. They are like us, only with no possum-fur bands round their heads, arms or waists."

Gradually the story unfolded. It seemed that there were three spirits living with the Ningi whose backs, at least, showed evidence of some earthly existence, in that all had scars, probably gained in fights with knives. There were, however, no special distinguishing marks on their chests, so it was not really possible to say with any degree of certainty to which people they had belonged while they were alive.

"And what about their canoe?" Buruda wanted to know. "Where is it?"

"There is none," Darvoi told him. "I think they had one, but it is not certain. There have been rumours, but that is all."

The rumour was that the Gowar-speaking people from the island with the big sandhills had found them on the beach, and had tried to get them to go back the way they had come, for everybody knew that spirits ought to be with spirits, and not with people.

"I wish these spirits would realise that!" Buruda burst out. "There must be a lot of unrest in the land of the spirits!"

"Still, they wouldn't go," Darvoi went on. "Instead, they made their way right down to Unbounba, opposite Bulan, and a Nunakul bu-ul saw them there. Their pale colouring frightened him, so he got into his canoe to go over to Bulan. Then he met some friends on the way, and they all went back to have a closer look at the spirits."

One of the spirits had apparently then taken a tool that had two sharp fingers, and had cut the beards of the Nunakul men. The spirits had shown by signs that they wanted to be taken over to Bulan.

"But the Nunakul wouldn't do it, even though they owed a debt to the spirit who had cut their beards,"

"I don't blame them!" Buruda said vehemently. "Spirits belong with spirits!"

"But they got there, anyway," Darvoi continued. "Two found a canoe and crossed. Then a Nunakul man took one back to Unbounba, and this spirit brought his remaining friend across."

The more Darvoi spoke, the more incredible the story became. The Nunakul had, as the law demands, been hospitable to those who were travelling through their country in peace. At the same time, they had been anxious to get rid of the spirits, and had been overjoyed to see two of them hacking out a log with an axe they had with them to make a strange-looking canoe. They had even encouraged the third spirit to help, and had denied him food when he had refused, Indeed, this third spirit had been so unco-operative that he had let the others set out in their canoe on their own, and had agreed to leave only when the Nunakul had stranded him on a sandbank with the tide coming in fast.

"So should all troublesome spirits be treated!" Buruda grated, remembering the unfriendly spirits in Kaerwagum in the last season of wallaidhau.

These new spirits had certainly been persistent, Darvoi told them. They had succeeded in crossing to Kalen-Kalen, and had travelled through Gnalungpin land as far as Turrbal country. Naturally, whenever the bu-ul had seen them, they had fed them and then urged them on their way. Eventually they had ended up in Ningi country, and had taken a canoe with a catch of fish in it across Tungulba to Tambal.

Buruda's mouth fell open. He could not believe his ears. "You don't mean --?"

"Yes," Darvoi told him. "Kamkuri told me that he himself had been in the party that had caught the fish, and they were having a rest behind some bushes out of the wind. They were astounded to find when they woke up that the canoe containing the fish was half-way across Tungulba!"

"But --!" Buruda sputtered. He was having trouble coming to grips with the actions of those spirits. There was just no way he could put into words what he was feeling. To use a canoe when the owners weren't there – that was excusable and understandable. To use it when the smallest search would have revealed the presence of its owners was unforgivable. But to use it when some freshly-caught fish had proclaimed to anybody with eyes that the owners were not only close, but also that they would be returning at any moment, that was --!

There was just no word to describe such behaviour!

"The spirits need spears through their hearts!" he growled, but immediately reflected that that might not be so easy. How sure could you be that spears would kill spirits?

"That's just what Kamkuri was going to do!" Darvoi assured him. "But when they caught up with them at Tambal and saw how emaciated they were, and that they were not bu-ul but spirits, they took pity on them instead. They even caught more fish for them. The spirits have been with them ever since,"

"How long ago since they got to the Ningi?" Buruda wanted to know.

"Two moons," Darvoi replied. "But I don't think they will be there much longer. They seem to want to go further north. Probably that is where their people are. Kamkuri even thought they might belong to the Badtjala, but I told him they didn't resemble anybody among our dead people, as far as I could see."

Buruda felt a sudden misgiving. What if these spirits claimed to be Undanbi?

Aloud he said, "Where are they going next?"

"Kamkuri will hand them on to the Dhundubari, I think," Darvoi said. "But it is all very perplexing."

By the time Darvoi had told them all he knew, it was time for them to seek the warmth of the hut.

Next morning, before Darvoi left to continue his homeward journey, Buruda suddenly remembered something that had not been mentioned. "Their names, Darvoi?" he asked. "What are the names of the spirits?"

Maybe one was Midherbingul.

"They have strange names," Darvoi told him. "As close as my tongue can say it, one is called Pamplet. Another is Pinigan. The third is Pardhen."

So Midherbingul was not one of them. But that was only to be expected, since Buruda could not imagine Midherbingul taking a canoe with fresh fish in it.

But Darvoi's tidings had created ripples in the calm waters of Buruda's existence, and he found himself anxious to return to the Undanbi camp. What if they were to find the three spirits already there? What if they claimed to be some of their dead relatives? Perhaps more to the point – what if somebody among the people recognised them as such?

Endless numbers of possibilities chased one another in his mind.

By mid-afternoon they were approaching the camp. Buruda found himself unnaturally apprehensive, despite the reassuring tapping they could hear as the women prepared the bangwal. Everything sounded normal, but sounds could be deceiving. The women would pound bangwal, even if spirits were in the camp. Indeed, they might need to pound more, for there would be added mouths to feed.

But as they rounded the last bend in the creek and the camp came into sight, his apprehensions vanished. The bu-ul were sitting around yarning, and this was a sign not only that there was still a surplus of fish for the taking, but also that nothing untoward had disturbed the even tenor of their existence. But perhaps the most encouraging sign was that the children were as noisy as ever, racing in and out among the huts, their feet kicking up clouds of dust as they ran.

There was nothing strange in this camp.

Wungul's yell alerted the camp to their approach, and soon there were happy tears as they were embraced by as many as could get close enough. Bunbithin found himself plucked from the rug on Nerida's shoulders. He was immediately offered a breast, which he accepted greedily, as always.

No, Buruda reflected happily. All was as it should be.

That night he told what he had learnt from Darvoi, and there was much consternation. They had hoped that the last cold season had seen the last of the spirits. But when Buruda reached the part of the story that told how the three spirits had taken the Ningi canoe containing the fish, they exhibited open-mouthed disbelief.

Naruman had called the last spirit-visitors ill-mannered. But what word was there to describe the action of taking fish and a canoe whose owners were only a few short paces away?

These spirits were not only strange – they must be evil!

"Makaron!" Bulangga was heard to mutter. These spirits must indeed be evil spirits, to act like that!

Yet Kamkuri and the Ningi had befriended them. So were they really makaron?

And there still remained the possibility that these spirits might be Undanbi. Darvoi had said that they seemed anxious to be helped to make their way north.

A council of the bu-ul was called, and it sat far into the night, discussing possible action. One and all wanted, if possible, to ensure that the Undanbi were not placed in the position of host to the three, as the Ningi had been. If the spirits belonged to a northern nation, then the sooner they got there the better. The Undanbi would not stand in their way. But to have to act as long-term hosts to spirits who were so obviously lacking in manners was not to be tolerated.

The only redeeming feature of this spirit visit was that the bodies of the three were at least not covered up in the unseemly manner affected by those who had come earlier in their winged canoes. Besides, all three had normal footprints, and therefore could not be expected to herald the approach of the disaster foretold in Buruda's dream

And, despite their unwillingness to meet the spirits, there was still the possibility that they could be Undanbi. Someone would have to find out whether they were or not. And the sooner this was done, the better.

The final decision was that Bulangga, as one of the eldest bu-ul, was to go to Dhundubari and examine these spirits. Buruda would also go, for his dream connected him indisputably with the spirits, and he should be with Bulangga to try to ascertain if any danger existed for the people.

If the spirits proved to be other than Undanbi, then both men were to make it clear to the Dhundubari that the Undanbi wanted nothing to do with them. The Dhundubari could pass them on to the Tumbra, if they so desired, but not to the Undanbi!

The two men left next morning on their journey down the ocean beach of Yarun, reaching the Dhundubari camp on the mid-morning of the second day. They had not long sat down when Nganku hobbled over with a broad grin on his face.

"Welcome, friends!" he said. "I suppose you have come to see our spirits."

"True!" Buruda answered. "But what has happened to your knee?"

"Just a little fight," Nganku assured him, but then added grimly, "I've yet to pay back the Dhungwubera bu-ul responsible!"

"A spear wound?" Buruda wanted to know.

"Yes, but it's all right now. There was a small piece left in. Bomarigo couldn't get it, but Pamplet took it out with his knife."

"Pamplet?"

Nganku grinned again. "One of our spirits," he explained. "He sleeps at my hut."

Bulangga was interested. "*Your* spirits, you say?" he asked. "Are they Dhundubari, then?"

"Yes, there is no doubt about that. Bomarigo recognised Pinigan as soon as he saw him, for he has a special mark on his back that one of our Dimmangali had. Pardhen and Pamplet are also Dhundubari. The old people know them by their back scars."

The two Undanbi felt a surge of relief. There was no problem for their people, then.

"But come and see them!" Nganku urged them. "You will see that they are beginning to look more like people now!"

They arrived at Bomarigo's hut to find the old man rubbing one of the spirits with his ball of charcoal, goanna fat and beeswax. Certainly, with the exception of his ugly nose, this spirit did look quite presentable.

"He's getting blacker every day!" Bomarigo remarked cheerfully. "Soon he will always be the right colour!"

After he had finished blackening the spirit's skin, he turned him round and showed Buruda and Bulangga the long scar extending from right shoulder to waist that had made positive identification possible. "The Dimmangali brother of one of my

Dimmangali friends had just such a scar!" he said. "He picked it up in a kin-bumbe at Kungalba many seasons ago!" He chuckled at the recollection. "I remember the woman well, for she was lovely! Still, her husband later killed him on the baiyaba at Baroon. Now he is back, and his name is Pinigan."

The spirit smiled at the sound of his name and said, "Good! Good!"

"He knows a few words of Gubbi now," Bomarigo explained. "When he remembers all the words, it will be time for him to pass through the dhur."

A sudden commotion from the direction of Nganku's hut drew their attention. A bu-ul's voice rang out, tense with urgency, "Gubbi! Gubbi!"

Then other voices also screamed, "Gubbi!"

There followed a concerted rush away from the hut, and Nganku hobbled across as quickly as he could, followed by the two Undanbi visitors. The sight that met their gaze was indeed enough to make the stoutest heart tremble. The spirit named Pamplet appeared to have set some sort of black pikki on the fire, and the water in it was sending out smoke. At the same time it was gurgling and hissing and moving itself around in a way that could only happen if magic were being used.

With one accord the three yelled, "Gubbi!" at Pamplet, and took to their heels also, Nganku's knee holding him back, but only slightly. When they had caught up with the other Dhundubari, who were standing looking angrily back at this unseemly demonstration of spirit power, Nganku yelled again in a tone that brooked no misunderstanding, "Gubbi! Wa! Wa!"

The spirit reluctantly took a stick and removed the pikki from the fire, and they all returned. The water was still smoking, but at least it had become quiet. Nganku made signs to Pamplet to pour it out onto the ground. When he had done this, albeit with a rather bad grace, Nganku carefully covered the smoking wet patch with dry sand, continuing until not a sign remained that magic water had ever existed. This done, he pointed at the black pikki and then to the fire. "Gubbi! Wa! Wa!" he shouted.

To make sure he had been understood, he repeated the action and the command, and Pamplet nodded. Only then was Nganku satisfied.

Next morning Buruda and Bulangga began their journey home. Both were relieved that they could take news back to their people that these spirits would cause the Undanbi no trouble.

"And that is good!" Buruda stated emphatically. "I would much prefer these spirits to be Dhundubari rather than Undanbi, even though they are beginning to look like real people!"

Bulangga summed it all up when he asked testily, "Why can't the spirits be satisfied to stay in the land of spirits? Have the Dhundubari been lax in performing the death rites?"

"We must be very careful ourselves!" Buruda agreed. "We must make sure Undanbi spirits return to the people only as babies!"

"Particularly when they use magic to bring water to life!" Bulangga added vehemently, and both men looked fearfully over their shoulders for a moment as they remembered this horrific experience.

Notes on Chapter 13

The axe-grinding grooves at Landsborough (Warudhra) in Mellum Creek are still visible.

Pamphlet, Finnegan and Parsons were cedar-getters wrecked on Moreton Island in 1823 in a storm. The "rumours" heard by Darvoi and related by him to Buruda were reasonably accurate. They lost their clothes in the wreck, but managed to hold on to a knife, a pair of scissors, an axe and a billy-can. The Gowar-speaking people of Moreton Island helped them, and they made their way in the manner described in this chapter from Unbounba (Campbell Pt.) on the south of Moreton Island to Bulan (Amity Pt.) on Stradbroke.

It was Finnegan who gave trouble by refusing to help in the building of the dug-out canoe, and the Nunakul refused to give him any food until he did, but they gave plenty of food to the working two. They even put the axe in Finnegan's hands to force him to give assistance. When he refused to get into the canoe with the other two, the Nunakul took him out in a canoe of their own and stranded him on a sandbank. If Pamphlet and Parsons had not picked him up, he would undoubtedly have drowned. In short, the Nunakul on Stradbroke Island "encouraged "them (as described by Darvoi) to cross in the dug-out canoe they had made to Kalen-Kalen (Wellington Pt.)

They used canoes they found on the bank to cross the Brisbane River, and then Ningi canoes to cross Tungulba (Hay's Inlet) to Tambal (Woody Pt.)

The billy-can incident on Bribie (Yarun) has to be interpreted in its proper context. No doubt Pamphlet wanted a hot cup of something – maybe tea made from tea-tree leaves. The Dhundubari, however, had every right to be terrified, never having seen water boil before.

The castaways were always, right up to the time of their "rescue", under the impression that the storm had blown them to the south of Sydney. In reality, they were hundreds of miles to the north of this town.

✧

Chapter 14

1823: Oxley "rescues" Pamphlet and Finnegan. He leaves John Uniacke in Pumicestone Passage and, taking Finnegan with him, "discovers" the Brisbane River.

There was a gathering of nations at Nambour, where the Tumbra were hosts to a number of others, all of which had kivar ready to pass through the dhur. The Nalbo, Kombobura, Dallambara and Dhungwubera were all represented. Although no kivar of the Undanbi were to take the test, Buruda had been invited to officiate at the baiyaba after the ceremony, for his fame was such that his presence was sure to add lustre to the proceedings.

As Buruda was preparing to leave for Nambour, Nganku turned up at Currimundi, where the main body of the Undanbi were camped at that time. Four Dhundubari bu-ul accompanied their manngur. Their boomerangs were painted white, but the number of weapons each carried left no doubt that they were prepared to take part in the baiyaba.

"The Dhungwubera bu-ul who wounded me will be there," Nganku explained to Buruda. "It is high time that I paid him back!"

Buruda took Turugun with him, since any piece of knowledge the young man could gain would help prepare him for his own dhur. The different fighting techniques that would be demonstrated at the baiyaba would allow him to perfect his own particular fighting style.

On the way Buruda questioned Nganku at length about his spirit visitors. How were they fitting into the life of the people?

"I don't know," Nganku told him. "They are learning the Gubbi tongue quite reasonably, considering that they knew none of it when they first arrived among the Ningi. They are even becoming fairly proficient in the use of the spear, as befits a dhan of the Dhundubari. They are becoming a better colour too, for we have been careful to rub them as we would a small boy twice a day. But" – and here his voice took on a note of puzzlement – "no matter how often we suggest it, not one of them wants to go through the kivar-yangga! We've tried to explain that they can't be given a wife until they become full bu-ul, and that they can't become full bu-ul until they first become kivar, but they don't seem to understand. Whatever the cause, they don't want to receive the marks of the Dhundubari!"

Buruda too was puzzled. "Do they want to remain boys, then? Surely you'd expect them to be trying hard to learn enough so that they can be given the test!"

"They seem happy as they are," Nganku admitted. "If any Dhundubari male were as old as they appear to be and had not become a full bu-ul, he would be too ashamed to live with us. But these spirits don't seem to be affected in any way."

"Maybe there is a reason why spirits don't want to be bu-ul," Buruda wondered aloud.

But for the life of him he could not understand why anybody, even a spirit, would not want to participate fully in the life of the people. Again he found himself wishing that these spirits had taken the recognised method of rejoining the land of people, and had been born as babies. This unorthodox system of return from the land of the spirits seemed to be somewhat dangerous to all concerned.

But Nganku had more to tell him, and Buruda listened with astonishment. Despite the fact that the Dhundubari knew that the spirits belonged to their nation, the spirits themselves did not seem to know. Or if they did, they were acting in a very strange manner, for they kept insisting that their home was to the north, and they were continually trying to make their way in that direction. Pamplet and Pardhen had tried early to make their way along the ocean beach of Yarun, but had been turned back by lack of food.

"Lack of food!" Buruda could not believe his ears.

"They were like babies, really," Nganku explained. "They did not even know about the yugari that can be collected so easily from under the sand!"

"So they do not have a choice, do they?" Buruda said. "They have to stay, whether they like it or not!"

"They're getting better at finding food now," Nganku said. "And right now the three of them are making their way north again. We tried to persuade them to return, but they got so impatient with us that we just had to let them go. After all, you can't punish boys for just being ignorant, can you?"

Buruda agreed. The way of all people was to be lenient with young children who were still learning to live. Only after they had been through the kivar-yangga did the full weight of the law descend heavily on the backs of men. And these spirits were still boys.

Nganku informed him that they had come across the tracks of the three since they had left camp on their way to Nambour. The spirits had taken one of the canoes the Dhundubari always left at Woorim and had crossed Kaerwagum, leaving the canoe near the site of the creek camp there.

Hardly had Nganku finished his story than Turugun pointed at the ground ahead. There, plain for all to see on the banks of the Maroochy, were the spirit tracks.

"Pamplet has sore feet," Buruda remarked. "I don't think he'll want to go much further."

Bending down to peer closely at the tracks, they all saw that it was so. The tracks of Pinigan and Pardhen exhibited an even distance between prints, showing they were striding easily. But the distance covered by Pamplet's left foot was not as great as the distance travelled by his right, showing that the left foot was painful. Indeed, he was walking on the outside edge of this foot. And even the right one, though it was coming down flat on the ground, was at times leaving vestiges of blood.

The tracks were so fresh that some blades of grass were still straightening themselves. Soon the party was able to see the three picking their way along the river bank ahead, with Pamplet bringing up the rear.

"Wait!" Nganku called out to the three. And as they looked back, startled, he told them, "It's Nganku!"

Then for a long time Buruda and Turugun stood aside while Nganku and the other Dhundubari pleaded with their spirit relatives to return to Yarun. But the visitors were adamant, explaining as well as they could that they must go "home" to the north. In vain did Nganku point out that Yarun was their home.

"Obviously they are talking of the spirit-land," Nganku said to Buruda at last. "They will go, I suppose." He turned to Pamplet. "But your feet are too sore!" he argued. "You'll have to stay with us!"

Pamplet really needed little persuasion, and agreed to accompany the party making its way to the baiyaba. Nganku gave him a stick to lean on, and he was able to keep up with them after they had slowed their pace somewhat. But the other two doggedly followed the river, intent on crossing and going north as soon as they found a spot shallow enough.

"They will find the spirit-land one way or another!" Buruda predicted grimly. "Either they will eventually reach it, if it does indeed lie to the north, or else they'll be sent on their way more swiftly by a spear or a club in the hands of someone who doesn't recognise them as spirits of the Dhundubari!"

The baiyaba at Nambour continued for three days. Only once did Buruda have to intervene personally, and that was when a Tumbra bu-ul continued his fight with a Dhungwubera warrior after Buruda had decreed that honour had been satisfied. A few strides brought Buruda to the side of the two combatants, and one swift stroke of his club laid the recalcitrant bu-ul unconscious on the ground, after which his friends quickly carried him away from further possible harm.

A murmur of approval rose from the ranks of the assembled nations. The laws of the baiyaba stated flatly that the appointed master-of-ceremonies had complete control over all proceedings. Anybody disobeying his instructions could expect to be summarily dealt with.

Nganku's fight was shorter than expected. The two contestants had had plenty of time to prepare themselves, so the flow of vituperation from both sides that preceded the fight was well appreciated by the spectators. Both were seasoned warriors, and both kept their eyes on their opponent as they picked up their spears with their toes, preparatory to placing them upright in the ground beside them. When the spears did eventually begin to fly, both caught them skilfully on their hardwood shields. Nganku's third spear, however, was only half parried by his opponent, and it penetrated the shoulder.

The fight was over. Four Dhungwubera bu-ul quickly carried their friend away to have his wound attended to. Then, as the law demanded in a pay-back fight of this kind, the three Dhundubari bu-ul who had accompanied Nganku entered the baiyaba and loudly challenged the same number of Dhungwubera bu-ul to do battle with them, if they considered that the matter was not settled.

But this was, of course, only a matter of form. While the Dhungwubera had every right to accept the challenge, everybody knew that Nganku had only paid back the Dhungwubera bu-ul for a wound he had been given earlier. The law had been satisfied in every respect.

During these proceedings Buruda stole a glance at Pamplet. There was no mistaking the look of pride on the spirit's face at Nganku's accomplishment. As Buruda remarked to Turugun on their way back to the Undanbi camp, which had again shifted back to the creek opposite Woorim, it was just possible that Pamplet would some day make a useful dhan of the Dhundubari, once he had made up his mind to pass the kivar-yangga. But it was certain he was of no use to them as a boy.

Three days after they had arrived home, a Dhundubari bu-ul and his wife stayed the night at the Undanbi camp. They had Pinigan with them. Apparently he and Pardhen had had an argument when they had reached Noosa. The Dhundubari bu-ul, who had been visiting relatives in that area, had eventually prevailed on Pinigan to accompany him back to Bomarigo, rather than try to continue his crazy journey to the north.

"Now only Pardhen will reach the spirit-land to the north," Buruda remarked to Wungul. "It would not surprise me to find the Badtjala making it a swifter journey than he anticipates!"

Another ceremony was to take place within a moon's time at the kivar ring just inland from Kuturrumba. The Ningi had invited representatives of the Kurpuru, Dhepara, Turrbal, Dhundubari and Undanbi. The main purpose of this ceremony was to release tension that had been building up over some time among members of these groups. Kamkuri had sent messengers around to the nations, suggesting that the recent spate of visits by spirits might be due to the fact that too many wrongs were going unavenged.

Buruda thought that Kamkuri might have a point. Since the bunyi festival, where he had alerted them all to the necessity of ensuring that all rites – birth, death, or increase – be observed meticulously, all the clans had been particularly careful in this regard. Still, since that time there had seemed to be even more activity among the spirits – first Midherbingul, then the ill-mannered spirits on the second canoe, and finally Pardhen, Pamplet and Pinigan. Maybe it was tension between the nations that was the trouble.

Certainly something had to be to blame!

When the Undanbi contingent arrived at Kuturrumba, however, Buruda was surprised to see that, while Pamplet had stayed at home with those Dhundubari who had not come, Bomarigo had allowed Pinigan to attend.

"Don't you think it would be better if he did not witness the fights that are meant to bring the harmony that will rid us of the spirits?" Buruda asked.

And Bomarigo admitted that he had done his best to persuade Pinigan to stay at home with Pamplet, but the spirit had insisted on coming. "Still, I'll leave him with my wife while the fights are on," he promised.

But this was more easily said than done. When the fights began, Bomarigo's wife could not hold Pinigan back, and had to follow him to the baiyaba, complaining bitterly all the way. Eventually Bomarigo was forced, for Pinigan's own safety, to take away his spear. This done, he spoke to the other manngur, apologising for his inability to keep this spirit away from things that it would be better for him not to witness. At the same time, he asked them to explain to their people that, although this being looked like a bu-ul, they would see from his lack of marks that he was really only a child, and was therefore not to be attacked under any circumstances.

Fittingly, since the baiyaba was being held in Ningi territory and he had been the one to call the nations together, Kamkuri was master-of-ceremonies.

Buruda hoped that Kamkuri's wish to clear away all disharmony would come true. He also hoped that the result would be worth the price. Probably it would be, if the spirits stopped troubling them.

But the day did not go smoothly. The second fight of the day between a Turrbal bu-ul and another from the Dhundubari left both sorely wounded. Within a short time the death-wail was heard from where the Dhundubari were tending their wounded comrade.

The fourth duel, too, was unsatisfactory. It brought a cry of foul from the Dhundubari, who claimed that the Ningi bu-ul had not held his opponent correctly round the neck while using the knife. Kamkuri disagreed, and the Ningi bu-ul was declared the victor.

Kamkuri may have acted correctly, but he was no Buruda, and did not command the respect of all. Despite the fact that the law stated that the opinion of the master-of-ceremonies had to be accepted, there was a howl of protest from the Dhundubari, and within the time it took to draw two breaths, three lots of four Dhundubari bu-ul were drawn up on the baiyaba facing the same number of Ningi, and spears were flying thick and fast.

The battle raged for a long time, with wounded men retiring to have their places taken by others, for it was important to ensure that the warring sides had equal numbers. The Dhundubari eventually began to give way. At last, a Ningi spear took a Dhundubari bu-ul through the throat, and the Dhundubari took to their heels, closely pursued by their enemy.

The other nations remained aloof from the battle, since it was no concern of theirs. Buruda hoped more than ever that the result would be worth the price. A second Dhundubari dead! Would this mean more harmony? He was fairly certain that it would only increase friction. Kamkuri's plan had not been blessed with a successful conclusion, well-meaning though it had been.

But even in tragedy there was a lighter side, and the spectators had to laugh as they saw Pinigan running for dear life from the Ningi. Even the Ningi pursuers laughed as they ran past him, for he could not even keep up with the fleet-footed women who had done their best to help him flee. The funny part, of course, was that he apparently did not understand that a child was quite safe from attack.

This spirit had a lot to learn!

Later they heard that a Ningi kivar had died in the chase.

That night Buruda sat with Kamkuri and the other manngur until the early hours of the morning. Their hearts were heavy. The wailing of the Dhundubari and the Ningi as they mourned their dead reminded them all that the heaviness of spirit that Kamkuri had hoped to dispel was worse than ever. They knew that sometime soon Bomarigo and Kamkuri would have to hear the bones of the dead speak. Then there would be further tension until these deaths were avenged.

"One death we could expect from so many fights on the baiyaba," Buruda said. "Three deaths are far too many!"

They all agreed. Buruda could not help feeling a deep sense of foreboding. When he eventually sought his bed, he tried in vain to drive the feeling away by seeking the sweet solace of Nerida's body. But his sleep was disturbed by vague, unnamed fears and he was relieved when, after tossing and turning till daybreak, a sharp squeal from Bunbithin jerked him awake.

Next day the Dhundubari left, wearing the red clay of mourning. They would take their time getting to their canoes near Ningi Ningi, for it was important for them to pay proper respect to their dead, whose skins had already begun to cure in the smoke of their fires the night before.

Buruda and the Undanbi stayed at the baiyaba all next day. Kamkuri had asked Buruda to officiate at the remaining fights, which involved not only the Undanbi, but also the Turrbal, Kurpuru and Dhepara. Kamkuri himself had to ensure that proper early funeral rites were carried out for the dead Ningi kivar.

Buruda made certain that each fight this day was terminated before any serious injury occurred. There had been too much mourning already. At the conclusion of each bout, his shout of "Gubbi!" was always followed immediately with "Yugara!" There would be no reason for any bu-ul of any nation to claim that he had not understood what was had been said.

And with Buruda in charge, no bu-ul attempted to strike a blow after the order to stop had been given. An arm might be raised with a club ready to descend on an unprotected head, but at Buruda's shout, that arm would stiffen into immobility. Full well they all understood the penalty for non-compliance.

That night he again slept fitfully, and next morning the Undanbi took their leave early. Buruda was anxious to cross Daki-Bomon into their own country as soon as possible. His feet were yearning for the feel of Undanbi soil. Lately he had spent too little time on it.

But his feet would have to wait yet a little longer. As they reached Gibunba, they caught up with Bomarigo and the Dhundubari and, out of respect for the Dhundubari dead, slowed their pace to match that of their mourning friends. Then, as they rounded the point where Kaerwagum stretched out before them, they caught sight of a huge canoe sitting over near Yarun, with those Dhundubari who had remained at home gathered on the shore facing it.

Two Dhundubari kivar were waiting for Bomarigo at Ningi Ningi, where their canoes were drawn up. They informed him that the spirit canoe had entered Kaerwagum the afternoon before, and that Pamplet had rushed into the water, calling out in his strange tongue. Soon the spirits had sent a smaller canoe to shore, and Pamplet had left with them.

Bomarigo asked Buruda if the Undanbi would accompany them to Yarun. "I know you want to get home, my friend," the old manngur said, "but you may be able to help us find out more about these spirits."

More than anything he had ever wanted before, Buruda wanted to go home. He had had enough of spirits! Still, he had to admit that Bomarigo was right. He might glean more knowledge about the spirits, and why they were becoming so troublesome. Reluctantly, he agreed to cross to Yarun with the Undanbi contingent.

Pinigan could hardly contain his excitement. The closer they got to Yarun and the huge canoe, the more the tears flowed unchecked down his cheeks. He tried to say something to Bomarigo, but his command of the Gubbi tongue proved insufficient, and he burst out instead into a flow of incomprehensible words.

As their canoe approached Yarun, they found themselves the focus of curious eyes from the spirit canoe. Pamplet, whose body was now covered, called out something to Pinigan, and Pinigan began to laugh almost uncontrollably. After a while he managed to collect himself and yelled a reply. A shout of laughter came from the watchers on the spirit canoe.

But there was no laughter from those Dhundubari still waiting on the shore. They had early seen the red clay of mourning, and some had already begun the death-wail. Here and there could be heard some curses and threats. Which one of the Dhundubari nation would they mourn? Whose name would this day be consigned to the silence?

The canoes grounded and were pulled out of reach of the tide. The cries became more poignant as some of those waiting realised that the faces missing were close relatives. Jagged shells were dragged down faces to release the blood of grief.

And in the midst of the crying, the small spirit canoe arrived and, almost unnoticed, took Pinigan out to join Pamplet.

The rest of the day and a great part of the night were given over to mourning, the Undanbi joining in out of respect for their friends. Time enough for the spirits tomorrow. Today their Dimmangali demanded their attention.

Next morning a small canoe with small wings above it left for the south with Pinigan and some other spirits. It had hardly begun its journey in the direction of Kuturrumba before another canoe left the side of the big one, with two spirits poling Pamplet and another one to the shore.

Nganku raced down to the water's edge to greet his friend. But somehow Pamplet looked less like a man in the ungainly coverings he now affected. It was disappointing to see him like that.

Pamplet pointed to Nganku and said to the spirit with him, "Nganku!" and the spirit smiled and said, "Nanku!"

Pamplet then pointed to the spirit and said something that sounded like "Midherunak!" When Nganku tried to repeat the name, the spirit laughed, pointed to his own chest and said, "Dhon!"

Nganku was delighted. This was an easy name to pronounce, with none of the strange ripping sound. He pointed to Buruda and said, "Buruda!"

And the spirit with the name of Dhon laughed again as he echoed the name.

As with Midherbingul, Buruda found himself liking this jovial spirit. He seemed anxious to learn all he could about the world of people, making interested sounds and talking animatedly to his companions every time he discovered something new. Even the huts excited his close attention, and he seemed overawed by simple things like dhilla, mula and merbung. When the dhan took their mula and caught fish for the evening meal, he appeared excited at their expertise, jumping up and down as the catch was brought ashore and he was given some for himself. He even looked closely and earnestly at the way the women pounded the bangwal.

Every now and again he would take a queer piece of equipment out of one of the dhilla sewn into his outlandish outer coverings, and make strange marks on it with a piece of charcoal that appeared to be stuck on the end of a small stick.

Inexplicable behaviour, indeed! But there was one thing about this spirit that seemed to set him apart from any of the others they had met so far, and that was his eagerness to learn all he could about the world of people. Nganku remarked, and the others agreed, that here was a spirit who might make a very useful member of any community, for he was as thirsty for knowledge as any boy anxious to prepare himself for the kivar-yangga.

Still, there was one piece of information that had to be gleaned from the spirit before any serious instruction could begin. To whom was he related, and in what way? Until this was known, he could not be assigned a skin, let alone a nation. And there was no way of discovering that unless the spirit removed his coverings. If they could only get a look at him, they might be able to tell from any marks remaining on his skin to what people he belonged. Some living person might recognise scars that remained from some long-forgotten battle. Maybe a footprint could give a clue, for everyone knew that a footprint was as foolproof a means of identification as you could get.

But although they begged him repeatedly to divest himself of these useless trappings, Dhon refused to comply. Indeed, once or twice he tended to show some impatience as a few of the more importunate dhan took hold of the coverings as if to take matters into their own hands.

So they would have to leave him alone. Perhaps he would take them off after he had been with them for a few days, when he realised how important it was that they know whom he should avoid close contact with, particularly among the women.

Buruda slept a little better that night, but found himself beginning to lose patience with Dhon by the end of the next day. Dhon wanted to know all about people, but didn't seem to understand whenever they asked him questions about the world of spirits. The burning question, of course, was why the spirits were coming here at all. But there was no way of getting an answer.

On the third morning, when Dhon returned to his canoe after watching the children playing murun murun, he cried out in sudden anger. Pamplet explained to those round about that Dhon wanted his axe back, since it had been stolen from the canoe. Hurriedly word was passed around, and it was Bomarigo's son, the young kivar who had brought the Undanbi news of Midherbingul's visit, who eventually brought it forward.

He was understandably angry.

"I did not steal it!" he shouted. "These spirits ale the fish that I caught! Surely they owe us something in return!"

Buruda placed a hand on the young man's shoulder as Bomarigo took the axe and handed it back to Dhon. He did not like to see this promising young man embarrassed. "You are right!" he told him. "It seems that spirits, even friendly ones, do not exhibit the rudiments of good manners! But maybe they have different laws. So let us forget it."

For his part, Dhon had regained his good humour, apparently completely unaware of the embarrassment he had caused. He talked long and hard to Pamplet, who then explained in his broken Gubbi that Dhon would like anybody who wished to visit the big canoe. When nobody came forward, Pamplet added that no harm would come to them, and that they would be returned to shore safe and sound.

Buruda quickly reasoned that, if any treachery was intended, he would be able to jump into the water and make his way to shore, so he stepped forward, as did Nganku. Four other bu-ul joined them.

"We must learn more about these visitors," Buruda said earnestly to Nganku as they were being carried out over the water. "We may find out what the canoe's wings are made of."

Watched carefully by the crowd on shore, the group climbed nimbly over the side of the large canoe. They immediately made their way to where they could see some of the wings folded on a big log. "It is like the covering on their bodies, only thicker and stiffer!" Buruda exclaimed in amazement. He could see that it was spread and furled by means of cords like those in their nets. There was no magic of clouds here! The only magic consisted in how the stuff made the canoe move.

But there were more wonders to examine on the canoe. Something soft and smooth like possum-fur rubbed against Nganku's ankles, making him jump with fright. Looking down, he saw a funny little animal that made a strange noise as it rubbed against him once more. Dhon picked the animal up and placed it in Nganku's arms, where it continued to make the soft throbbing sound as Dhon stroked it. Buruda felt it also, and broad grins broke out on the faces of all the bu-ul as they passed it from one to the other.

Dhon pointed to the animal. "Kata!" he said very carefully.

At least this animal had an easy name to say.

Triumphantly Nganku held the animal up for all on shore to see, and a great cry of delight rose from the people as they saw for the first time that the spirit-world at least possessed animals that were not harmful to hold.

Another sound, like the cry of a fretful child, attracted Buruda's attention, and he turned to see another creature in some sort of enclosure. It had two ears – and an extra pair as well!

Buruda looked fearfully at Pamplet. "What is that animal with four ears?" he wanted to know.

Pamplet spoke to Dhon, and all the spirits roared with laughter.

"Gota!" Dhon spluttered mirthfully as he gave the name of the animal. And, in between laughter, Pamplet explained that the animal had only two ears.

Dhon went over to the animal and grasped it by its second set of ears, signing for Buruda to do the same. But Buruda recoiled in disgust as he realised what he was touching. "They are bones!" he shouted to Nganku. "The gota is an animal with bones sticking out of its head!"

What strange animals the spirit world had! A kata so soft and warm that it would be warmer than a possum-fur rug to sleep with on the cold nights of wallaidhau! And a gota so ugly that its bones could not be contained within its own body! Buruda could not bring himself to touch those offending bones a second time, so alien was their feel. The remainder of the party, however, would not rest until they had felt them.

Then Buruda looked down, and as he did so he felt the blood drain from his face.

"What is wrong, Buruda?" Nganku wanted to know, concerned at the expression on his friend's face.

But Buruda shook his head and said nothing, not wanting to tell his friend what he had seen. For he realised that, if the others knew, there would be a general stampede for the water. As it was, it was all he could do to stop himself from jumping over the side himself.

For there on the feet of the gota were the small bony toes that were just the right shape to make some of the tracks on the sands of Yarun in his dream! There could be no mistake! This animal was the stuff of which nightmares were made!

How he managed to preserve a semblance of normality as his friends joked with the spirits and held the kata up again and again for those on shore to see, he did not know. But he managed to do so. Then, after what seemed like an eternity, Dhon spoke to Pamplet, who told them they would now go back to shore.

How good it was to set foot once more on the sands of Yarun – to be away from that alien animal! It had even smelt wrong! Indeed, nothing about it had been right!

And as they landed, the canoe which had gone south a few days before reappeared. Dhon waved his hand in its direction, and said something so unpronounceable that Buruda could not believe his ears. Noting the quizzical look on Buruda's face, Dhon repeated what he had said, and Pamplet explained that this was the name of the man standing in the canoe making its way back toward them.

Valiantly Buruda tried to get his lips round the name. "Midherodhli!"

Dhon clapped him delightedly on the shoulder, and despite the terror of his time on the canoe, Buruda again found he could not help liking this spirit.

But that night at a council of all the bu-ul, Buruda told them of the gota, and warned them against the spirits. He told them that in his opinion these spirits meant dreadful danger for the world of people. They acted differently from the way men acted. They had different manners from those of people, as Bomarigo's son and the incident of the axe demonstrated. They appeared to be well-meaning in their way, but they found it necessary to hide their bodies from the gaze of people. Even Pamplet and Pinigan, who had given promise of trying to fit in with their relatives of the Dhundubari, had appeared with covered bodies the instant they had rejoined their spirit friends.

"Spirits belong with spirits, and men with men!" he thundered to the council.

But worst of all, he was convinced that the danger that was yet to come was beyond imagination. "We have already seen the toeless footprints of my dream," he reminded them. "True, the spirits have demonstrated that in reality they keep their toes covered, and that they have footprints similar to our own. But it is also true that in my dream their toeless prints were all about, while there were no prints of men on the sands of Yarun! And it is also true that there were other prints, the like of which we have never seen. Today Nganku and four other bu-ul saw an animal that could make such prints – the gota – a spirit animal with bones growing out of its head!"

A groan came from the assembly.

"What can we do?" Bomarigo asked.

"I do not know," Buruda admitted. "My dream gave me no help there. Even my old friend, the manngur Dimmangali, gave no inkling as to what we might do, although he did warn me that there was something dangerous in my dream."

"Spirits belong with spirits, and dhan with dhan!" Naruman shouted. "We should use the spear, the boomerang and the club on these spirits to ensure a speedy return to their land! That is the only way we can avoid having our footprints replaced by the footprints of ghosts!'

But Nganku did not agree. "Do you mean you would spear Pamplet and Pinigan, relatives of ours – or Pardhen, who may yet return from the north?"

Buruda had too much respect for the Dhundubari manngur to suggest that that was exactly what should be done. But he suspected that there were many present who agreed with Naruman, and he was himself half inclined to think that the Undanbi bu-ul was right.

After the meeting broke up, Buruda slept not at all. Supplanting all other thoughts was his great longing to feel Undanbi soil once more beneath his feet. He could hardly wait for day to break to be on his way. Despite the humid heat in the confines of the hut, he clasped Nerida tightly to him, ignoring Bunbithin's protests. He needed to feel the closeness of her familiar body.

They left early, crossing Kaerwagum in borrowed Dhundubari canoes. Buruda preferred to go this way, rather than take the way up the ocean beach of Yarun. This way they would cross Daki-Bomon into Undanbi country before Bigi reached his highest point.

As they beached their canoes on the Ningi side of Kaerwagum, they looked back and saw the winged canoe making its way back toward the open sea, with Pamplet and Pinigan waving frantically to the Dhundubari.

Buruda hoped he would never again see a spirit canoe!

Notes on Chapter 14.

The fighting described, where Finnegan had to be divested of his spear in case he caused trouble, and where he was left with the women, probably took place close to the ring at Kippa Ring.

✧

Chapter 15

1824: Parsons "rescued". First Settlement established at Red Cliff Point. Oxley explores the Brisbane River.

Nerida felt uncharacteristically restless, her brow furrowing as she pounded the bangwal. But she could find nothing to explain why she was feeling this way. There was no shortage of food. Bangwal and water-lily bulbs were plentiful. The dhan were still catching plenty of fish, even though the big shoals of mullet had disappeared with the imminent approach of the heat of nguruingan. There was also plenty of variety in their food, for here near their camp at Daki-Bomon there were lots of emus, and the big bodies of these flightless birds always provided sufficient meat for the whole camp. Besides, two days ago the dhan had successfully netted and speared a dugong, one of those huge sea animals that come up to breathe, and whose delicious meat was so sought after – and there was still enough left over for yet another meal.

She could hear Bunbithin playing contentedly nearby with the other children. So what was there to worry about? Nerida mentally shook herself as she brought her mind back to the task in hand. How pleasant it was to feel the strong play of her muscles as her arms moved rhythmically up and down, forcing the bangwal to yield up its nutritious flour! What a delight to see the healthy Bunbithin come hurtling toward her from the squealing mass of children, and to have him stand beside her on sturdy legs to take a quick refreshing drink from her left breast, before taking off once more to resume his place in the chasing game that seemed to have no purpose other than running and yelling!

By now she had plenty of bangwal for roasting, so she laid her pounding tools aside. And as she moulded the cakes, Garwidha and Buldarin, each nursing a babe at her breast, dropped down in the shade beside her. Soon they were joined by Baldhin, who asked, "And how are the happy mothers?"

Garwidha beamed as she looked down at her nursing infant. "Just happy!" she replied.

Nerida reached out to touch Baldhin's shoulder. She knew full well what had sparked the question. For no matter how many times Baldhin had searched for a place where a spirit might be lying in wait to enter the binang of a passing woman, she had not been able to persuade one to take up its abode in her body. Wungul had prepared her binang well – of that there was no doubt. But it seemed that, although Baldhin was a handsome woman, and although she was careful to frequent those places where all the women knew spirits were lurking, no baby spirit appeared to wish to use her body as a means of entering into the world of people.

Buldarin also understood the longing behind the innocent question, and wordlessly handed over her own little girl so that Baldhin could offer her a breast. Baldhin might not have an infant of her own, but there was no reason why she should not experience some of the joys of motherhood.

For some time the talk was of inconsequential matters – the delicious taste of the dugong, the balmy weather, the ease of procuring bangwal in this place where they had not camped for some time. Then they talked of the forthcoming bunyi feast, due in a couple of moons, and of how far each had progressed in fashioning dhilla and necklaces for barter.

Suddenly Baldhin, who had been looking fondly down at the infant nuzzling at her breast, said absently, "The smoke is still rising from the direction of Warun."

There it was at last! Nerida thought. That was why she had been feeling apprehensive earlier. True, bushfires were often a fact of life, especially after the dry, cold season of wallaidhau. They were not particularly worrisome. Indeed, they were often followed by storms which made the grass shoot and allowed the animals to flourish. At times the dhan even fired the grass themselves to encourage the bush to replenish itself in a more fruitful fashion.

So why were they worried about the smoke they had seen for the past few days rising from Warun in Ningi country? There was enough dead grass there, surely, for a fire to burn fiercely. In fact, the Ningi themselves might have lit it.

Yet there was something not quite right about it, just the same. Bushfires moved. Granted, they sometimes caused trees to smoulder and smoke for days. But the smoke from Warun did not seem to move, nor did it seem like smoke from smouldering trees. In any case, there were not enough hollow or dead trees round that area to cause such a smoke.

"Wungul and Buruda have been talking about the smoke, and wondering what has been causing it," Baldhin told them. "They have been looking out across Daki-Bomon, hoping to see a Ningi dhan who might be able to explain it."

"Naruman reckons the Ningi must have gone mad," Garwidha said. "He says no people would make such a lot of smoke from one place unless they had lost their wits."

But the women weren't convinced Naruman was right. There had to be some reason for the smoke, but what it was they couldn't imagine.

"Maybe it is spirits!" – this from Buldarin, her eyes rolling in her head as she made the suggestion.

"Spirits do strange things," Nerida admitted, not sure that Buldarin wasn't right. "What about Pardhen?"

They all turned their eyes up in disgust as they recalled the latest news from the Dhundubari.

Barely a moon since, a Dhundubari bu-ul and his wife had stopped for the night at their camp on the creek opposite Woorim. The wife had confided to the Undanbi women that her husband was travelling north to spend some time with Badtjala relatives, and it was all because of her.

"You know Pardhen returned from the north some time ago," she had told them. After they had nodded that, yes, they knew, she had continued, "Since Pardhen is really a boy, we women all have to take turns in supplying him with bangwal, just as the dhan have to take turns in giving him fish and meat."

The visitor had paused, and the Undanbi women had waited impatiently for her to go on. She was not telling them anything they did not already know. What the Dhundubari were doing for Pardhen was exactly what the Undanbi would have done in similar circumstances. But the woman had seemed hesitant about going on.

"And –?" Nerida had prompted her.

Then the words had tumbled forth, and the revelation had shocked them to the core. It appeared that Pardhen had been sitting near Bomarigo's hut as the woman had approached to give him his share of her bangwal cakes. She had noticed that his dhun was enlarged, but had come near nevertheless, for everyone knew that sometimes a man's dhun did this remarkable thing unbidden, and the most polite way of handling such a situation was always to ignore it. But Pardhen had waited until she was near enough, and had then touched her binang!

"No!" The shocked cry of the Undanbi listeners had been one of utter disbelief. No civilised being could possibly act in this fashion! No bu-ul could possibly do this! And any boy, even a spirit boy, would know better than to attempt to touch a woman's binang!

And all before the gaze of the whole camp!

What sort of a creature was this Pardhen, anyway?

In any case, he had soon learnt his lesson. The roar of disgust from the dhan had sent him scampering into the darkest depths of the hut.

In the long run it had probably been his very openness that had saved his skin. For, even though no man would think of harming a boy, leaving it to the women to discipline children when necessary, there had been a short time when the woman's husband had been on the point of splitting Pardhen's head with his club. But Bomarigo had intervened, pointing out that no person in his right mind would do what Pardhen had done with everybody looking on, and that his wits must have been scrambled by some evil spirit for the moment.

"Leave him be!" he had pleaded. "I will talk to him and teach him the law relating to women! He will not do it again!"

And, after the first shock had passed, the husband had admitted that such must be the case. Pardhen must surely have been visited by an evil spirit. Still, he had talked it over with Nganku, and together they had reached the conclusion that it might be better if he were to visit his Badtjala relatives. The fact was that he wanted to be away from Pardhen for some time, in case he remembered too much all of a sudden, and ended up with the blood of a boy on his hands.

"I am pleased Pardhen is a Dhundubari!" Buldarin remarked vehemently. "I would hate to have to put up with such a person in our camp!"

And they all agreed.

"So maybe spirits are making the smoke at Warun," Baldhin said again, handing the sleeping bundle in her arms back to Buldarin. "It would make just as much sense as what Pardhen did to the Dhundubari woman!"

"But surely what Pardhen did makes him a makaron!" Garwidha said fearfully, rolling her eyes at the thought that an evil spirit could be as close as Pardhen was. "Maybe they are all makaron!"

But the other three bade her be silent, for even the mention of such evil things might call them forth. You could never be too careful.

While they had been talking, a canoe carrying a lone man had grounded at the mouth of the creek, and a young Dhundubari bu-ul had alighted, to sit on the sand and politely wait to be noticed. His boomerang was painted white. Buruda recognised him as the messenger who had brought the news to the Undanbi of the visit of Midherbingul. At that time he had been a kivar, but he had since undergone the test of the dhur – and with distinction, Buruda remembered. Nor could anything else be expected, since he was the son of Bomarigo, and Nganku himself had taught him. His name was Dharvurin.

The dhan did not let Dharvurin wait long. Piringa went across and invited him to join the Undanbi men, who were mending their mula in the shade of the casuarinas fringing the banks of Daki-Bomon.

"What news do you bring from our Dhundubari brothers?" Buruda asked him. "Is your father well? And Nganku?"

Dharvurin assured him that both were well, although his father was, of course, getting old and a little tottery. Still, he would be able to make it to the bunyi feast this coming season of nguruingan. "But they want our Undanbi friends to know that there has been much movement of the spirits on Yarun and down past Kuturrumba at Warun!" he concluded.

Buruda's face grew grim. "I suspected as much!" he grated. "Have they been causing the smoke of the last few days?"

"We think so," the young warrior replied. "It is Midherodhli who is back, and he has brought a lot of other spirits with him – Pinigan, too!"

"Is Pinigan back with his Dhundubari brothers, then?"

Well, he had come back, but he had gone again. "And they took Pardhen with them."

"So there are no spirit brothers left with the Dhundubari?"

"None."

"Then what is happening at Warun?"

Dharvurin did not know. But it seemed that the spirit canoe might have stopped there, although it would be hidden from the view of those on Yarun by Kuturrumba. "But we are only guessing," he admitted. "Kamkuri has sent no word from the Ningi, and all we can see is that great cloud of smoke."

"Yes, and that is all we can see!" Dhubal exclaimed. "It is not reasonable to make so much smoke!"

"Nganku wondered whether we should send messengers to the Ningi to find out what is happening," Dharvurin told them.

There was no doubt that many of the Undanbi were also consumed with curiosity, and would dearly love to know what was happening in Ningi country. But, as Buruda pointed out to them, it was, after all, not the business of the Undanbi – nor of the Dhundubari, for that matter. "If it is the spirits making smoke," he said, "it may be that our Ningi brothers are helping them, and are even now taking part in some sacred ceremony that it would be impolite to interrupt. We do not know what is happening. If Kamkuri wanted our advice, I am sure he would send word quickly enough. Whatever is happening at Warun, it seems that the Ningi are content to handle it themselves. We will find out soon enough, no doubt, when they attend the bunyi feast. Meanwhile, my brothers, let us be content to remain where we are." He took a handful of soil and let it trickle through his fingers. "There is something good about being on our own ground."

So it was agreed. What was happening in Ningi country was the business of the Ningi people. Let them look after it themselves. There were no strange occurrences in Undanbi territory yet – no unexplained smoke, no spirit canoe. Time enough to deal with it when it affected their own land.

"Tomorrow we move back over Coochin," Wungul reminded them. "It will be enough to keep our eyes peeled in this direction. We can move quickly enough if the smoke makes its appearance over Undanbi country."

"Tell Nganku that, if he needs us, we will be only too willing to come to Yarun if the spirits cause trouble there," Buruda told Dharvurin. "We will wait for his message."

But Buruda felt a heaviness of spirit long after Dharvurin had left. It was almost as if the very nature of existence was being altered. Why could these spirits not dwell happily within the land of spirits, as they had always done since the Before-Time? Try as he might, he could come up with no other reason than that the Dhundubari and the Ningi might have been remiss in some aspect of the funeral ceremony. But somehow he was not convinced that this was so. He had been present at some of these ceremonies, and there had been nothing lacking in their observance. He also had a sneaking suspicion at the back of his mind that what had happened to the other nations could just as easily happen to the Undanbi. And more and more he was beginning to suspect that these spirits, even the likeable Midherbingul and Dhon, were evil.

Makaron!

If so, it could be that the Undanbi and their brothers might be called upon to fight – and that despite Bomarigo's remark that it was not possible to fight the wind and the eternal!

Naruman's suggestion that the spirits should all be attacked with boomerang, spear and club might have some virtue!

There was a blight over the bunyi festival that season.

True, the feasting was just as enjoyable, and the dancing and singing at night just as companionable. The competition for prizes at the games was as vigorous, and the bargaining at the exchange was as eager as ever.

But always, after the feasting and the playing and the dancing, the talk would turn to the makaron.

Makaron!

The name hung like a threatening cloud over the huge camp at Baroon.

Both the Ningi and the Turrbal had tales to tell of the uncivilised behaviour of these ill-mannered creatures, and of their use of Mumba the thunder to kill and maim. There was no doubt any more – these makaron were worse than evil!

Kamkuri told of how Midherodhli and a large party had landed from their canoes at Warun, between Kuturrumba and Banda-Mardo, not far from the kivar ring. There they had started to erect their huts – and what strange huts they were – right in the area that was reserved for huts when the kivar-yangga or dhur ceremonies were in progress. Nor had they waited to be shown, as visitors ought, just where they ought to erect their camp. Nor had there been a period of sitting and waiting, before being invited onto Ningi land!

Not only that, but they had brought strange animals from the canoes and turned them loose to eat the grass. Unlike animals of the real world, these animals seemed obedient to direction, apparently content to be pushed hither and thither by makaron who kept an eye on them. And every one of these animals left a deep, two-toed footprint!

"Similar to the tracks in my dream!" Buruda reminded them.

True! But they were of three sorts. There was the gota, which had bones growing out of its head, and which the Ningi had heard about from Buruda and Nganku. There was also another short-legged animal that made grunting noises that bore some resemblance to the noise made by the koala when he was mating. Or perhaps a better description of the sound was that it was like the flatulence from the nulla mumu of a man who had eaten too prodigiously of roasted bunyi nuts. And there was yet a third animal that made noises like the gota, but which had a thick coat of queer, thick hair that matted together and did not singe easily when the meat was being cooked.

"Did the makaron cook this meat, then?" someone asked.

"Ah!" Kamkuri smiled. "They may or may not cook it – but we did!"

Laughing, he told them of how a number of these strange animals had come close to the line of trees where the Ningi dhan had been lying hidden, watching the actions of the makaron. As soon as they were close enough, two bu-ul had crept behind them and moved them without trouble into the shelter of the trees.

"They ran further into the trees, and some of our dhan followed them," Kamkuri said. "They made a terrible noise, and those of us who remained watching saw the makaron looking in our direction. We thought they might chase after them, but they let them go."

"I think they were afraid to come after them!" a Ningi bu-ul called out, and there was a general laugh at the thought of the timidity of these makaron.

"Maybe so," Kamkuri agreed. "But we took no chances, and moved the animals further away before we speared them. They may be spirit animals, but they fell to our spears with no trouble!"

"What did they taste like?" a Badtjala bu-ul wanted to know.

"Good!" yelled a Ningi bu-ul. "Different, but good!"

"Yes," Kamkuri said. "They tasted a little like dugong, a little like goanna, and a little like echidna – but quite good!"

At that point the Ningi manngur had signalled to one of his men, and the bu-ul had brought forward part of the skin of one of these animals. This was passed round for days, until everyone knew what Kamkuri had been talking about when he had mentioned the thickly-matted hair that refused to burn easily.

But the Ningi had only just begun to tell their tale. Apparently the makaron were not content with stripping bark from the trees to build their huts. Instead, they used the whole tree. First, they chopped it down with their sharp axes until it fell, and the earth shook with the agony of its dying spirit. Then they hit its body until it split apart, and again the groaning of the tree-spirit could be heard. And at last they placed the parts of the tree upright, holding the pieces together in some strange way that the Ningi could not understand.

"Probably magic," a Tumbra man ventured.

Yes, it was probably magic. But whatever held the pieces together, the sad part was that many beautiful gum-trees had fallen prey to the makaron need for wood.

"How many?" Buruda wanted to know. "How many trees did they kill?"

Kamkuri spread his hands, and the way he said, "Gurwindha!" drew a gasp from the assembled host. Such devastation was unimaginable!

The more Buruda listened, the more horrified he became, as he realised that what he was hearing was too close to his dream for comfort.

Another Ningi told of how some of the makaron had taken their special digging-sticks and dug in the ground.

"We were interested to see what they were digging for," he said. "There was no bangwal where they dug. Nor was there any food of any other kind that we knew about. We wondered whether they knew the secret of some other food. But, no! What did they do? They burnt everything they dug up – grass, trees, bushes, everything! Then they put other plants in the ground to take the place of those they had destroyed! And they have kept giving these plants water to drink as if they are trying to take the place of the clouds that bring rain to all living things!"

No wonder the Ningi had wondered what was going on, and had stayed close to discover the meaning of these strange events! Their curiosity had even overcome to some extent the shock and horror of seeing these ill-mannered creatures laying waste the beautiful land around Warun.

"But didn't you try to stop them?" Bulangga called out incredulously.

"Yes," said Kamkuri. "We did protest, at first from a distance, for we could see the thunder-sticks in the hands of those whose upper parts were covered in red. Then, when we could stand it no longer, we sent in a group of bu-ul to tell them to stop. And one of the red ones lifted his stick, the Mumba roared, and a fine bu-ul, Dimmangali, the son of my sister, fell dead!"

"You cannot fight the thunder!" Bomarigo's quavering voice was heard.

"We ran!" another Ningi bu-ul shouted, daring all present to call him a coward. "We could do nothing else! We picked up our Dimmangali friend and ran!" Then he cursed as he went on. "But we came back! One red-covered makaron fell to our spears later, and two animal-watching makaron also fell!"

A great shout of approval rose from the throng. It was good to see that even makaron were not exempt when it was necessary for them to be paid back for a killing.

But the story from the Turrbal was not so heartening. They told of how Pinigan, with Midherodhli and two others, had spoken with them at Yowoggera.

"There were some strange things left on a log, and also the dhilla which Midherodhli carried on his head. Since they had been killing and eating our ducks and swans, we naturally thought that these must be the articles they wanted to leave in exchange!" The speaker was becoming more agitated as he spoke. But one of the dhugai used his thunder-stick, and our manngur had to take some stones out of the side of the bu-ul who had the strange things in his hand!"

"Have you still got these things?" a Dhungwubera bu-ul wanted to know.

"No. He got such a shock to feel the pain that he dropped them! But we kept the dhilla!"

"Where is it?" another called.

"We threw it away!" he was told. "The things are rather useless, for they have no cord to loop over the shoulder! Our women make far better dhilla!"

But that hadn't been the end of it. They had come across the dhugai again a few days later at Baneraba, and Pinigan had told them that Midherodhli wanted his dhilla back. When the bu-ul who had taken it laughed and threw a stick, showing his contempt for those who took from Turrbal land and wanted to give nothing in return, Midherodhli had used his thunder-stick.

"And our brother Dimmangali died!" the Turrbal bu-ul who was telling the story screamed. "He died from a magic hole no bigger than my fingernail, which bled hardly at all!"

"Death to the dhugai!" the other Turrbal warriors yelled, remembering once more the outrage they had suffered.

And the assembled host joined in. "Death to the makaron!"

When the noise had died away, Bomarigo's quavering voice was heard once more. "But you cannot fight the thunder!"

At the meeting that took place on the final night before the nations were to return home, there was a hush as Buruda rose to speak.

"I am filled with sorrow for our Ningi and Turrbal brothers whose names are Dimmangali because of the thunder-sticks of the makaron!" he began. "But more – I am filled with dread as I hear what has happened at Warun! You will remember that three seasons ago I told you that in my dream I saw tracks of toeless makaron, and no tracks of dhan! I saw tracks of strange animals! I saw no trees, and the land was desolate and lifeless, the earth turned over as if every woman in every nation had taken their digging-sticks and killed the plants!"

He paused to let what he had said sink in. Then he went on. "Think, my friends! What we have heard from the Ningi is very like my dream! And I fear it is only the beginning!"

Once more he paused, and the listening bu-ul scarcely breathed.

"There is more to come!" he reminded them. "In my dream I saw unspeakable things – bodies dead by means I could not fathom! And I heard the death-wail of the Undanbi!"

A groan escaped his audience.

"The bones of the old Undanbi manngur spoke," he went on, "and accused the makaron of causing his death! And on his death-bed he warned me about my dream!"

Again a groan from the assembly.

"Three seasons ago," he reminded them, "we determined to be very careful in our observance of all sacred things. I know we have all done this."

A grunt of assent swept the throng. They had been careful to obey the law in every respect.

"Yet it was not enough! The makaron came! Some were able to take the form of relatives of our brothers the Dhundubari, and lived with them!"

"They were our relatives!" Nganku called out angrily. "Their marks proved it!"

"They may have been," Buruda admitted. "I have too much respect for the Dhundubari who claimed Pamplet, Pinigan and Pardhen as their kin to suggest they were wrong! But I wonder if these makaron have the power to assume the marks of our kin, simply so that we will accept them!" He hurried on as he saw Nganku's mouth open once more. "No, my friend, I do not believe you could do other than accept them. We Undanbi would have done the same."

Nganku sat down, satisfied.

"But" – and Buruda's stabbing finger in the firelight was like a spear – "I can tell you this! Any makaron setting foot on Undanbi land will not be found to be our kin! Of course, all nations must do as they wish. But we Undanbi will take the covering from a makaron only after our spears have dyed that covering red! If we find then that we have killed some spirit relative of ours, so be it! Spirits belong with spirits, and the spirit of our kin will have returned to the land of spirits!"

A roar of approval rose from the throats of the Undanbi. They rose as one and stamped their feet.

Buruda's nose-bone quivered. "Bomarigo, my old friend, you have said we cannot fight the thunder! We will bear this in mind and, wherever possible, will not let the makaron see us before our spears fly! We can fight the thunder if the makaron don't know they have to use it! Our spears may yet prevail! The Ningi have shown us the way!"

Not all who listened agreed with Buruda. Yuonmandi, the Kombobura manngur, thought he was wrong. But nobody doubted his sincerity, and nobody wanted to stand up and challenge the logic of the powerful Undanbi manngur.

And not one, even among the Undanbi, realised how Buruda's heart quailed as he thought that, in any case, the end was probably inevitable. His dream had given him no reason to hope that the outcome would be other than disastrous. Still, he was determined that the Undanbi would try to fight the wind and the eternal! Birral grant strength to their arms!

Tomorrow they would be back once more on their own soil. The bunyi feast had been good, but it would be better to be home.

Notes on Chapter 15

"Makaron" was the Gubbi word for "evil spirit(s)". The Yugara word was "Dhugai".

According to Oxley's account of the Turrbal man who threw a stick at him at Breakfast Creek, his shot had only wounded the man. But the author is convinced, after reading the account in Steele's The Explorers of the Moreton Bay District.1770-1830, that the man died. I have come to this conclusion after reading that there was a great deal of wailing heard from the camp throughout the night.

Chapter 16

May, 1825: Settlement moved from Red Cliff Point to Brisbane.

The Ningi remained hidden in the trees before the devastated clearing in which stood the strange huts of these makaron interlopers. They had not returned as a nation to this area since the makaron had taken up their abode. At irregular intervals, however, parties of bu-ul had come silently through the bush, their nose-bones gleaming, their bodies painted for war, to hurl their spears at unwary makaron. Since that first angry spearing of the three in retaliation for the killing of their brother Dimmangali, they had accounted for three others.

"Buruda was right!" Kamkuri exulted. "Their thunder-sticks are useless when they cannot see us first!"

At all times on these expeditions they had left their women and children behind, with a contingent of bu-ul to guard them. One thing about these makaron – they seemed content to sit in one place, and did not move about to get food, as people did. This made it easy to elude them, for they did not turn up unexpectedly in another hunting-place. Nor did they seem to have any religious ceremonies to perform at the proper places, as people did.

But, while the fact that the interlopers stayed in the one place suited the Ningi, they could not help feeling contemptuous of creatures that did not move around to allow the land to replenish itself. Did these evil spirits not realise that their remaining in this place had depleted it of most of its animals? Did they not realise, too, that their strange animals ate all the grass, and left none for the animals – brothers and sisters of the Ningi – who roamed free in the bush?

"How will we ever be able to hold a kivar or dhur ceremony at Kauin-Kauin again?" one bu-ul had yelled angrily at one of their meetings. "Where are the animals to help feed the assembled nations?"

They would never forgive the makaron for driving their animals away.

They would never forgive the makaron for camping so near their sacred ceremonial grounds.

Every now and again – out of anger rather than necessity, for there was no shortage of food in the rest of Ningi country – a dhan would dispatch one of the makaron animals and carry it home to be roasted.

But today was different. Something had happened since the last time they had been here. One of the big huts – the one constructed of flat logs that had been brought on the big canoe – was missing. The land where the grass and plants had been burned was once again bare. And there was feverish activity, as makaron followed makaron carrying bundles down to the seashore, where those same bundles were conveyed by small canoes onto the large one, which was sitting out in the sea. No strange animals could be seen.

Kamkuri could hardly believe his eyes. "Are they leaving?" he asked incredulously.

"That would be too much to hope for!" Poldha said.

"If they are not, we could help them do so!" This remark came from Badu, and his muscles bulged as he hefted his spear in readiness. But almost immediately he relaxed again. There was too much open ground between the waiting bu-ul and the makaron. It would be sheer suicide to dash over that gap in the face of their thunder-sticks.

Still, the more they watched, the more they became convinced that the makaron were indeed leaving. Kamkuri could feel his heart pounding more rapidly in his breast as he thought how marvellous it would be if they could only be rid of these pests forever. The animals could come back and thrive. The grass and the trees would be able to grow once more. The sacred ceremonial ground could once again be used.

Dazzled by the prospect of these delightful possibilities, he had become for an instant unaware of the scene before him. A sharp intake of breath and a curse from Poldha brought him back to reality.

No bundles and no makaron remained on the land. But, just as it had begun to look as if they had all gone, two makaron were coming back in their small canoe! Yes, they were walking back to the huts!

This was too much to bear! Did not these makaron know they were dead, and belonged in the land of the dead – not the living! Did they intend always to leave someone behind in the land of people, to remain like sores on the face of Ningi land?

Gubbi! Gubbi! Wa! Wa!

Angrily Kamkuri stood upright in full view of the makaron, and the other bu-ul did the same, their nose-bones quivering in righteous anger. "Come, brothers!" Kamkuri screamed. "Let us perform the proper funeral rites on these huts! Let us send these two makaron back to the land of the dead!"

They needed no urging. And, as the rest began their rush at the startled makaron, Badu already had smoke rising from his fire-making sticks.

There was a sudden shout of laughter from the bu-ul as the two makaron ran for dear life back to the canoe and tumbled into it. The bu-ul would have no need to worry about them. They turned their attention to Badu, who had caught up with them, flames crackling from the bunch of grass in his hand. In no time they all had fiery bundles and were excitedly running from hut to hut, each eager to be the first to ensure that these huts of the dead were destroyed, as all huts of dead people were destroyed.

While this was happening, Kamkuri was screaming out to the makaron on the canoe, whose wings were now unfurled. "Go back to the dead!" he yelled. "These huts are no longer of any use to you! They too are dead! They have been dwellings for the dead, and they are no more! Do not come back, you dead makaron! These huts belong to dead people!"

And, as the fires gained firmer hold on the huts, they all went down to the seashore, the better to make sure the makaron could hear them. "Dead huts!" they screamed, pointing at the blazing buildings behind them. "Dwellings not even good any more for dead people like yourselves! Gone! Do not come back, you evil makaron! You are dead!"

How good it was to see the creatures go!

They laughed. They clapped one another on the back. They looked at the smoking embers of the camp behind them, to make sure they had not imagined it all. They looked at the canoe growing smaller and smaller as it went away. Tears of joy streamed down their faces. They hugged one another.

Kamkuri spoke. "We should tell Buruda," he said. "He would be very pleased to hear what we have done."

Badu stepped forward. He would like to see the look on the great manngur's face when he heard the news. "What is the message?" he asked. "I will take it."

Kamkuri thought about it. No message should ever be sent without a great deal of thought. Indeed, if a message was not important enough to consider carefully, it was probably not important enough to send at all.

At last he said, "Tell our brother Buruda that he was right. The makaron can be fought. We Ningi have fought them, and they have left. Let us hope that they have left for the land of the dead. But if they have not, at least they have left Ningi land. We have burned their huts, as it is proper to do with the huts of the dead. Perhaps that will stop them returning."

He paused, and Badu waited for more. "And tell Buruda that the Ningi, like the Undanbi, will never take the covering from moving makaron to see if they are our kin. We will, like the Undanbi, remove the covering only after our spears have pierced it!"

The bu-ul leapt into the air, yelling their agreement. They had seen enough of makaron on Ningi land.

Badu turned his face north to carry the message across Daki-Bomon to the Undanbi.

That night there was much laughter and dancing in the Ningi camp. Their hearts had not been so light since the desecration of their land by the makaron almost a full season before.

At the same time as the Ningi were celebrating the departure of the makaron from their shores, a party of Turrbal were staring aghast at what was happening at Miandhin. For days past, there had been much coming and going on the big river. As at Warun, the dhugai – or makaron, as the Gubbi called them – had been cutting down trees with their sharp axes, and the groans of the falling giants had found an equally despairing echo in the hearts of the watchers. Even mei trees, whose succulent beans had always supplied the Turrbal with flour, were being destroyed.

Soon a track scarred the landscape from Miandhin across the creek to the river above, as dhugai carried bundle after bundle from the big canoe sitting near the sandbank. Other dhugai were striking the fallen trees until they split apart under the strain, to be used for huts – exactly as the Ningi had described it at the bunyi feast.

Were these the same dhugai who had used the thunder-sticks at Yowoggera when two bu-ul had taken the dhilla and the strange gleaming things? Were they the same ones who had killed their brother at Baneraba three days later?

It was impossible to say. But one thing was certain – they were equally ignorant and evil.

What sort of creature would not wait to be invited before building huts? What sort of creature would not sit and wait before barging through a stranger's country? What sort of creature did not paint his weapons white to show his peaceful intentions – or red if bent on war?

But worse – what sort of creature would ignore the clear markings showing the boundaries of the sacred ground surrounding the tree near the creek, which contained the bones of the Turrbal Dimmangali? And even worse – what sort of creature would cut down one of the trees upon whose bark was the mark that told anyone coming near that the ground must be entered only on the most sacred occasions of burial?

"Maybe they are their own bones!" Madha suggested. "They may want to be close to their own bones!"

But their manngur Gariwar did not agree. "If they were the spirits of Turrbal," he argued, "they would surely show more sensitivity to those of us who are left behind. These dhugai who barge back and forth over Turrbal land without waiting for permission must surely be the spirits of some ill-mannered race from so far away that we could never visit it ourselves! None of the nations we know, even as far north as the Badtjala, would behave in such a fashion!"

"They may forget how to behave in the land of the dead," someone suggested.

"Then let us teach them how!" a young kivar grated. It had been his brother who had been killed at Baneraba.

"Buruda says we should fight," Gariwar admitted. "On the other hand, Bomarigo wasn't so sure. If you look carefully, you will see the thunder-sticks in the hands of those with red covering! And if you look more carefully, you will see that they are extremely watchful as the other dhugai are busy with their tasks! I do not think we could attack them without losing many bu-ul! What do you think, Davur?"

Davur was the bu-ul who had been wounded at Yowoggera. In his mind, he could still feel the pain of the stones entering his side, and he could still hear the frightening roar of Mugara the thunder that had accompanied the pain. He shook his head.

"The magic is hard to fight!" he told them. "The pain comes at the same time as the thunder! You can see a spear and fend it off. You cannot see the stone that is put there by the magic of Mugara!"

Gariwar nodded. He remembered that Buruda had said not only that they should fight, but also that they should be careful not to let the dhugai see them.

"Those red-covered ones are too watchful!" he muttered. "There would be too much mourning for Turrbal dead!"

Those with him agreed. There were too many with the magic thunder-sticks.

They looked at the strange new animals being driven along the new track from the canoe toward the huts. Buruda was right – these were too strange for anything but nightmares! Indeed, the whole scene of devastation had a nightmarish quality!

"Buruda told us this would happen," a grey-bearded bu-ul reminded them. "It was hard to believe when we first heard it, but it is not hard to believe it now. Perhaps the Undanbi manngur should be told."

So it was decided. The Turrbal could do nothing against the brutal show of strength of the dhugai, but at least they could let Buruda know. After all, it was Buruda who had dreamt of this before anything at all had happened. His wisdom might yet help them find a way out.

The Undanbi cry for the dead had just finished when Badu arrived on the southern bank of the creek opposite Woorim. He had taken a full day and a half to complete the journey from Warun. Making sure his white boomerang was visible in the gathering dusk, he waited until a loud "Kui!" invited him to cross to the camp.

Nerida herself handed him some leftover bangwal cakes and mullet on a sheet of dibing bark. As he wolfed it down - for he had not stopped to hunt that day - he told Buruda of the departure of the makaron.

And after darkness had fallen and the fires were lit to illuminate the meeting ground in the centre of the camp, he had to tell it all again. Here was something that was not only for the ears of the bu-ul. The whole camp could listen and appreciate the great victory of the Ningi over the makaron. Again and again they wanted to hear how the two makaron had tumbled over each other in their haste to reach the canoe as they had seen the Ningi racing out from the trees.

When the camp eventually sought their huts, only a short time remained till dawn. But no matter – they could sleep late today. There was still food left over from the day before, for the season of wallaidhau was on them, with the mullet schooling in great numbers. Their guest was provided with a woman to keep him company, for surely he deserved every comfort, having provided them with the most welcome news they had heard in a long time.

Buruda slept soundly, but Nerida stayed awake for some time, contentedly listening to his heavy breathing. She was happy. Bunbithin lay within the curve of her body, strongly insulated against the cold by the possum-fur rug covering them all. Their dog was curled on the rug nearer the entrance of the hut, where the warmth from the small hearth-fire could more easily be felt. And the way her husband was breathing showed that his sleep was dreamless.

Truly it was good to be alive in this beautiful spot in Undanbi land. The muted roar of the ocean on Yarun, the lapping of the water in the creek close by, the occasional sound of a leaping fish as the tide reached its full, the soft whispering of the cold night breeze through the needles of the she-oak trees along the bank – all were like a soothing lullaby.

No evil spirits could be abroad on such a night. Her eyelids drooped at last, and she slept.

Next day had all the atmosphere of a bunyi feast, so light-hearted were all the people. The children seemed to be playing more boisterously than ever. The women chattered more loudly than usual as they left to dig bangwal. Even the dhan acted a little more frivolously as they sat repairing their nets.

Badu was feted. He took very little persuading to remain another night.

The hated makaron had gone!

But, towards the end of the day, just as they were about to go to their separate huts for the evening meal, Bagara of the Turrbal arrived with his news.

So the detestable makaron – or dhugai, as Bagara insisted on calling them – had not returned to the land of the dead! Even as the Ningi and Undanbi were celebrating the release of the land from the thrall of the spirits, they had been laying waste Miandhin, that sacred place of the Turrbal in the bend of the big river!

"You say they even killed a tree with the warning signs on it?" Bulangga wanted to know. Surely he had heard wrongly!

Yes, they had done that.

"And did they not fall dead?" Naruman asked.

Yugara! No! They seemed to be immune from those spells which would kill an ordinary man. The Turrbal had expected to see them suffer prodigiously for this act of sacrilege, but nothing had happened. Perhaps even the spirits of the land were afraid of them!

A groan escaped his listeners. Once again Buruda heard the voice of Bomarigo saying, "How do you fight the wind and the eternal?"

There was no rejoicing that night. The elders called a meeting of the bu-ul, and they moved well out of earshot of the women, the light of their fires reflected on the surface of Kaerwagum.

Dhubal spoke. "Our Turrbal friends have asked our advice – particularly the advice of our manngur. But before our manngur speaks, is there any bu-ul who can suggest what the Turrbal ought to do about these makaron?"

Naruman needed no second invitation. Jumping to his feet, he flung a spear with all his strength at a dibing tree whose white bark stood out starkly in the firelight. It struck truly, the point deeply embedded in the trunk, the shaft quivering. And, even before it became still, he was shouting, the movement of his nose-bone accentuating the passion he felt.

"Kill them all!" he yelled. "Bury your spears in their bodies, Bagara! Cast your throwing-clubs so that the bones of their faces crack before their force! Hurl your boomerangs and let them sever the heads of the makaron from their bodies!" He leapt into the air as he spoke, his arms flailing as he mimed the action needed for each weapon. "And let your clubs smash them to pulp as you come to close quarters! Let none escape!"

A number of bu-ul leapt to their feet as he finished, their roars of approval showing where their sympathies lay.

Bulangga waited for the noise to die down, and then turned to Bagara. "What do you think of that, my friend?" he asked.

Bagara rose. He took his time, looking round at the assembled bu-ul. When he began to speak, his voice was controlled. "You Undanbi have never felt the force of the magic thunder-stick of the dhugai," he pointed out softly. "One of our bu-ul – Darvu – has! And he says that the hurt and Mugara the thunder come at the same time! Darvu told you this at the bunyi feast! And we had another bu-ul – Dimmangali – who was killed at Baneraba! You were also told this at the bunyi feast!" He turned to look squarely at Naruman. "Do you still think we should go against the sticks of thunder with our spears?"

But Naruman had no intention of being out-argued by a Turrbal. He rose swiftly to his feet once more. "The Ningi have used their spears against the makaron!" he pointed out, and there was just a faint trace of contempt in his eyes as he looked across at Bagara. "Badu of the Ningi is here to tell you that himself, if you like!" He paused for effect, and then added more quietly, "Is a Ningi a better fighting-man than a Turrbal?"

The insult was open, obvious. Bagara was shaking with rage as he sprang to his feet. "I will show you that a Turrbal is a better fighting-man than an Undanbi, if you like!"

But as both men belligerently faced each other, their spears half raised, Buruda's voice cracked out as he came to his feet. "Yugara! Gubbi! Enough!" The ring of authority in his voice caused the two to lower their weapons. "We are not here to challenge one another!" he reminded them. He turned to Naruman. "You have no right to suggest that the Turrbal, who have sent to us for advice, will not fight when they need to, or when they can! You have seen their bu-ul on the baiyaba many times, and you know full well that they acquit themselves honourably, as all bu-ul must when the time comes to fight!" Turning to Bagara, he said,

"We do not doubt that the Turrbal could do to the makaron what the Ningi have done. What does Bagara have to say to Naruman about that?"

Buruda sat down. Again Bagara took his time before answering. "At the bunyi feast," he said at last, "the Ningi told us that they had speared one with the red covering and two others. But these dhugai were not alert at the time." He looked across at Badu for confirmation before continuing. "We, too, wanted to attack, but we saw that the red-covered ones with the sticks of thunder were too watchful. Gariwar said there would be too much mourning for the Turrbal."

He sat down, looking across at Naruman, daring him to say more. But the Undanbi bu-ul remained silent.

No other bu-ul rose to speak. Here and there one muttered something to his neighbour. At last Bulangga asked, "Is there more? Or do we ask our manngur to speak?"

"Buruda!" they called. "Buruda!"

Buruda rose. "I believe," he told them, "that there is some sense in what Naruman has said. The makaron should be speared and clubbed at every opportunity! You will remember that Bomarigo has said that they cannot be fought, but the Ningi have shown us that this is not so! Still, their thunder-sticks have far too much magic, and we must always bear in mind that that magic works at the speed of Bulla-Bira, the forked lightning that comes with the thunder! And the makaron seem immune to our magic, or they would have died the instant they destroyed the tree marking the sacred burial-ground of the Turrbal!"

He paused, as if a sudden thought had just struck him. When he began to speak again, it was almost as if he was thinking aloud, so that many of the bu-ul had to lean forward to hear him. "If they are indeed immune to our magic," he said, "it seems useless to weave spells with intent to do them harm. Nor do I, as a reputable manngur, approve the use of the minkom."

The use of the word drew a gasp of dismay from his audience. They were all only too aware of the power of those malignant black crystals in the hands of some unscrupulous manngur! They could all remember cases –

But Buruda gave them no time to dwell on this aspect. His voice rang out more strongly, showing he had come to a decision. "Bomarigo told me once that he had composed a chant to rid the Dhundubari of Midherplinda and the makaron with him. Midherplinda left, and it was a very long time before our people were again plagued by makaron. Maybe it is time once again to compose a chant to rid us of these ignorant creatures!" He turned to Badu and Bagara. "Tell Kamkuri and Gariwar that I will attempt to compose a chant that will help us send these makaron back to the land of the dead. If they also compose chants, it is just possible that we may be able to sing them back to where they came from, as Bomarigo sang them back so many years ago!"

A murmur of approval rose from the whole assembly. It was worth a try.

Buruda spoke once more. "It may work – it may not," he told them. He turned his attention once more to Bagara. "And tell Gariwar that my advice is to stay clear of the makaron. Do not camp any more at Miandhin. Make your camp instead at Yowoggera, Barrambin, Baneraba, Mirbarpa, Buyuba, and Kupidabin. If you do not place yourselves in view of the makaron, they will not be able to use their thunder-sticks on you! Keep clear of them! Do not, under any circumstances, try to make friends with them! You will remember that the Dhundubari made friends with Pamplet,

Pinigan and Pardhen – and after that a whole horde of makaron descended on us!"

A loud "Yau-ai!" came from the assembly.

"There are some nations," Buruda went on, "who are convinced that these makaron are spirits of dead relatives returned to visit them. I once thought so myself, and excused their ill manners by saying that, in the land of the dead, they had forgotten about their life with people. This could be so, for we all know that babies, who return to us from the spirits of the land, have forgotten what they once knew when they were with people at an earlier time."

He paused, knowing that among his listeners would be those who would wonder why makaron could not be like infants, and therefore spirits of dead relatives. He waited until he knew that their doubts had increased to such an extent that they would be wondering if he was wrong. Then he went on. "But how many babies bear the marks of dead relatives to prove their identity?" he asked them. "Do they not come to us completely unmarked, the marks of their living having been taken away from them?"

"Yau-ai!" Many agreed.

"And if a woman gives birth to an infant who does have unseemly marks of some kind, do not the other women attending the birth immediately kill that infant?"

"Yau-ai!" They were all now following his relentless logic.

"These makaron," he continued, "have marks of living that may or may not prove their relationship to living people. But, as we do with babies who are marked or deformed, we must kill them!"

They all leapt to their feet, spears and boomerangs clashing. "Kill the makaron!" they yelled.

Naruman yelled loudest of all.

Buruda waited until quiet had descended before he continued. "Tell Gariwar," he said to Bagara, "what we have decided here tonight. But do not forget to tell him also to keep clear of Miandhin! If any Turrbal do go to look at what is happening there, let them leave the women and children behind! And let them look from the cover of trees! If a makaron is foolish enough to come within reach of a spear before he has time to use his thunder-stick, well and good! But Gariwar is right --it would be foolish to give the makaron any chance to use their magic! Too many times since the coming of the makaron have we heard the death-wail of the nations!"

There was nothing more to be said. The council broke up, and the bu-ul made their way back to their camp beside the creek, blazing torches lighting their way.

Notes on Chapter 16

"Umpi Bong!" were the words yelled by the Ningi as the whites left Redcliffe. They mean "Houses of the dead", and the name still sticks. (Now called "Humpybong")

"Mei" was the name for the black bean tree, sometimes called the "Moreton Bay Chestnut".

"Mugara" was the Yugara word for "Thunder". The Gubbi word was "Mumba".

The manngur used the "good" stone, the "kundir", to heal. Only a few manngur used the "bad" stone, the "minkom", to bring evil to those they did not like.

Chapter 17

*1825-26: **The settlement at Brisbane expands. Convicts escape into the bush. Major Lockyer, taking Finnegan with him, explores further up the Brisbane River. A Pilot Station is set up at Amity Point on Stradbroke Island.***

The songs had been sung.

Buruda had patterned his song on the one that Bomarigo had used successfully with Midherplinda half a lifetime before and, after he had taught it to the bu-ul, they had spent three whole evenings separated from the women. During these times they had concentrated their thoughts wholly toward the south, directed at Miandhin, willing the makaron to return to the land of the dead, at the same time loudly singing Buruda's song and dancing the dance of the spirits.

They knew that similar sacred ceremonies would be taking place with the Ningi and the Turrbal, for Kamkuri and Gariwar would also have composed powerful songs. Birral grant that, taken together, the songs of the three nations would prove powerful enough to make these makaron release their strangling grip on the land!

But the season of wallaidhau came full upon them, and the news from the south was as gloomy as ever. Gariwar sent word that many beautiful hoop pines, those graceful trees among whose needles the king parrots and black cockatoos loved to fly about and feed, had been cut down and their bodies carried away on the winged canoe. And after the trees had been killed and the stumps burned, still more ground had been dug up by the strange digging-sticks of the dhugai, so that no sign remained of the living spirits that had once occupied the now lifeless space.

The Turrbal, however, had not been idle. Now and then a dhugai axe would be left unattended on the ground for a short while, and a bu-ul who had concealed himself nearby would take it for his own. Even the heads of the dhugai digging-sticks were useful, being made from the same sort of stone as the axes. Their blades made excellent knives. After a while, though, the red-covered dhugai tended to become more watchful, and the Turrbal had to be content with what they had already managed to acquire.

As the hot season of nguruingan approached, Gariwar once more sent Bagara to the Undanbi to acquaint them with developments. There was much to tell. A new sort of animal had been brought in on the canoe – an animal that, like the gota, had bones growing out of its head. But it was much bigger than the gota, and it made a frightening noise that resembled nothing known, although it was something like the roar of a great number of bu-ul yelling out all at once before a battle, as they rattled their spears to increase their anger. This sound, though, was enough to make the hair rise on the back of the neck – so eerie was it.

"And the tracks?" Buruda wanted to know.

Bagara's drawing of the two-toed tracks made Buruda's heart skip a beat. They were the very ones he had seen in his dream, mixed with those of the gota and those of the animal with the thick matted hair and short legs.

All of these tracks were two-toed. The only other dream-track yet to make its appearance was that of the animal with no toes.

And, according to Bagara, always round the new camp the dhugai had set up at Miandhin was the sound of loud banging. It was as if the very existence of these evil creatures depended on the making of noise. The bush animals had long since learned to give the place a wide berth, for they too had found out that the thunder-sticks meant danger. The kangaroos had hopped away to graze elsewhere, and the ducks and swans were scarce, preferring to fly to other waters where they would find more peace and quiet. Miandhin was no longer the useful hunting-place it had been only as short a time ago as last season of nguruingan.

"Luckily these creatures don't hunt much!" Dhubal muttered.

Bagara was quick to take him up on this point. "Not all the dhugai hunt," he admitted. "They spend their time on meaningless tasks at Miandhin. But the red-covered ones go out daily in their ones and twos to use their sticks of thunder on such unwary animals as they might stumble upon. They go up and down the river in their small canoes, and have even ventured out to Barrambin and Binkinba to kill kangaroos."

"And they still don't ask permission to hunt on Turrbal land?" Buruda asked. "They still give nothing in return for the animals and the trees?"

"Yugara! No!"

"And do they still destroy the bangwal and other ground food, and cut down the mei trees?"

"Yau!"

Truly the ways of the makaron were unfathomable! They seemed to hold nothing sacred! Even women knew they had to be careful to preserve the bounty of the earth! And where the bu-ul and the women always occupied themselves with ensuring increase by performing all the necessary sacred rites, these creatures seemed to ignore the need for doing anything of the kind! Indeed, they seemed to get some sort of perverse pleasure out of the act of destruction! Did they not realise that, if they did not take care of the other living things that were the brothers and sisters of people, there would soon be nothing left? Did they not realise that it was necessary to move away from a place while that place was yet full of the things that made life pleasant and possible?

"It worries me what they will do when the food around Miandhin does run out completely," Buruda said. "Is that why they left Warun? And if so, where will they turn up next?"

Nobody had an answer.

"They seem to have some ceremonies," Bagara told them, and his listeners paid close attention as he began his account, for it was some small comfort to know that there was at least a vestige of religious observance amongst these creatures. "Two of our bu-ul were watching one day as they dragged one of their number to a tree and tied his hands up above his head, after taking the top covering from his body. Then one took a heavy cord and began to strike his back and shoulders, while the other dhugai stood round and looked on. It must have been very painful for the Dhugai tied to the tree, for he turned his head from side to side as the heavy cord was swung at him. At last the cord broke his skin, and blood began to flow – almost as much blood as flows when we make our bu-ul at the dhur."

Naruman's face showed his keen interest as he asked, "Did the makaron at the tree cry out?"

Bagara shook his head. "No. The two who were watching saw him clench his teeth, but heard nothing other than the grunts of the dhugai swinging the cord. Every now and again the red-covered ones standing nearby would laugh, as if they were appreciating the courage of the one undergoing the test, and the other dhugai seemed also to be full of admiration for the way he stood the pain. But no – he did not cry out!"

Here was something his listeners could understand. All had been through the kivar-yangga, and most through the dhur as well. They knew how much concentration was required to turn the mind sufficiently from the pain to allow the ecstasy of entry into manhood to come to the fore. They knew how, at times, the merest suggestion of a whimper could almost escape the lips, if concentration lapsed even for an instant. It was a true test of manhood.

"So they do have ceremonies!" Buruda breathed, relieved to find that some trace of humanity lingered in these otherwise evil creatures. "It is strange that they mark the back and not the chest, true! But at least they do put some identifying marks of manhood on their people! How did the makaron taking the test react when the charcoal was rubbed into the wounds afterwards?"

Full well they all knew the pain of the charcoal, which made the cicatrices stand out so proudly on a bu-ul's chest and shoulders. They waited expectantly for Bagara's reply.

"They did nothing about that," Bagara told them. "When it was over, they untied him and put his top covering on again. Then he went back to what he had been doing before the ceremony – digging with his digging-stick. They all went back to digging, except for those with red coverings."

The shock of this information on his Undanbi audience was evident. They drew breath incredulously. What a travesty of a ceremony this makaron rite was! There appeared to be no careful marking of the pattern before they began! Then they marked the back instead of the front! There were no steps taken to ensure the permanence of the marks of manhood! And, perhaps worst of all, there was no celebration afterwards – no presentation of the newly-made man to the people! They simply went back to what they had been doing before!

"This ceremony," Buruda remarked, after he had thought for a time, "could be worse than if they had none! It simply demonstrates their depravity – how far removed from civilised behaviour their actions are! It also shows how dangerous it is to look at the marks on the body of a makaron and attempt to decide from those marks what person he had been in real life! These marks are made by the makaron themselves! We must tell all the nations about this so that they can beware of falling into this error!"

But even as he spoke, he knew that not all nations would take notice of this warning. There would always be those who would rather trust their own eyes when confronted with unmistakable identifying marks on a makaron. Nor could he find it in his heart to blame them. Marks – be they footprints or body markings – had always given irrefutable evidence of a person's identity, ever since the Before-Time.

"There is another ceremony which I myself witnessed," Bagara told them. "I couldn't understand everything that happened, but others have seen it at different times, and we all agree that it seems to have something to do with the cry for the dead, since it comes about that time every night."

"Ah!" Bulangga brightened up at the thought. "Creatures who mourn their dead cannot be completely depraved!"

"What exactly happens?" they all wanted to know.

"I saw them all standing round," Bagara said, "and one of the red-covered ones took two sticks and beat them on a round thing hanging from his neck. As he beat the thing, the other red-covered ones danced round, their legs moving in time to the noise. Then they, too, stood still, and the noise stopped. One – perhaps the most important one – yelled in a loud voice, and then there was a sudden screaming noise from a stick that another red-covered one put into his mouth."

Again there was a sudden intake of breath from his audience. What manner of creature could make sticks scream?

But Bagara had not finished. "Then the red-covered dhugai lifted their thunder-sticks and, after the thunder, another one let down the piece of beautifully-patterned bark, which they leave fluttering in the wind all day at the top of a big stick they have put into the ground. It has colours of white and red clay as well as a beautiful blue. I have never seen clay of this colour. This bark seemed to be held up with a thick string."

"And then –?" Buruda urged him.

"Nothing more. That is all."

What a strange ceremony! As Bagara had remarked, it was probably some sort of mourning rite, for it seemed to come at about the same time as the cry for the dead. But how could such a ceremony make sense? There was no decent wailing to show sorrow, no calling for retribution, no cursing of those responsible for the death of the loved ones being mourned. There was nothing logical about it at all.

"But then," Buruda commented after much discussion, "it probably doesn't make a great deal of sense for dead people to be mourning for the dead. Or is it that they are mourning for the loss of their own lives?"

But surely even that would evoke more emotion than that described by Bagara!

Bagara was indeed full of news, none of it heartening. Pinigan had returned and, from all accounts, the Nunakul at Bulan had been overjoyed to see him.

"That cursed makaron!" Dhubal shouted. "He came before the great influx of the evil ones! What will follow next?"

They all agreed that it was probably not a good sign. Pinigan and his two companions had been the harbingers of disaster for the Ningi. Were they the ones the makaron sent ahead to find out where the best place was to cause trouble among the people?

"Where did Pinigan go?" Buruda wanted to know.

"He went with others up the big river," Bagara said. "Messengers from the Yuggera and the Garumngar sent word that they had been seen. The Yuggera were quite taken, apparently, with the red-covered ones, two of whom also had red hair."

He added with dry humour, "Gariwar told the Yuggera messenger to take word back to his people that these dhugai also have red blood, and that they ought to test this for themselves!"

A short, sharp laugh from his audience showed that the joke was appreciated. Gariwar had spoken well.

"The Yuggera were also interested in the animals with the matted hair."

Wungul could contain himself no longer. "It is always the same!" he shouted. "These makaron blind the people with new things – things like new-fangled axes and knives that are not as good as the old ones! And people do not see them for the evil things they are!"

And Naruman brandished his spears and shouted, "Death to the makaron!"

"The Garumngar were a bit more suspicious," Bagara continued when the noise had subsided. "Pinigan and his party came upon some Garumngar women and gave them something that looked like solid water you could hold in your hand. It did not feel like water, they said, but at least they could look into it and see their own faces, just as you can see your own face in a pool of water that is not disturbed by the wind. The women were quite interested in the thing, and looked at themselves for some time. The dhugai wanted the women to go down to their canoe, but they suspected that, if they did so, they would surely be taken away. Besides, what self-respecting woman would go with strange men down to their canoe? To make matters quite clear, one of the women gave her dhilla to the dhugai, so that they could see that a proper exchange of goods had taken place, and could expect nothing more from them."

A murmur of approval rose from the listening bu-ul. This Garumngar woman had handled things well, and had acted as they would have expected their own women to act – in such a way that had left the makaron in no doubt as to her virtue. But there was a muffled curse or two from some who remarked that Pinigan, who had spent so long with the Dhundubari, should know better than to lend himself to actions that could be construed as trying to buy the favours of women! The makaron might be excused for being ignorant – Pinigan could not!

One final piece of news Bagara had for them before the meeting ended. The makaron had built a hut at Bulan, and three red-covered ones were there at all times.

"May the Nunakul kill them one by one!" Naruman shouted.

"On the contrary," Bagara told him, "the report is that the Nunakul are treating them as friends, and are keeping them supplied with fish. And because they are without women, they are also giving them some degree of comfort in that regard."

"The fools!" Naruman shouted. He could not believe his ears.

"Maybe," Wungul agreed. "But the Nunakul have never suffered at the hands of the makaron."

"Nor have we!" Naruman rejoined tartly. "Yet we are sensible enough to know you cannot deal with them! We have heard of the killing of our brothers in other nations, and have learnt from that!"

"And don't forget that you have a manngur who has also warned you against them!" Dhubal reminded him. "The Nunakul have no such manngur."

Naruman became quiet. It was true that much of the opposition to the makaron had been aroused by Buruda, who had prophesied long before the coming of these creatures that only disasters could result. It was hard to blame the Nunakul for acting in time-honoured ways toward guests who were sojourning peacefully in their land. With a different manngur, the Undanbi might do the same.

It was Turugun who first heard the frightened squeals of the women.

Some of the dhan were engaged in hunting ducks at Coochin. A number had moved quietly upstream where the ducks were known to congregate, their task being to frighten the birds downstream toward other waiting dhan. It was the task of those waiting to throw returning boomerangs over the heads of the approaching ducks as soon as they came in sight. At the same time they were to whistle like tilgonda the hawk. The birds, tricked into thinking that the sounds of the boomerangs and the whistling of the dhan heralded an imminent attack by hawks, would naturally dip quickly down over the water to escape. Turugun and his waiting companions would then easily dispose of the panicked ducks by hurling their heavy fighting boomerangs amongst them.

All had gone according to plan. But the waiting dhan had just caught sight of the approaching flock when Turugun had heard the first shriek from the direction of the swamp where the women were busy collecting water-lily bulbs. The squeals that had followed had galvanised him into action.

"Follow me!" he had yelled, grabbing his spears and racing away. "The women are in trouble!"

As one the waiting dhan raced after him, the forgotten ducks wheeling to safety. Time enough for them some other day. All could now hear the screaming and yelling of their women, and the sound made them discover speed they had not known they possessed.

Just before Turugun burst through the bushes surrounding the swamp, he could hear, even above the screams, the thumping of the women's digging-sticks against flesh. Some person or animal was being dealt terrible punishment at their hands.

Then they came into view. Most of the women had formed a protective phalanx round the children, who were huddled together on the left-hand margin of the swamp. But directly in front, the digging-sticks of two cursing groups of women were rising and falling as they flailed at two creatures on the ground. Through the women's legs Turugun could get glimpses of the outer coverings affected by makaron.

The hair rose on the back of his neck. What were these interlopers doing here? How dared they venture on to Undanbi land?

"Stand back!" he yelled. "Stand back and give me room!" And as they did so – but only after delivering some final blows at the shapes on the ground – his right arm shot forward, and his spear took one of the makaron through the throat.

Almost simultaneously a shower of spears whistled past him as the other dhan released their weapons.

For a long time after that there was much confusion. Each woman wanted to be the first to tell what had happened. The result was that, even by the time a runner had brought those men who had been engaged in fishing, none of the dhan had been able to piece the events of the morning together.

Buruda soon brought order. He looked at the faces of the dead makaron, beaten to an unrecognisable pulp by the digging-sticks of the women, and a deep satisfaction filled his heart. He knew that the spears, which had by now been retrieved from the bodies, had probably not been needed.

"You women have done well!" he commended them. "This is the way to treat makaron who stand on Undanbi land!"

A great roar burst from the throats of the men, and they stamped their feet. No makaron was welcome to the Undanbi.

There was really not a great deal to tell, after all. The women had been busy getting water-lily bulbs, when a sudden shriek from one of the children had made them look up. There coming toward them from the safety of the bushes had been these two creatures, holding out their hands, their faces twisted into unnatural grins. The women had acted without hesitation. They had, of course, not been told everything that had gone on at council meetings, but they did know that any makaron entering Undanbi land would be done to death. And they could all remember distinctly the sudden look of desperation on the faces of the evil spirits as they had turned to run.

"They cannot run fast!" Mundul said contemptuously, spurning one of the bodies with her foot. "Even old women can catch them!"

"Let us see whether these makaron have marks to show they are our relatives!" Dhubal remarked. "Perhaps we will yet need to give them decent burial!"

A short laugh from the other bu-ul applauded his grim humour.

The coverings proved extremely resistant to tearing, but at last they had the top parts off. The bottom parts came more easily, since they were made with some sort of fastenings on the outside of the leg-parts. Both bodies had many marks on the back, which undoubtedly were the result of the same sort of ceremony witnessed by the Turrbal. The ankles also showed signs of having at some stage been encased, perhaps by some ornamental band. Various partly-healed sores were visible on many parts of the bodies.

They took their time, the older bu-ul and the women minutely examining every portion of skin, in case there was some slender piece of evidence that these grotesque creatures had, indeed, once dwelt with the Undanbi. But there was nothing. Nor had they really expected to find anything. In any case, they would not have believed the evidence of their eyes if there had been an identifiable mark. Unlike the Dhundubari, they did not trust the makaron.

When they had finished, Buruda once more took charge. "These makaron are already back with their own kind!" he told them. "It only remains to put them where their spirits will no longer have the power to bother us!"

The women went back to their bulb-collecting, and the dhan carried the bodies some distance away, leaving the coverings where they had fallen. They had no need of these useless things, and they had no intention of providing the makaron with their use in the land of spirits. They dug the grave in the sand and lined it with sticks, finally dumping the bodies face down in the bottom. If the spirits wished to re-enter these bodies, let them see nothing but dirt below them! Let them dig further into the earth – away from the world of people!

By the time the heat of nguruingan had begun to abate, the Undanbi had accounted for four more of the makaron. In each case there had been no time for the creatures to communicate with them.

First Piringa, making his way home after a short visit to the Nalbo, had found himself coming up behind one of them. A throwing-club had split the back of the makaron's skull before he had become aware of Piringa's presence. Turugun had dealt with a second one, his spear penetrating so deeply that the point projected a full hand's breadth beyond the back of the makaron, who had died with a foolish look on his face. And Buruda and Wungul had used their clubs on two others, dashing suddenly out at their surprised quarry with bloodthirsty yells, preferring to use weapons that would give the satisfying feel of hand-to-hand combat, rather than strike from a distance.

In none of these cases were any identifying marks discovered that would indicate that the evil spirits had, in their earlier lives, been Undanbi. They were all buried face down. Let their spirits search the depths of the earth!

News came from other places. The Nalbo had killed a makaron who had been seen near the great trading track. The Ningi had dispatched two others.

But when Buruda led a group of Undanbi bu-ul to Kupidabin to participate in a dhur, he was dismayed to learn that the Turrbal had taken a number of makaron back to Miandhin, when they had come across them wandering helpless in the bush.

"You did not kill them?" Buruda could not believe his ears.

"No. We had no need to. They were harmless enough," Gariwar said.

"Harmless!" Buruda found himself hard put to it to keep his temper. With difficulty he held himself in check, mindful of the fact that for this moment he and the other Undanbi were guests of the Turrbal. "Harmless, when -!"

But Gariwar could see the effect of his words on the Undanbi manngur, and held up a hand. "My friend," he pleaded, "please don't make up your mind about us until you see what has happened. Tomorrow we will go to Miandhin, and you will see for yourself the power of the dhugai!"

With that Buruda had to be content. Next morning they left early for Miandhin, arriving there as Bigi reached his highest point.

The scene that met his eyes seemed, if possible, even more horrifying than his dream had been, and the longer he looked at the devastated site, the more unlovely it appeared. The destruction was so great that his mind had difficulty encompassing it. No cyclone, no fire, no flood could affect the earth as these makaron had done! If he had not known he was looking at Miandhin, he would never have recognised it! Gone were the beautiful mei trees, the graceful hoop pines! The creek that tumbled down toward the big river was unrecognisable! Even the character of the cool waterholes had altered, the layer of water-lily leaves having disappeared from their surface! And over and above all, the desolate appearance of the bare earth added its own horror to the ugliness of the strange huts of the makaron!

Nothing made sense. Even the actions of the makaron themselves were incomprehensible. The red-covered ones with their thunder-sticks strutted round in the most indecent fashion, their actions quite different from those whose coverings were not red. It almost appeared as if the whole aim of the red-covered ones was to humiliate the others, whose shuffling gait spoke of something so alien as to be inexplicable. Nothing in Buruda's experience had prepared him for this. He thought of the proud carriage of the Undanbi bu-ul, the walk that proclaimed to the world that no man was better! Even the Undanbi women – and the children, with their wide-eyed wonder – were prouder than these shuffling creatures! Surely this difference among the makaron pointed to something unutterably evil!

Gariwar had watched with interest the play of emotion on the Undanbi manngur's face. He touched his arm and pointed, drawing his attention to a line of makaron shuffling toward one of the huts. "Look at their feet!" he urged Buruda.

Buruda looked, and held his breath. What was this? There were bands of some sort round the creatures' ankles, and these bands were joined by some thick material that clanked. The stuff seemed so heavy that the makaron had to hold it up before them in their hands to allow them to walk. Why would anyone use ornaments like these? he wondered. Surely it was better to walk freely and boldly! What could be the purpose of using something that hampered movement so much? If this was what happened in the land of the spirits, it was a land to keep clear of as long as possible, and escape from at the earliest opportunity!

He almost found it in his heart to feel pity for all but the red-covered ones.

But Gariwar was drawing his attention to another hut, in front of which one of the makaron had been tied up, stripped of his top covering.

Buruda was interested. "The man-making ceremony?"

"We thought so once," Gariwar admitted. "But now we think we were wrong. We have seen it happen to the same dhugai too often for it to be that. We don't know what it is, but" – and here his voice trailed off thoughtfully – "we have begun to feel pity for those who are marked like this. We think it is done to humiliate them."

And as Buruda watched the scene unfold before him, he began to understand what his friend was talking about. This was no man-making ceremony! And even the worst insult on the baiyaba could never hope to make anyone feel as downcast as this wretch looked!

Before they left their hiding-place to return to the camp, he caught sight of one of those large-toed animals that Bagara had described. How repulsive it looked! And when it lifted its head with the bones protruding, how monstrous was the sound that escaped from its ugly mouth! There was nothing to compare the noise to, except perhaps the sound of a badly-formed bondaban – though he had to admit that he had never really heard a badly-made bondaban. All bu-ul were very careful when they made one of these.

That night he talked with the Undanbi bu-ul about what he had seen. They could not hope to fathom what was going on at Miandhin, he explained. But they could at least understand why the Turrbal did not kill the wandering makaron.

But Naruman was impatient with such talk. "Do you mean we should take them back, too?" he demanded.

"No," Buruda assured him. "We do not know why there is this difference between the red-covered makaron and the others. It does seem, indeed, that the red-covered ones are worse than the others. But we do know that no makaron, whatever his covering, has any right to be on Undanbi land – or on Turrbal land, for that matter! If we kill enough, it may be that they will all go away and leave us in peace!"

But in his heart was a feeling of great despair. The strange actions of the evil ones had left him in doubt as to whether or not he was any longer capable of thinking straight. What he had witnessed was so horrible, it almost made him believe he might have lost his reason.

He could almost hear the death-wail of his dream.

✦

Chapter 18

1826-28: Captain Logan explores to the South, discovers Coomera and Logan Rivers. Logan explores to the Fassifern, climbs Mt. French, reaches Mt. Barney. A Windmill is erected at Brisbane on Wickham Terrace. Limestone Kilns are built at Ipswich. On Stradbroke Island, Dunwich is occupied. Cunningham, Fraser and Logan journey to Mt. Barney. Cunningham discovers Cunningham's Gap.

Buruda stood on the very top of the high hill, the sacred stones in their bark covering held under his right arm.

From this eminence his sharp eyes could easily pick out the limits of Undanbi land in all directions. To the south he could see the flat ground round Daki-Bomon, where Ningi country began. To the west, although he could not pick out the trading track itself, since it lay in thickly-forested country at the foot of the Nalbo mountains, he could follow its course in his mind's eye as it snaked northward toward Nambour, past the foothills of Baroon. This trading track separated his land from that of the Nalbo and the Dallambara. To the south-east he could see the northern end of Kaerwagum, and his memory followed its winding course southward, for Kaerwagum separated Undanbi country from Yarun, the home of the Dhundubari. And to the

299

north of Currimundi he could just distinguish the darker green of the line of trees following the course of Mooloolah, the river that defined the southern boundary of the red-nosed Tumbra, the people of Maroochy.

Buruda had come to this spot for a very important ceremony. And as he stood there, he reflected on how the Undanbi bu-ul had carefully observed every rite of increase, as had always been done since the Before-Time. Thus, as the people moved from any campsite, those whose brothers and sisters were kangaroos never neglected to beg these animals to replace their numbers before it came time for the people to return to that place in the future. Those who were ducks did the same, as did the swan and the goanna people – and, indeed, people of all animal totems. These rites had always achieved their purpose admirably, for at no time had the Undanbi found a shortage of food within their boundaries, nor yet within the seas that stretched beyond their eastern border.

Truly there was a great deal to be thankful for. The earth provided bountifully.

Still, in order to guarantee a perpetuation of this bounty, from time to time it was necessary for the manngur of a people to perform secret ceremonies which went far beyond the observance of these everyday religious rites. Today was one of those times, and this hill-top which commanded such a panoramic view of Undanbi country was the place where the sacred pieces were kept.

He was in no hurry to begin. He found himself experiencing a feeling of exaltation as he looked around him. And this feeling was too precious, too holy, to allow it to be shattered too quickly. Here was the land from which his spirit had come, the land to which it would one day return. Within the trees and rocks of this beautiful land were the spirits of all the Undanbi – all Undanbi who had been and Undanbi who were yet to be. As he stood there, the sensation grew within him that he was enclosed within some sort of great ball where there was no discernible beginning or end.

How long this feeling lasted he did not know. But when it eventually did leave him, and his eyes once again picked out the land of the Ningi in the haze to the south, he felt the exaltation unaccountably give way to a sense of desolation and sorrow so acute that tears started from his eyes.

For this Undanbi land was untouched, unspoiled, used only as the creators in the Before-Time had meant it to be used – for the good of the people and the preservation of the spirits. But not so Ningi land. There the makaron had laid waste the area round Warun, killing trees and plants in wanton fashion. And the purpose of such destruction could not be comprehended, so senseless was it.

And Buruda groaned aloud as he recalled what he had seen at Miandhin in Turrbal country only two short seasons before. How could any beings perform such sacrilegious acts? He shuddered as he wondered what might happen if the makaron ever did these things on Undanbi land. How would it be possible to continue to live after one who belonged to the land saw such desecration?

From all accounts, Miandhin was now in far worse case than it had been when he had last visited it. And, more frightening still, the accursed makaron were continuing to reach out in all directions into the country surrounding Miandhin, spreading devastation wherever they touched.

What would happen to his Turrbal brothers?

What would happen if they came north toward the Undanbi?

These accursed makaron! They had apparently not been content with erecting their outlandish huts, which must surely become infested with all manner of vermin as they continued to occupy them season after season! No! Now they were using even the rocks of the earth itself as hut-building materials! On the very hill from which Buruda and Gariwar had looked on the devastation below, there was now a structure of stone as tall as a fair-sized tree and much thicker – or so he had been told! And from its top hung a huge contraption shaped something like the toy boomerangs that children made by tying two small pieces of bark together to form a cross!

What on earth could the makaron want with such a thing?

And it appeared that other huts were being built of big rocks that were being hacked unceremoniously from the bank of the river opposite Miandhin. Surely even the makaron would know that this rock had been put down by the creation giants of the Before-Time! Surely they would know that there was religious significance to this place, and that to disturb it might allow evil spirits – more evil that the makaron themselves, perhaps – to wreak havoc among the people!

At the thought, Buruda involuntarily clutched the bundle beneath his arm more tightly.

And it seemed that it was not only at Miandhin that the rocks of the earth were being desecrated by the hard tools of the makaron. At Tulmur they were digging up the white rock and putting a fire to it! Why would anyone do that? What sort of creatures were these, to think that they could burn rock? Did they possess some of the secrets of creation? For there were, Buruda knew, some stories dating back to that time that talked of rocks that burned and glowed!

But surely it was not the task of the makaron to make rocks burn! Surely that should be done only by the creation figures, those giants who had left their mark on the whole of the great land in the time of creation!

But that was not all they had been told. Apparently, not content with committing sacrilege by destroying that which should be eternal, the makaron at Tulmur had, as they had at Miandhin, objected when the Yuggera had picked up the tools left lying around. The Yuggera had thought, as any right-thinking person would, that these were their due – some sort of recompense, however slight, for allowing the makaron to use the land and camp on it, even though the makaron had never asked permission! The red-covered ones had made their appearance soon after that, and the others had stopped leaving their tools lying around.

Was there no sense of justice at all among the makaron? Was it so hard to understand that you just did not hunt on another's land without permission, that you did not take something belonging to another without first asking, that you must always ensure that there was an equitable exchange?

And was there no religion at all among them? Did they not understand that the land was sacred, as everything that was on and within it was sacred?

In the whole of living memory, no dhan had ever acted as these makaron were acting. If there had been one bu-ul who had perpetrated the smallest of the crimes committed by these evil ones, he would have been immediately put to death!

But how did you execute punishment on these powerful makaron? How did you fight the thunder?

The news was that the Turrbal had discovered that the new plants that had come up in the patches laid bare by the makaron were good to eat. It stood to reason that, since these plants were growing in areas where the mei trees had grown as long as anyone could remember, it was only fair that the Turrbal should be able to partake of this new food. But no! The makaron had set a watch, and whenever the people had tried to avail themselves of this food, the watcher had set up a terrible clattering, and the red-covered ones had come running with their thunder-sticks!

Again a groan escaped Buruda as his eyes stared unseeing toward the south. It was difficult to imagine that any creatures could possess such a degree of depravity.

As far as this new food was concerned, the worst incident had apparently taken place last wallaidhau, when there had been a man-making ceremony on the south bank opposite Miandhin. The people involved had been the Turrbal, Yugumbir and Garumngar. The messenger who had brought the news had described the scene so vividly that it still stood out starkly in Buruda's mind as he stood atop the hill.

It appeared that the bu-ul on the south bank had determined to take the new food, since it was theirs by right. And as he remembered the story, Buruda almost felt as if he himself had been there, had heard the angry yells of the bu-ul as they faced the watcher guarding the food plants, had sensed the sudden panic of the makaron as he had turned to run, had seen the spear as it cleft the air in pursuit of the runner, had heard the thud as it struck the wretch in the hand.

And he shuddered as he recalled how the messenger had told of how the bu-ul, sitting round their campfires later that night, the incident almost forgotten, had been suddenly shocked out of their wits as the thunder had roared out of the darkness, where the red-covered ones had crept up unobserved.

Gariwar and the other manngur had had to suck stones out of four bu-ul that night. And one had died, turning the time of rejoicing into grief. The Garumngar had covered themselves with red clay to mourn their Dimmangali brother, and had sorrowfully left the ceremony to carry his remains homeward.

How could you fight the thunder? How could you reason with creatures so devoid of understanding?

As he recalled other things he had heard, Buruda shuddered once more. What was worse, he wondered – the theft and desecration of a relative's skin, or the sacrilege of removing bones from where they had been laid to rest in a sacred tree? So incredibly horrifying was the thought of either, that it was only by a supreme effort of will that he could force himself to think about them at all.

Yet both had been done!

It had been Darvu who had brought the tidings of these events and, since there had been no reason to go aside, the women had also heard them.

Buruda could still see the pale shock on Nerida's face as the full import of what Darvu had been saying had sunk in.

"The skin of a woman!" she had breathed. "Surely not the skin of a Dimmangali woman!"

"The skin of my brother's wife!" Darvu had assured her, tears rolling down his cheeks at the recollection. "My brother and his family were visiting the Yuggera, and his second wife had left the skin in a dhilla in the shade of a hut near Tulmur while she was collecting mei beans with the other women. When she returned, the skin was gone!"

"Ai-ee! Ai-ee!" The whole Undanbi camp had mourned with Darvu the loss of this most sacred relic. Even the children had understood why the tears were coursing down the news-bringer's face. They had all known how Darvu's brother would have touched that skin lovingly every day, keeping alive the precious memory of one they had lost. They had all known how Darvu's brother and his children would have periodically spread the skin out, to view once more those tender breasts that had nurtured the children during the lifetime of the Dimmangali mother.

How could this happen? How?

Even Naruman had been shocked into silence by the enormity of this crime.

"You know who did it?" Buruda had asked gently.

"Yes." Darvu's face had become bleak. "The tracks were those of a red-covered one. My brother and I waited near the food plants for many days until we saw that this particular red-covered one would be the one that would come when the watcher made a noise. I walked in boldly while my brother hid. When the red-covered one came to the noise, my brother speared him."

A fierce growl of approval had arisen from his audience. Although Darvu had later explained that he did not know if the red-covered one had died, at least there was some satisfaction in the knowledge that he had not gone unpunished.

But what sort of creature would want to profane the memory of a dead person by taking a skin? Who would even want to touch the skin of a dead stranger? You would see any number of these relics in any camp. You might even want to see and touch the skin if it was that of a dear friend, but you would always ask permission first. Any other skins – surely they would mean nothing to you, and you would not even consider touching them!

What sort of twisted mind would even envisage stealing one?

Again Buruda mentally shook himself, trying in vain to blot out the horror of the tidings that came periodically from the Turrbal.

Darvu had had more to tell. The makaron had apparently not been content with destroying the tree whose markings had warned all and sundry that they were approaching the ground wherein stood the sacred tree containing the bones of the Turrbal dead. They had taken their sharp axes and cut a hole in the base of the tree containing the bones, and had extracted the bones of long-dead Turrbal, even leaving some scattered near the tree! Two bu-ul had witnessed this act of sacrilege, and had noticed that the makaron had held up a number of skulls in apparent triumph as they had reached into the hole they had made. They had taken these away to one of the big huts. Soon others had returned to the tree, to carry away more skulls!

Why would any creature want to separate the skull from the rest of the bones of a dead person? Even on the rare occasions when they had heard of a dog digging up the bodies of those whose people buried their Dimmangali in the ground, not one of Darvu's listeners had ever heard of these animals running away with the skulls and leaving the rest behind!

These makaron were even worse than dogs!

If these interlopers would only be content to sit down where they were and leave the rest of the people alone, it might be half tolerable. Let them keep one skin – let them keep the skulls they had! But let them leave the rest of Turrbal land and that of the surrounding nations in peace!

But that wasn't the way they worked. As had been expected, Pinigan's trip up the big river had heralded a further expansion of evil. Tulmur had been taken not long after that. And now the island-dwelling Nunakul as well had more to contend with. The huts at Bulan and the red-covered ones in them were still there. But, not content with that, the makaron had put red-covered ones and huts further down the island at Gumpi!

Where would it all end?

Surely Undanbi country could not remain immune for ever!

Still, so far they were safe. The journeys of the makaron from Miandhin had reached out in other directions – to the west and the south. There was a new important makaron at Miandhin who seemed to love to wander with those strange animals with bones growing out of their heads. He had gone with others through Yugumbir country as far south as Baga Baga, and on the way he had climbed to the top of Pundhagin. He had, of course, not asked permission to traverse the country, and the Yugumbir had not been able to see just what he had hoped to gain with his aimless wanderings. Nor had they been able to fathom why he had bothered to climb Pundhagin, since he had not seemed to perform any sort of religious ceremony at the top.

In the face of this apparently insane wandering, the Yugumbir had been careful to keep out of his way.

Just a short two moons ago this makaron had again returned to Baga Baga with two other important-looking makaron. One of these, shortly after they had returned, had left Tulmur with a party and had travelled across Yuggera country until he had come to the great range extending as far north and south as the eye could see. The Yuggera had watched the party disappear into the gap separating Kunyinnirra and Niamboyu. A few days later they had caught sight of them making their way back toward Tulmur.

Nobody could work out why these makaron wandered as they did. It wasn't that they were changing campsites, for they always returned to Miandhin. It didn't seem to be for the purpose of procuring food, for they never seemed to bring back as much as they took with them. And they never stopped long enough in one place to perform anything that resembled a religious ceremony.

And their purpose certainly wasn't to visit the people. They never sat down long enough to be invited over to any camp.

But Buruda knew that the Yuggera and the Yugumbir were terrified that these wanderings might presage the arrival of some red-covered makaron who would sit down in their land and refuse to leave. And well they might be fearful! Buruda himself was fearful that this sickness on the land would spread northwards to Undanbi country! No place seemed safe from these creatures!

He forced his mind back to the present. Suddenly there was a sense of urgency about his actions that had been lacking as he had been busy casting his mind back over recent events. Now he must do what he could to ensure that Undanbi land remained untouched by these unholy makaron.

Sitting down, he unwrapped the bark to reveal four smooth crystals. Of all living things, only he was aware of the significance of each. The old Dimmangali manngur who had been his mentor had, over a period of time, taught him what power each of the crystals had, and had shown him how to bring out that power by rubbing each in a special way, while singing the appropriate chant and facing in a special direction. If used correctly, these crystals had the ability to focus the strength of the land so forcefully that nothing could harm it.

Buruda was well aware of the awesome power he possessed. He knew that the hands of countless manngur had caressed these stones, and it was therefore not only the power of the stones themselves he was about to call into being, but also the power of all those manngur who had preceded him. One day Buruda himself would pass on to the land of the spirits, and another manngur would be able to call on the power of his spirit to assist in the protection of the land.

He must start Turugun's instruction immediately. No time must be lost. It was Turugun who would be the next Undanbi manngur, if Buruda had his way.

He turned to face due north and, as his hands began their careful rubbing of the first stone, he began the chants that would protect the people and the land from harm. He had a long task ahead of him. It would be nearly dark by the time he had finished.

But by that time he would once more have ensured the safety of Undanbi land for the present.

Notes on Chapter 18

The material for this chapter has been mainly gleaned from Steele's The Explorers of the Moreton Bay District. 1770-1830. In this, Fraser (a botanist) writes of how he had been told that many of the skulls from the gum-tree cemetery in Creek Street had been previously carried away by "scientific persons". It was Private Platt, of the 57th Regiment, who took the skin from a hut just above the junction of the Bremer and the Brisbane Rivers. He presented it to the explorer Alan Cunningham!

Chapter 19

1829: Cunningham Explores the Brisbane River Valley as far as Linville.

Nobody could remember when there had ever been such a vast concourse of people gathered together in one place for a dhur. The crowd might at times have been slightly greater at a particular bunyi feast, but the occasion of a dhur normally involved at most four or five nations, each of whom had kivar ready for the full test of manhood. At this dhur, however, there were gathered people from the Yugumbir, Yuggera, Dungidau, Garumngar, Dungibara, Turrbal, Dhundubari, Tumbra, Kombobura, Badtjala, Nalbo, Dallambara and Dhungwubera, as well as the Undanbi, who were hosting the event.

Not all these nations had kivar who were ready for the test. But when the message-stick had gone out from the Undanbi inviting them to participate, all had eagerly accepted. They knew that this was more than a simple dhur. This dhur was the dhur of Turugun, favourite son and pupil of Buruda, whose fame had grown enormously as, one by one, the events he had foretold so many seasons ago had come to pass.

The power to dream dreams was inherent in all people, but the power to have dreams like Buruda's was very rare indeed.

Even the women had at last been told of most of Buruda's dream, since by now it had become common knowledge, as the makaron had blighted the land. Only the horror of the final oblivion was still kept from them. And all the bu-ul – including Buruda himself – still hoped against hope that this was only a symbolic part of the dream, capable of less literal interpretation than that of the complete annihilation of the people.

Certainly at this joyous assemblage there was reason to hope that the strength of the people would go on forever. Here at the northern end of Kaerwagum there were no makaron to mar the proceedings, nothing to twist out of all recognition the laws set down in the Before-Time.

Only one dark shadow lurked in the background to remind them all that not everything was as perfect as it ought to be. The nations to the south and south-west had all been careful to leave a fairly strong contingent behind in their own country, with orders to bring news with all possible speed if the makaron started anything new. This was not the time to forget that the actions of the makaron were quite illogical, and therefore unpredictable. It would not pay to be taken by surprise.

In this season of wallaidhau the mullet and the tailer easily supplied the needs of all. This was the reason why the Undanbi had decided to hold the dhur at this time. This year, too, there had been a lack of rain in the inland, and the people away from the coast in such a year always asked permission to come and partake of the bounty of the sea. When the dhur was finally over, some of the Nalbo and Dallambara would undoubtedly remain for some time with the Undanbi, while others would sojourn temporarily with the Dhundubari, Tumbra and Ningi.

Turugun had long since passed the time when he could have first taken the test of full manhood, but Buruda had deliberately lengthened the period of his protege's youth. Turugun was fully aware that it was Buruda's wish that he further his education sufficiently to allow him one day to become a manngur of the Undanbi. The young man was also aware that to assume the title of manngur in the nation that claimed the most famous manngur among all the nations would be fraught with difficulty. He might too easily be found wanting in comparison with Buruda, and might therefore labour unsuccessfully all his life to gain the respect of the people. And Buruda had pointed out to him again and again that this respect was vital. For the faith of the people in a manngur's ability to perform the ceremonies of healing and increase was just as important to the success of those ceremonies as the performance itself.

Thus Turugun had already been led a long way into the study of the intricacies of the human mind. And he had been warned that from now on the pace of instruction in this area would increase tremendously, that there would be little time for at least a full season for his mind to be occupied with anything else. Then, if the spirits moved the surface of the still water and he was able to find his own kundir, he would become a manngur. Until that time, though, there could be no thought of marriage, for a wife would distract his mind greatly and so impede the development of its full power.

Nevertheless, Turugun knew, as did all people from a very early age, who his promised wife was. Her name was Guluwa, and he had helped grow her up by supplying her father with meat and fish since he had become a kivar. She had already had the joint of her little finger removed, and was as graceful and delicate as the moonlight she was named for. He was glad she had been born a Dhuroingan to match his Balkuin, for of all the young women in the Undanbi she was without doubt the most desirable.

At the beginning of the dhur, as the candidates were being lined up to be taken away, there had been a gasp of admiration as Turugun had responded to the call of his patron. Those who had seen him grow season by season were not surprised, for they had become used to being bested by him on the baiyaba, whenever custom had allowed kivar to be matched against bu-ul. But those who had never caught sight of him gazed open-mouthed at his magnificent physique, and wondered aloud how it was possible for another to be so like Buruda,

Wungul had grinned secretly at these remarks, reflecting that his young pupil Bunbithin, who had already far outstripped other boys in all things and was already demonstrating remarkable mental and physical ability, would one day arouse just as much admiration. He felt impatient for that time to come. The boy could already throw a man-sized spear more accurately than some kivar.

As expected, Turugun's induction into manhood went off perfectly. When the graduates, after almost a moon of testing, were brought back to the people, the marks of full manhood standing out boldly on their shoulders, the roar that greeted Turugun rivalled the sound of the surf on the stormiest day. Tears of joy coursed down Buruda's face as he held the hand of his favourite son. This was indeed a day for pride.

The baiyaba that followed had never had an equal, even at a bunyi festival. It continued for four full days, with grudge fights and demonstration battles taking place continuously. And on the afternoon of the fourth day Buruda and Turugun appeared on the field and loudly challenged any two bu-ul to face them. Never before had two such bu-ul, magnificent in their battle regalia, been seen together on the baiyaba.

There was no shortage of opponents. Just to be seen on the same field of honour as the two Undanbi was something any bu-ul would almost give his wundu for. Two by two they came out and faced them – and two by two they retired with wounds they had not had earlier. All afternoon it continued, and when Bigi at last disappeared, the two left the field with only slight scratches.

But the bu-ul who had managed to inflict these slight wounds on the two would boast about it for the rest of their lives.

Nerida, her belly swollen once more with the expectation of her second child, found the dances at night exciting and interesting. The mix of people at the big camp ensured an infinite variety. The story she had liked most was the Dungidau story of the platypus. This furry little animal that poked its duck-bill round the mud and rocks of the creeks searching for food was a favourite of all, but it was held in particular regard by the Dungidau. They even gave its name - Mairwar - to their part of the big river that ended up flowing through Turrbal country. As everyone knew, these small animals, like all others, had been people in the Before-Time. And the Dungidau story told of how these little people (for, of course, they were no bigger than the mairwar they were to become) journeyed from the sea, killing sea-snakes as they went. When they reached Dungidau country, however, the sea-snakes overpowered them and turned them into mairwar, which they had been ever since.

Nerida smiled to herself that last evening as she recalled the wonderful mimicry of the Dungidau as they had sung and danced this story. She wondered what stories would be told to entertain them on this final night.

But they were to find that all thoughts of entertainment would be driven from their minds long before the time came to assemble round the campfires.

The messengers from the Yuggera and Dungibara arrived just after the cry for the dead. Their news caused a great flutter in the crowded camp. By whatever name they were called – makaron, dhugai, or moi – a party of evil spirits had once again invaded Yuggera and Dungibara land, crossing it and hunting without permission.

Baribah, the Yuggera messenger, told of how the dhugai had first appeared on the banks of the Urarrar beyond Tulmur, travelling with some animals with bones on their heads, as well as some huge dogs which made must un-doglike sounds.

"We know these dogs!" Gariwar had interrupted the messenger. "They are dogs to keep clear of, as we found out at Miandhin with the food plants!"

Baribah had agreed that that was indeed the case. These dogs were as big as bu-ul, and were not to be taken lightly.

"The dhugai came suddenly upon two of our women and their children at Gudhabila," he told them. "What they would have done to them if they hadn't taken to their heels straight away we don't know, but our women have had strict instructions to stay clear of the evil ones. They ran to us, calling for help. We stood on a ridge some distance from the dhugai to take stock of the situation, since there were only two of us. Just as it began to get dark, they made signs for us to approach them, and because we thought it would be a good idea to find out more about them, we did so."

A babble of conversation rose from the Yuggera, people voicing varying opinions about the wisdom of this action. Some praised the courage of the two, while others thought it was scandalous that they would take such a risk with so many fighting men away.

Baribah dismissed their opinions. "Whether it was sensible or not," he told them, "we went. And even one of our women and two kivar came as well." He hurried on to forestall any other interruption. "The dhugai took a tool that moves when you put your fingers in it, and cut our beards for us."

Those close enough could indeed see for themselves that Baribah's beard was almost non-existent. They were not sure they liked it as much as their own flowing beards.

In the press of so many people trying to get close enough to hear what was going on, there was a small space left around the group of manngur. Buruda's voice rang out clearly from this group. "Tell us what this tool was like," he said.

It then became evident that Baribah had been waiting for just such a request. Like a magician, he reached into the dhilla under his left arm and extracted the tool. Then, putting his fingers into the loops at one end, he used it on the beard of the bu-ul nearest him. As the hair fell to the ground, the tool made a sound like the twittering of a bird.

"E-e-e-e-e-e-e!" - this from the appreciative crowd.

Even Buruda was impressed. Baribah must have run considerable risk to take the implement, if the stories from Miandhin and Tulmur were any indication of the value the makaron placed on their tools. At both these places, they used red-covered ones to ensure nobody took any.

"How did you get it?" he asked Baribah.

"The dhugai gave it to me. I suppose it was to pay for crossing and hunting on our land." Then his voice changed tone, became harsh, as he continued. "But as you can see, it is only a little thing, and not even very useful – unless you break it apart and make two knives out of it. I let the dhugai know that they would need to give a lot more if they wanted to continue further!"

"And -?" Gariwar prompted him, as he paused.

"The most important dhugai made signs for us to go away!" Baribah told them indignantly. "We didn't want to go until they had given us fair payment for their trespass, but they went back to their shelters. And when we went to follow, their savage dogs growled and bared their teeth, pulling so hard on the cords that were tying them to a tree that we beat a hasty retreat! We did not want those cords to break!"

Baribah had been talking loudly, but so great was the multitude that those furthest away were dependent on those nearer to convey the message. Buruda decided that the messages brought by the two southerners were so important that all should have a chance of hearing better. He shouted that all people should gather in their usual evening places round the great campfires, and there all would be able to hear what the makaron were doing.

After they were all seated and order once more prevailed, Baribah continued his narrative. "Four of us followed them next day. We kept a long way away, hoping that their thunder-sticks wouldn't be able to harm us at that distance if they decided to use them. Later in the day, when they were near Milgero, three others who had been away hunting came and joined us. We decided to see if fire would make them turn tail!"

"A-a-a-a-a-a-a-ah!" The audience breathed deeply. This was more like it! All Yuggera knew how dry the grass was round Milgero at this time, and the others could guess!

"The wind was gusty," Baribah went on, a smile flickering across his face as he remembered. "The dhugai started to yell as soon as they saw what we were doing, but they didn't use their thunder-sticks. They were coughing and spluttering, and it looked as if we had them trapped. Then they got the idea of lighting a fire back towards ours."

A sigh of disappointment rippled through the audience.

But then Baribah laughed. "They were so clumsy at what they did that their own fire nearly caught them!" He waited for the roar of laughter to subside before he went on. "But the spirits were on their side. The wind changed and they were left safe, though they coughed and spluttered for a long time afterwards."

A murmur of conversation broke out on all sides. It was always the same! some said. The spirits were always on the side of these evil ones! Others suggested that their manngur could maybe devise ways of securing intervention of the spirits on the side of people.

But Buruda was interested in something else that Baribah had said. He did not believe that the lack of use of the thunder-sticks by the makaron had been motivated by kindness. "How far away did you keep?" he asked Baribah, and was interested to note that it was about two spear-throws' distance.

This information might prove important at some future time.

"The fire seemed to work," Baribah said. "They turned north toward Dungibara country. Since we knew most of the Dungibara were also here with the Undanbi, we followed, but kept out of sight."

Dharara, the Dungibara messenger, then stood up to take up the story. "The Yuggera told us about these interlopers when they came up with us just south of Gallanani. There were two of us. Baribah stayed with us as we followed these accursed moi along the banks of the Mairwar. From time to time we called out to the moi to get out of our country, but they took no notice." He paused, his face showing puzzlement as he continued. "They said nothing at all! You would expect them to say something, surely – even if it was just to yell back at us, or to ask our forgiveness for crossing our country! But they said nothing! They didn't even seem to see us!"

His listeners, too, could hardly believe their ears. What sort of beings would completely ignore the yells and curses of bu-ul? Even animals would look up, or run away. And these makaron hadn't even looked up to acknowledge that they were being addressed!

"We did notice that the animals with bones growing from their heads, which the moi seem to use to carry their loads, looked frightened every time we yelled," Dharvara went on. "So we wondered what would happen if we kept quiet for a while and then scared them suddenly. We stayed out of sight, keeping pace with them until they came to a bend in the river where there was a steep cliff. Then we jumped out and yelled at the tops of our voices. It took the moi all their time to stop the animals running over the cliff!"

Again a murmur of appreciation swept over the assembly. It was good to hear of attempts to unsettle these interlopers!

But Dharvara's story was one of failure, despite their courage. The makaron had used a thunder-stick, which luckily had done no harm. But they had then released their dogs, and the bu-ul had been hard put to it to outdistance these savage beasts, which had pressed them so hard that they had not even had the opportunity to turn and use their spears.

From then on Dharvara's group, with Baribah, had gone on ahead of the moi, alerting all those in their path to the danger. They had missed one small family, however, and had found out later that the bu-ul had yelled defiance at the trespassers, who had at least given this bu-ul some compensation. They had set their dogs at a group of feeding kangaroos and, after the dogs had killed two, the moi had presented the family with some choice cuts of meat.

"Were these small kangaroos?" Buruda wanted to know.

"No. The bu-ul told us that the two killed were full-grown kuruman."

"How many dogs to each kuruman?"

"He said it took only one dog for each kuruman, and that the kuruman were dead almost in the blink of an eye!"

A sharp intake of breath showed that the impact of this statement was not lost on the assembled people. What size of dog could be expected to deal with a full-grown old-man kangaroo on its own - and so quickly? These must indeed be formidable animals!

"We followed again," Dharvara went on. "We tried to trick them once by putting our throwing-clubs in our belts along our backbones and pretending to want to trade with them. But they would have none of it, and signed with their thunder-sticks for us to leave them. Then when they erected their shelters for the night near Wungar, we crossed the river lower down, hoping to surprise them. But two came after us with thunder-sticks, and we only just managed to escape with our lives. We could hear the stones from the thunder crashing through the leaves over our heads, and tearing up the ground around us!"

The listeners were becoming angry now, and curses punctuated the night. Who did these makaron, these dhugai, these moi think they were, to trespass and hunt on their land, and then try to kill those who rightfully objected?

And Dharvara told of how the Dungibara bu-ul who had watched the progress of the moi had at last lost patience, and had armed himself to the teeth. Then, when the moi had reached Kannangur, having begun to retrace their steps, the bu-ul had thrown caution to the winds and, with another bu-ul called Kunya, had openly defied them.

Again Dharvara paused as a murmur ran around the assembly. Most of them had heard of Kunya. He was a Dungibara bu-ul of no mean courage, and one to be reckoned with.

But there was consternation when they heard that the makaron had again used their thunder-sticks without warning, and the two had been forced to run, routed even before they had had a chance to use their spears. And Kunya had been struck in the leg, so that he had even had to drop his weapons to allow him the chance to escape.

Dharvara hastened to allay their fears about Kunya. Two stones had hit him in the legs, and he was limping badly. But neither stone seemed to have lodged there to render it necessary for him to seek out the help of a manngur. There was a hole in each case where a stone had gone in, and another where it had come out.

In his mind Buruda could hear the voice of the old Dhundubari manngur, who had been too frail to attend this dhur. "How can you fight the thunder?"

How *could* you fight the thunder?

And for a long time there was cursing and shouting among the assembled bu-ul, as they discoursed at length on the uncivilised behaviour that was always exhibited by the makaron. What sort of fighting men were these creatures, not to respond decently to insults and defiance hurled at them by an honourable enemy? Even a dog would growl before it attacked! The rules of warfare obliged all bu-ul to honour the time of cursing, insults and defiance that must always precede the first flight of spears.

No bu-ul would meet defiance with ignorant silence!

Luckily this time no great harm had been done. But again the depredations of the makaron had marred a meeting of the nations. What had been a time of great rejoicing had become a time for worrying, a time of anxious tension as they waited for the next unpredictable event.

Despite the shortage of food back in their home countries and the surfeit of it along the coast, no Yuggera, Dungibara or Dungidau would now stay with the coastal people beyond tomorrow. They might need all their fighting men if trouble erupted.

But before they left, Wakadho, the Dungibara manngur, invited Buruda and Turugun to attend a great kivar-yangga to be held by the Yuggera, Dungibara, Dungidau and Garumngar after next wallaidhau. They would, of course, send a formal message-stick as the time drew near, but he would like the two to be prepared for the occasion.

At the back of their minds, though, was the thought that many things might happen before that time came round – in Undanbi country as well as in the lands to the south-west. No longer could they look to the future with the assurance they had felt in the past.

Notes on Chapter 19

"Moi" was the Wakka word for "Evil Spirit".

✦

Chapter 20

1830: Captain Patrick Logan, Brisbane Penal Commandant, meets his death at the hands of Aborigines.

As one spirit leaves, another arrives.

So it was after Turugun's dhur, in that hot time of nguruingan. Word had hardly arrived that the spirit of the old Dhundubari manngur had left his body, when Buldarin and Ngita took Nerida away to have her baby.

They named the little girl for the time she had made her appearance – early in the morning, even before Bigi had poked his head above the horizon. Little Dhuluru was assiduously rubbed with charcoal twice a day to make her a presentable colour by the time they brought her back to be shown to the people, even though she complained vigorously each time. And Ngita and Buldarin were both amazed at the strength with which Dhuluru sucked at their breasts each time she was hungry. Bunbithin had had a formidable suck, it was true, but this little girl might have an even more powerful one.

For his part, Buruda took advantage of the time of Nerida's absence to take Turugun on a long hunting trip, for this was a fine opportunity for him to expound further on the secrets that were closed to all but manngur. Turugun's education was proceeding excellently, it was true, but it would be foolish to neglect to take advantage of a time when they would both be able to bend all their energies to exploring the secrets of the laws that made possible the existence of all life.

They returned, highly satisfied with the progress they had made, in time to welcome Buruda's little daughter to his hut.

Piringa, who had taken his family on a hunting trip toward the Nalbo mountains, came back to report that he had dispatched yet another makaron who had been making his way north on the trading track. After he had stripped the body of its covering, he had found no evidence to suggest kinship with the Undanbi. He had buried the body face down.

"Two others had gone ahead of that one," he warned. "Let us hope the Tumbra deal properly with them!"

But Buruda did not think that Girrimar would act quickly. The Tumbra manngur had not been as vociferous in his support for the Undanbi course of action as the Ningi had been.

Then suddenly there was more news from Miandhin, and the Undanbi wept loudly as they heard what had transpired with the Turrbal.

The most important man amongst the makaron – the one whom the makaron called "Komidi" – had committed one of the greatest atrocities possible.

It seemed that the Turrbal, sick and tired of being denied access to the food plants that had replaced their succulent mei beans, had stepped up their attempts to gain justice as far as this food was concerned. They had become particularly irate when the makaron, not content with the amount of devastation they had already caused, had put another camp out beyond Yowoggera, on the flat land toward Doomben, and had cut trees down there. They had also become extremely worried as they noticed that the canoe that travelled across the sea to Bulan always returned with more makaron than it had set out with. The number of interlopers at Miandhin was now so great that it rivalled even the number of people at the bunyi feasts.

That these makaron might become so numerous that no land would be left to the Turrbal seemed a distinct possibility!

Gariwar had therefore organised a concerted raid on the food plants at Binkinba, and a savage battle had ensued. Two Turrbal and one guard had been killed. The next day two bu-ul, relatives of those killed, had returned to exact vengeance, and one of them had been killed.

Such actions were understandable. After all, not all attempts at vengeance were successful. But the Undanbi found it difficult to accept what Paldha, the Turrbal messenger, told them next. Surely not even an evil spirit – a makaron – could do that! The utter horror of what the evil Komidi had done was beyond belief, surely!

But Paldha assured them that it was so, and tears coursed down their cheeks and they cried aloud. Yes, it was true! Komidi had taken the dead bu-ul and had him skinned! He had then had the skin stuffed with straw, finally putting it on a stake among the food plants!

"He is still standing there!" Paldha told them. "And we dare not go and get him, for there are many red-covered ones in attendance there!"

Such a volume of curses broke out that it was some time before Paldha could continue.

At last Buruda said, "The Turrbal won't let this evil Komidi go unpunished, surely!"

"No. But there are always many red-covered ones round him. And he sits on a big animal with no toes on each foot, and this animal goes very fast, so it would be very hard to catch him, even if he didn't have the red ones! He also has a small thunder-stick of his own!"

"No toes?" Buruda was interested. "Draw this animal's tracks for me."

Paldha obliged, and Buruda found himself staring aghast at the last tracks of his dream. He had hoped against hope that no more of his dream would come to pass – but here it was again. What would be next?

"The Yugumbir have seen this animal, and call it a yeraman," Paldha told them. "I don't know why they gave it this name, but perhaps it is because it has its beard growing out of the back of its neck."

First the gota – and last the yeraman. No more animals were left to come out of his dream.

But he could not continue this line of thought for long, for Paldha was speaking again. "This Komidi often travels far from Miandhin. He has been to Yugumbir and Yuggera country before, and Gariwar says he will wait until he sees this evil one set out again. It may take two seasons – it may take four – but we have vowed that he will not escape!"

Buruda placed a hand on Paldha's shoulder. "Tell Gariwar that, if we see this evil one first, he will have no need to worry about him!"

But even then Paldha had not finished. He told them of how two Yuggera women had been collecting mei beans near where the Urarrar joined the big river, when they had been surprised by three dhugai who had been hiding in the nearby shrubbery. "They took them from behind, and tied some of their bark round the women's mouths," Paldha said. "Otherwise they would have been able to call for help. They struggled, but the three were too strong, and threw them to the ground! They then forced their legs open and used them horribly!"

A great cry broke out from the women who were listening, and the bu-ul reacted with a great roar, cursing these things that were worse than even the most evil of spirits. There had been reports of cases of violation among the people of the past, to be sure, but they were so rare that nobody could recall a case in their own lifetime.

"One dhugai held one woman while the other two forced the other," Paldha explained. "Then they took it in turns on both!"

Again came that great cry from the women mixed with curses and threats from all sides.

Surely nothing but death was a suitable punishment for such a deed!

"The Yuggera have decided that the three will die!" Paldha agreed, and a great shout of approbation rose from all. "Their tracks have been examined by the Yuggera, and some of our bu-ul who were visiting at the time also saw them. These three are known, and they will die – be it at the hands of the Yuggera or the Turrbal! We have sworn it!"

Again a great shout heralded the news.

But still Paldha was not finished. He explained at great length how the two women had suffered at the hands of the dhugai, and the more he told – of bruises, split lips, and worse – the angrier his listeners became.

The women felt nauseated at this description. How could this be? Surely the way of a man with a woman could not be distorted in this fashion!

"Perhaps Gariwar will now see that the makaron, even those not covered in red, are not as harmless as he thought," Buruda suggested. "Perhaps he will not be so kind to those who are wandering away from Miandhin in the future."

"There are many Turrbal bu-ul," Paldha gritted, "who have vowed never again to return the wandering dhugai! Gariwar is not so sure, but he is beginning to think as we do. I don't think there will be as many taken back now."

"I will tell you exactly how to send them back, if you like!" Piringa said, and the savage burst of laughter from the others was all the explanation Paldha needed.

It was, after all, the Turrbal who exacted retribution for the violation of the two Yuggera women.

It was the season of wallaidhau. Paldha, who happened to be keeping watch upstream from Miandhin, noticed the three who had been identified as the attackers get into a canoe and pole it up towards him. He ran quickly to alert other bu-ul, and soon a large party of Turrbal, making sure they kept out of sight, were keeping pace with the canoe as the three, assisted by the incoming tide, made their way upstream. They made good time, eventually stopping, well out of reach of their friends at Miandhin, to fish in midstream.

The waiting bu-ul cursed under their breath, for the three were out of range of their spears, and there was no way they could get at them. At last Bagara hatched a plan and, taking half the bu-ul with him, moved to a point upstream out of sight and sound of the three dhugai, and there the three spent some time spearing fish. Fortunately at this time of wallaidhau the mullet were plentiful, even so far up the river.

When they rejoined the watchers on the bank, they were told that the three had not caught many fish. "They don't seem to know how to catch mullet," Paldha had whispered. "Their cords are no good for that."

Why the dhugai persisted in using their cords when there were so many better ways of ensuring a good catch of fish had often been the subject of discussion with the Turrbal. In many ways these dhugai, despite their knowledge of the magic of thunder, were like babes when it came to procuring food.

Bagara and another man took all the mullet and, leaving their spears behind, stepped out boldly into the open, calling loudly to the three in the canoe. "Come here!" Bagara shouted. "You can have fish for nothing, if you like! But if you've got something to trade, we'll take it!"

The three looked up, startled, and began to jabber together in their outlandish tongue with the harsh hissing sounds.

The two on the bank smiled, making signs as they continued to call out. They held their catch high to show the quality of the goods they wanted to trade. They knew their fish were far superior to anything the dhugai had in their canoe.

For a while, as the three argued among themselves, it looked as if they were not to be hoodwinked. But eventually they pulled in the weight holding their canoe steady and began to pole toward the shore.

Bagara and his friend gave as good a performance as they could, trying to convince the still hesitant dhugai that their intentions were nothing but friendly. They smiled broadly at the oncoming three, and the hidden bu-ul grinned appreciatively at their acting prowess. And while he waited, Paldha found himself formulating an idea for a dance to commemorate this day, and he gave a silent chuckle as he thought of the dramatic effect he could impart to the dance by exaggerating the antics of the two with the mullet.

But the grins faded as the serious business began. The canoe had hardly touched the shore when the Turrbal rushed out, their savage war-cry shattering the peace of the bush. For the space of three whole heartbeats they froze, their spears poised, for it was important to them that their victims experience some of the horror that had been the lot of the violated women. Then, with a fierce joy, they released their weapons, and the three fell in their canoe, the protruding spears making the bodies look like kakkar the echidna.

The two who had been holding the mullet dropped them and raced in with sticks, anxious to get in at least one hit before life left the bodies. But their blows, satisfying though they were, were not needed.

There was to be no burial face-down for these three. The Turrbal and the Yuggera had had many moons to decide what would be the ultimate fate of these violaters of women. Pulling them from the canoe, the bu-ul first stripped them and examined the bodies. There were no marks to connect them with the Turrbal. Then carefully, almost ceremoniously, they placed the bodies face up, and three bu-ul took their knives and slashed into their wundu and dhun. After they had marked the parts beyond recognition, they replaced the mutilated bodies in the canoe and shoved it out into the river.

They wanted these bodies to be discovered.

Surely even the most ignorant dhugai would be able to tell from the way the bodies were presented just why these three had been killed!

Afterwards, Paldha went upstream toward Urarrar to take the glad tidings to the Yuggera.

And after Gariwar had been told, he immediately sent Bagara to tell Buruda. "He will be pleased to hear that the Turrbal can still execute sentence on those condemned by the law – even dhugai!" he said.

The great Dungibara kivar-yangga was in progress.

Buruda looked proudly across at Turugun. His favourite son was in the process of testing the kivar in the laws relating to food, and Buruda had to admit that he himself could not have done it better.

Ever since the great kivar-yangga had begun, the young man had conducted himself like a true manngur, which he was indeed in all but the final test at the pool. The other manngur had been content to stand back and let Buruda's protege take a leading part in the ceremony, and it had been Turugun who had been entrusted with pointing out to the women the boundaries of the sacred ground. And finally, it had been Turugun who had dismissed the women of the four nations – the Garumngar, Dungibara, Yuggera and Dungidau – to their allocated area some distance upstream from the kivar ring, which was situated at a point near the river where the territories of the Garumngar, Yuggera and Dungibara met.

The kivar-yangga had gone off smoothly, and tomorrow would see its conclusion. At that time the kivar, all of whom had borne the various ordeals with great fortitude, would receive the marks of young manhood appropriate to their particular nations. It had been a good ceremony, and Buruda was pleased he and Turugun had been invited, for the young man had learnt a lot by participating with the other manngur from these nations of the south-west.

Buruda himself also felt he had learnt something. He had been particularly intrigued to find that Maltagara, one of the manngur of the Yuggera, had accepted one of the wandering makaron into his people. Boraltju – for such was the name of this Yuggera makaron – had been accepted into full manhood only last season at a dhur held by Maltagara's people in conjunction with the Yugumbir.

Boraltju had been presented to Buruda by Maltagara as something of an oddity, for Maltagara was far enough removed from Miandhin to ensure that his people had not felt much of the impact of these evil ones. Maltagara had, however, been earlier alerted by the other manngur to the fact that this Undanbi manngur was highly suspicious of claims that the dhugai were returned spirits of the dead. He had therefore taken great pains to show Buruda the marks that proved beyond all doubt that Boraltju was a member of the Yuggera.

Although Buruda had politely acknowledged that there was no doubt about the genuineness of the makaron's claim, inwardly he remained extremely dubious regarding its authenticity. Something was not quite right. When Buruda had questioned him about his progress in remembering the things he had forgotten since his death, Boraltju had been eager to explain in his halting speech that he was remembering more each day. But there was something that did not quite ring true – perhaps it was only that the creature was a little over-eager to prove he could remember.

Even when Boraltju had told him that the makaron name for the spirit world was Inglun, there was something about this information that made him wonder why the man had bothered to tell him. After all, what did it really matter what these creatures called the world of spirits? It did not alter the fact that they ought never to have left it!

Even the marks of manhood did not look quite right on Boraltju. True, they were there for all to see, but they did not stand out nearly as boldly as did those on Maltagara and the rest of his bu-ul. To Buruda, it was almost as if the marks were proclaiming the falsity of his claim to relationship with the Yuggera.

Still, he kept his thoughts to himself. Maltagara had every right to claim kinship with the makaron and, indeed, the claim might be justified.

The afternoon was well-nigh gone when a breathless Yuggera bu-ul arrived to say that the dhugai they called Komidi was approaching the sacred ground on his yeraman. He had four others with him, one of them in a red covering. And two more were bringing two animals with bones growing out of their heads.

There was consternation at this news. A strong party of bu-ul was immediately dispatched to ensure that the sacred ground of the kivar-yangga was not profaned. They returned after dark with the tidings that the dhugai had camped for the night only a short distance from the first tree upon whose trunk were the marks that all but shouted to anyone approaching that the penalty for proceeding further was death.

Discussion as to what action to take went on well into the night. Only those whose duty it was to ensure that the young candidates obeyed the law of the kivar-yangga were not present. First one and then another offered suggestions regarding the alternatives available to them, to ensure that the kivar-yangga could proceed to its conclusion on the morrow.

"There is no doubt that the dhugai Komidi can use the thunder!" one reminded them. "We cannot stop him coming on into the sacred ground! Therefore we should leave the making of the marks of manhood until another day!"

But a roar of disapproval drowned him out. That had never happened before, and would not be tolerated this time. The kivar-yangga must proceed as planned.

"Let us make the marks in another place," another suggested. "We could move to another ring in a very short time, even though it hasn't been prepared."

Again a derisive roar silenced this one. Were they men or were they women? The marks would be made at the proper time by the proper officials in the proper place!

But there was no dodging the fact that this dhugai, who was used to roaming over the country of any nation as if it was his own, would probably tomorrow desecrate the sacred ground by bringing his party through. And there was no blinking the fact that his present path would lead him straight toward the ring!

Buruda stood up, and silence descended. He looked across at the makaron sitting uncomfortably near Maltagara, and asked, "Do you know this Komidi, Boraltju?"

"Yau."

Boraltju was finding it hard to meet the eyes of the Undanbi manngur. Buruda suspected that the makaron had already guessed that the questions that were to follow would be awkward in the extreme.

"Can you still speak his language?"

"Y-yau." The answer was given hesitantly.

"Then could you not paint your boomerang white and go and tell him tomorrow that he must not enter the ground that is sacred to the kivar-yangga?"

"Yugara! No! No!" The strangled cry from Boraltju left them all in no doubt that he meant what he said. There was no way he would go and treat with Komidi.

But even Maltagara was nonplussed at his kinsman's vehement refusal. What Buruda had suggested had struck him as a reasonable request. "Why?" he wanted to know. "Why, Boraltju? Surely the white boomerang would protect you!"

By now Boraltju could sense the extremely adverse reaction of the whole meeting to his refusal, and he hastened to explain. "This Komidi is an enemy of mine!" he told Buruda. "He does not know that the white boomerang is a sign of peace! He will kill me!"

And Buruda recognised that in this the makaron was entirely sincere. This Komidi must indeed be an evil one! For a long time he remained standing, thinking, and none interrupted, all waiting silently for what the Undanbi manngur would suggest next.

At length he said, "Tomorrow we must send a number of bu-ul to move the women from the river, for it seems that Komidi, if he keeps on, must cross their path higher up. This must not happen! The women must be kept away at all costs!"

"Yau-ai!"

"It is also vital that the kivar-yangga proceed to its conclusion tomorrow. Turugun and all the manngur with the exception of Maltagara and myself will remain with the kivar, as will half the bu-ul, including all those who are most closely connected with the candidates. These boys must receive their marks with honour tomorrow, for all their lives they must remember the sacredness of the occasion when they reached young manhood! Nothing must be allowed to interfere with that!"

"Yau-ai!" The roar of approval echoed from the surrounding hills.

"The rest of us will meet this Komidi. We will try to turn him back. If we cannot, we will do our utmost to keep him down near the river bank, away from the ring. The ground they will be on will be sacred, but at least we will be keeping them away from the most sacred part of all. And if they will not remain near the river bank, then we must fight! Some of us will die, but we must at all costs keep them from the kivar!"

"Yau-ai!" Spears rattled against shields as battle-fury mounted in his listeners.

After some degree of quiet had again descended, Buruda turned once more to Boraltju. "You can call out to Komidi to go back, when we are all with you to protect you?" he asked.

"Y-yau!" Again the hesitant answer gave some indication of the mortal fear this makaron held for the one camped such a short distance away.

"Then tomorrow that is what we will do. Will this Komidi take warning and go back, do you think?"

"He is afraid of nothing!"

"Then, so be it!"

But even in his mounting anger at the cheek of this makaron who apparently would not listen to reason, Buruda felt a sneaking regard for such a one who would not run from danger. If Komidi had been a bu-ul instead of a makaron, Buruda would have liked to measure himself against him on the baiyaba.

There was still one thing to be said before they slept. "This Komidi," Buruda told them, "is under sentence of death for having a Turrbal skinned and stuffed with grass!" They had all heard of this atrocity, and a low growl greeted the Undanbi manngur's words. "It may therefore be best if we execute this sentence some time on Komidi's present journey! But, for the moment, let us labour under no misapprehension! If Komidi persists in coming forward and enters the sacred ground, his life is forfeit under the law! There is no other course open to us! We may perhaps let those with him go free, for the word is that they must do what the Komidi tells them to do." He looked across at Boraltju, who nodded agreement. "But, in any case, the only way Komidi may return to Miandhin this time will be if he takes our warning tomorrow and turns back!"

"Yau-ai!"

Against such logic there was no answer.

Early next morning Buruda's plan was put into action. A number of bu-ul hurried upstream to take the women and children out of harm's way. Half the remainder made their way downstream to where Komidi's party was camped.

The makaron were already moving forward toward the tree marking the sacred ground, and the hidden bu-ul watched in horror as the party passed the tree without so much as a sideways glance, and then entered the river to cross to their side. With one accord they rose out of the grass that had been hiding them and roared their defiance at Komidi, who had pressed on ahead of the others.

"Tell him!" Buruda said sharply to Boraltju. "Tell him to go back over the water, or he will be killed!"

With a voice that at first quivered, but gradually gained strength, Boraltju called out words that Buruda hoped would be understood by the makaron. Sure enough, Komidi halted the animal he was sitting on – which Buruda promised himself he would study in greater detail later – and called out something in reply.

"What did he say?" Buruda asked.

"He said he will come forward, and won't do us any harm!"

Buruda spat. "Tell him the ground is sacred!"

Once more Boraltju called out, but this time Komidi lashed out at the yeraman, making it rear up and run toward the waiting bu-ul. But he had not taken into account the steepness of the hillside.

With a roar of anger, the men began rolling huge rocks down in front of the yeraman, and those rocks bade fair to take both yeraman and dhugai into the water. Komidi turned tail, followed by a chorus of derisive yells from the hilltop.

Next the red-covered one hurried forward and lifted his thunder-stick to his shoulder. The roar came and, as the stones from the stick were heard crashing through the leaves above their heads, the bu-ul retreated over the brow of the hill. Buruda could not help noticing that Boraltju had led the retreat.

The makaron party continued to advance.

"Komidi will die," Buruda told the waiting bu-ul, "but it will be of no advantage to us if some of us die at the same time! If we can keep them away from the sacred ring, we will have done enough for this day! It is only if they make directly for the ring that we must put ourselves in danger! Let us keep them down near the river if we can!"

All that day they harassed the dhugai party, advancing and retiring as the occasion demanded. At one time, for one heart-rending moment, as the bu-ul stood on the brow of the hill with the kivar ring in sight behind them and the dhugai passing below them, it seemed that Komidi would bring his party in sight of the ring by following more even ground than that afforded by the river bank. But the bu-ul had charged at the crucial moment and had managed to keep Komidi in his place.

But for many seasons the kivar of that ceremony would boast that they had been receiving their marks of manhood at the precise moment when stones from a thunder-stick had been crashing into the trees around the ring! Nor had the hand of any bu-ul engaged in making the marks faltered in any way!

By nightfall the dhugai had put themselves well and truly beyond the sacred ground, and had stopped near the spot where only yesterday the women had been camped. Four bu-ul were detailed to keep watch.

"We have done what we wanted to do," Buruda told them all. "The boys are now kivar. Still, there is more to do. Tomorrow they will be presented to the women. Then there is the baiyaba, which in a kivar-yangga of this size should continue for at least three days. Let us honour these sacred obligations! These makaron will go on further. If they do start to return, the four watchers will send us word in plenty of time. Let us complete the kivar-yangga before we deal with this accursed Komidi!"

The baiyaba was conducted without further molestation from the dhugai. As Buruda had suggested, it lasted a full three days, and in all that time there was no sign that Komidi was on his way back. His party was still camped upstream, and a messenger from the watchers told of how Komidi had gone off on his own from Gunundhin with his yeraman, and had travelled almost as far as Bumgur.

The Dungidau bu-ul rattled their spears at this news. What right had this moi to barge over Dungidau land like that?

Then, as the baiyaba ended, a bu-ul by the name of Kaldhu arrived from the Turrbal. It had been Dimmangali, his brother, he explained to Buruda, whose skin had been placed among the food plants, He wanted the task of killing this Komidi to be left to him.

"You will be there!" Buruda assured him. "But there are some others involved in the kivar-yangga who would feel cheated if they were also not there! This makaron deserves to die, and die he will! Let us all be content with that! Who strikes the fatal blow is not important!"

Then, just as some of the people were beginning to think of returning home, word came at last that Komidi and his party were on their way back.

All that day watchers were set to follow the party. Komidi again went off on his own in mid-afternoon. And it was fortunate that four bu-ul decided to follow him for, although they had expected him to rejoin his party at nightfall, he in fact made solitary camp in one of their own huts very near the sacred ground he had profaned only a few short days before.

Buruda could hardly believe his ears when the news was brought. Komidi on his own! This time the spirits seemed to be on the side of the people! But they would need to wait to take this law-breaker till they could see what they were doing. Attack in the dark was always a chancy business. There must be no chance of escape for this one! Another night was not too long to wait for revenge.

Making no noise, they made haste to a spot not far from the hut, arriving there after the first stars had begun to twinkle. All night they waited, shivering in the cool of the night air, which was always bracing in this place so far from the sea. At times they found themselves envying Komidi his warm hut and the fire smouldering in front of it. But they would put up with much more discomfort than this to ensure that this evil dhugai received justice.

Kaldhu hardly felt the cold. The image of his Dimmangali brother had kept his wrath warm for a long time.

Afterwards, many claimed to have struck the first blow. But Buruda knew that Kaldhu's spear had struck home just as the panic-stricken Komidi, shocked by the sudden appearance of the bu-ul just as he was about to roast some mei, had raced toward his yeraman. And even in the heat of battle, Buruda found it in his heart to admire the iron will of the makaron, who managed to get onto the back of the frightened yeraman even with the spear protruding from his back. But Turugun's throwing-club split the back of the evil one's skull even as the animal rose to jump the gully that separated him from his freedom.

After that, there was much thudding as clubs were brought into play. This Komidi would never stuff another skin, never desecrate another sacred ground. And just as they had finished burying the naked body, a large party of bu-ul raced off to attack the rest of the dhugai party who were approaching.

Although the other dhugai were able to make good their escape, since their thunder-sticks were well in evidence and there was too much open ground to allow the possibility of a surprise attack, the bu-ul were well content. The profanation of their kivar ground had been avenged.

Before he and Turugun left, Buruda examined the yeraman, that strange animal with its beard on the back of its neck, and that was content to let makaron ride on its back. It had not been able to make the jump over the rocky gully, and had fallen with a terrible scream, to be put out of its misery at last with blows from countless clubs.

It smelt strange – like all makaron animals, with the possible exception of the kata. And its bony, toeless feet were so alien that Buruda had to steel himself to touch them. But there was no doubt that it was this animal which had made some of the prints in his dream. The evidence was all around him on the ground. And as he touched the feet, he heard once again in his mind the death-wail of his dream, and his heart sank.

Was there no possibility that some part of his dream would yet prove false?

Notes on Chapter 20

The word for "beard" was "yeran". It is thought that this is the reason why the Aborigines of the region called the horse "yeraman". The town of Yarraman is named after the word for horse.

Boraltju was John Story Baker, a convict who escaped in January, 1826. In the book he has been put at this particular ceremony because there is some evidence that someone did call out to Logan, warning him to go back over the water.

Many historians believe that it was the convicts who were with Logan who killed him, rather than the Aborigines. But there is enough evidence to give the Aborigines the credit for so doing, particularly in view of the fact that he had had the skin of one stuffed as a "scarecrow"! The account of Lt. G. Edwards in a letter written in 1830 also gives weight to the version presented here. Edwards' description points very strongly to the idea that a sacred ceremony was being interrupted.

Chapter 21

1830-1833: More convicts run. Women convicts are moved to Eagle Farm, and they are put to work at the cutting on Hamilton Reach. The Nunakul fight a pitched battle with the soldiers on Stradbroke Island.

Once more the great bunyi feast at Baroon was in progress, and from near and far the nations had gathered to partake again of the largesse of the earth. There was, however, something different about this feast. While to most of the people this difference was not noticeable, to Buruda it screamed aloud of the dangers of changing times – of infiltration into the world of people by the evil spirits who might destroy them.

Turugun was just as concerned as Buruda, and so was Kamkuri. Since the death of the evil Komidi that morning three seasons before, the Undanbi and the Ningi had each sent four more wandering makaron back to the land of the spirits. The Nalbo also had accounted for some – just how many Durbai could not say. And the Turrbal, since their disenchantment with the interlopers over the stuffing of the skin, had killed a number.

Gariwar's reply to a query about numbers had been terse. "Gurwindha!"

Nevertheless, there was about the Turrbal an ambivalence that made Buruda feel uncomfortable. His discomfort owed its existence not only to the inconsistency of the Turrbal regarding their treatment of the makaron, but also to the fact that he could understand this inconsistency. On the one hand, the Turrbal were now much more committed to the idea that dhugai who wandered away from Miandhin or the plant-food place beyond Yowoggera were fair game, and should be dealt with summarily instead of being taken back to their friends. But at the same time, many of the Turrbal bu-ul had apparently taken to wandering about among the dhugai huts and exchanging articles with the dhugai. Or they might simply take the articles, if they happened to be left lying around. Therefore, there were among the Turrbal at the feast a number of these alien articles, particularly knives which had such sharp edges that they could cut the hair of a dhan's beard.

Buruda had tackled Gariwar about this one evening. "Such a knife could give a bu-ul an unfair advantage on the baiyaba!" he said. "Why do your people mix with these makaron?"

And Gariwar had sighed. "You Undanbi don't have dhugai in your country who look as if they are there to stay," he explained. "We do! And their numbers are so great that there is nothing we can do about it! This and their thunder-sticks make them too powerful to drive from our land! So what is there left for us to do but to try to turn their presence to our advantage? What would you do if you were a Turrbal?"

Buruda had had no answer. There was none. He knew Gariwar was already doing all within his power to ensure that the makaron did not take more Turrbal land. All religious obligations were being meticulously fulfilled. Confrontation was out of the question. What more was there to do?

And even though the makaron had not spread out any further during the last three seasons, there were small signs that they might not be content to stay where they were forever. Buruda had visited the Turrbal only four moons before, and had been shocked to see the extent of the destruction in the cliff on the south shore opposite Miandhin. Here the very rocks of the belly of the earth had been pillaged and laid bare. And the bank of the river at Yowoggera, past which the new track led to the makaron camp near Doomben, was in like case. Here the makaron had set their women to digging the rock – for what purpose, no one could tell.

What distorted mind could ever consider digging into rock? There was, after all, no food to be gained there! Besides, the rocks had been laid down in the Before-Time, and were still to this very day the abode of the mighty spirits of that time of creation!

Were these makaron deliberately trying to provoke these mighty beings?

If so, why?

No, Buruda could not find it in his heart to blame the Turrbal for their actions. If the makaron had set up their huts in Undanbi land, he did not doubt that the Undanbi would be just as helpless, and would react in the same way. But that did not stop his skin crawling every time he heard a strange word that was part of the language of the makaron, which the Turrbal were now at times inclined to inject into conversations.

Nor were the Turrbal alone in this. There were at the festival a number of makaron whom the various nations had claimed as their kin, and who were therefore living as dhan of those nations. The Dhindhinbara people had among their numbers a makaron named Daramboi. There was also word that the Tumbra had adopted one, although he had not attended the feast. And the Kombobura had two – Wandi and Moilu. Moilu had even taken a Kombobura wife named Namba. Indeed, it had been Namba who had claimed Moilu as her Dimmangali husband.

Buruda and the Undanbi could find no warmth in their hearts toward these strangers who claimed kin with the people. They had seen too many marks on the backs of too many dead makaron to be easily led into believing that these evil ones were kin to anything other than evil itself! Still, they held their peace. But at the same time they did not indulge in the minute examination given these makaron by many members of the visiting nations. They were just not interested.

However, Turugun did remark to Guluwa one evening, as their little baby boy was busy at her breast, that he thought Moilu was looking somewhat downhearted, and that his wife Namba was far too thin for her own good. "The way she looks," he said, "I would not be surprised if Moilu finds himself with no wife before this moon is finished."

His words proved prophetic. That very evening the death-wail of the Kombobura was heard, and for four days that nation mourned the passing of Moilu's Dimmangali wife. At the end of the fourth day Moilu himself disappeared, and Younmandi sent two Kombobura bu-ul after him to bring him back. They returned after half a day to report that, with the death of his wife, Moilu could no longer bear to stay with his brothers, and was returning to Miandhin to live with the spirits.

Yuonmandi looked downcast at the news, but the Undanbi were pleased to see the back of at least one of the accursed makaron. Piringa even said aloud that it was a pity the other two hadn't joined Moilu in his pilgrimage back to Miandhin. Naruman remarked even more loudly that it was a pity all makaron, especially those at Miandhin, did not leave for the spirit-land!

But unsettling news was also coming from places other than Miandhin. This season the Nunakul were attending the festival, and they brought stories of the red-covered ones at Bulan which, while entertaining in many ways, were nevertheless worrying in the extreme.

It seemed that the red-covered ones had gotten into the habit of visiting the Nunakul women in their camp. This habit had obviously grown out of the generosity first shown by the Nunakul when the degga, as they called them, had first arrived. But, as always seemed to happen where these degga were concerned, the problem was that they could not tell the difference between a privilege and a right. Thus they did not always wait to be asked before they took advantage of the women who, if their men happened to be away fishing, felt powerless in the face of the demands of these degga.

Some of the degga were more unreasonable and importunate than others. By far the worst was one they called Dhurong, and he had made such demands on one of the younger wives of an old bu-ul, that this bu-ul turned up at Bulan one day and threatened Dhurong.

"You keep away from my wife, you dog's turd!" he had yelled, brandishing his spear. "If you don't, this spear will go into your dhun and come out your nulla mumu! We'll see then if you can make my wife lie down on her back for you, you piece of dung!"

The old man had then left, and all seemed to quieten down. But Dhurong had only been biding his time. The next time the old man turned up at Bulan, he had used his thunder-stick, and the husband had fallen down dead.

"Those degga are not to be trusted!" the Nunakul bu-ul who was telling the story had said. "This Dhurong had left the old man's wife alone, and the old man had thought he had learnt his lesson!"

His listeners had cursed at the mention of the makaron's treachery.

"We waited a whole moon," the story-teller had continued. "Then one day, just after we had finished fishing, Dhurong came down to our camp at Pirrenpirrenpa. He seemed to think we had forgotten all about it, and we smiled and offered him the best of our fish. We even emptied all the fish out of our mula so that he could see them better!" The bu-ul had paused for a moment to give greater effect to what was to follow, and then had gone on. "But what he did not know was that nets need to be empty if you are going to throw them over someone's head!"

A great roar of laughter had greeted this piece of information. They had already guessed what had happened to this evil red-covered makaron. The mula had effectively pinioned his arms while the Nunakul bu-ul had used their heavy clubs to good effect. He had been dead within a very short space of time. No more would he molest a woman of the Nunakul or any other nation!

But the sequel to the story had excited even more interest than the death of Dhurong. The Nunakul had composed a dance about it, and this dance proved so popular that they had been forced to perform it on three successive nights.

As they had expected, the other red-covered ones at Bulan had reacted strongly the instant they had learned of Dhurong's death, and had come out in full force against them. But the Nunakul had selected their battle-ground well, their fighting men taking up position south of Kuroignkuroignpa, where there was plenty of deep mud. From the start the red-covered ones had found it hard to keep their footing, as they had been forced to jump from tussock to tussock on the muddy flat. One or two had become stuck so fast that, even in the midst of battle, their friends had been forced to help pull them out. The Nunakul, meanwhile, had been able to use the cover of the mangroves each time they had come forward to hurl their spears. And every time the degga had retaliated by using the thunder, the bu-ul, quite used to the terrain, had been able to melt into the shadows once more, lying flat in the mud while the stones had whistled over their heads.

Buruda and Turugun had looked at each other with delight the first time they had heard this. "You can fight the thunder!" Buruda had remarked triumphantly. "These makaron are not invincible!"

But the Nunakul supply of spears had given out, since the degga had not thrown them back, as would have happened in a normal battle. So they had been reduced to boomerangs and throwing-clubs. A few of the degga had been knocked over, but they had managed to crawl away and return later to the fray with white coverings wrapped round their wounds.

The Nunakul, too, had suffered casualties. One bu-ul had been forced to retire from the battle with a hole in his side, and another had had a piece knocked out of the side of his nose with one of the stones from a thunder-stick.

(At the feast, both these bu-ul became firm favourites in the dance, for they took their own parts in the play. Indeed, the one with part of his nose missing was feted for days because of this deformity gained honourably in battle. Bu-ul of all nations – and women, too – wanted to look more closely at the damage a stone from a makaron thunder-stick could do.)

But to return to the battle:- As the day had worn on and supplies of boomerangs and clubs had also been exhausted, the Nunakul had been reduced to manufacturing makeshift spears on the spot. Feverishly they had used their axes to hack down saplings, which they had then sharpened roughly to points. Then once more they had crept through the reeds, to stand suddenly and hurl the makeshift spears at the enemy, and just as suddenly to drop flat to let the stones whistle harmlessly over their heads. And even while they had been engaged in these manoeuvres, their women had begun breaking off more saplings for them to use in the next charge. Even the older boys had worked frantically to supply the bu-ul with weapons.

All day the battle had continued, with neither side gaining the advantage, Then, as Bigi had sunk below the horizon, the degga had all stood up and called out, "Dhandai! Dhandai! Enough!"

The Nunakul had also had enough and, since honour had been satisfied, they too had stood up. And soon the two parties had mingled. Then they had all walked to Gumpi together, where they had exchanged presents and food.

On the whole, the story of the battle, together with the performance of the dance to commemorate it, made Buruda feel a little more contented. As he explained to the rest of the Undanbi, the Nunakul had proved that the makaron could be fought. Their thunder-sticks were no more effective than spears if you could only come to close quarters with them. Indeed, part of the dance had shown a bu-ul taking shelter behind a tree and emerging unscathed after the makaron had used their thunder-sticks.

Yes, this news was a little more heartening than the news you normally got about the makaron!

And there was another thing, too. The makaron had not fought completely fairly, true. If they had, they would certainly have thrown back the spears, as happened in all battles. But they had nevertheless shown that they could honour a truce at sundown, as all civilised nations did. Nor had they shown any ill-feeling toward the Nunakul since the battle. This lot of makaron seemed to be aware that there had been a balance on both sides as far as damage was concerned.

Perhaps there was, after all, some hope that individual makaron could learn to live with people.

Still, they should never have come without invitation in the first place! No matter which way you looked at it, they were interlopers!

Each night this dance was performed, at its conclusion one of the Nunakul would take a piece of bark and, using it to wrap around some of the stuff given as presents by the makaron, would set it alight and put it in his mouth. He called it "baki". Some of the other bu-ul had been invited to try this new fad, and even Buruda had attempted to breathe in the smoke in the way he was instructed to do. But his lungs had rebelled, and he had refused to try a second time.

A present such as this he could well do without!

At the back of his mind, too, was the uncomfortable thought that the bunyi feast, a time of plenty though it was, was becoming a caricature of its former self, twisted out of all recognition by an all-pervasive fear of the makaron that underlay every vestige of human contact. Where once the talk had been of inter-national rivalry in games, of mighty deeds on the baiyaba, of tales of the Before-Time, of the increase or decrease in animal or plant life – now the talk was only of the evil ones. And whatever you called them – makaron, dhugai, moi or degga – it all came down to the one topic of conversation.

Not that the games didn't continue, or that mighty deeds were no longer mentioned. But somehow, all the games and mighty deeds seemed to be inextricably linked to the makaron.

At this feast, for example, Daramboi had become the focus of attention as he had taken part in the wrestling and other games. But, like Boraltju, there was something about Daramboi that did not ring true. His beard was not as flowing as those of the other Dhindhinbara bu-ul. The marks of manhood were insignificant when compared with those of his brothers. And, although he did manage to distinguish himself in wrestling, it seemed to Buruda to be mainly through subterfuge and trickery that he had prevailed each time.

This Daramboi was a puny individual, hardly reaching the ear of an average bu-ul. It seemed almost as if he had not had enough to eat in his youth, as if his development had been arrested because of famine in the land. Perhaps that was why the spirits were at Miandhin. It could be that there was a great shortage of food in Inglun, the land of the spirits.

At the baiyaba which finished the festival, Daramboi was called out by a Dulingbara bu-ul. He claimed that Daramboi had abused his hospitality by looking lecherously at his wife when he had taken him into his hut for part of the festival. There was a great stir at this challenge, and Buruda found himself interested in spite of himself. How would the Dhindhinbara makaron handle himself?

The contrast between the two contestants was stark. At one end of the baiyaba stood the Dulingbara bu-ul, black and tall and straight, his beard waving in the cool afternoon breeze. At the other end stood Daramboi, pale in comparison and slightly stooped, his rather skimpy brownish beard barely hiding his neck from view. And even in the way they arranged their weapons there was a difference, with Daramboi immediately placing his three spears upright in the ground, while the Dulingbara bu-ul laid his on the ground, deftly picking them up in his toes only after the first flurry of insults had been traded.

This contest was appearing uneven from the start. Turugun, who was the presiding manngur on this the last day of the baiyaba, found himself wondering how this scrawny, undersized creature would last against the magnificent specimen of manhood opposing him. Even the insults lacked balance, the fine oratory of the Dulingbara bu-ul easily surpassing the broken Gubbi phrases used by Daramboi, as he tried unsuccessfully to express himself in a language he had long since forgotten.

Then at last the first spears flew, and a different picture emerged. The Dhindhinbara makaron and his marks of manhood might look unimpressive, but it soon became obvious that he had gained those marks honourably. His spears flew as straight and far as his opponent's, his shield deflecting the missiles just as deftly. And when they eventually flung their shields down to race toward each other and lay about them with their clubs, the smaller man showed he was just as capable of delivering equally powerful blows, and could fend them off as well. In the final bloody moments, as they slashed at each other with their knives, locked together in that deadly embrace, the spectators even got the feeling that, in this unlikely-looking contest, the smaller of the two opponents might be proving slightly superior.

Then, as Turugun at last shouted, "Gubbi!" the makaron broke just as cleanly from the contest as the Dulingbara bu-ul. And he grinned just as broadly at his late enemy.

A loud "E-e-e-e-e-e-e-e!" showed how much the spectators had enjoyed the show. Even Buruda found his opinion changing. Whether or not this makaron had been a member of the Dhindhinbara before his death, there was little doubt that he did deserve the title of Gubbi bu-ul. He had proved himself a dhan indeed.

That night, the final one of the festival, Paldha and the Turrbal bu-ul performed the dance portraying the avenging of the Yuggera women. Each bu-ul took his own part in the dance, which proved extremely entertaining. Just as Paldha had envisaged it on that fateful day three seasons ago, the exaggerated antics of Bagara and his friend as they tried to entice the three dhugai into bringing their canoe closer to shore was hilarious. The spectators howled with laughter and rolled on the ground as the two held imaginary mullet in their hands and greatly overstated the degree to which the corners of their mouths had been drawn back in the attitude of smiling. And the more the spectators reacted, the more the two over-acted. Indeed, it became somewhat difficult for the actors to decide just how to make the change from this shameless burlesque to the final savage denouement. But at last they managed it, and all proclaimed the dance to be an unqualified success.

So once more the feast had been held. But, as at the last two, there had been that shadow hanging over all their heads that had prevented a complete surrender to enjoyment. Rugs, necklaces and dhilla were exchanged, but the final bargains were struck just a little more hurriedly than usual – concluded, as it were, before the last vestige of enjoyment had been drawn from the haggling.

At the back of all their minds was the thought that time was no longer an infinite resource. The makaron might have moved during their absence, and could at this very instant be altering their lives to such an extent that they would nevermore be the same.

They needed to get back to their own country.

Notes on Chapter 21

"Moilu" was John Graham, a convict who absconded in July, 1827. He lived for six years with Yuonmandi, returning to Brisbane in 1833 after the death of his wife Namba.

"Wandi" (meaning "Great Talker") was David Bracewell, a convict who absconded during Logan's time.

"Daramboi" (meaning "Kangaroo Rat") was James Davis, a convict who absconded in 1829 and lived with the Dhindhinbara people and others till 1842, when he returned and was pardoned. Despite many attempts to get him to do so, he could never be persuaded to divulge any secret regarding the "dhur" or man-making ceremony.

The account of the battle on Stradbroke Island is taken from Steele's Brisbane Town in Convict Days 1824-1842.

✦

Chapter 22

1835-36: Tuberculosis and Smallpox break out among the Aborigines. A convict on Stradbroke Island is sentenced to 50 lashes for concealing the venereal disease and communicating it to an Aboriginal girl. Quakers Backhouse and Walker visit Brisbane.

Turugun had made his fire at Warudhra, where he intended to remain until the fingernail moon had turned to the half-ball. Once more he needed a new axe, the old one having become so chipped and ground-down that it was no longer able to perform all the tasks he demanded of it.

"We have had a great deal of bad weather lately," Buruda had said to him as he had left the camp. "Sometimes the markings on the trees guarding the sacred area can become defaced and blurred if flying branches hit them. It would never do for any Undanbi to stumble unwittingly onto the sacred area, for the penalty would be death! And it would be even worse if a stranger, however innocently, managed to come within reach of the stones, for this would result in untold damage to the Undanbi nation!"

So on his way to Warudhra Turugun had turned aside from his family for a time to check on the safety of the stones and to re-mark the weather-worn signs. He had even unwrapped the stones and performed a short form of the ceremony, turning to the four directions as the rite prescribed. In these evil times there could be no harm in once more invoking the protection of the mighty guardian spirits of the Undanbi.

He felt a deep contentment as he worked at grinding the hard black stone he had selected from the bed of the creek. There was something intensely satisfying in the physical labour involved, in feeling his muscles at work as he bent tirelessly over his task. And added to this was the calming influence on his spirit of the almost religious aura surrounding this grinding-place, where dhan had shaped their axe-heads since the Before-Time, as the deep grooves attested.

Out of the corner of his eye he could see Guluwa pounding the bangwal, while little Banawa played in the dirt nearby. The boy's little black body, such a short time ago glistening from the coat of charcoal and goanna grease Guluwa had applied, was fast becoming dull as the dust collected on it.

For a time his hands became still, so lost was he in the idyllic scene before him.

It was good to be with people, he reflected. There was something intensely satisfying in hunting with the dhan, in coming home to a camp noisy with the chatter of women and children, in eating a meal before his hut while the smoke of other fires mingled with his own, in sitting round the great campfire at night to indulge in conversation and enjoy the dancing and singing.

But at times it was also good to be in a quiet place such as this, with only his own family and the smoke of his own fire to contemplate, with only Banawa's squirming and chattering to disturb his meal, with only the deep silence of the bush to share his rapture in Guluwa's body when they eventually sought their sleeping place within the hut.

He noticed that Banawa had begun sucking at Guluwa's breast, and that his wife was looking quizzically across at him. He grinned at her, guessing that she would know his thoughts without being told. And, as his hands once more returned to their task of shaping the axe-head, he marvelled at this uncanny ability of hers. Buruda had once told him that Nerida also possessed this power.

He reflected idly that perhaps this was the way of the spirits of the Undanbi. Perhaps they ensured that their manngur always had the help of superior wives. Certainly this was the case with Buruda and himself. He had not noticed it with the manngur of other nations. Their wives did not seem to stand out from the rest.

He held up the axe-head for closer inspection. It was nearing completion. The two shallow grooves for holding the handle had been completed, and the blade where he had earlier roughly flaked out the shape was approaching the desired smoothness. Tomorrow it would be ready to receive the handle.

Guluwa called out to attract his attention. A man and a woman were approaching from the south along the trading track. Even from this distance he could see the white boomerang in the dhan's belt, so there was no need for him to rush for his weapons. As evening was drawing nigh, he was not surprised to see the two sit down not far away and wait for an invitation to visit. After a suitable time had elapsed, he went over and saw that it was Boldavur of the Badtjala and his wife.

But even while he was extending the invitation to visit his fire, he was shocked to see the difference in this bu-ul. He remembered him from the last bunyi festival as a strong warrior, clear of skin. The man before him looked considerably weaker, and something had happened to his skin, which seemed to be pitted as if somebody had poked him all over with a stick and the dents had refused to come out. Not only that, but the pits were of a lighter colour than the rest of the skin. Even his beard looked patchy.

The skin of his wife was in like case.

After the meal was over, to which the visitors contributed a goanna and some mei cakes, Boldavur told them the answer to the question that they had been too polite to ask. The story was not a cheerful one.

"I have seen you looking at our marks, friends," the Badtjala bu-ul said. "You will remember that when you saw us last we did not look like this. You might also remember that we had two children, a boy and a girl. We have them no more."

Tears gathered in their eyes as they listened.

Boldavur had gone with his family to visit the Turrbal, and had also taken his wife's father, who had relatives in that nation. One night the old man had become very sick, and had become so hot that they had had to keep sprinkling water on him to try to cool him down. His head had also begun aching terribly, and they had kept crushing plenty of leaves of the headache plant so that he could inhale the scent. But since that hadn't seemed to do any good, the old man had begged them to wind his headband more tightly about his scalp, as everybody knew this sometimes helped with a headache. Luckily this had seemed to give him some relief, and he had been able to fall asleep.

Next morning, however, he had become worse, complaining of excruciating pains in the back. At the same time he had begun to vomit, and his bowels had become so loose that they had had to keep replacing the bark under him as it became soiled. No amount of wattle gum had helped to settle his belly. Nor had Gariwar's kundir been able to alleviate the terrible back pain.

This had continued for three whole days, and then they had heaved sighs of relief as the old man had recovered. But their relief had been short-lived, for next day the two children had gone down with the same terrible pain. At the same time they had noticed that hard pimples had begun to appear on the old man's face and forearms, and he had once more become extremely hot. Within a very short time these pimples had covered his whole body.

Bodavur took a deep breath, and his wife began to moan, swaying from side to side, as he continued his story.

The two children had just seemed to be getting better when the old man's pimples had filled with pus, and he had found great difficulty in breathing. Then he had died. Their Turrbal friends had hurried to bury him - for this was the way of the Badtjala. Besides, the Turrbal were anxious to get rid of the body as soon as possible. They had not been able to remember a similar death, with the body apparently beginning to decay while it still contained life. They could have understood if there had been a bad spear wound with the spear-point left in, for in some such cases there was a rotting of the flesh before death. But never before had there been such a strange case as this.

Horrified, Turugun realised that what he was hearing bore a strong resemblance to the description Buruda had given of some of the dead bodies in his dream.

But Boldavur had more to tell. "The children died just as the old man had died, and as we buried them I could feel the sickness coming on me." He shook his head in disbelief. "I could not imagine such pain as I suffered! I have been in many battles, as you know. But the pain of a spear wound is as nothing to the pain I felt in my back when the pimples came!"

Gariwar had by now decided that it was time to destroy the influence of the evil spirits causing the sickness, and had burnt the hut in which the old man and the children had died. The Turrbal women had helped Bodavur's wife build another hut, and then the Turrbal had left, fleeing that place of corruption and death.

"I do not blame them," Boldavur said. "When evil spirits are abroad, it is necessary to do all in your power to save your people from their influence. Gariwar and his people did what they had to do. I hope they managed to escape the evil spirits."

Turugun was aghast. "You don't know if they did?"

"No. We haven't seen them since. I lay there close to death for I don't know how long, while my wife made me eat bangwal, even when my stomach rebelled. I don't remember much, except that at one stage my wundu swelled horribly and I had to scream with the pain. I can tell you that there is no pain like it at the kivar-yangga or the dhur!"

Luckily Boldavur had begun to recover and his scabs had begun to fall off by the time his wife had succumbed to the sickness. The evil spirits must have lost some of their strength by then, for she had not been quite as ill as he had been. For days he had dragged himself around, tending his wife and foraging for food when he could.

"It is a full moon since the scabs fell away from me," he said, "and I am feeling almost as well as I did before. Four days ago we burnt our hut and left. We are travelling slowly back to Badtjala country."

"It will be wonderful to feel our own soil under our feet once more!" his wife added, and then commenced moaning again. "But our lovely Dimmangali children and my Dimmangali father will never again feel the warmth of Badtjala land!"

There was great meaning in the cry for the dead in the small group that evening.

Boldavur had other news of the Turrbal that was also disquieting. "There seems to be a sickness among them that makes them cough until they don't seem to have the strength to cough any more," he told them. "I saw three or four bu-ul and a couple of women who were coughing all the time, and even a couple of children. One was coughing blood. I have never seen anything like this before. This sickness seems to make them very thin."

The two Badtjala left next morning to resume their homeward journey, and Turugun hastened to return to the Undanbi camp with his family. The final grinding of his axe could be done on the grinding stones at Caloundra. But the axe was not as important as getting word to Buruda. Was this sickness described by Boldavur the one that was to cause the death-wail of Buruda's dream?

Turugun's news greatly unsettled Buruda. It was almost as if he could smell death in the wind, particularly when it came from the south. Again he saw the twisted masses of suppurating flesh, smelt the stench of corruption, heard the death-wail of his dream. What Boldavur had described was too close to what he had seen in his dream for comfort.

There was now nothing in his dream that was closed to the knowledge of women, so there was no point in excluding them from the discussions that must follow. Guluwa already knew about the deaths from the sores, and by now all the women would have heard about them.

That night there was a meeting of the whole nation round the great campfire, and Turugun told them what Boldavur had experienced. When he described the pit-marks in the skin of the two Badtjala people, and of how the old man and the children had died, there were exclamations of horror.

"What can we do to stop this sickness coming to the Undanbi?" they wanted to know. "What is the cause of it?"

Buruda let Turugun explain. After all, the young manngur knew more about it than he himself did, since he had seen the marks left by the sickness. And they were both agreed as to its cause.

"Since the Before-Time," Turugun said, "there has never been a sickness like this one. Only evil spirits could cause such a sickness as this, and so it is to the makaron that we must look for its cause! Just how they do it we can't tell. Perhaps they sang the Badtjala Dimmangali man and children to death. Perhaps they are in touch with evil spirits in the land of the dead, and bring invisible ones in their canoes from Inglun, as well as those we can see. But however they do it, there is no doubt they are to blame!"

Naruman stood up and yelled, "The Turrbal have been too kind to the makaron! They should use every opportunity to kill them! And so should the Nunakul! There is altogether too much talk of friendship, as I told them only a moon ago!"

Naruman had only just returned from a visit to the Nunakul at Bulan, where he had taken part in a kivar-yangga. He had steadfastly refused to have anything to do with the makaron – or the "degga", as they persisted in calling them. Indeed, he had had the temerity to tell his host one night that he ought to be ashamed of himself for comforting the makaron with his wife. The fact that his host had afforded him the same comfort hadn't made any difference to Naruman!

Buruda had heard that Naruman had not been the most popular guest at the Nunakul ceremony. A fine bu-ul and thoughtful husband he might be. And Naruman had also shown that he was a wonderful provider, finding no trouble in procuring enough food, even though he had taken Damira as a second wife three moons ago. But he was just too forthright for words.

Bulangga, his grey beard shaking with indignation, rose and faced Naruman. "And how, might we ask, do you think the Turrbal should go about this extermination of the makaron? There are more makaron at Miandhin than there are people at a bunyi festival! And they have thunder-sticks, too!"

Piringa stood up for Naruman, however, pointing out that he had not suggested killing off all the makaron – only killing when the opportunity arose.

"The Turrbal are already killing those who wander off!" Dhubal said. "More they cannot do!"

So the talk went back and forth. Generally they had all agreed that the mistake had been made in the very beginning, when the numbers of makaron might have made it possible to kill many and drive the others off. But it was too late now. Now only magic could help. The manngur should all seek the help of benevolent spirits.

"We are already doing so – Gariwar as much as the rest of us," Turugun pointed out.

"Maybe Naruman is right as far as the Nunakul are concerned," Wungul remarked. "There are not too many at Bulan and Gumpi to drive off."

"But they keep coming in their canoes!" Naruman grudgingly admitted. He was remembering the arguments the Nunakul themselves had levelled at him. "It would be hard to get rid of them. The Nunakul have already fought them, and didn't kill any. And even if they had killed a few, the makaron would simply have brought more red-covered ones from Miandhin, and many Nunakul would have died."

Then the women had their say. Let the makaron keep to themselves and not force themselves on the women! Not only was it against the law to force women in this way, but it was also degrading and shameful to have to lie with another of uncertain skin!

"And the Nunakul should stop giving comfort to the makaron by letting them have their wives! Naruman was right there!" Ngita called out.

But another said it was the business of the Nunakul, and what harm could there be in that, apart from the fact that nobody knew the skin of any makaron?

Then Buruda rose to speak. "Everything you say makes sense," he told them. "But we are here to talk about ways and means of stopping the makaron using their magic against the people to bring sicknesses such as the one Turugun told us about. This sickness is something that I have been waiting to see, for you are all aware – even the women now – that a long time ago I had a dream that foretold the coming of the makaron, the bringing in of their strange animals, and this terrible sickness. We have got used to their thunder-sticks, and have heard from the Nunakul how we might stand up in battle, even against the red-covered ones. But we do not yet know how to stop the sickness-making magic. We do not even know how they work it. If we did, we might be able to do something about it."

Again he sat down, and silence followed. Nobody could suggest how the makaron worked their magic. The manngur should know more about such things than ordinary people.

Turugun stood up once more. He had had time to think. "Gariwar argued at the bunyi feast that his bu-ul had every right to go amongst the makaron at Miandhin to take advantage of trading opportunities," he reminded them. "It seems to me that it is only by close contact such as this that we have a chance of finding out how these evil spirits operate. I will travel to Miandhin tomorrow and talk to Gariwar. He may know something already. I may even go among the makaron myself to try to find out how they perform this magic."

Bulangga pointed out that there was no guarantee that Gariwar and his people were still there, and a long shudder shook the whole of the audience at the thought of this grim possibility. Surely this couldn't happen!

Buruda said, "We must just hope that that is not the case. If Boldavur and his wife managed to get better, then surely some of the Turrbal would escape. No, friends, let us not look upon such possibilities until they are really upon us! Gariwar is a very astute manngur, and I think we can trust him to find ways of averting danger threatening his people." He turned his attention to Turugun. "You have spoken well. But it is the older manngur who should look into this business. I will journey to Miandhin myself."

Turugun knew that Buruda was trying to ensure that he did not run into danger at the camp of the makaron, but he did not argue. There was a lot of sense in having the older and wiser manngur at Miandhin. Things which might escape the notice of a less experienced bu-ul would not be missed by Buruda.

Before he sought his hut that night, Buruda talked with Naruman. He had noticed in the firelight, when Naruman had stood to speak, that he had a greyish sore on his dhun. He was fearful that it, too, might have something to do with the sickness the Badtjala family had suffered. And as he also remembered that some of the bodies in his dream had had such chancres on their dhun, he was terrified that this death-sickness might already be among the Undanbi.

But Naruman shrugged it off. "I must have got a splinter in my dhun," he told Buruda. "A pimple came there a few days ago, and then it burst." He laughed. "I can hardly feel it, even when I lie with Damira at night."

Buruda was relieved. There was no doubt that Naruman did not look sick at all, so this must be something quite different from the Badtjala sickness. Naruman was probably right. He must have got a splinter there - although how any bu-ul in his right mind could allow this to happen was beyond Buruda.

But at the back of his mind was a nagging doubt. Naruman would not die from a small sore like that, certainly. But why had his dream shown him similar sores on dead bodies?

Gariwar was glad to hear from Buruda that Boldavur and his wife had survived. The Turrbal had kept clear of that camping spot since the deaths, and would not return there for many moons.

"After we left them, one of our families went down with the same sort of sickness," he told Buruda. "The council of the bu-ul discussed what was best for us to do, and the father of the family advised us to leave them, as we had left the Badtjala. It was his daughter who had become ill, and he urged us to let him and his wife attend to the girl themselves. He argued that the evil spirits in the girl might kill her, or go. But if we stayed there, it might escape from her body and do damage to many more people." He shook his head. "We did not like leaving them, but of course he was right. We haven't heard from them since, so we think they must have died. We have not gone back to the place to bury them, for the evil spirit could still be searching for other people to enter. I think we will wait a full season before we try to find their bones and give them burial."

Buruda's heart felt heavy. Just to be at Miandhin and to see the deterioration there since his last visit was extremely depressing. The Turrbal had certainly borne the brunt of the trouble brought by the makaron.

He said, "My friend, I am here to see if there is something we can find out about how the makaron are getting these evil spirits to cause sickness. Last time I saw you, you told me that some of your bu-ul make periodic visits to the camp at Miandhin for trading purposes. Do you think one of these bu-ul would take me there?"

In the end, three men accompanied Buruda. As soon as they heard what he was after, Bagara, Paldha and Kaldhu had eagerly offered their services. They seemed quite eager to be guides to the well-known Undanbi manngur. It would be a novelty for them to be able to teach this wise one something they knew and he didn't.

So for the first time Buruda found himself close to the heart of all the evil, and even the assurances of his three companions were hardly sufficient to calm his fears. Kaldhu said he had been here often and that these dhugai were friendly enough, although he didn't always understand what they were doing. Paldha had been there only once before, but no harm had come to him, and he had been able to procure the blade of some sort of implement that had proved to be a marvellous thing for getting bark off trees. Who knew – today they might get some other valuable thing! Bagara was quite nonchalant about the whole affair, strolling between the huts and pointing out the food plants as if everything belonged to him.

They noticed that great crowds of the makaron were converging on one of the larger huts. There were red-covered ones with their thunder-sticks, as well as the ordinary makaron with the downcast expressions. But Buruda was most interested in others who had things round their ankles that clanked as they walked, and which they apparently had to hold up in front of them to allow them to move. He had seen these before from a distance. They looked much worse close up.

Kaldhu noticed Buruda's look of horror. "You get used to those!" he assured him. "There are lots of them around. I don't see why they have those things – but that is what the dhugai are like!"

To Buruda they looked nothing like ornaments, as he had once believed them to be. They filled his mind with a sense of hopelessness. What sort of creatures would allow their brothers to walk round encumbered like this?

The large track they were on suddenly seemed empty. Then two black-covered makaron approached, accompanied by an important-looking one, and another covered in a long flowing covering. Buruda was interested in this covering, since it looked for all the world as if the makaron in it was carrying round a small hut.

Again Kaldhu noticed his puzzled look, and laughed. "That is one of their women!" he said.

A woman? Surely not! Where were her breasts? Buruda wondered if Kaldhu was joking.

Then one of the black-covered makaron smiled at the four bu-ul and signed for them to enter the big hut. Buruda felt he wanted to run, but Kaldhu did not hesitate. "Come on!" he urged his companions. "They are friendly enough if you don't take their tools or try to get at their food plants!"

The remaining time at Miandhin seemed like a bad dream to Buruda. It was only by the exertion of a great deal of determined self-control that he was able to force himself to remain within this alien hut with the stench of the makaron in his nostrils.

And what happened inside the hut made no sense at all, and even the experienced Kaldhu could later shed no light on what the makaron had been about. It was obviously some sort of meeting, but unlike any other meeting Buruda had ever been to. There seemed to be a rule at this meeting that only certain makaron could speak. First the important-looking makaron spoke at length to the others, who were all sitting down on what looked like some logs facing in the one direction. Surely they should have been sitting in a circle, so that everyone should have a chance to speak! But no! After the important-looking makaron had spoken, one of the black-covered ones got up and went on and on for a long time, while all the others stared intently at him, saying nothing!

Did they not have an opinion of any kind?

At last this black-covered one sat down, and nobody seemed to move for a long time.

Despite the discomfort in the situation, Buruda felt that this might be the time to get answers to his questions. So he called out from where he was standing, "What are you all doing here? Is this the place where you cast spells to bring sickness to the people? If not, where do you weave these wicked spells? Where do you commune with your evil spirits? And why do you want to bring harm on the people, in any case?"

Buruda was pleased to see that they all looked at him as he spoke. The two black-covered ones looked at him in a friendly fashion, and then asked something of the first speaker, who only shrugged his shoulders.

But he was not pleased to see the broad grins on the faces of many of the rest of the makaron. Even the red-covered ones had these grins, and they gave him the impression that they were not looking at him in a friendly fashion, but rather as if he were a figure of scorn.

One of the black-covered ones said something in reply to Buruda, but he could not make out the meaning.

Once more he tried. "Do you have anybody here who speaks in a language people understand?" he asked. "Tell us what you are doing!" He pointed to the black-covered one who had beckoned them in in the first place. "Why did you ask us to come into this hut if you are not going to show us something?"

But it was all useless. Kaldhu added his pleas to Buruda's, only to be met with the same blank looks that showed a complete lack of understanding.

"Let us leave!" Buruda said finally in exasperation. "We will learn nothing here!"

He was sorely tempted to use his spears on the ribs of some of these rude grinners!

His visit to Miandhin had been fruitless. If makaron behaved in this strange way, where those covered in certain colours could speak while others in other colours could not, what did it all mean? Why did they put those heavy things on the legs of some, and not others? Why did they invite you into a hut, and then ignore you while they spoke to others? Why had they all gone into the hut in the first place? Could they not have held their meeting out in the fresh air, where their stench would not be so noticeable, and where more of their kind might have had a chance to speak?

As he said to Gariwar, if that was the way they cast their spells, he did not see how those spells could ever be effective! There was no sense to anything he had seen!

But perhaps worse than his inability to understand what had gone on inside the hut was the despondency he had felt when he had seen the two thin Turrbal bu-ul who were suffering from the cough. His heart bled for the Turrbal manngur, who admitted that he had no answer to this scourge that made some people so sick. Luckily not many people had the cough.

Birral grant that no Undanbi would ever cough like that!

Notes on Chapter 22

In Brisbane Town in Convict Days. 1824-1842 Steele mentions the fact that, while the Quakers Backhouse and Walker were giving a service in the barracks, a few Aborigines came into the barracks, and seemed to want to know what was going forward, but nobody could interpret into their language.

Chapter 23

1836: The *Stirling Castle* is wrecked on Fraser Island. Eliza Fraser is "rescued" from the Aborigines by Moilu, assisted by Wandi.

The first thing Buruda did after he returned from Miandhin was to seek out Naruman. The similarity between the sore on Naruman's dhun and those he had seen in his dream had continued to prey on his mind. His dream had not been wrong before in any detail. He only hoped that in this case it might be found wanting.

To his great relief he found Naruman bouncing with energy. The ulcer on his dhun had almost healed, and Naruman laughed at his concern. "I told you it was nothing, Buruda!" he scoffed. "The splinter must be out now, and it's almost better. It gave me no pain at any time. But I'll be more careful of my dhun from now on! There are better uses for it than putting it in the way of splinters!"

Both Garwidha and Damira kept their eyes modestly downcast as their husband said this, but could not totally suppress their giggles. Both of them appreciated Naruman's use of his dhun!

Once again Buruda found himself contentedly becoming lost in the easy tempo of life in the Undanbi camp. With such a life it was easy to put to the back of his mind the problems associated with the makaron. But he knew this was not the case with other nations. The Turrbal were confronted almost daily with evidence of the devastation caused by these interlopers. Even the Dhundubari were seeing more of them, as small parties of makaron now frequently visited Yarun to catch fish with their cords. But Undanbi soil was still unsullied by the taint of their presence, and the deep throbbing pulse of the earth could still be felt by those who listened, as day followed day, with men and women involved in tasks that had been the lot of people since the Before-Time. And children still ran squealing about the camp, free of restraint until the time came for them to take up the responsibility of adulthood.

It was good to be alive.

Then, as the moon once more became a fingernail, so thin it was scarcely visible in the evening sky, Naruman fell ill. One day he did not turn up with his mula as usual to take part in the fishing. Buruda lost no time in getting Turugun and hurrying to Naruman's hut. They found him lying on his bed of dibing bark, groaning.

When Naruman spoke, his voice was hoarse. "I have a terrible headache and sore throat," he grated. "My bones are all aching, and I feel hot, too!"

Turugun was concerned. These were some of the things that had been wrong with the Badtjala and Turrbal families before they had died, when their bodies had started to decay even while they were yet alive. Was this the same illness?

There was no doubt that Naruman was hot. Within the hut the heat from his body was palpable. Even in the coolness of the air in this season of wallaidhau he needed no covering, and was sweating profusely. But it was the pain in his joints that seemed to be causing him most trouble. Groaning loudly, he lifted his arm to show the two manngur how difficult it was with the pain in his shoulder.

"You have a lump under your arm!" Turugun remarked.

"Under both arms, and in my groin as well!" Naruman groaned.

The air within the hut was heavy with the scent of the crushed leaves of the headache plant that Garwidha and Damira had used to try to ease the pain in his head which, he said, was not as bad as it had been since they had tightened his headband. And his throat was a little easier since he had chewed the guligba leaves they had brought him.

"But my accursed bones!" he complained. "Why won't they stop aching?"

Garwidha's second little boy of four summers ran into the hut, and Naruman groaned for her to send him away. "He makes my bones feel worse!" he explained.

Buruda took hold of the sick man's hand to comfort him, and a startled look came over the manngur's face. He could feel tiny hard pieces in the palm of the hand. Turning it over, he could just make out a rash similar to that caused by the sting of the gimpi tree – only these were brownish instead of red. Nor had he ever known the rash caused by the gimpi to bring up these little hard pieces beneath the skin. It was for all the world as if someone had put tiny grains of sand under the skin.

The other hand was the same.

"Where did you get these?" he wanted to know.

"I don't know," Naruman moaned, "but they are all right! They don't hurt at all! It's my bones that need fixing!"

The two manngur spoke together for some time. Buruda asked Turugun to recall precisely what Boldavur had told him, in case there was anything he had missed. Then they compared the sickness of the Badtjala family with what Naruman had told them. There were many similarities, but they did not seem to be identical.

"The heat is there," Turugun said, "and the headache, too. But they said there were terrible pains in the back, whereas Naruman says they are in his bones."

"True. But there are still these marks on the hand. They could spread further. This may yet be the scab disease of the Badtjala."

Naruman groaned when he heard this, and his two wives held their hands to their mouths in dismay. Full well they knew what the dreaded scab sickness could do!

"Yet this has one more thing," Buruda said. "Just over a moon ago Naruman had a sore on his dhun." He showed Turugun the small scar. "I don't know whether that is connected with this sickness or not. But it could be that it is not the scab disease."

Later, in private, he would tell Turugun about the chancres on the dhun of the dead bodies in his dream. Naruman and his two wives might draw some hope from this difference when compared with the scab disease, but Buruda himself was filled with foreboding.

They used their kundir stones, passing them over the affected parts of the sick man's body. Such treatment was often effective when all else failed, for it afforded the sick man the protection of benevolent spirits. Then, since it was fairly obvious that this sickness had been caused by the makaron – for only evil spirits could have introduced the small things beneath the skin on the palms of both hands – they put green bushes on the fire in front of the hut opening. The dense smoke would assist in driving out the evil from the sick man's body and all the area surrounding the hut.

Then came the part that Buruda had been dreading, but which he had known from the start he would have to do. "Gariwar of the Turrbal," he told Naruman and his two wives, "saved his people by moving away from the huts of the families that had the scab sickness. The evil spirits could not find their way to the rest of the Turrbal, and had to be content with killing the old man, the Badtjala children, and one family of the Turrbal." He put a hand on Naruman's shoulder, withdrawing it quickly as the bu-ul winced at the pain of even this slight touch. "It may be that this is not the scab sickness, that it is something that will go away now that we have used the kundir stones and the smoke. But the good of the people must come first, and we will all leave for Currimundi as soon as we can. You and your family will stay here."

At this Damira began to wail and rock back and forth, tears cascading down her cheeks.

Buruda placed a kindly hand on her head. "Your family will not be left completely alone," he told her. "We dare not take any risks for the sake of the people. But every afternoon a bu-ul will leave something for you to eat at the spot where the women camp when we hold a dhur at Caloundra." He turned to Garwidha. "Your eldest son will go there every afternoon before the bu-ul arrives, and he will leave a sign for us. He will place a stone in a line for every one of you who is sick. If there is only one stone, we will know that only one is sick, and so on. And if everyone is well, he will put four stones like this."

Bending down, he placed four stones in the form of a square, one at each corner.

Garwidha nodded her understanding. She was pleased Buruda was not deserting them completely. Even Damira had stopped her wailing.

"But," Buruda warned them, "your boy will go back two spear-throws from the stones and hide behind a tree before the bu-ul arrives each afternoon. If he does not do this, no bu-ul will visit the place again, and it could be many moons before we return to this camp! We dare not risk the safety of the people in any way! No doubt, unless we have already succeeded in driving the evil spirits away, they will try to follow the people and do them harm! We must make sure they do not find us!"

The people cast many backward glances at the forlorn little group of two women and two boys standing near Naruman's hut as they left the camp near the creek and turned north toward Currimundi. Would they ever see their friends alive again?

For three days the messenger returned to them at Currimundi with the news that there was still only one person sick. On the fourth day there was great jubilation as they heard that all were well. And for the next four days, the same good news was hailed with joy. There was even talk of returning to the camp where the lonely little group would undoubtedly be longing for the companionship of their friends.

But Buruda warned them against too much optimism. "Turugun has told you", he reminded them, "that in the case of the scab sickness the old Badtjala man and the two children each thought they had recovered before the worst came! Let us hope that Naruman is really better, and that no other persons in his family become sick. But we will wait longer before we return, just the same!"

They waited a full half-moon further before the two manngur decided that the four stones had been in place long enough to signify that Naruman had really recovered.

What rejoicing there was when, upon their return, they found that Naruman was as robust as he had ever been. He explained that the pains had disappeared as if by magic three days after his treatment with the kundir stones and the smoke. "I went to sleep one night feeling not quite so bad," he explained to the two manngur. "The next morning I woke up feeling as well as I'd ever felt!"

But they examined him carefully just the same, paying particular attention to his hands and armpits. Naruman was right. There was no trace remaining of lumps or hard rashes.

"The best thing about this," Buruda later said to Turugun, "is that none of the others got sick at all. Maybe my dream was wrong about sores on the dhun. Perhaps the makaron can't hurt us too much with these."

Nevertheless, they determined that they would follow the same course of action if ever anybody else showed signs of these sores and lumps. You could not be too careful where the safety of the people was concerned.

Wungul was inordinately proud of his favourite son. Bunbithin had for the past season shown increasing signs of body-hair growth and, since the Nalbo, Dallambara and Ningi also had lads old enough to be put to the test, the Undanbi had sent word to these nations inviting them to a kivar-yangga to be held near the trading track in the vicinity of the Nalbo mountains. Wungul and Buruda had chosen this spot because of the fact that it was near this ceremonial ring that Bunbithin's spirit had first entered Nerida's body.

And what a lad Bunbithin was! He was already as tall as a bu-ul, and his arm could hurl a boomerang or spear as accurately and as far as most of those many years his senior. Besides, his eye could discern the signs showing the passing of an animal long after they had ceased to be visible to many bu-ul. He was a pupil to make his mentor proud.

Everything had gone smoothly at the ceremony. Nerida had held onto her son with just the right degree of protectiveness as Ngalumun, the Dallambara manngur, had fought to tear him from her grasp. And in the ring the boy had stood up to the tests as well as any boy had ever done. Now the marks of young manhood stood out proudly on his chest, and Wungul's own chest had swelled as he had presented him finally to the women.

The young Bunbithin had gone, and in his place stood a young man with a different name. Wungul's eyes filled with tears of pride as, in response to his challenge, the women boomed out the new name, "Kaldaru!"

Like Turugun before him, this young kivar performed so creditably on the baiyaba following the kivar-yangga that no other kivar could come near him – even those who had been kivar for two or three seasons.

How could there be another so like Turugun and Buruda? people asked. These Undanbi were formidable dhan indeed!

The return to the camp on the creek was triumphant. But, as with most ceremonies since the makaron had arrived, they found that even on this joyous occasion there had been problems.

Like most nations in these troubled times, the Undanbi had fallen into the habit of leaving some families behind in their most-used camping-spot during ceremonial occasions, just in case the makaron suddenly appeared in their land. This time Bulangga and

Dhubal had stayed behind with their wives. These two, though their beards were grey and their arms not as strong as in their youth, could still give a good account of themselves in a fight. Not only that, but they could still have made it quickly to the kivar ground if it had become necessary.

While it had not been necessary to send a message to the ceremonial grounds this time, much had been happening. Halfway through the time of the ceremony a group of Tumbra had arrived at the camp with four makaron who had been passed on from nation to nation from K'Gari to the north. The Tumbra had wanted Bulangga to take charge of the four and pass them on to the Dhundubari, but the old man had refused, pointing out that he and Dhubal were acting as caretakers during the kivar-yangga. The Tumbra had therefore crossed to Yarun themselves and taken the makaron down the ocean beach.

"You did not kill these makaron?" Naruman wanted to know.

But Bulangga was in no mood for Naruman's bluster. "What would you have done, when the Tumbra were carrying white boomerangs?" he asked testily, and Naruman looked at the ground, crestfallen. "Besides, these makaron were in poor condition, and it is not in the nature of Undanbi bu-ul to kill those so obviously in need of sustenance!"

Two days later another makaron had been brought south by another Tumbra. This man's feet were in a sad condition, and he had been met by another makaron as soon as he had been taken over to Yarun.

"The one who met him was from Miandhin," Dhubal explained. "He had apparently been fishing on the southern part of Yarun when the other emaciated makaron had arrived, and this fisherman had walked north to meet this last one."

Naruman couldn't help muttering that the Dhundubari ought to be ashamed of themselves, letting the makaron come and go as they pleased, just as if they were friends! And Buruda thought that Naruman was probably right. There was something very dangerous about letting the makaron take liberties. The Ningi had shown what ought to be done when they had attacked the interlopers at every opportunity. The Turrbal could do nothing about the makaron because of their vast superiority in numbers. The Nunakul were aware that any attack would be met with the bringing in of more red-covered ones from Miandhin. But what excuse did the Dhundubari have? None, except that they themselves were friendly people who had suffered no harm at the hands of the makaron. But then they had always been ready to see the best in the makaron – right from the time of Pamplet, Pinigan and Pardhen.

Still, it was fruitless thinking this way. The Dhundubari were a nation on their own, and would do what they thought was best, as all nations did.

From what Bulangga and Dhubal could tell them, it was obvious that the time of the ceremony had seen exciting times for the nations to the north. It appeared that a number of makaron, one of whom was a woman, had beached their canoe somewhere near Binngi on K'Gari. Some of them had left to walk south and these, obviously in need of assistance, had been handed from the Ngulungbara to the Badtjala, and thence to the Dulingbara. Trying to cross from K'Gari to Karah, two had drowned. The rest had been taken across by canoe and eventually handed over to the Kombobura, who had then passed them on to the Tumbra.

"But the woman!" Dhubal said. "The Tumbra had it from those further north that the Badtjala, who ended up with her, were sorry they had ever clapped eyes on her! They rubbed her with charcoal and goanna grease to save her from the mosquitoes and to make her a more acceptable colour, and she screamed every time they did it! They gave her tasks to perform that every woman does, and she screamed at them for getting her to do them! When they couldn't help smiling because she always seemed to have to bend over to pick up sticks for the fire, instead of using her toes to save her back, she screamed at them! Nothing they did seemed to please her!'

Bulangga took up the story. "There was a makaron with them who had such a fat belly that they say it hung down almost below his dhun. He was weak from the start, and died soon after the Badtjala took him in. And this screaming woman seemed to blame the Badtjala for his death, even though they had given him food and tried to get him to see that he would feel much better if he moved around more, instead of sitting down all the time!"

Truly there was no understanding the ways of the makaron. But this woman seemed even worse than the others they had seen, if the Badtjala were to be believed.

"The Tumbra think the Badtjala have handed her over to the Kombobura," Dhubal said.

Buruda smiled to himself. He wondered how Younmandi would cope with this termagant.

Half a moon later they learnt that the woman was again back with the other makaron. She had apparently been Moilu's wife, the one who had died at the time of the bunyi feast, and Moilu had come back from Miandhin to tell Yuonmandi he wanted her back, as he couldn't live without her. But Moilu had tricked Yuonmandi by taking her away from the Kombobura by night. And it seemed that Wandi had also helped in the deception!

Whether or not Yuonmandi was worried that the woman had been spirited away, their informant couldn't say. But Buruda was of the opinion, from what he had heard of the woman, that the Kombobura manngur would have been pleased to see the back of her.

The stir caused by these events had hardly subsided when there was a dhur held at Gullirae, and the highlight of the festival following the ceremony was the performance of a dance the Badtjala had made to commemorate the arrival and departure of the screaming woman, as they called her. All the nations present were so entertained by the consummate acting of the performers that they were forced to perform it every night. Buruda noticed that Yuonmandi was just as amused as anyone else, rolling about helplessly on the ground as he roared laughing. So probably he had been quite pleased to see Moilu's wife disappear.

But, Buruda reflected, in a way it was very strange. Moilu's wife had been nothing like that when he had seen her at the bunyi feast.

On the final night, after one of the performances, Damira told Naruman and Garwidha that she had felt a spirit enter her body just as she had been passing a small stone on her way to fetch water in her pikki that morning. So the little family that had such a short time before been face to face with possible annihilation was overjoyed. They wondered whether it would be a boy or a girl. Garwidha hoped it would be a girl. She already had two boys, and it would be nice to have a little girl to bring balance to the family.

Although the Dhundubari had had no kivar ready to enter manhood, Nganku had been invited. He took the opportunity to talk long and earnestly with the other manngur, and his talk was disquieting. He had heard that the Nunakul had had more than their fair share of still-births lately. Just what sort of baby had been emerging from the binang of the Nunakul women he couldn't say, since the women themselves had been very secretive about it, saying only that the babies had been born dead. But there had been murmurs of monstrous things so that, from all accounts, the Nunakul women were no longer crying with joy when they felt a spirit enter them, but instead were fearful of what the birth might bring.

No matter how much Buruda pressed him for more information, Nganku could tell no more. That was all he had heard, and the Dhundubari woman who had passed the information on to him had been reluctant to tell him even this. Birth was the business of women, and only when death threatened did it ever become the business of the manngur.

But Buruda's hair had risen on the back of his neck as he had listened. This was without a doubt some more work of the makaron!

When would they leave the people in peace?

Notes on Chapter 23

There is a monument to Eliza Fraser on the shores of Lake Cootharaba. The exact place where the Aborigines were camped when Graham took her away is slightly beyond the northern end of the lake. Graham told the Aborigines she was his dead wife returned to life. He took her away during the dancing at night. After her rescue, Eliza Fraser took to the stage to tell her story. She seems to have had a very lively imagination, and embroidered her tale to make it interesting enough to make money for her. Some writers say that the attacks that were made on Aborigines of the area from that time on can be attributed to the lies she told about the way she had been treated.

✦

Chapter 24

1837-1838: The first steamer ("*James Watt*") arrives at Dunwich. It brings Andrew Petrie and his family to the colony. Dr. Lang brings German missionaries to Humpybong. They move to Nundah very soon after their arrival, for the Aborigines at Humpybong prove hostile.

The expression on Garwidha's face was enough to tell Nerida that something had gone badly wrong.

At that instant there was the cry of an infant, and Damira looked down excitedly into the hole lined with dibing bark beneath her feet. Her face assumed a sudden blank appearance. Then the three women froze in horror.

This baby was not right! It was a girl, true – but such a girl as you would meet only in nightmares! The head was normal. But the body! The belly was so large that it poked out beyond what you would expect even in a girl three seasons old! It looked horrible!

A look of anguish came over Damira's face. She screamed, shutting her eyes to the monstrous sight. And even as the scream rent the stillness of the bush, Garwidha acted. Her digging-stick was close at hand and, her face set determinedly, she raised it high and brought it down. The dull thud cut short the wails of the new-born infant.

The women all knew what had to be done. There was no time to be lost. This misshapen thing had to be disposed of as quickly as possible, before the spirit that had caused it could collect its wits and enter the binang of some other unsuspecting woman. Leaving Garwidha to tend Damira, Nerida quickly wrapped the thing in dibing bark and, taking her digging-stick, hurried away some distance. She ran in a direction to take her further from the main camp, taking care to make her course devious, going first one way and then another. Everything must be done to confuse the evil spirit. When she was far enough away, she hurriedly dug a deep hole in the sand and hid this thing from the sight of people forever.

By the time she returned to the other two Garwidha had already taken care of the after-birth. Damira was sitting in the smoke of the fire, her head between her knees. She had been looking forward so much to having a baby at her breast! Why had she given birth to such a monstrosity?

"Hush now!" Nerida kept her tone practical. "This happens sometimes, and you've just got to get used to it! The trouble must be that the spirit entered you while you were away from Undanbi land!"

Garwidha hastened to agree. "It was at the time of the dhur at Gullirae!" she reminded Damira. "Goodness knows what sort of spirits you would find up there in that country! Next time you will get a good Undanbi spirit to enter your binang!"

By next morning Damira's breasts were hurting, so Garwidha hurried to the main camp, returning with a small girl of four moons, whose mother had been filled with pity to hear of the tragedy that had befallen the birth party. "Tell Damira I'll feed some of the other babies till the time comes for her to come back," she told Garwidha. "Then she can give me back my little girl and she can help feed as many as she likes!"

All the women could guess at the anguish of losing a baby at birth, and it went without saying that all the women would be willing to alleviate the pain by sharing their babes with the one who had suffered such a loss. Among the people there was no feeling of compulsion to grieve endlessly, and Nerida and Garwidha were comforted to see the look of tenderness that was mixed with Damira's tears as the little girl drew nourishment from her breast.

By the time the period of seclusion was over, the birth scene had lost its harsh edges for the three. It would be talked about among the women for a long time, of course, for it was necessary at all times to draw as much knowledge as possible from every life experience. In this way future disasters could often be averted. But it still remained that on very rare occasions such things did happen. Among the Undanbi, indeed, it was only the very old women who could remember a baby born long ago with a misshapen foot. But they did happen.

Soon it was the occasion of a large dhur at Kauin-Kauin, and the Ningi had invited the Undanbi, the Dhundubari, the Turrbal, the Nunakul, the Gnalungpin and the Kubenpil. There was great rejoicing as old friends of these nations who had not seen one another for many seasons met again, and the dances at night had everybody at a fine pitch of excitement. Particularly interesting was a new dance from the Nunakul which commemorated the arrival only a few short moons before of a new sort of canoe that the degga had brought in from the ocean past Bulan. It had gone down to Gumpi.

The Nunakul had kept this dance a secret for the first night, and when they had performed it on the second night, there had been many sceptics.

Most had agreed that it was a fine dance. But why put such a huge fire and such great clouds of smoke in the middle of the canoe? Everyone knew you could carry fire in a canoe – why, even in a bark canoe made by people there was room for a small fire to be carried on clay and sand. So it was really no surprise to anybody to find that the makaron carried fire, too. But such a big fire? No!

A Turrbal bu-ul remarked that such a big fire would be sure to burn down the sticks that the dhugai always had sticking up in their canoes. Another wondered if the wings they used might not also catch alight.

But, no! The Nunakul assured them all that this particular canoe had gone along without wings! And it had two great round things – one on either side – that made a terrible splashing noise as they beat at the water. And the fire and the smoke had been as big as the dance had said – bigger, even!

At last their audience were convinced that it was not some fanciful tale dreamt up to trick people and give the Nunakul a great laugh at everybody else's expense. The makaron apparently did have a new sort of canoe that could go along, not only without the need of poling, but also without the normal wings they used. And it huffed and puffed like a huge monstrous thing as it moved, belching out smoke and sparks from a great thing that went up in the middle of it. Altogether it had presented a truly frightening spectacle and the Nunakul admitted that, even though they were used to the vagaries of the degga, this time they had run for dear life to put as much distance as they could between themselves and this contraption.

So the second time they performed the dance there was much more interest than there had been the first time.

But later, after the Undanbi had returned to the area set aside for them by Kamkuri, Piringa voiced his dissatisfaction with the popularity of these new dances. "Who cares if they've got a new sort of magic canoe?" he wanted to know, spitting disgustedly. "Always these makaron! What is wrong with our own canoes that we have been making since the Before-Time?"

Nobody disagreed.

Even here at Warun, which the makaron had laid waste so many seasons ago and from where the Ningi had succeeded in driving them away, there had lately been further interference by the makaron. Kamkuri told them that three moons before the dhur a canoe had dropped a number of makaron and some red-covered ones off here, and they had even built a hut. What they wanted he did not know, but the Ningi had made it very plain that they wanted nothing to do with them. Once was more than enough, as far as they were concerned.

"We set fire to the hut early one morning," Kamkuri said. "Then next day we rattled our spears and threatened them, taking care to keep a long way from the thunder-sticks. After a couple more days, they left."

Buruda was pleased to hear that the Ningi were taking such a hard line against these makaron. It was a pity other nations wouldn't follow their example. But he sighed to himself, realising it was not so easy for others.

Nevertheless, Birral grant that the Undanbi could do as well as the Ningi if they were ever threatened.

The news from the Turrbal was not so heartening. Some dhugai had sat down at Nundah, that beautiful chain of waterholes.

Indeed, after listening to Kamkuri, Gariwar was of the opinion that these might be the very dhugai who had built the hut at Warun!

This was unsettling news indeed! "Not at Nundah, surely!" a Kubenpil bu-ul said. "Where will we camp on our first night now when we are on the way to the bunyi feast?" A similar outcry rose from the Nunakul and Gnalungpin. Nundah was an ideal camping-site for nations on the move, and the Turrbal had always been happy for those coming through their land to the feasts to use this finely-watered area with plenty of game as an overnight stop.

"Surely the makaron could see the well-used tracks that go past there!" Buruda said, outraged. "Can't they leave anything alone?"

"We did think of driving them away – even killing them!" Gariwar admitted. "Bagara pleaded with us to allow him to lead an attack, especially after they began to use their tools to dig up the ground for their food plants!" Then his voice took on a helpless note as he continued. "But we dared not! Miandhin and the red-covered ones are too close, and they are far too many for us!"

Somehow these makaron resembled muthar, the spider, which often spun its sticky web until, from a very small beginning, it eventually took up a large space in the forest! Not only that, but the web was too often placed inconveniently over a track, so that the unwary hunter could find his beard and hair unexpectedly enmeshed in a sticky mess! A curse on these spider makaron, who dared to spin their webs in lovely places like Nundah!

When the main business of the dhur began, the enforced segregation allowed the women plenty of time to bring themselves up-to-date regarding recent events. The women of all other nations were told in hushed tones of the death of Damira's misshapen babe, and the Undanbi women were in turn told of similar events elsewhere. The incidence of such occurrences seemed greatest amongst the Nunakul, but each nation had some tale to tell. There had been infants who had never begun to breathe, infants with sightless eyes, and infants with other deformities too horrible to mention. These had presented no real problems apart from the anguish suffered by the mothers as the babies had been done to death. But there were other cases which had proved far more painful – for example, babies who within a few days of birth had found difficulty in breathing because they had developed a bloody discharge from the nose, so that they had to be killed.

But - and here the voices became even more hushed in case the children who were the subjects of discussion could hear – perhaps the most tragic of all the cases involved infants who had been presented to the nation after the period of seclusion, only to succumb to some strange maladies afterwards.

You could see them here and there playing with the other children as the women went about their daily tasks. Here was one who was always snuffling, grey matter oozing continually from its nose. Here was another with sores round its mouth, here another where the sores seemed to have gone, only to be replaced by skin which perpetually sloughed away, leaving the lips raw and bleeding. One Kubenpil woman had a small babe of a few moons who had, she said, been perfect at birth – but now it had terrible blisters on the palms of its hands and the soles of its feet, and it cried whenever she touched its arms and legs. Another Turrbal boy of four summers was finding it hard to get around. His legs seemed too weak to hold him, and his shin bones had even bowed forward, for all the world like the side sticks of a mula! There was even one case of an older Nunakul girl who could no longer hear, and whose eyes were so inflamed that her family had remained at Bulan to care for her.

There were altogether too many of these children for comfort. And they had all happened since the degga - dhugai - makaron had arrived!

Perhaps the greatest tragedy, Nerida reflected, was that all these children were as dearly loved as any other. It was one thing to dispose of deformed children at birth, before the mothers had held the tiny bodies to their breasts, as had happened with Damira. It was quite another thing to find out later that this perfectly-formed baby who had become a part of you was itself marked with a taint similar to one that had led to the death of others. No mother - indeed, no nation - would consider allowing one of these whom they accepted and loved to perish.

Better by far, though, if they had perished at birth!

Meanwhile at night, at the dhur itself, the manngur were also considering the same question.

"I heard of a Yuggera boy whose teeth, after the first lot had fallen out, grew all crooked!" Gariwar informed them. "He even finds it hard to talk. At times he even acts as if he is out of his mind!"

"There was a girl of the Dhundubari," Nganku told them, "whose mouth went bad. She could hardly eat at all, and in the top of her mouth there was always a sticky stuff that had a rotten smell. I used the kundir stone on her many times, but eventually the top of her mouth got holes in it, and she died."

A horrified gasp went up from the others. This was the most fearful thing they had heard. Never before had anything like this happened to the people!

"Why are these things happening?" Turugun asked. "They must be connected with the makaron – but how? It does not seem that they started to happen the instant the makaron arrived. If they had, it would make more sense."

"Perhaps it took the degga some time to release these evil spirits in the land," the Nunakul manngur suggested. "It may be that they did not bring these spirits in on their first canoe, but brought them in later, and then sent them out to infest the birth-spirit places which our women frequent when they are wanting a child."

Whichever way they looked at it, there seemed to be no getting away from the fact that the problem was connected with the birth-spirit places. These, after all, were the sites from which the spirits had jumped to take their places in the binang of the women. How had the makaron changed the spirits of the land, which had always been so benevolent, into evil things that brought disaster and deformity to the nations?

But then, how did the makaron do anything? Nothing they did made sense!

The Gnalungpin manngur drew their attention to the fact that the children they were talking about – the deformed ones that they could see daily round the camp – were only some of the cases. "There are others the women tell us nothing about," he explained. "In our nation there have been two still-births, and I am sure that you will find similar cases among your own people." He waited for signs of agreement before continuing. "The women tell us nothing about them – only that they were born dead. But I stumbled on a group of women one day who were saying something about a misshapen baby, and they suddenly fell silent when they saw me. The trouble is they consider it none of our business. So all we know is that the problem is worse than it looks."

There was no doubt that this was true.

Buruda wondered whether Nerida would tell him more if he asked her directly. He determined to find out when he saw her after the dhur.

But here and now it was his turn to speak. He had listened to the others for many nights now, for it was in these other nations, particularly those with close contacts with the makaron, where the majority of the cases were. The Undanbi had had one – Damira – and he knew little enough about that. But something had been going over and over in his mind for some time now, and it was time to speak. He rose, and the others fell silent. Whenever the Undanbi manngur spoke, it was a time for listening.

"You have said it is the fault of the birth-spirit places," he began, "and you may be right. It could be that there are many more evil spirits in these places since the arrival of the accursed makaron! But there are also babies being born who are, as has always been the case since the Before-Time, perfect in every way. There have also been cases before the coming of the makaron of babies who were born dead. The difference is that these were once very rare. But let us not lose sight of the fact that the evil spirits have always been there, waiting to take advantage of any woman they could enter."

He paused to let them digest what he had said, and then went on. "There is something else besides the birth-places to consider," he said, gratified to see their awakening interest at his change of direction. "Before a spirit can enter a woman's binang, it must be prepared by a bu-ul's dhun. We have always known this to be so. Even in the case of animals, we know this happens. Even with the kangaroos, the koalas in the trees, it is so. So it is with all living things."

Turugun thought he could see where Buruda's logic was leading them. The Nunakul manngur was also beginning to get a glimmer of understanding. The rest waited expectantly.

"It would be easy to understand," Buruda pointed out, "if all these malformed babies had entered the binang of our women only after the makaron had prepared them. We know that the makaron put their dhun into a woman's binang as all do. It may be, then, that the makaron prepare a binang in such a way that evil spirits in the birth-places find it easy to enter, while good spirits find it harder."

Now they all understood. There was a great deal of sense in this.

"But there is one thing you seem to have forgotten," Kamkuri pointed out. "These evil spirits did not all enter our women after makaron had prepared their binang."

"That is true," Buruda admitted. "Damira, for instance, had not been with a makaron, and yet her baby was born dead – or worse." He suddenly changed the direction of his argument once more. "But let me return to something you have heard about many times – my dream of many, many seasons ago, that told me of the disasters that were to befall us. It showed me the tracks of the makaron and their strange animals. It showed me the way the makaron would destroy the trees and dig up the land. It showed me the scab sickness."

Again he paused, and they waited expectantly.

"It showed me something else," he went on after a while, his eyes seeming to focus on something in the far distance, "and I have been trying for a long time to work out just what this meant. At last I think I may have some sort of answer, although I am not sure." His voice trailed off into nothingness, as if in his mind he was once again viewing that horrifying scene, and could once again hear the death-wail of his dream.

"This other thing?" Gariwar prompted him.

Buruda brought his mind back to the present. "These other things I saw," he told them, "were sores on binang and dhun!"

They looked blankly at him, not understanding.

"If I had not seen this in my dream," Buruda explained, "I would have missed it. But I saw such a sore on the dhun of Naruman, Damira's husband."

Gariwar wanted to know what the sore looked like, and Buruda explained.

Then the Nunakul manngur said, "I have seen such sores. I even had one myself at one time."

They all looked and saw the small scar where the sore had been.

But they were still not sure that Buruda was talking sense. What could such a small sore on a dhun do? The Nunakul manngur said it hadn't even hurt – had hardly been worth thinking about - and Buruda admitted that Naruman had said the same thing. Then surely Buruda wasn't suggesting this would have anything to do with the number of evil spirits which had, since the coming of the makaron, found their way into the binang of the women! How could this be?

"It may be that I am wrong," Buruda admitted. "It would certainly never have entered my mind if I had not seen the sores in my dream. But I did see them, and everything in my dream has so far proved true. Even these sores have occurred, although I must admit I have not seen any such on the binang of a woman. Still,

I have kept reminding myself that everything else in my dream foretold disasters, and I must therefore think that this, too, is a disaster. These sores look and feel harmless, but in the dream they were far from harmless. I think that, if a bu-ul has such a sore, his dhun might also prepare the binang of a woman in such an unusual way that evil spirits might find it easy to enter, just as they find it easy to enter after a makaron has prepared the binang."

The other manngur admitted, albeit grudgingly, that Buruda might be right. But only Turugun was completely convinced. The others found such an argument too far-fetched to accommodate easily.

But whatever the cause of the deformities, they were all agreed that they would need to be very exact in their religious observances, particularly in the way they each used the magic stones to ensure the protection of the benevolent spirits in their own particular lands. There was no room for slackness in this regard.

And after the dhur, Buruda asked Nerida about Damira's baby. But she proved quite evasive, mentioning only that it must have had something wrong with its belly, for it couldn't breathe.

Her husband might be a great manngur, Nerida said to herself. But even manngur had to leave women's business to women.

Chapter 25

1840: Runaway convict John Story Baker (Boraltju) returns to Brisbane and leads Gorman via Flagstone Creek and Gorman's Pass to the Darling Downs. Surveying begins preparatory to free settlement. German missionaries, Schmidt and Eipper, journey north to the Undanbi.

Buruda smiled to himself as he saw Yingera approaching the hut. Nerida would once again have to turn her back and pound her bangwal facing the opening of the hut, or else give up and go and visit a friend for a while.

Dhuluru, now nearly old enough to have Nerida wind the cord round her little finger, also saw the young bu-ul, and put her hand to her mouth to hide her smile. Yingera seemed to find plenty of opportunities to visit her father – more than necessary, perhaps.

At that instant Nerida caught sight of him and turned her back. "He was here only this morning with some fish!" she muttered disgustedly, digging Dhuluru in the ribs with her pounding-stick. "Does he think you need to be as fat as a dugong before you can become his wife? Anyhow, he's got plenty of time to fatten you up yet! It will be at least three seasons before you go to his hut!"

Dhuluru said nothing in reply, but grinned and looked modestly at the ground as her promised husband came closer. She had seen the mullet he was carrying, and grinned even more broadly, knowing that they already had enough for the evening meal from his earlier visit. Still, she took care to keep her mouth covered with her hand, since she had no desire to embarrass him.

"N'gara!" Yingera was always formal on these visits to his future father-in-law. He sat down and deposited the mullet on the stones near the fire.

"Nara!" Buruda answered dryly, reflecting that the dogs would eat well tonight. He hoped for Nerida's sake that this visit would be short.

But Yingera was in no hurry. He wanted to discuss the advisability of putting more logs in the creek, for here at Coochin, where they presently had their camp, the teredo were not as plentiful as he remembered in the past.

Privately Buruda thought there were enough teredo to keep them going for many seasons to come, but nevertheless he politely voiced agreement that one or two extra logs would not do any harm. He knew that it wasn't teredo the young man had on his mind, that all Yingera needed was a topic of conversation – any topic would do – while he took the opportunity of casting sidelong glances at the girl sitting quietly and shyly near the fire.

Yingera must have spent much time thinking over what he would talk about, for he seemed to be in no danger of running out of conversation. Buruda managed to keep his end up while his hands remained busy, scraping and hardening a new spear he had cut out of a bloodwood tree a couple of days ago. Periodically he would hold it over the fire to get it hot enough to change its shape as his hands and feet pressed it into a perfectly straight line. At times even his teeth came into play.

And all the time Yingera's voice droned on. The kangaroos were plentiful at Coochin. Even the emus were more numerous than they had been the last time they had camped here. What were the makaron doing at Miandhin? They had put up even more wara-wara barriers at Tulmur, and at Nundah, too – or so Yingera had heard.

Buruda found that a grunt every now and again was enough to satisfy his visitor, so he concentrated on his spear. At last he was satisfied with its straightness and, picking up the piece of sharkskin he had set aside for the task, he smoothed the weapon until, when he hefted it in his hand, it felt easy and beautifully balanced. Then with only half an ear attuned to what Yingera was saying, he blackened the spear over the fire until he was satisfied that it was sufficiently hard to perform whatever task he would require of it.

At last his visitor appeared to have exhausted his repertoire, and stood to go – but not before he had cast one last glance in Dhuluru's direction.

Nerida was apoplectic as she turned her face once more to the fire. "The very idea!" she gasped. "How could he think that those things are interesting? And how could he possibly think we need more mullet? I'll - I'll -!"

But what Nerida was going to say was drowned in a roar of laughter from Buruda and Dhuluru, who now considered that Yingera was far enough away not to be embarrassed by their outburst.

"Sometimes I wish we had betrothed Dhuluru to somebody with more sense!" Nerida went on, still smarting from her enforced inaction at this busy time of day. "When does he think we women make our bangwal cakes, I wonder?"

Buruda looked fondly across at her, and she calmed down quickly enough after seeing the look of disappointment that crossed her daughter's face. "Not that he is a bad fellow!" she admitted. "But I do wish he'd come once a day and be satisfied with that!"

"He is the most outstanding Dhuroin in the whole of the nation," her husband reminded her. "Unless you want to look further, he is the best bu-ul for Dhuluru among the Undanbi."

"Oh, I'm satisfied enough!" Nerida laughed, her ill-temper forgotten as she placed the cakes at the edge of the fire. She turned to Dhuluru. "Are you satisfied enough?" she asked, her eyes twinkling.

"I am," Dhuluru assured her. Her breasts had not yet begun to swell, but she was already old enough to know that Yingera would make a good husband. She'd have hated to have a suitor who was content to see her only once a day.

But Buruda had no intention of letting Nerida off so easily. All at once he looked very serious. "Of course," he said, "we may have done better if we had looked among the Dhundubari or the Tumbra – or even the Nalbo." He paused, and then his face lit up at a thought that had only that moment occurred to him. "The Turrbal – that's where we should have looked! Gariwar told me there is a fine young lad of about Dhuluru's age who is a Turrwan! I wonder -?"

"That's enough of that!" Nerida told him. "We don't need to look anywhere but at Yingera!"

But Buruda hadn't finished with them. He had noticed the look of curiosity in Dhuluru's eyes, and grinned to himself. His daughter was still young enough to wonder if there might just be someone more suitable. "Yes," he went on. "I believe the lad's name is Tompitri."

"Tompitri?" Neither Nerida nor Dhuluru had ever heard of this boy.

"Yes. I think he has lovely eyes, the colour of the sky, and his hair is like dibing bark – nice and white! So is his skin!"

"Ugh!" Dhuluru's face wrinkled in disgust. "I didn't think people could be so ugly!"

He laughed. "The makaron are!" he told her. "And this is a makaron child I am talking about!"

Nerida aimed a stick at him, and he was forced to dodge. "That's not funny, Buruda!" she chided him. "You of all people – to make jokes about the accursed makaron!"

He was immediately contrite. She was right, of course. The joke had been in extremely bad taste. Still, what he had said was correct. This makaron lad who had come to Miandhin a few short seasons before had taken to staying with the Turrbal for a night or so every now and again, and from all accounts had learnt to speak the language as if he had been born to it. Gariwar even claimed that the boy could make himself understood in Gubbi, having learnt it from the visiting Dhundubari.

"The boy assures us he would rather live with people than with the dhugai," Gariwar had said to Buruda. "And even though he is a dhugai, there is something about him that you can't help liking. Our boys are always excited to see him, and look forward to having him spend the night. We made him a Turrwan, for that is the skin he mostly resembles, and I can tell you he was so proud when we told him! If only dhugai were all like him, it would be much better!"

No, Buruda thought to himself, that was not so! It would be much better if all makaron kept to themselves and went back to the spirit-land! But he could sympathise with Gariwar, nevertheless. To fight fully-grown makaron and kill them was one thing. But since it appeared they could have children, that was a different matter. No bu-ul would ever consider harming a boy unless he really had to. And Buruda could also understand why Gariwar had been forced into deciding which of the four skins the boy fitted into. Since he had shown a definite preference for living with people, there was a distinct possibility that one day he would take the test of manhood, and perhaps even marry. It was therefore very necessary that he learn from an early age, as all boys must, just which girls he had to avoid, in case they one day became his mother-in-law.

Still, Buruda thought wryly, his joke had recoiled on itself. It wasn't till today, in his teasing of Nerida, that he had realised that this Tompitri had the skin that would legally allow him to marry Dhuluru! That would never happen! The very thought made his skin crawl!

With Yingera gone and the bangwal roasting, his thoughts turned to Miandhin, as they were wont to do when not occupied with other things. Kaldhu had called in half a moon before to let the Undanbi know that Boraltju had left the Yuggera to return to his makaron friends at Miandhin, and Maltagara had been quite put out about it. Not only that, but this Yuggera makaron had then gone back through Yuggera country and taken the head makaron from Miandhin through the pass that led from Yabarba to Gunibara land! This was treachery indeed!

And at Miandhin itself there were changes afoot. There were nowhere near as many makaron with the heavy leg things.

Instead, more and more makaron seemed to be coming in who stood up like men. And there were two makaron who kept going south with others into Yugumbir country, and then returning to Miandhin with their bony-headed animals. They had big cords that they kept stretching out and taking in again, and every now and again they would place three sticks in the ground that were joined at the top, and bend down to look carefully at the thing on the top.

These makaron were mad for sure, Kaldhu had assured Buruda. If a bu-ul carried such a thing, he would not need to check every so often that the thing on top hadn't fallen off! Nor would he need to look so closely. Perhaps these two were nearly blind.

But whether they were blind or not, the Yugumbir were fast losing patience with them, and Kaldhu was of the opinion that not many moons would pass before the two blind makaron would be consigned swiftly back to the spirit-land. Korbenbob and Bogi had both been heard to utter dire threats, and Meredeo had said that anybody – dhugai or not – who came onto Yugumbir land without the protection of a white boomerang should never even be given the opportunity of drawing two breaths of Yugumbir air!

Kaldhu had also told the Undanbi that the Turrbal had still not worked out what the dhugai were doing at Nundah. Indeed, their presence was quite puzzling. There were no red-covered ones there, and their sole purpose, apart from growing food plants, seemed to be to perform actions without meaning. Even the growing of the food plants was inexplicable, for they had more than they could eat themselves, and unlike the other dhugai at Miandhin, seemed only too pleased to share their food with the people. So strange were they, that the bu-ul had taken turns staying at Nundah to try to find out what they were up to.

Some sort of pattern, insane though it was, had begun to emerge. They would share the food only if you did something for them. That made some sense. There were all sorts of things you could do. You could dig in the ground like a woman, chop wood with their sharp axes, bring in sticks for them to make their strange wara-wara barriers to keep their animals in, and so on. For all these things they would give you good food. You could even be extremely lucky and get some of their yams, those ground roots that were even more succulent and delicious than the yams from the forest.

But the easiest thing you could do was sing songs. Kaldhu had even sung one of these, but it was so alien-sounding that it had set the teeth of his Undanbi listeners on edge. He had explained that you got used to the sound after a while.

And how excited these mad dhugai got if you managed to repeat one of their chants! Kaldhu had not yet been able to master it all, but he had repeated the beginning of one of them. "Aufather widhartin evanalloh bithainem thaikingdum –!"

According to Kaldhu, when two of the bu-ul had shown they could repeat this chant from beginning to end, the dhugai had been beside themselves with delight, loading the dhilla of the two with yams and other food.

Gariwar had set the two bu-ul to teaching others this chant. It could even be a magic spell that would help get rid of these pests! But in any case, it seemed to be effective in getting the dhugai to part with their delicious yams.

According to Kaldhu, Paldha had shown himself to be quite a linguist, and had learnt some words from the mad dhugai at Nundah. Paldha even claimed to know the meaning of these words, although from what he had told the rest of the Turrbal, they remained sceptical about this claim. It just did not make sense that any dhugai would spend their whole time talking about a spirit of a dead bu-ul who had come back to live with the people! Paldha surely must have got it wrong!

In the midst of his reverie, two things happened that brought Buruda's mind back to the present with a jerk. The first was the appetising smell of the roasted bangwal and mullet that Nerida was handing to him on a piece of bark. The second was a loud "Kui!" from the south bank of Coochin, where Karperi was standing with Paldha, who had a white boomerang in his belt, and two makaron.

Buruda wasn't going to stop eating for any makaron. If they had been on their own, yes. In that case, he'd have had no hesitation in poling across and putting a spear between their ribs! But the boomerang of peace prevented it, so he had to content himself with glowering over his meal, while Piringa poled Karperi and his visitors across.

Soon a whole crowd of people – Paldha and the two makaron in their midst – were gathered in front of Buruda's hut.

"N'gara, Buruda!" Paldha said. "These two dhugai are from Nundah, and they have asked me to take them to the people so that they can tell them why they have come to visit the nations."

Buruda was interested. This was something he had been waiting to find out ever since the makaron had begun to infest the land. Perhaps he had been wrong to be upset when he had first seen Paldha with his two companions. It could be that, for the first time, the puzzle was about to be solved.

"Sit down, friend," the Undanbi manngur told Paldha. "And get the makaron to sit, too. We have plenty to eat for all."

Yingera had seen to that, he thought to himself.

A curse from Nerida and her sudden departure into the interior of the hut alerted Buruda to the fact that Yingera was among those crowding around these strangers. It was therefore left to Dhuluru to set some mullet and bangwal out on dibing bark for the visitors.

Luckily the crowd soon dispersed, and Nerida could once more emerge.

It was interesting to see that, before they began to eat, both the makaron closed their eyes and clasped their hands in front of them, and then one of them said something. Buruda turned to Paldha and asked him what they were doing, but he replied that he didn't know. The makaron's voice got louder as Buruda and Paldha were speaking.

As they ate, Buruda had ample opportunity to observe the two. They had the distinctive nasty odour of their kind, but there was little to make them stand out from others he had seen. Perhaps the covering on their bodies was a little darker than most – something like the covering of the two who had been in the big hut at Miandhin that time, when he had been invited inside for no apparent reason.

The three visitors had hardly finished eating when the cry for the dead began from a hut just down the creek. Soon all members of the camp were involved, but the makaron sat silent throughout. Buruda thought that that possibly made sense – the dead might not bother mourning for themselves.

When it was over, Buruda asked Paldha when the makaron intended to tell him why they had come, and the Turrbal bu-ul said some strange words to one of them, who said something in reply.

"They would rather wait and tell all the people at one meeting," Paldha explained.

"Then so be it. Soon the people will be gathering round the great campfire. But before that time comes, tell me something of what is happening at Miandhin."

"I haven't been there much lately. Instead, I have been spending a lot of time at Nundah, trying hard to get to know their tongue, for Gariwar is becoming anxious that we should get to know as much about the dhugai as we can. More dhugai are coming and going at Miandhin, and he is beginning to get worried."

Buruda agreed that this made a great deal of sense. Some of the problems of the people undoubtedly stemmed from the fact that there was no way of finding out the intentions of the makaron. "And have you learnt this tongue?"

Paldha grinned. "It is a hard tongue, full of breathing and other sounds. But yes – I have learnt enough to know something of what they do."

"So perhaps you can tell us why they have come."

Paldha's grin widened. "I'll let you hear it from them later," he said, and then burst out laughing. "You'll find it interesting."

Buruda could see that Paldha was not going to explain the joke, so contained himself in patience for the time being. In the meantime he asked about life at Nundah. Was it true that the makaron were making lots of wara-wara barriers out of sticks, and had an extremely succulent sort of yam which they gave to the people?"

Paldha's brow darkened at these words. "Yams!" he spat. "Yes, they do have yams which we put in the ground for them, and which they then feed us. But a moon ago they used the thunder-sticks on the people who were digging the yams!"

Buruda was dumbfounded. "But I thought you said they gave the people yams!"

Paldha's voice became calmer. "Yes, they do – but only if the people do things for them, like digging, or cutting trees, or building their wara-wara." He suddenly grinned again. "They give most if you can sing their songs or say their chants."

"But they used their thunder-sticks! Why?"

"The people were digging the yams without doing anything first."

"But surely they understand that the land is Turrbal land!"

Paldha sighed. "I have tried telling them that, but they don't seem to be able to grasp it. They just keep saying that we must work for the yams."

"Did the thunder-sticks kill anybody?"

Again Paldha's expression became dark. "No. But Gariwar had to take lots of little stones out of the heads and chests of two bu-ul! And one of them can no longer see out of his left eye!"

Buruda's hand tightened round an imaginary spear, and the eyes of the two makaron darted back and forth before the anger in his face. "If you had not come with a white boomerang, I would kill them now!" he grated at Paldha.

Paldha reached out and touched his arm. "Steady, my friend!" he told him. "The other makaron at Nundah know that these came with me! So if anything happens to them, I would never be able to go back to Turrbal country! There are too many red-covered ones at Miandhin!"

Buruda began to understand even a little more clearly than before the frustration that the Turrbal must experience daily. He forced himself to relax.

By now the people had begun gathering round the great campfire, so he led the way in that direction. When they were all settled, Bulangga was the first to rise and ask Paldha why he had brought the makaron to the Undanbi.

"I brought them here, Bulangga, because they asked me to," the Turrbal bu-ul replied. "They say they have some good news to bring to the people, and that they will tell you why they came to Turrbal land in the first place."

A buzz of conversation greeted these words. This should be interesting. They had wanted to know this for a long time.

One of the makaron said something, and Paldha spoke again. "The dhugai would like to say something, and I will tell you what he says."

"Yau-ai!" came from many throats.

The makaron then stood and spoke. Every now and again he would pause, and Paldha would tell the people what he had said. Often Paldha would appear to have some difficulty understanding the meaning, and would need to ask a number of questions before he could interpret. But the more Buruda saw of Paldha in action, the more convinced he became that he was indeed something of a linguist.

At the same time, however, the Undanbi manngur could understand why some of the Turrbal had not been convinced of Paldha's ability to translate. The problem was that the makaron was talking nonsense. What he was saying was quite childish. Indeed, so childish was it that many of his listeners had begun to hide their grins politely behind their hands.

"Surely he can tell us more!" Turugun muttered. "We know all this!"

But then it was over, and Paldha said that the dhugai was going to talk to Birral for a while.

What a strange way he used to talk to Birral! He clasped his hands in front of him, and then droned on and on. And just as Buruda was about to tell him to stop because he could stand no more of it, the other makaron and Paldha joined in, and Buruda recognised the chant that Kaldhu had told him about – "Aufather widhartin evanallow bithainem thaikingdum - ." But, unlike Kaldhu, Paldha struggled valiantly on until he got to the final word, grinning widely all the time.

The makaron sat down, and there was silence at last.

Throughout the discussion that followed, Paldha's grin remained wide. He knew only too well that the Undanbi would have been full of expectation, wondering what the message of the dhugai would be, wondering why they had come in the first place. And he also knew that, like the Turrbal before them, the Undanbi would not be able to see what all the fuss was about.

"The makaron gets excited, simply because the spirit of a bu-ul called Dhidhu came back to live with the people!" Piringa scoffed.

"Surely he knows that every baby contains the spirit of one who has already died!" Naruman said.

"There are two makaron with us at the moment who have been dead already, and are now messing up the lives of people by coming back!" Bulangga's words raised a ripple of laughter.

"Ask them why they didn't bring Dhidhu with them!" Turugun called out. "Or is one of them this Dhidhu?"

"I can answer that," Paldha said. "The Turrbal asked that, too, and they told us that this bu-ul is up in the sky."

This time there was a great shout of laughter. "Then he is dead again!" Naruman said. "Ask them why they don't leave us alone and go back to the sky, the same as this other makaron!"

Once more Paldha spoke with the two and, as one answered, his grin grew even wider. "They say we'll all go there one day!" he told them.

Even the children chortled. What a great piece of news this was! Why, all children learnt, almost as soon as they could talk, that there was a time after death when spirits jumped off into the sky, remaining there for some time before returning to earth! If the makaron had cared to ask, the smallest child could have taken them by the hand and led them to the very spot on the headland at Caloundra from which all Undanbi spirits jumped into the sky!

Buruda shook his head. No wonder Paldha had seen this all as a big joke! This news was about as interesting as saying that Bigi came out of the ocean every morning and went behind the mountains at night to sleep, or that mullet lived in the sea, and died if you took them out of it!

A makaron had died and his spirit had returned! There were far too many makaron at Miandhin who had done the same thing!

Turugun summed it up. "Tell them", he said to Paldha, "that we Undanbi would be far more interested in hearing stories of makaron who had died and never returned!"

The rest of the evening was spent more productively in dancing and singing. To give the makaron their due, they tried to look interested. But there was no hiding the disappointment in their faces.

Still, nobody could see what they had to be disappointed about.

These were no different from all the other makaron. Their actions were unpredictable and insane – one moment giving yams to the people, the next using their thunder-sticks on those who were taking yams that were growing in the people's own soil!

Nor did their stories have any sense to them, simply stating the obvious, with no attempt made to dress up the story by dancing and singing!

The Undanbi were not sorry to see the grinning Paldha take the two makaron south next morning.

Notes on Chapter 25

In her record of her father's life in early Brisbane, Constance Campbell Petrie says that her father told her that the Aborigines called him "Turrwan", which meant "Great Man". This meaning is even given again on the last page of the book. Yet "Turrwan" was the Yugarabul equivalent of the Gubbi "Dhuroin", a marital skin, and Tom Petrie spoke both these languages fluently. One can hardly accuse Tom Petrie at this great distance in time of making a linguistic mistake. But was he having a great joke with his daughter? Perhaps the best explanation might be that his daughter had mistaken one of the things he told her, or that her memory played her false. (Or, of course, there may be a VERY remote possibility that the word could have two meanings.)

The Aborigines gave the name "Wara-Wara" to the early fences built round Brisbane, since they resembled the figures children produced with the string game they played on their fingers.

Paldha describes the difficult language of the whites as "full of breathing". There was no "h" sound in the Aboriginal languages.

✦

Chapter 26

1840-41: Surveyors Stapylton and Tuck are killed by Aborigines near Mt. Lindesay. The Leslie Brothers take up land on the Darling Downs. Five stations are established in the Brisbane area: Cressbrook Station on Cressbrook Creek, Bigge Brothers at Mt. Brisbane Station, Mackenzie Brothers at Kilcoy, Archer Brothers at Durundur, George Mocatta at Grantham (with the notorious "Cocky" Rogers as manager).

Buruda and Turugun were in earnest discussion atop the high hill where they from time to time performed the ceremony to assure the Undanbi the protection of benevolent spirits. The ceremony was over once more, and the crystals had been reverently replaced in their protective bark covering and hidden from prying eyes. The marks on the trees roundabout had also been retouched so that there could be no mistake about the penalty awaiting any person who trespassed on this sacred ground.

"The time has come," Buruda said, "to think again about the makaron. Makaron we call them, and makaron they will remain forever. But it has come to me that they may not be spirits at all – evil or otherwise. Perhaps they are just evil men!"

"But Boraltju said they come from Inglun, the land of spirits!" Turugun protested. "Surely he would know, being one of them!"

"Boraltju said they came from Inglun," Buruda replied. "He did not say it was the land of the spirits."

The thought was too new for Turugun. He waited patiently for the older man to continue.

Buruda rose and strode about while he talked, having found long ago that thoughts came more easily while he was active. "We know that babies are spirits returned from the spirit-land to the land of people," he said. "There is no doubt about this thing, for it is obviously true. Women have always felt the moving of a spirit within their bodies at the exact moment when they have passed a spirit-place."

He paused and looked into the distance for some time, and the young manngur still waited. At last Buruda continued, his voice soft as if he was trying to bring order to the ideas that had lately led him to doubt the origin of these interlopers.

"We know that babies are pale," he said, "and our women rub them with charcoal to make them turn the proper colour. We know that this paleness is caused by the roasting of the bodies of our dead, so that the spirit itself is pale when it returns to the people, though it has grown a new skin. But what about the makaron?"

"The makaron have pale skin," Turugun pointed out. "Doesn't that mean that they, too, must be spirits returned from the spirit-land, just as babies are?"

"That sounds reasonable," Buruda agreed. "But the makaron from Nundah who spoke to us did not seem to think that he was a spirit."

Turugun found it hard to keep the derisive tone out of his voice, remembering that he was talking to a manngur older and wiser than himself. But he felt he still had to correct Buruda over this one thing.

"He spoke utter rubbish!" he said. "Even our children know the things he was telling us about!"

"I know. But what he said has troubled me ever since. The reason it has troubled me is that I cannot imagine how anybody, even a spirit, could be so stupid as to utter such drivel when speaking to grown people! I have asked myself again and again why this makaron tried to tell us that a bu-ul had come back from the spirit-land, when we had the evidence before our very eyes that a large number of spirits had done the very same thing!"

In the slight pause that followed, Turugun protested, "But he was mad!"

"That is what we have thought," the older manngur said. "We have looked at what these makaron do, and nothing makes sense to us. Yet what about our babies? Are they mad, too? Certainly not! What they do is very simple, and they learn very quickly. Why, then, should these makaron all be mad, when our babies are not – if they are both from the spirit-land?"

A long silence followed. Buruda was thinking. He was not yet satisfied with the way he had expressed himself. Indeed, he was not yet sure of what exactly he wanted to say. And Turugun was trying to come to grips with what his mentor was saying.

They continued thus for a long time.

At last Buruda said, "I could not understand why the makaron from Nundah looked so sad when we took what he said so lightly. I looked closely at him while the singing and dancing were going on, and I saw no sign of madness. He did not grin foolishly, as some people do who are not possessed of all their wits. He did not run around wildly, or fling his arms about. He just looked disappointed, that's all."

Turugun waited for more. He could not yet see where Buruda's thoughts were heading, but he had to admit that there was no doubt that what he had said so far made sense. He had also noticed the sadness on the makaron's face.

Buruda spoke again. "I was troubled," he said, "and I could not leave these doubts of mine alone. I was troubled, because many of the things I had believed might turn out to be false – if the makaron from Nundah was not mad. But I could not convince myself that he was mad, even though I, too, had laughed at the stupidity of the things he had said!"

Turugun blinked, confused. His mind was beginning to become as troubled as Buruda's.

"I said to myself," Buruda told his favourite son, "that I would try to believe that the makaron was neither mad nor stupid. If that was true, though, some of what he had said ought to make some sense. And what had he really said? Nothing much, except that this bu-ul Dhidhu had been killed, and had come back as a bu-ul – not a baby – to live with people."

"But we already knew this could happen!" Turugun spluttered.

Buruda remained patient. His thoughts had begun to come more clearly.

"How do we know?" he asked Turugun.

"Because we have seen many spirits return."

"And who were these spirits?"

Then, at last, what Buruda was trying to say came through clearly to Turugun. He, too, began to pace excitedly back and forth. Finally he became still. "The only way we know that spirits can return freely from the land of the spirits is that we have seen the makaron," he said pensively. "If they are spirits, then the makaron from Nundah is mad! If the makaron from Nundah is not mad, then they may not be spirits!"

"I have thought long and hard about this," Buruda said. "Our people on K'Gari saw the first winged canoe, and thought of spirits. They came to Yarun, and then to Warun and Miandhin, and we thought of spirits because of their colour and their ignorance."

"But they are not spirits?"

"No, I do not believe any more that they are spirits. I believe they are evil men!"

Still, Turugun could see other problems. "But their magic thunder-sticks! The way they make their canoes move without poles!"

"Even men can use magic," Buruda reminded him. "I have seen bu-ul use magic songs that they sing in the direction of a young woman they want to attract, and it has worked. We manngur use the magic kundir stone, and it works. No, the fact that they use magic is not proof that they are spirits!"

By the time they had finished talking it was getting dark, so they descended the hill to the shelters where they had left their families. They agreed to keep the subject of their discussion secret. There was no point in trying to convince others of something it had taken Buruda so long to wrestle with before he himself had been able to reach a conclusion. Buruda reminded Turugun that he had not been able to convince the other manngur that the sore on Naruman's dhun had had something to do with Damira's dead child. Yet Buruda was still convinced that the sore had made Naruman prepare Damira's binang in such a way that it had made it easier for an evil spirit to enter. He was not prepared yet to try to convince others of this new thing that had come to him – that the makaron were simply strange, evil men.

If he wasn't careful, it would not be too long before others began to think it was Buruda who was the mad one!

"There would be no point in trying to convince others, in any case," Buruda said. "After all, this does not alter anything at all. It makes it no easier to get rid of these evil beings. Indeed, it might have been easier to get rid of spirits. If these are men, they are acting in ways that we have never seen men act before. They seem to have no religion, no laws laid down in the Before-Time. They sit down on anybody's land, with no thought of the people whose land it is. And they seem to have no land of their own, for if they did, they would want to return the bones of their dead to that land, as people have always done. They may not be mad, but they are certainly lawless – and this makes them worse than spirits!"

Next day, when they and their families had returned to the camp by the creek, they found that Darvu had arrived with news from the south, and some of this news confirmed their fears that the makaron had no laws whatever.

The first piece of news was cheerful, in that it concerned the two dhugai who had continued to go out from Miandhin into Yugumbir country with their long cord and three sticks. Darvu reported that these two, in company with others, had set up camp near Dhalgumbun, near the very southern end of Yugumbir land. The Yugumbir had been cunning, for they had hung around the camp quietly, coming and going for days, to allay the suspicions of the dhugai party. Then one morning they had struck while five of the party were away. The main one who used the three sticks had been speared quickly, and then another, who had been sick in one of the shelters, had also been killed. Korbenbob had also used his club on a third one, and had thought he was dead, too. But they had later found out that he had recovered.

Darvu laughed as he told them this. "We heard from the Yugumbir messenger that Korbenbob was very angry when he found out he had not killed the dhugai! He and Meredeo and Bogi each claim to have had a hand in killing the other two, but Korbenbob had been so pleased that he alone had struck the third one down! When he found out that he had failed, he was very unhappy!"

The Yugumbir had taken some shiny pieces from the tools the dhugai had been using, intending to make spearheads and knives from them. But they had had to scatter some days later when a party of red-covered ones had surprised them in their camp, and they had been forced to leave some of these things behind.

"Still," Darvu said, "they are pleased they have shown these dhugai that they are not welcome in their land! They even burned their shelters to stop the spirits from returning!"

Buruda held his peace. The burning of the shelters would certainly prevent the spirits of the dead makaron from returning, but he very much doubted it would stop the others who, he was now convinced, were not really spirits.

While this section of Darvu's news was heartening, the rest made the hearts of his Undanbi listeners heavy. Many of them could remember the coming of the makaron to Warun, and then to Miandhin. They recollected the way the makaron had, like the expanding web of muthar the spider, spread out to sit down in Nunakul land at Bulan and Gumpi, and also in Yuggera country at Tulmur. And not many seasons ago they had built their huts at Nundah.

Now they were going further into country they had hitherto left alone!

There was talk that they had taken their alien animals into country far away – west of the great range that marked the western limit of Yuggera country. As in other parts, they had not asked the people in whose country they sat down for permission!

If that had been all that had happened, the Undanbi would still have felt reasonably secure, for the western edge of Yuggera territory was far away – much further than they would ever want to travel in their lifetime. Besides, it was in a direction opposite to the one the makaron at Miandhin would have to take to reach Undanbi land.

But there was more.

In Yuggera land, still far to the west but too close for comfort, the makaron had brought their animals to Goanumbi.

Buruda cursed when he heard this. It seemed to be as he had often claimed. The makaron first sent some of their kind to live with the people, and then followed them to sit down in the land! So it had been with Pamplet, Pinigan and Pardhen! So it had been now with Boraltju, who had stayed with Maltagara in Yuggera country! So it would probably be with Daramboi, Wandi and Moilu! He must remember to talk once more to Yuonmandi and the Dhindhinbara manngur about Wandi and Daramboi, who were still living with the people! They must be made to understand that it was highly dangerous to allow the makaron to stay!

The Undanbi would never let such a thing happen while he breathed!

The story of the makaron at Goanumbi was uglier than anything the Undanbi had heard before. True, there had been incidents that had made people feel sick inside ever since the makaron had arrived. Every killing with a thunder-stick had caused an uproar among the people. The theft of the woman's skin had made their blood run hot. And perhaps the most horrible incident up to now had involved the Komidi who had had the skin of the Turrbal bu-ul stuffed with straw.

But many of these wrongs had been avenged.

Now at Goanumbi there was a dhugai called Kokki, who had Maltagara and his Yuggera at their wits' end. This Kokki had plenty of helpers, and they all had yeraman, which not only made them very hard to catch, but also made it impossible to run fast enough to escape. A number of Yuggera at Goanumbi had already fallen to Kokki's thunder-stick, as he had led his evil helpers in thundering raids on helpless people in their camps.

But worse than the thunder-sticks, these wicked dhugai possessed a number of huge dogs, so savage that their slavering jaws seemed to like nothing better than to tear people apart. There were stories that had drifted in to the Turrbal from Goanumbi of strong bu-ul who had had their entrails ripped out by these vicious animals, the like of which had never been seen before.

Darvu had to pause in his story at this stage to allow the angry threats and curses to run their course. If this Kokki had been within reach at that moment, the Undanbi bu-ul would have used their bare hands to pull off his wundu and dhun, to tear his tongue from his mouth and his eyes from their sockets! Their own teeth would have ripped open his throat and severed his windpipe!

They were pleased to hear that Maltagara had vowed vengeance. They could imagine the awesome sight if the whole of the fighting men of the Yuggera ever assembled in one place to face this Kokki! They were many times more numerous than the Undanbi.

The rest of Darvu's news was even more unsettling. There were no more tales of cruelty, certainly. But the fact that the makaron had sat down in so many places was extremely disturbing, to say the least.

There were makaron in Dungibara country. Two lots had sat down in Dungidau land – one lot near Gunundhin, and another at Bumgur. And there was yet another group at Durundur.

Durundur! That was just west of the Nalbo mountains, two of which they could see from where they were standing – only one sleep away! Their consternation was great, and they looked fearfully in that direction, almost as if they might be able to discern these evil makaron, even at this distance!

That night there was a meeting of all the people at the great campfire. For once the children were quiet, for the fear that possessed their elders had communicated itself to them, and they huddled together, waiting for someone to speak.

Dhubal rose and addressed the assemblage. "These makaron are so close to our land," he said, "that it is possible they may even try to sit down on it! We must sharpen up the points of our spears, and make sure our fighting boomerangs and clubs have no flaws that will cause them to shatter! All our weapons must be kept in perfect fighting trim, for we never know when we may need to use them! The makaron are too close!"

"Yau-ai!"

Naruman was of the opinion that they should not wait for the arrival of the makaron. "Let us paint ourselves for war!" he yelled, jumping into the air. "Let us go to our neighbours, the Nalbo, and help them drive these makaron from Durundur!"

About half the bu-ul yelled "Yau!" and rattled spears against shields.

But Bulangga pointed out that there were two things wrong with this course of action. First, such an action might be interpreted by their neighbours as a hostile act against the Nalbo themselves. Second, the Nalbo had not asked for help, so they had no right to trespass on Nalbo land. "Besides, they have not even let us know that the makaron are at Durundur," he said.

"They haven't been there long," Darvu explained. "It was only three days ago that we got word. I have no doubt they will send you news before long."

Then Turugun stood. "The movements of these makaron follow some sort of pattern," he said. "There were makaron many seasons ago in the country beyond the western mountains bordering Yuggera land, and the head makaron at Miandhin went with Boraltju over these same mountains only two seasons ago. Now the makaron are sitting down beyond those mountains. Boraltju himself lived with the Yuggera for many seasons, and now the makaron are sitting down at Goanumbi."

A curse or two punctuated the night as they recalled Darvu's account of what the villanous Kokki was doing at that place.

Turugun continued. "Many seasons ago you will remember we killed the Komidi while there was a kivar-yangga in Dungibara country. This Komidi had come on his yeraman and travelled through Yuggera, Dungibara, Garumngar and Dungidau land. Now the makaron are sitting down with their animals in Dungibara and Dungidau country. More makaron always seem to follow where small numbers have been before."

He paused before adding, "No makaron has ever come on to Undanbi land like these others."

"What about the mad makaron with Paldha?" someone wanted to know.

"And what about Nalbo country?" another asked. "We have never heard of small groups going into Nalbo country!"

Buruda rose, and they were quiet. "You are not right when you say that makaron have never visited the Undanbi," he told them. "Indeed, the old Dimmangali manngur of the Dhundubari told me long ago that, even a long time before many of us were born, Midherplinda crossed Undanbi land to the Nalbo mountains. But Turugun is also right. These makaron seem to like to send some of their sort in first before they arrive in their hordes with their accursed animals. That is why I have long argued that no makaron should ever be allowed to live with the Undanbi! That is why I have warned the other nations against claiming kinship with these evil ones!"

A fierce murmur of agreement swept through the throng.

"The Nalbo may ask for help," Buruda went on, "and if they do, we will give it. But we are used to looking after ourselves in our own country, and undoubtedly that is what the Nalbo will want to do. Likewise, we must look after our own business, and our business is to ensure that no makaron who sets foot on Undanbi soil breathes for too long! We have done this in the past, and we must continue to do so! Many makaron have already been sent to the land of spirits by our spears and clubs!"

Boomerangs rattled against spears. "Yau-ai!"

He waited for the noise to subside before he continued. "But what has happened in the past may not be good enough for now," he warned them. "In the past, some makaron may have gone through Undanbi country without our knowledge. Particularly when we have had our camp on the seashore, as we do in the seasons when fish are plentiful, one or two might have slipped past on the trading track – or even within Undanbi land on this side of the trading track! Daramboi, Wandi and Moilu probably did!" He paused to let this sink in. "And this may not have mattered too much in the past, for they did not sit down. But now that the makaron are sitting down with their animals in different places, we must make sure that we know immediately if one single makaron dares to enter our sacred land!"

"Yau-ai!" Again the rattle of weapons was heard.

Much discussion followed Buruda's speech. Eventually it was decided that from that time on, even in the seasons of plentiful fish, some Undanbi families would always be camped on the southern and western approaches. They would take turns in watching for the accursed makaron. They would not be taken by surprise as some other nations had been. At the first approach of the makaron and their animals, the fighting men would paint for battle and drive them out.

Next day the messenger from the Nalbo arrived, as Darvu had predicted. The Nalbo did not intend to cause trouble with the makaron at Durundur.

Buruda cursed long and loudly. When would people learn some sense?

✧

Chapter 27

1840-41: Massacre at Grantham by "Cocky" Rogers, manager of Mocatta's station. Two Aborigines hanged at the Wickham Terrace windmill for the murder of Stapylton and Tuck.

Turugun and Buruda were engaged in earnest conversation before the older manngur's hut, their faces mirroring their concern. Nerida and Guluwa were also listening, for what was being said concerned women as well as men, and there had already been much discussion about this particular problem whenever people gathered, with opinions almost as varied as the number who had ever voiced a point of view. But by and large the general feeling was that Buruda had been right in the beginning.

"It has to go back to the sore on Naruman's dhun," he was telling Turugun for the umpteenth time. "There is no other way that little Bandhuru could be as he is! Naruman must recognise from now on that his dhun does not prepare a woman's binang in the correct way! That little scar on his dhun must somehow affect a woman's binang, so that evil spirits find it easier to enter!"

As if to emphasise what they were talking about, at that very moment a group of children ran past the hut, one of the older girls carrying Bandhuru, whose hoarse laugh could be heard amongst the squeals of the others.

"At least the little fellow is happy enough," Turugun said. "And the blisters on the palms of his hands and the soles of his feet are clearing up, so that he can toddle round again."

"Yes," Guluwa said. "But what a pity those sores round his lips left those cracks and peeling skin!"

"No matter what I have done, nothing has helped," Buruda muttered. "The kundir seems useless, as does every bit of medicine that we have ever used for sores! The sicknesses that come from the makaron seem to be beyond our powers!"

"My kundir was also powerless," Turugun reminded him, concerned at the dejected tone in the older man's voice.

"But it is strange that no medicine we try has cleared up his running nose or husky voice," Nerida said. "Never before have we failed to cure these with the proper medicines!"

"There is nothing we can do with these illnesses that have arrived since the time when the makaron first arrived," Buruda admitted dispiritedly. "All we seem to be able to do for the scab sickness is leave the families behind and run!"

For a while there was silence as they remembered the family they had been forced to abandon in a hut between Coochin and Daki-Bomon only four moons before. The sole survivor had been the eldest daughter, who had rejoined them only half a moon ago after her scabs had healed and she had set fire to the hut that had been the death place of her parents and two younger brothers.

The accursed makaron! Why did they bring these disasters on the people? How did they bring the scab sickness? How had they put the sore on Naruman's dhun?

At least the sore on Garwidha's breast healed up," Nerida said, anxious to inject some mood of optimism into the conversation. "And Garwidha said it didn't hurt."

"Naruman said that about the sore on his dhun!" Buruda reminded her. "And the little scar on Garwidha's breast is very like the little scar on Naruman's dhun! I don't think we can take much comfort from the fact that they both healed!"

Nerida caught her breath fearfully. By now all the women knew about Buruda's dream, even the fact that there had been no trace of people left on the bare earth. They knew he had seen the scabs and sores on dead people. But surely there would always be people! Surely the sores would not kill them all! Surely the makaron would leave them in peace!

"Can't you do anything?" she asked Buruda. "Is there nothing?"

Buruda heard the fear in her voice, and was saddened that he could offer so little comfort to this still-beautiful wife of his. "We have learnt a little about the sicknesses," he told her. "Every time there is an outbreak of the scab sickness, we will run from the evil spirits causing it so that they cannot find their way to the other families. But this sickness of Bandhuru – it is different. Even by the time Damira came to rejoin the people after his birth, there was no sign of it."

"Only that his cry was husky," Nerida reminded him. "Other than that, there was nothing."

"And it was after that that Garwidha got the sore on her breast," Turugun said.

"Yes. And now Damira is expecting another baby," Buruda mused. "By the size of her belly, it won't be long before you will once more take her away to give birth."

Nerida waited for him to say more, the look on her face showing her inner turmoil. She remembered the first time. She could still hear the thud of Garwidha's digging-stick as she had dealt with the misshapen thing that had emerged from Damira's binang, could still see the look of horror on the mother's face. And the second time – how happy Damira had been to suckle her little baby! The worrying had not come till later, as little Bandhuru had weakened, refusing to become as black as he ought, for all the world as if he was bent on keeping close to the spirit-land from which he had come. Then had come the blisters and the cracks and the peeling skin.

What would this next babe be like? Nerida knew that Damira was terrified that her baby would come out like the first one. She had even confided to Garwidha that it might be worse if it came out like Bandhuru for, much as she loved her little boy, she was not sure that it might not have been better if he too had been clubbed to death. Then he would have been spared the suffering he had been forced to endure.

Had Naruman's dhun been able to prepare Damira's binang better this time? This was the thought in all their minds.

It was Turugun who broke the silence. "Let us hope that Damira's baby will be a proper person in all respects this time," he said. "But it seems that Bandhuru had nothing wrong with him at birth apart from his husky cry." He paused a moment, and then went on. "I know it is the women who must make the decisions at this time, but it seems that, if this next babe also has a husky voice, it might be a sign that an evil spirit has once more entered Damira's binang. Perhaps the women should act accordingly."

Nerida looked imploringly at Buruda.

"I think Turugun is right," he admitted unwillingly. "There seems to be nothing we can do to save our children from this new sickness other than to do away with those born with it, as the women have always done when some monster has found its way into a woman's binang. It could be better to make a mistake or two in this regard, rather than end up with so many sick children that the nation becomes too weak to survive – which seems to be the wish of the makaron!"

Nerida's heart sank at these words. She knew how hard it was for any mother to lose a baby after she had carried it in her belly for so many moons. The spirit might be evil, but a mother could easily overlook that in the closeness she always felt for the spirit-child who had chosen to make her its home. Bandhuru was proof enough of that. Not only Damira – but all the women – found it easy to spoil this boy whose health was so delicate.

No, it would not be easy to follow the advice of the two manngur. It had been hard enough for Garwidha to act out of necessity with the first baby. How much harder it would be to put to death a small child simply because it had a husky voice!

Nevertheless, it would have to be considered. Next morning, after long discussion with other women, she and Garwidha came to the conclusion that it might be best to take no chances with Damira's baby-to-be. Damira might hate them both for a while but, even if there was even the faintest sign that an evil spirit resided within the small body, it should be sent back to the spirit-land without delay.

A week later they built Damira's birth-hut well away from the creek camp. Two mornings after that a little girl made her appearance, and they heaved sighs of relief to hear its lusty cry.

Damira seemed intent on allowing none but herself to suckle this miraculously healthy child, and the two older women looked on happily while the young mother nursed her little girl.

But on the fourth day Nerida began to suspect that the infant's cry was sharper, and next morning was horrified to see that its head was larger than it had been. By the end of that day even Damira could see the effect of the fluid that was swelling the skull.

Nevertheless, she grimly held on to her baby as the two midwives fought to wrest the now obviously monstrous child from her arms.

This time it was Nerida's digging-stick that delivered the death-blow, and it was Garwidha who hurried away to bury the body in such a way that the evil spirit would be thwarted in its attempts to find its way to the camp, where it might bring harm to the people. But, despite all the arguments Garwidha and Nerida could bring to bear, Damira scored her face with the marks of sorrow. And that night, as a fierce storm hit the area, she insisted in sitting outside the hut in the pelting rain, loudly lamenting, pleading with Bulla-Bira the lightning to put an end to her sorrow.

"Why?" she kept moaning, rocking back and forth. "Why? I did nothing wrong! I ate no food that is forbidden to women carrying a spirit-child! Why?"

But there was no answer. Nor did the lightning oblige by striking her dead.

For a long time after they had returned to camp, Nerida found it hard to rest. The nights seemed punctuated with the scream of the grief-stricken mother and the sound of the thud of her digging-stick on that grossly-misshapen head. Again and again Buruda had to awaken her and hold her sobbing in his arms until the sounds faded.

And Buruda began to wonder if this was how the makaron would ensure the death of the people. Would these evil beings put such a heavy curse on them that eventually all babies would be born with the shapes of monsters?

But two other women gave birth soon afterwards – one to a boy and another to a girl – and both babies showed no signs of the curse whatsoever.

Then, as the days became as long as they ever did, the Undanbi were reminded that the makaron had other ways of getting rid of people.

It was Baribah who brought the news from Maltagara. He had taken some time, going first to the Yugumbir and then to the Turrbal and Ningi on his way to the Undanbi. But Maltagara had impressed on him the importance of letting the Undanbi manngur know what had happened.

"Let Buruda know," he had said to the emissary before he had left with his white boomerang, "what has happened to us at Goanumbi! Tell him we are beginning to learn that he is right! We should never have let the dhugai near us in the first place! We should have used our spears and clubs on every dhugai that ever barged across our territory, and that includes Boraltju! Tell Buruda that Boraltju is no longer kin to us! And tell him that the dhugai can be kin to nobody but their own evil selves!"

Buruda listened carefully while Baribah spoke. Then he said, "Tell me, my friend – does Maltagara still believe that the makaron are spirits returned from the land of the dead?"

A gasp went up from most of the listening Undanbi. They were surprised to hear this question. What could Buruda mean by it? Surely everyone knew that the makaron were evil spirits! Surely there was no doubt about that!

But Baribah shook his head. "No. We do not know where the dhugai come from, but we no longer believe that they are spirits! The perfidy of Boraltju convinced us of that, when he showed the head dhugai the way to the high places beyond the mountains!"

The Undanbi people found this new idea puzzling. Only Turugun found it easy to understand, since it was only to him that Buruda had expressed his doubts as to the origins of the makaron.

But the Undanbi would have to think about this some other time, for Baribah was once more speaking.

"I think you have heard of the dhugai called Kokki, who has many dhugai to help him and savage dogs huge enough to pull down a bu-ul and rip out his entrails." He paused for signs of assent before proceeding. "This accursed Kokki came upon our main camp at Goanumbi two moons ago while we were away hunting and took all the sheets of bark from our huts, carrying them away on his yeraman to build his own huts in the place on which he has sat down! When we returned, there was no place for us to take shelter from the rain!"

Now the Undanbi had things to consider other than the origins of the makaron. A roar of disgust rose at Baribah's tidings. Who would do such a thing? Huts were something that strong winds sometimes destroyed, and at times fires also took their toll. But to every nation it was important to have semi-permanent bases where they could be sure of shelter, where they would not need to go to the trouble of building fresh huts every time they came back to that area. It was always comforting to know that there were shelters to come back to, even though they might need to be renovated to some degree.

Besides, there were the trees to consider. It was not right to expect trees to give new bark to make shelters, unless the old bark had deteriorated to such an extent that it was no longer serviceable. The spirits of the trees were always pleased to supply more once this had been explained to them. But how did you explain such a thing as had been done by this makaron?

"Is Kokki still alive?" Naruman called out, and a number of bu-ul rattled their weapons to show their feelings in the matter.

"Unfortunately, yes," Baribah replied. "He is strong, with many helpers, and his savage dogs are always alert. It is not easy to surprise him."

All knew there would be much more information to come from Baribah. Maltagara and his people would not easily accept the desecration of their camp.

"What did the Yuggera do?" Buruda asked quietly.

Baribah smiled grimly. "There are many helpers, and there are many dogs and thunder-sticks. But there are also many animals which the dhugai call dhipa."

"Dhipa?" Buruda had never heard this word before.

"The thick-haired animals which make a funny noise, and whose feet have two toes." Baribah mimicked the sound of the animal, and Buruda realised he was talking of the same sort of animal that the Ningi had killed so long ago when the makaron had first come to Warun.

Baribah's brow darkened at the thought of these animals. "These dhipa have eaten the grass so that most of the kangaroos have hopped away from Goanumbi. And the huge dogs have eaten the rest of the kangaroos! Even the emus are scarce! All you can see most of the day are dhipa and more dhipa! We Yuggera have decided that, since the dhugai have driven the animals away from our hunting land, it is only right that we should hunt the dhipa!"

A roar of approval rose from his listeners, only to subside as they saw the sudden look of pain that crossed the face of their visitor.

"One day we came across a lot of these animals which were not under the eye of any dhugai," he went on. "We had speared very few kangaroos that day, so naturally we availed ourselves of the food that presented itself to us. But as we were in the process of roasting some, Kokki appeared with his helpers on their yeraman and, almost before we knew what was happening, our bu-ul were falling to their dogs and their thunder-sticks! We threw our spears and boomerangs, but there was too much confusion, and they did no good! We could do nothing but run as fast as we could! And even as we did so, their dogs were snarling at our heels and pulling bu-ul down, and more bu-ul were falling to their thunder-sticks!"

There was a long silence, and then there was a clatter of weapons from the listeners as loud as Mumba the thunder. This was not to be borne! These makaron must be obliterated!

At last there was enough quiet for Buruda to ask the question that was in everybody's mind.

"How many?"

"Gurwindha!" The long-drawn-out word left nobody in any doubt as to the number who had fallen. "Most of our families, Maltagara's included, are mourning Dimmangali brothers, fathers, and sons!"

Again came the rattle of weapons and shouted curses.

But it was all very well to threaten, Baribah pointed out. All Yuggera bu-ul were now permanently painted for battle, with their weapons in constant readiness. But how could you fight dhugai who had thunder-sticks and dogs, and whose yeraman moved faster than a bu-ul could possibly run?

"All we can do is take the dhipa when we can," he said wearily. "And every now and again, when we are lucky enough to surprise a dhugai alone, we can let our spears and boomerangs speak for us!"

For many months after Baribah's visit the Undanbi kept themselves in a state of instant readiness. No makaron must ever be allowed to set one foot on Undanbi soil! What had happened to the Yuggera must never happen to the Undanbi!

And gradually the idea took root that these interlopers were only men – but evil men indeed, who must be made to return to whatever country they had left.

Then, as the cold of wallaidhu once more heralded the return of the big shoals of mullet and tailer, a messenger arrived from Gariwar. The dhugai at Miandhin had brought in two bu-ul of the Yugumbir, and had put them into one of their huts. Paldha had spoken to some of the dhugai, and they had told him that they would kill these two bu-ul within half a moon.

"Why?" Buruda wanted to know. "Why will they kill these Yugumbir?"

"They told Paldha that it was because the Yugumbir had killed the two dhugai near Dhalgumbun," the messenger told him.

That was understandable, at least. Apparently the makaron understood the principle of a death for a death. But why on earth bring them back to Miandhin? Surely it would have been easier and kinder to kill them in their own country! The fact that one of them had been nowhere near the earlier killing was beside the point. A death was required for a death, and the Yugumbir would understand that.

But why bring them back to Miandhin?

"We don't know," the messenger said. "But Gariwar thought you might like to come to Miandhin and see what happens, for Paldha says the dhugai will do this thing in the open."

There was no understanding the ways of the makaron. Why would anyone want to do this thing in the open? After all, from what the messenger had been able to tell them, it did not seem that there would be a fight on the baiyaba, or anything like that. But what else could it mean?

Perhaps the makaron did have something like the baiyaba, after all!

Turugun went with Buruda to Miandhin. More and more lately Buruda had found himself depending on the young manngur, drawing power from the strength and virility of the younger man. And more and more he was becoming content to allow Turugun to speak while he listened.

They arrived at the Turrbal camp at Barrambin at sunset on the third day, just in time to join in the cry for the dead. Afterwards, it did not take Gariwar long to give them the latest news. Paldha had been to Miandhin that very day and had learnt that the two Yugumbir would be killed tomorrow.

"Is there to be a fight on the baiyaba?" Turugun asked.

Paldha laughed shortly. "No! You wouldn't get a dhugai to stand out on a baiyaba and face a bu-ul man to man! These Yugumbir bu-ul will be strangled!"

Buruda was horrified. This was surely not a death befitting a fighting man! Had Paldha perhaps mistaken the meaning of the words of the makaron who had given him the information?

But Paldha was adamant. He had made no mistake. The two Yugumbir would be taken to the round stone hut on the hill overlooking Miandhin the following morning, and there they would be strangled in full view of anybody who cared to turn up!

Next morning Gariwar, accompanied by the two Undanbi manngur, led the whole of the Turrbal nation to the hill, and there they saw what must have amounted to the whole makaron nation crowding round the strange stone hut. These makaron were laughing and joking as if they had just arrived at a bunyi feast and were greeting old friends.

When the dhugai saw the Turrbal approaching they began to shout and laugh even more. And as the procession drew closer with the three manngur in the lead, they moved aside a little as if to allow these newcomers a better view of what was about to happen. But then the laughter became more subdued as it became obvious to all that the bu-ul had appeared fully armed, contrary to their usual practice.

As the dhugai moved to one side, a number of red-covered ones ran around to place themselves between them and the Turrbal.

But Gariwar had achieved his aim, and Buruda smiled grimly to himself. The makaron might kill two bu-ul today, but they would be aware always that the Turrbal had turned up at this killing fully armed, and they would wonder why Gariwar had led his men into Miandhin in this fashion.

It was good to see the red-covered ones jump and the others start back in fear as a number of bu-ul rattled their weapons. And Buruda found himself almost laughing at the thought of what their reaction might have been if Naruman had been present. A more accomplished rattler of weapons and curser of the makaron than Naruman would be hard to find!

But something was happening at the top of the hut, and the people were surprised to see a dhugai appear whose face was covered as if he was avoiding contact with his mother-in-law. He came out onto a high platform made of logs and tied together in some fashion. Above this platform was a stick protruding from the hut, and from this stick hung two thick cords with loops.

There was an audible intake of breath from the people. The significance of those two loops was not lost on them.

Then the two Yugumbir bu-ul came out onto the platform, their hands tied behind their backs. They looked down and grinned as they saw the sea of black faces amongst the dhugai.

"It is good to see people again!" one of them yelled. "These dhugai do not smell good!"

The Turrbal laughed. This bu-ul had courage.

"Don't forget to die like a bu-ul!" Turugun called out, and the two grinned down at him.

"Don't forget to live like a bu-ul!" the second man yelled back. "And don't ever forget that a bu-ul can kill a dhugai!"

The rattle of weapons that greeted these words caused a sudden stir among the red-covered ones, who half lifted their thunder-sticks to their shoulders.

But now the people were interested in something else that was happening above them. The dhugai whose face was covered put the two looped cords over the heads of the two bu-ul. And then a second dhugai, draped in colourful covering, stepped out onto the platform and, holding a piece of white bark before him, was yelling out words that all could hear.

Paldha was standing nearby, and Turugun asked him what was being said. But even Paldha could make neither head nor tail of the flood of words, understanding only the word "death".

Then the dhugai whose face was covered pulled on a stick and the two Yugumbir fell through a hole that appeared suddenly beneath their feet. Their bodies jerked to a halt as the cords tightened, and then began a horrifying series of jerks and contortions that seemed to the onlookers to go on for a very long time. Only when the eyes were bulging from their sockets and the tongues were protruding from the swollen faces did the movements cease.

A roar came from the watching bu-ul, and spears rattled on shields. Even the women rattled their digging-sticks together. The red-covered ones jumped and brought their thunder-sticks up to their shoulders. At the same time the rest of the dhugai stopped laughing and scattered, pausing only after they had put quite a distance between themselves and the menacing people.

But no spears cleft the air. There were too many red-covered ones for that. Gariwar held his shield aloft for all to see, calling out that any precipitate action could only bring sorrow to the people.

Then Buruda stepped forward. He had been shocked beyond belief at the method used by the makaron to kill the two Yugumbir, whose bodies swung lifelessly at the ends of the cords. This was no death for any bu-ul!

In the silence that followed his appearance alone at the front, magnificent in his rage, his voice boomed out for all to hear. And as he spoke, his spear stabbed the air above his head.

"You have killed these two bu-ul from the country of the Yugumbir," he called out to the makaron. "But it is a shameful thing you have done, no matter how justified you think the killing was! You makaron will have to take care from now on if you venture too far into the land of the people without protection, for you will not return! And above all, do not come into Undanbi land, for our dhan are pledged to make sure you never leave it! And you had better make sure you dispose of the bodies of these two Dimmangali properly, or their ghosts will wreak havoc among your shelters, even when you sleep at night!"

The ensuing rattle and clatter of weapons from the people caused the red-covered ones to jump back still further. But they took great care to keep their thunder-sticks at their shoulders.

Still the people remained in their places, waiting to see what would be done with the bodies. Four Yugumbir bu-ul who had come to Miandhin to see the killing edged their way to the front, eager to claim the bodies in order to allow their people to perform the proper rites of burial. But the red-covered ones pointed their thunder-sticks in their direction, and the four became still.

Then a container on rollers pulled by a yeraman was brought under the bodies and the dhugai with the covered face cut the cord. The thud as the two bodies hit the floor of the container sent a shock-wave through the people, and some began to cry aloud. The four Yugumbir in particular could not contain their grief, and refrained only with difficulty from launching their spears.

Again Gariwar held up his shield, and quiet descended. The people remained still then for a long time, facing the red-covered ones and the other dhugai beyond them, who seemed too fascinated by the spectacle to run, despite their obvious terror.

Finally, Gariwar spat deliberately on the ground and turned his back. As one, all the people did the same. And as they walked slowly in the direction of Barrambin, they heard the great sigh that escaped the lungs of the dhugai still gathered on the hill.

These dhugai would think twice before again using such an uncivilised method of getting revenge.

Notes on Chapter 27

At the inquiry into the Grantham massacre, "Cocky" Rogers and his men claimed that NO Aborigines at all were killed, because none of the guns would fire!

Apparently a convict took young Tom Petrie to see one of the bodies of the executed Aborigines in its coffin. He was horrified at the gruesome sight.

Chapter 28

1842: Shepherds poison between fifty and sixty Aborigines with arsenic at Kilcoy station.

Buruda looked at the small party departing along the narrow track leading up the creek in the direction of the Nalbo mountains, and a sudden feeling of foreboding overcame him. Nothing seemed to have caused this sudden disquiet. Indeed, only a few short heartbeats before he had been thinking of what a beautiful day it was for Bulangga to be starting his visit to the Dungidau at Bumgur, and nothing had changed in that short time. Above him wuruma the sea-eagle could still be heard whistling as he circled, eyes searching the waters of the creek for signs of an unwary mullet. Behind his hut, in front of which Nerida and Dhuluru were busy collecting their digging-sticks and dhilla preparatory to going out after bangwal, he could hear dinda the peewee calling as he searched for insects.

Nothing was amiss.

And yet suddenly nothing seemed right. Gone was the sense of well-being, gone the feeling of contentment, gone the sensation of peace and harmony

In their place – only this uneasiness of spirit that could not be explained.

He could hear the women and children coming from the other end of the camp, and made up his mind quickly.

"We will move out today and hunt toward Warudhra," he told Nerida. "It is time our family took their turn watching the trading track for signs of the makaron. I'll go and tell Wungul while you prepare."

"But," Dhuluru protested, "you said nothing -!"

"Quiet, girl!" Nerida told her shortly, guessing the reason for her daughter's reluctance to go. "You'll be with Yingera as his wife before next wallaidhau, I expect! You'll have plenty of time with him then!"

By the time Buruda returned to the hut, the two were already moving through the trees in the direction of Warudhra. He collected his weapons without haste and, as he did so, tried to come to grips with his sense of unease. He had told Turugun and Wungul simply that he had become concerned that the makaron might enter Undanbi land, and that he was going toward the west to strengthen their watch in that area. He was, indeed, not sure that it wasn't this concern that had given him the prickly feeling up the back of his neck in the first place.

He left the camp heavily laden, for he would need all his fighting gear if he were to encounter makaron. Ever since the coming of these invaders all bu-ul who took turns in protecting the fringes of their lands always took all their weapons. His throwing-club was tucked into his belt parallel to his backbone, where it was not only out of the way but also out of sight of an unsuspecting enemy.

He did not follow the path taken by Nerida and Dhuluru. They would dig bangwal and hunt small game on the way, and he would meet them at Warudhra for the evening meal. But he had other things to do first. Perhaps his dark premonition had to do with the magic crystals that protected the Undanbi from harm. Had someone entered the sacred area and disturbed them? He would need to check.

As he swung along, he cast his mind back over the last few seasons. It had been a long time now since he had felt that inner peace that comes from knowing that all things are in their right place. No longer could he feel the throbbing heartbeat of the earth when he stood in the stillness if the bush.

Perhaps it was simply that he was getting old. His beard was grey and, although he could throw spear and boomerang as accurately as ever, so that there was still no bu-ul who could stand against him on the baiyaba –with the exception, of course, of Turugun, whom he would never face - he felt as though he had lost his zest for living. He no longer looked forward to the gathering of the nations at the great bunyi feasts as he had in the past. The blood no longer sang through his veins as it had in days gone by.

Yes, perhaps he was just getting old. But even that thought troubled him, for he knew that many of his own age – Wungul, for instance – still felt more of the zesl for life than he did this morning. Why was it that he felt so old?

Perhaps it was the makaron, for he above all men had early seen the danger of these evil creatures, so that by now it seemed to him that his whole life had been taken up thinking only of them. Where others had been able to lose themselves in the joy of the hunt and the thrill of the contests on the baiyaba, at the back of Buruda's mind had lurked the evil shadows of the makaron. He had not for a long time been able to eradicate the thought of impending doom, the feeling that it was only a matter of time before the whole fabric of civilised society would collapse and leave nothing in its place except the chaos, lawlessness and barbarism of the makaron.

Where were the great spirits of the Before-Time? Why did they not rise up and expel these evil makers of magic?

He found the stones untouched in their protective bark, and the marks on the trees fresh and clear. So these had not been the cause of his mental malaise. Still, he found some comfort to his spirit in handling the crystals that had felt the touch of countless manngur before him, and he once again performed the ceremony invoking the protection of the mighty beings who had created this great land.

He wondered how many nations would attend the coming bunyi festival. The council of the bu-ul would have to decide which families would remain at home to bring news of any makaron incursions.

And a wave of resentment swept over him as he remembered the time –such a short time ago – when all families would attend the festivals and the other ceremonies, when there was no need to leave some behind to protect the land.

The accursed makaron!

He wished he knew a curse strong enough to bring death and destruction to the whole of that warped and twisted nation!

A family of kangaroos which had been resting in the shade of a bloodwood tree sprang up almost at his feet and hopped frantically away, but he ignored them. He could easily have brought one down, but he did not need one. He knew Nerida could be counted on to have enough to eat.

And once more the picture rose in his mind of the party that had gone off that morning to the Dungidau dhur. It had mainly been the older ones who had gone – Bulangga, Dhubal, Ngita, Wimbur, Koppakkin – for the younger and stronger bu-ul might be needed to repel the makaron and their animals. The only bu-ul of Buruda's generation to go had been Piringa, and he had left his family behind.

Still he could not shake off the feeling that he should have gone with them.

Why should such a thought keep returning? It was quite unreasonable, particularly in view of the fact that he could not raise any enthusiasm at the thought of meeting old friends.

Perhaps he felt this way because Bulangga had joked as he left about coming to the end of his life, about soon attending the dhur in the skies. Somehow the thought of never again seeing the father who had taught him to throw his first spear was not to be considered. There was so much he owed to the older man who had taught him everything he knew. Only the use of magic and medicine had come to him from another.

Still, thinking about the patient tutoring he had received in his youth helped to alleviate his heaviness of spirit to some extent. By the time he could smell the smoke rising from the fire Nerida had lit before the hut they usually occupied at Warudhra he had begun to feel somewhat easier. He had been foolish to succumb to this mood of depression. Bulangga was old, but not so old as to be tottery, and would undoubtedly live for many seasons yet. He would not be surprised to hear when they returned home that the old man had accepted a challenge on the baiyaba.

Nerida looked carefully at him as he strode toward the hut, and was relieved to see that his smile of greeting was almost back to normal. She had worried all day about the dark mood that had appeared to envelop him suddenly that morning. It was good to see that he had regained the spring in his step.

"You will like your meal tonight," she said, and laughed as he told her that he knew she had a spiny echidna, for he could smell it baking in the ashes.

Dhuluru too was pleased to see her father in a lighter mood. True, she had been disappointed when he had first sprung the news on them that they were coming to the trading track, for it would mean that Yingera would not be able to visit her until she returned to the main camp. But her naturally bright nature had reasserted itself during the day, and she had found herself looking forward to being alone with her parents. Her mother was right – she would shortly have a lifetime with Yingera. Besides, she had inherited from her parents the capacity to think deeply, and did not object to being alone with her thoughts, free from the burden of having to make conversation. When she was on her own in the bush, she could sometimes even hear the spirits of the trees divulging secrets for her ears alone – and beyond this whispering, on rare occasions, she could sense the existence of some great truth waiting to be understood.

No, time would not hang heavily during the period of her absence from Yingera.

That night, after a short early sleep, she awoke to become aware that her parents were finding pleasure in each other's body, and she was glad. Her small breasts tightened as she listened. There was something comforting in this age-old ritual which she had often witnessed when her parents thought her asleep, and which the women had explained to her in great detail to ensure that she would understand her part in it when her time came for her to go to her promised husband.

She heard the sighs of contentment as they finished, and in her mind she imagined herself and Yingera giving those same sighs.

It would be nice to be a wife, she thought to herself, as she drifted off to sleep once more.

Next day they moved south parallel to the trading track until they reached the country near the foot of Tibrogargan. That night they feasted on kangaroo, for Buruda's mood had lightened still more, and he had enjoyed stalking the small family whose ears he had seen poking up above the grass as they had rested in the shade during the warm part of the day. And when he had reached the hut that Nerida had freshened up for them, he had also been pleased to see that the women had dug some yams to add to their diet of bangwal cakes.

"These yams are good!" he told them later, and added as an afterthought, "I'll warrant they are better than the yams the makaron grow at Nundah!"

Next day, after they had dug bangwal, Nerida and Dhuluru stayed at the hut making dhilla, while Buruda made a leisurely trip to Beerburrum, the southernmost point of Undanbi land. He was searching for any sign that might proclaim the trespass of a makaron, but there was none. He returned late that evening to partake of some more of the kangaroo, more contented than he had been for some time.

That day the land had seemed to him to be more alive than he could remember it for many seasons.

But that night, just as he was on the point of falling asleep, he suddenly heard the death-wail calling to him from beyond Tibrogargan, and he sat bolt upright. Loud and clear it came, just as it had all those years ago in his dream, and he knew that something was terribly wrong. And even as he raced out of the hut, the death-wail still rang in his ears, and a feeling of deepest sadness swept over him, so that he did not even hear Nerida's sharp cry asking what was wrong.

He found himself joining in the cry, his voice rising and falling in time to the cadence of the chant. And always before his eyes floated the ghostly form of his favourite father.

And still the cry of death was in his ears, coming to him beyond the mountains of the Nalbo. He raked his face with his fingernails until the blood flowed, staining his beard. He raked until Nerida and Dhuluru flew at him and grabbed his hands to prevent him doing himself further harm.

And then he rocked back and forth, sobbing uncontrollably, refusing to be comforted.

His teacher-father was dead! Never more would he see his face, hear his voice, feel the touch of his hand!

Dimmangali! O, my father Dimmangali! Why did you die?"

For a long time he sat, his eyes vacant, gazing into the fire. The night turned cold, and Nerida threw a rug over his shoulders, while Dhuluru fed the flames of the fire. And all the time he gave no sign that he was aware of what they did.

Only now and again did he move, and each time it was to moan, "Dimmangali! Dimmangali!"

As the sky began to lighten in the east, he rose and threw off the rug. He took no notice of the crisp coolness of the morning, his mind now intent on the task ahead. Taking a ball of red clay from his dhilla, he coated himself all over with the red of mourning. Then he coated his boomerang with the same paint. And after that, he painted the designs on his body that would declare to all who saw him that he was determined to do battle.

Finally, he placed his nose-bone in position.

His father was dead, and someone was responsible. Whoever saw him coming with his red boomerang and his battle-paint would be left in no doubt that he was after revenge.

At no time had it occurred to Nerida to question the fact of Buruda's father's death. He knew, and that was enough. Nor did she try to stop him. She knew that what he was doing had to be done, and her heart was heavy within her.

Nevertheless, he would need food where he was going. She placed the remains of the bangwal cakes and the kangaroo in his dhilla.

Before he left, he looked deeply into Nerida's eyes and said quietly, "Tell Turugun to look after the Undanbi until I return!" Then, after resting a hand on Dhuluru's head for an instant, he turned his face to the west.

The two women looked listlessly after him for a time. Then, picking up their paraphernalia, they began to walk in the opposite direction.

All that day Buruda strode west, making camp that night near a stream beyond Durundur, which he skirted to keep clear of the makaron in that area. He had hardly noticed the country he was going through, his mind set on what he would meet when he got to Bumgur. How had his father met his death? It could not have been on the baiyaba, for that would not happen until the conclusion of the dhur, which must surely not even have started yet. What, then?

He would get no answer until he got to Bumgur.

Next morning, however, as the sun's heat was increasing, he saw a figure staggering toward him through the trees from the direction of Bumgur. As it got closer, he saw it was Piringa.

But this was not the Piringa who had left the creek camp only a few short days before. This was a Piringa whose face was pale, whose eyes were staring, and whose stomach kept trying to disgorge whatever was within. This was a Piringa who, no matter how much Buruda gave him to drink, never seemed to get enough.

And from Piringa he heard the story of what had happened at Bumgur. It took him most of the day to piece it together, for the sick man found trouble speaking, and Buruda had to bring all his medical knowledge to bear to relieve his suffering. But the story did come through, and Buruda discovered within himself a fury so great that he thought his body would burst under the pressure.

And again it was the makaron, those turds of things from that evil land of Inglun!

As the nations had gathered for the dhur, they had found that game was not as plentiful as it should be, since the makaron dhipa had eaten the grass. The Dungidau had therefore suggested that they kill some of the dhipa which had strayed beyond the watchful eyes of the makaron. But before they could do so, the makaron themselves had turned up at the big camp where all the nations were gathered, and had made signs to the people to wait while they brought them food.

"We were quite touched by their kindness," Piringa gasped. "We thought they must be different from the other makaron. One of the Dungidau even remarked that Maltagara of the Yuggera would be surprised to learn that not all moi killed people!"

The makaron had returned with meat – enough for many people. And many people had eaten. It was not until the evil ones had gone that people had begun to groan and void their bowels. Then they had found that they could not get enough to drink, and soon the stench of vomit and dung had hung over the whole camp as people, young and old, had writhed on the ground in agony, calling out for help. And always the cry had been for water – more water!

Then they had begun to die, and the dying had gone on for a long time, with the death-wail of the different nations signalling how many had been affected. And even the death-wails had been feeble, intoned as they had been by the sick and the dying.

Piringa began to cry once more as he again experienced the horror of the death scene, so indelibly etched on his mind.

"How many?" Buruda asked.

"All! All the Undanbi but me!"

And Buruda rocked back and forth, singing the song of death.

His other father! His mother! Nerida's father and mother! "How could you leave us, you Dimmangali? How could the makaron do this? Why should my wife have so much sorrow to bear? O, Nerida, my poor wife! O, my father-in-law and mother-in-law!"

But then Piringa gave him the news about the Wuganbara. Half that small nation had perished!

Half a nation! So many! How could that possibly be?

All next day he stayed with Piringa. He speared a kangaroo, and the sick man managed to keep some of it down. Gradually the raging thirst eased. Buruda got some wattle gum and managed to bring Piringa's diarrhoea under control. And the pains began to be less severe.

"You should leave me!" Piringa kept weakly insisting. "The makaron may be dead before you get there!"

But Buruda did not think that would be likely. There would be plenty left for him.

In any case, there was no hurry now. He was too late to perform the last rites on the bodies of the Undanbi. He knew his Dungidau brothers would have done everything correctly, since all knew the way used by the Undanbi to honour their dead. The skins and the bones would be kept for him. And even if he did not live to reach Bumgur, the Dungidau would themselves take the sacred remnants to the Undanbi.

Thus did all civilised nations behave.

And as a manngur his duty at the moment was to Piringa. But that did not mean there was less fury in his heart, less determination to exact payment for the deaths of his loved ones.

By next morning Piringa was so much better that it was obvious he would be able to make his way back to the creek camp unaided.

Leaving him plenty of food, Buruda once more turned his face toward Bumgur.

Notes on Chapter 28

The information in this chapter about the poisoning of the Aborigines at Kilcoy station has been taken from Queensland Ethnohistory Transcripts, Vol. 1, No.1, Book 1: "The Aboriginal Perspective. In this transcript, Bracewell and Davis's account of the incident is mentioned. These two (i.e. "Wandi" and "Daramboi") told Andrew Petrie that, at the great bunyi festival at Baroon in 1842, there had been many threats levelled at the whites, and that some reprisals had already occurred and others were sure to follow. They maintained that Andrew Petrie's party itself would have fallen victim to the vengeance of the Aborigines had it not been for their (i.e. Wandi and Daramboi's) intervention.

✦

Chapter 29

1842: Dimmangali!

Buruda took only enough time with Koradha, the Dungidau manngur, to assure himself that all necessary rites had been completed to ensure the safe passage of the Undanbi dead to the world of spirits. Nothing had been forgotten, and Koradha led him to the spot where the people had deposited the earthly remains of his loved ones. And here he remained grieving for the whole afternoon, chiding these Dimmangali for leaving their friends and relatives without so much as a goodbye, at times dragging his nails down his face to add to the marks of sorrow already there.

"We will not need to break your bones to find those responsible!" he told them. "And you can be sure they will pay!"

That night he talked quietly with Koradha.

"I see no Wuganbara here," he said.

"No. They have all gone home. There were too many dead!"

"How many?"

"We Dungidau lost four. The Wuganbara lost as many of their people as are still alive!"

Buruda groaned. "How many makaron have you killed?" he wanted to know.

"Two have already gone to the spirit-land!" Koradha stated flatly. "But there are still many more moi, and when the dhur is over, we will wage war on them!"

"Tomorrow at dawn I take the track to punish these makaron!" Buruda told him. "I will try to take my revenge as far away from the dhur as possible, so that those makaron who remain will not think those in this place are to blame! But take my vengeance I will! There will be at least one makaron in the spirit-land for each Undanbi they have killed!" He spat savagely on the ground as he spoke.

The frost was still on the grass as he set out next morning. It was so early that the magpies had not yet begun to warble.

That night he kept watch at a hut which he had seen two makaron entering in the evening. He would have liked to follow them in and take care of both at once, but four dogs were outside the hut, and he knew they would alert those inside before he had any chance of approaching close enough to allow him to act. So he waited in a nearby gully, dozing now and then, shivering despite the rug Koradha had given him.

Luck was with him. As dawn was breaking he saw the door open and one of the makaron move toward a nearby clump of trees.

Taking only his club, Buruda moved like a ghost through the half-light to the clump, one eye on the curled-up forms of the dogs near the hut. The squatting makaron, grunting with the effort of voiding his bowels, was unaware of his approach.

The club descended and he collapsed in his own dung, his brains spilling onto the ground.

Buruda saw one dog sit up and look in his direction, its ears pricked. He remained stock-still, and after a short time the dog curled up once more. Only then did he move silently back to the gully to collect his weapons and melt into the surrounding hills.

That night Wungul found him, sitting near his smokeless fire in the scrub.

"Good!" Buruda said. "Now we will be able to finish the job sooner, my brother!"

Two days later they came across two makaron moving their dhipa over toward Dhini, and waited silently in a clump of bushes that stood directly in the path of the animals. So motionless did they remain that the dhipa passed them by without so much as a sideways glance. And the red clay of mourning must have covered their scent admirably, for the dogs also passed by. Still, only one makaron came close to their hiding-place, and he fell to Buruda's spear without knowing what had happened. But his yeraman took fright and alerted the other makaron, who thundered away on his animal, leaving the dhipa unguarded.

One of the dogs bared its teeth and growled at them as they emerged from the bushes. But this was not one of the dogs the makaron used for hunting people. It was no bigger than people's dogs, and so could safely be ignored.

Wungul speared a dhipa as Buruda retrieved his own bloodied spear and wiped it on the makaron's covering.

That night they ate well. The dhipa was by no means a bad animal to eat.

"But these accursed alien animals are eating all the grass while the kangaroos and other animals are starving!" Buruda grated. "They should all be killed!"

Next day they came upon a number of dhipa with no watcher in sight. Methodically they went about the task of spearing as many as they could, managing to slaughter quite a number before the scent of blood caused the others to scatter in terror. Later they kept watch from the cover of the deep scrub, and were delighted to see the angry reaction of the two makaron who discovered the dead animals.

That night, as they sat near their small fire in the scrub, they busied themselves fashioning new weapons. It was impossible to tell how long they would need to hunt these makaron before they had at last exacted just compensation for the Undanbi lives that had been taken. It was important to have a supply of new weapons to replace spears that could break and clubs and boomerangs that could split, and this task was one that would occupy them at every opportunity.

It was good to feel the warmth of the fire.

"The fish will be shoaling," Wungul remarked longingly, "and we could be filling our mula with mullet! And talobilla the dolphin will be ready to bring the tailer in to the beach at Caloundra for the bu-ul to spear!"

"Yes, my brother," Buruda agreed. "Undanbi land calls us, to be sure! But Undanbi dead call us to seek revenge, and we cannot ignore their call! There will be time for mullet and tailer when we have done!"

But he had to admit that it was hard to be away from home. It would be good when he could once again feel the warmth of Nerida's body next to his own under their own fur rug! It had not been long since he had seen her, he knew, but it felt like half a lifetime.

It would even be good to have to put up once more with the boring remarks of Yingera as he invented excuses to be near Dhuluru!

Next morning as they reached the edge of the scrub, they saw two makaron with no dhipa in attendance searching the ground as they rode along on their yeraman, two huge dogs ranging far and wide around them.

They themselves were now being hunted. The makaron were not going to sit down while their friends were being killed.

They stayed in the cover of the scrub all day, planning, watching. Late in the afternoon they saw the two makaron ride back, still searching the ground.

That night Buruda said, "Two makaron on yeraman, with thunder-sticks and two dogs such as those, are dangerous odds! I think we would die if we were to tackle them in the open!"

Wungul waited for Buruda to continue. He knew his brother well enough to know there would be more to come. Somewhere in that agile brain a plan was hatching.

"But I wonder –!" Buruda went on softly after a while, holding a new spear over the fire to allow the wood to harden. "I wonder how it would be if we could get them to follow us into the scrub!"

"There are still the dogs!" Wungul warned him.

"Yes," Buruda admitted, "there are still the dogs! And those dogs are evil ones indeed! I remember the Yuggera and the Yugumbir telling us about them, and I remember that we found it hard to believe there could be animals that could pull down a bu-ul! But they were right!"

Silence reigned for some time. Then – "I think the dogs would easily get to us in the scrub before the makaron could," Buruda said. "What do you think?"

Wungul saw at once where the argument was leading. "Yes!" he said eagerly. "If we had to deal only with the dogs at first, I think we could do it!"

"I am sure we could!" Buruda smiled grimly. "Those dogs are big, but their skulls are not too thick for our clubs, surely!"

Next morning found them again looking out from the shelter of the scrub and once more, as on the previous day, the two makaron rode past, their eyes sweeping the ground. Once more the huge dogs passed, ranging far and wide round the two on their yeraman.

Without haste Buruda led the way back into the scrub, proceeding slightly at an angle to the direction in which their makeshift shelter lay. Soon they came to a shallow depression formed by the decay of a once-mighty forest giant.

Wungul grinned. "Perfect!" he said, swinging his club in great arcs to test the space available. "The two of us can work here without getting in each other's way! We even have plenty of room to launch a spear, if we need to!"

Grinning, Buruda placed all but one of his spears on the ground. Wungul did the same. This was the spot where they would see if these dogs could be fought!

Again they returned to their original position on the edge of the scrub. Bigi rose to his full height and began to drop to the western mountains. Every now and again they dozed. They knew they had plenty of time. The makaron would, if they repeated their actions of yesterday, not return till they had searched as far as they could in the daylight.

They readied themselves soon enough. The afternoon air was cooling down when they rose and stretched. Then, unhurriedly, they moved to a spot out in the open where a passer-by could not fail to notice them.

Once more they sat down and waited.

The clatter of the hard toeless feet of the yeraman gave them the first sign that the makaron were returning.

They stood up in full view, eyes searching for the dogs. It was important for their plan that the dogs should give chase before the makaron had time to move swiftly in with their yeraman. Yes – they were again lucky! The huge beasts were closer to them than the yeraman!

Buruda and Wungul began to lope in the direction of the scrub. Suddenly there was a loud yell from one of the makaron, and at the same time there was an unearthly deep sound from both the dogs. Looking back over their shoulders, the two saw that the dogs were already racing full speed in their direction.

Their lope then took on the appearance of a race for life. But they had been on this ground for days now, and it was as familiar to them as the floor of their huts back at the creek. Every rock was a friend to them, and they simply flew over the ground. They could hear the howling of the dogs behind them, the sounds coming ever closer. And even above these sounds could be heard the clatter of the feet of the yeraman as the yelling makaron urged them to greater efforts.

Then the scrub reached out its protecting arms and they ran for the clear space where they had earlier left the remainder of their weapons, dodging in and out among the vines and the trees as if they presented no impediment to their progress.

The two grinned at each other as they heard the dogs crashing through the dense scrub behind them. These animals were much more used to hunting in the open, as they had suspected.

They were still breathing easily as they reached the clearing and turned to face the animals, their clubs at the ready.

But not everything went as they had expected. Both slavering dogs chose to spring at Buruda, and even as his club cracked the skull of one, the other had fastened its jaws onto his left leg.

But before the animal could start that tearing, rending action described so vividly by the Yuggera, Wungul's club had put an end to its life and the jaws relaxed their hold.

Both men bent to pick up their spears and melted quietly into the surrounding undergrowth. They knew that the makaron, if they followed the dogs, would be on foot. The scrub was no place for a yeraman.

But the makaron had gone quiet. Where the hunted men had earlier been able to hear them crashing along after the dogs, there was now nothing but silence.

They were obviously wondering why the dogs were no longer making a noise.

Suddenly Wungul jumped as he heard the sound of a dog growling savagely, for all the world as if it had its quarry by the throat. Were there other dogs, then? Surely the odds were now too great for them!

He looked across toward where he knew Buruda had gone into hiding - and then he understood! His brother was standing where he could see him, and the growls were coming from Buruda's throat!

Buruda did not intend that the makaron should return to their yeraman until they had come to see what their dogs had caught!

Gleefully Wungul added his contribution to the growling, and Buruda once more became invisible. The sounds of approaching makaron could again be heard as they crashed through the scrub toward the growls.

Now the two makaron made no attempt to hide their approach. They obviously knew that they would have no need to worry about the bu-ul their dogs had come up against! They knew those growls of old!

They did not even have time to level their two small thunder-sticks. The swish of the thrown spears was the last sound they heard on this earth.

Afterwards the two found the yeraman standing at the edge of the scrub. But both animals were able to break free before either of the men could launch a spear, and careered off in the direction the makaron had been heading before the chase had begun.

That night they talked long, deeply satisfied with the result of their plan. Wungul even suggested that the two of them could put on a play about today's fight to amuse the people gathered at the coming bunyi festival. He thought the people would appreciate the growling of the dogs!

Buruda's leg was painful, and he put some healing leaves and clay on the wound to ease it. But they knew that the makaron would not ignore this day's happenings. They would need to shift their camp as soon as they could see tomorrow.

Next morning they moved as early as they could. But, while it was important to vacate their present position quickly because the makaron would surely be here soon, it was also essential that they move only when the dark of the scrub lightened enough for them to see clearly. For it would be fruitless to leave the place if they left signs for anyone to follow.

They moved with care, every step studied. Every now and again one or the other would retreat a step to replace a leaf disturbed by their last movement. About mid-morning they heard, in the direction from which they had come, the sound of a thunder-stick.

The dead makaron had been discovered. And still they refused to be hurried, looking always as much in the direction of the last step as to the next one.

By mid-afternoon they were satisfied. They had left all sounds of pursuit far behind, and were far from the scene of yesterday's battle. And they were certain that nobody would be able to follow their tracks.

"I doubt that even Turugun could follow us here!" Buruda grinned. "I don't remember ever being so careful before!"

"You never had to be so careful before!" Wungul reminded him. "This is the first time we have had to act as though we are ashamed of killing vermin!"

"No!" Buruda let out a curse. "We have always been able to walk with our heads up! Whenever we had an enemy, we were pleased that he could see us, so that we could do battle on the baiyaba as bu-ul have done since the Before-Time!"

For days they did not move from their new temporary shelter except to procure food. There were still plenty of pademelons to be had, for they had not been affected by the arrival of the dhipa, which did not feed in the scrub. And it was in the scrub that the pademelon made his home.

Buruda had to use part of the time to tend the bite on his leg. By the second day it became swollen and red, and he had to use his knife to let out the pus that had formed in the flesh. He used hot clay and eagle's down to poultice it after he had lanced it, and by the fourth day he was once again able to walk without a limp.

Three days later he said, "The makaron ought to have given up the hunt for us by now. Tomorrow we will go and see where else we can strike!"

They found their target two days later. There was a makaron hut in the forest that was obviously used by a watcher of the dhipa. Before the hut were tracks of one makaron with a yeraman and one dog, and the tracks told the two that the makaron had been there that morning. There was a gully not far from the hut, and they would wait there for his return.

But the owner of the hut did not return that day. Bigi sank below the mountains, and there was still no sign of a yeraman approaching from any direction. Buruda motioned to Wungul, and they swiftly made their way to their shelter in the scrub-covered hills.

"This one may see the end of it!" Buruda said as they warmed themselves beside the fire. "Our dead will have had their debt repaid when we have seen this makaron dead! After that we can take our Dimmangali's bones back to our own land!"

"But we will wait for this one as long as we have to!" Wungul said. "This looks as good a place as any to kill our last makaron!"

Next day their vigil was rewarded. From their hiding-place in the scrubby gully they saw not one, but four makaron on yeraman, and with them a large number of dhipa – more dhipa than they had ever seen before.

Buruda looked across at Wungul and shook his head. "There are too many for us!" he whispered. "They don't have any of those huge dogs, certainly, but this is no place to fight a battle against makaron with thunder-sticks and yeraman! We are too far from the scrub!"

They watched the makaron tie their yeraman to a stick in front of the hut, and soon smoke was rising from the hole in the top. But only one makaron had gone inside. The others stood around talking to each other and looking at the dhipa and the dogs that were guarding the animals. Then the makaron who had gone inside came out again, and they all sat on logs drinking their smoking water.

Buruda was starting to get worried. They were all right while they remained concealed in the gully. But if they had to move for any reason, they would be in the open and within range of the thunder-sticks. There was no way they could retreat from their present position without being killed, for the makaron on their yeraman could easily run them down before they could ever hope to reach the protection of the scrub.

"Too many makaron!" Buruda muttered again.

And Wungul nodded. "Too many!"

They would have to remain motionless in the gully all day. And it was yet only mid-morning!

Bigi passed his highest point and began his downward journey, and still they kept their position. Buruda's leg began to hurt, but he ignored it. The makaron got on their yeraman and went out to the dhipa, but they did not go far enough away to allow the two to make a break from the gully and head for the scrub.

Buruda blamed himself. He had been so sure there would be only one!

And it was as if Wungul had read his thoughts. "There was the track of only one makaron!" he muttered.

The dhipa moved back towards the direction of the gully, eating the grass as they went. The dogs and the makaron on their yeraman followed them. The two in the gully started to get really anxious.

The dhipa got closer – too close!

A single dhipa moved toward the very spot where the two were hiding, and one of the dogs followed it. But the dhipa would not be told by a dog where to go, and ran down into the gully. At the same time a makaron yelled and came clattering along on his yeraman to bring the dhipa back.

As he came face to face with the two in the gully, his face showed shocked surprise. But the surprise gave way to a blank look as two spears pierced his body and he tumbled to the ground.

But the other makaron were already yelling as he fell, and the thunder of the feet of their yeraman told the two that there was no time for hesitation. Grabbing their weapons, they raced up the gully in the direction of the scrub. But, as they had known from the start, they had too far to go.

The thunder came, and Buruda heard the stones from the weapons hitting the bushes round his head. But Wungul seemed to trip, and dropped to the ground.

Buruda turned. He knew that his brother would never trip, that the thunder-sticks had indeed killed him. And before Buruda's eyes there appeared a blood-red mist, and like an old man kangaroo that had been driven beyond endurance, he stood at bay.

And suddenly everything seemed to be moving so slowly. The yeraman no longer seemed so close. The makaron did not appear to be lifting their thunder-sticks quite so swiftly to their shoulders. And his arm as it launched his fighting boomerang at the nearest makaron did not seem to launch it with its usual strength.

He was even surprised to see that it nearly decapitated the makaron it struck.

Somehow, almost unaware, his arm launched a spear, but the yeraman reared and it struck the animal in the throat.

The scream of the animal as it threw its rider mingled with Buruda's roar.

"Makaron!" he yelled, as he launched yet another spear, which took the falling makaron in the chest. "Accursed makaron! Die, makaron!"

He did not feel the stone from the thunder-stick that hit him as he grabbed for his throwing-club.

He did not hear the swish of Turugun's spear as it passed him and took the last makaron in the belly.

But before his eyes had completely glazed, he thought he saw Wungul holding his bloody head where the stone from the thunder-stick had grazed it.

He thought he heard Turugun weeping and saying, "Oh, Buruda! Why did you hide your tracks so well that it took me too long to find you? Oh, Buruda!"

And he thought he heard himself gasp, "Not Buruda, my son! Dimmangali! Dimmangali! Speak my name no more!"

He did not hear Wungul and Turugun begin the death-wail.

But he did see a most marvellous sight - his own land, the land of the Undanbi – spread out under him, as he floated through the air toward the spot on the headland at Caloundra where he would jump off to join the Undanbi spirits of the ages.

He could distinctly hear the deep, throbbing heartbeat of the earth, and he had a feeling that nothing had ever been as perfect as everything was at that very moment!

And like a sudden flash of light came the revelation that, whatever the makaron did or did not do, there would always be Undanbi people!

He could even hear them singing!

Epilogue

It may seem to the readers that the ending could have been a lot more pleasant than the one I have given this story. But I would like those readers to remember that the ending of many of the stories of the Aboriginal people alive at the time of the invasion of their country was not very pleasant. So I make no apology for the ending.

Indeed, I believe that I have correctly shown that, even though vanquished, Buruda saw at the moment of his passing that his people would continue to survive and prosper in a country that still belonged to them, even though they no longer had the exclusive right to it. The invaders might shoot and poison the people and rape the land, but the country would always remain faithful to its task of caring for the people who had so carefully cared for the land itself since the Before-Time.

That is what Buruda thought, and I do, too.

My hope is that we invaders will properly learn to respect and honour those indigenous people whose land we stole. It is all very well to say that invasion at the time was inevitable, because that is the way the world was then. It is all very well also to state that any other nation (e.g. France or Germany) might have been even harder on the Aborigines.

But all that does not alter the fact that dispossession, massacres and poisonings did occur, to the shame of us all. And the diseases we invaders brought certainly did not help.

I think it may have been better if an Aborigine had written this book. But at the time of writing, I had access to some small number of history books, all of which looked at their stories from the point of view of non-Aboriginals.

I thought it was about time we looked at it from the indigenous point of view.

I still do.

Select Bibliography

Berndt, R.M. & Berndt, C.H., 1977, *The World of the First Australians.* Ure Smith, Sydney. (2nd Ed.)

Dawson, Ailsa R. (Undated), *Early Chronicles of Cypress Land*, (Viewed in Caloundra City Library)

Dwyer, B. & Buchanan, N.,1986, *The Rescue of Eliza Fraser*, Noosa Graphica.

Foxon, C. (Ed.), 1985, *A Bonyi Gathering*, Maroochy Local History Project.

Holthouse, Hector, 1978, *Illustrated History of Queensland*, Rigby Ltd., Sydney, N.S.W.

Holthouse, Hector, 1985, *Up Rode the Squatter. Outback Classics Edition*, Angus & Robertson, NorthRyde, N.S.W.

Montagu, Ashley, 1974, *Coming into Being among the Australian Aborigines*, Routledge & Kegan Paul, London. (2nd Ed.)

Petrie, Constance Campbell, 1975, *Tom Petrie's Reminisences of Early Queensland*, Lloyd O'Neil Pty.Ltd., Hawthorn, Australia.

Queensland Ethnohistory Transcripts. Vol. 1, No. 1. Book 1, The Aboriginal Perspective. (Includes statements by escaped convicts, and "The Gaiarbau Story")

Steele, J.G., 1972, *The Explorers of the Moreton Bay District. 1770-1830*, University of QueenslandPress, St. Lucia, Queensland.

Steele, J.G., 1975, *Brisbane Town in Convict Days.1824-1842*, University of Queensland Press, St. Lucia, Queensland.

Steele, J.G., 1984, *Aboriginal Pathways in Southeast Queensland and the Richmond River.*University of Queensland Press, St. Lucia, Queensland.

Watson, F.H. (Undated), *Vocabularies of Four Representative Tribes of South-Eastern Queensland*, Supplement to Journal of the Royal Geographical Society of Australasia (Queensland)No. 34, Vol. XLVIII.

Winterbotham, L.P. (Undated), *The Gaiarbau Story.* (In The Aboriginal Perspective above)

✦

List of Peoples Mentioned in the Text

The following list does not attempt to set "boundaries" for the nations named. Indeed, some of the nations could rightfully be considered to be sub-sections of other nations mentioned. The list is intended simply to give the reader some inkling of the areas involved whenever these nations are mentioned in the story.

Nation	Location
Badtjala	Mid Fraser Island and adjacent mainland
Baiyambora	Yabba Creek
Carburrah	Lake Cootharabah
Dallambara	Blackall Range
Dhepara	Eight Mile Plains
Dhindhinbara	Inland from Wide Bay
Dhundubari	Bribie Island
Dhungwubera	Mt. Tuchekoi
Dulingbara	South Fraser Island and adjacent mainland
Dungibara	Esk, Moore
Dungidau	Kilcoy

Garumngar	D'Aguilar Range
Gnalungpin	Wynnum
Gunibara	Darling Downs
Kombobura	Noosa River
Kubenpil	Wellington Point
Kurpuru	Coorpooroo
Nalbo	Glasshouse Mountains
Ngulungbara	North Fraser Island
Ningi	Redcliffe, Toorbul
Nunakul	Stradbroke Island
Tumbra	Maroochy River
Turrbal	Brisbane
Undanbi	Coastal area from Mooloolah River to Glasshouse Creek (for our present purposes)
Wuganbara	Not known. Bracewell mentions them as losing 30 members in the Kilcoy poisoning.
Yugumbir	Gold Coast hinterland
Yuggera	Ipswich west to the Dividing Range

List of Places Mentioned in the Text

BagaBaga	Mt. Barney
Banda-Mardo	Scott's Point (undoubtedly from "bando" - white clay, which can still be seen there)
Baneraba	Toowong
Baroon	Blackall Range
Barrambin	York's Hollow (present Exhibition Grounds and Victoria Park)
Beerburrum	One of the Glasshouse Mountains
Beerwah	One of the Glasshouse Mountains (lit. "Up in the sky")
Binkinba	New Farm
Binngi	Waddy Point, Fraser Island
Buderim	Buderim Mountain
Bulan	Amity Point, Stradbroke Island
Bumgur	Kilcoy
Buyuba	Newmarket
Caloundra	Caloundra. (lit. "Place of the beech log") In 1944, Clarrie Diefenbach was told by Jack Grigor that an old Aborigine had informed him that this was the name after the coming of the white man, who cut beech logs and floated them down Pumicestone Channel.

Coochin	Coochin Creek
Coonowrin	One of the Glasshouse Mountains ("Crookneck")
Coolum	Mt. Coolum
Currimundi	Lake Currimundi (lit. "Place of the flying-fox")
Daki-Bomon	Glasshouse Creek (lit. "Stone standing up")
Dhalgumbun	Mt. Lindesay
Dhini	Mt.Kilcoy
Doomben	Pinkenba
Durundur	Near Woodford
Gallanani	Mt.Esk
Gibunba	Northern side of Deception Bay
Goanumbi	Grantham
Gudhabila	Grandchester
Gullirae	Double Island Point
Gumpi	Dunwich, Stradbroke Island
Gunundhin	Junction of Brisbane and Stanley Rivers
Kaerwagum	Pumicestone Channel
Kalen-Kalen	Wellington Point
Kannangur	Yimbun
Karah	Inskip Point
Kauin-Kauin	Redcliffe (lit. "Blood-red")
K'Gari	Fraser Island (Badtjala name)
Kow-Woi	Indian Head, Fraser Island
Kungalba	Yandina
Kunyinnira	Mt. Mitchell, Cunningham's Gap
Kupidabin	Samford
Kuroignkuroignpa	Flying Fox Creek, Stradbroke Island
Kuturrumba	Scarborough

Mairwar	Part of Brisbane River (name given by Dungidau people)
Maroochy	Maroochy River
Miandhin	Brisbane (Central Business District)
Milgero	Laidley
Mirbarpa	Indooroopilly
Mudjimba	Mudjimba or Old Woman Island
Mooloolah	Mooloolah River
Nalbo Mountains	Glasshouse Mountains (Name used to show position)
Nambour	Nambour (lit. "Red-flowered paper-bark")
Niamboyu	Mt. Cordeaux, Cunningham's Gap
Ninderry	Mt. Ninderry (lit. "Leech")
NingiNingi	Toorbul Point
Noosa	Noosa Heads (called "Nguthuru" by the Gubbi people)
Nulu	Long Island (in Pumicestone Channel)
Nundah	Nundah (lit. "Chain of water-holes")
Obi Obi	ObiObi Creek
Pirrenpirrenpa	Small sandhill at Amity, Stradbroke Island
Pundhagin	Mt. French
Tambal	Woody Point
Tungulba	Hay's Inlet
Unbounba	Campbell Point (Southern tip of Moreton Island)
Urarrar	Bremer River
Warudhra	Landsborough
Warun	Humpybong, site of first settlement
Woorim	Northern tip of Bribie Island (Name at present given to southern tip)

Wungar	Moore
Yabarba	Helidon
Yabba	Yabba Creek
Yarun	Bribie Island
Yowoggera	Breakfast Creek

Dictionary of Words Used

(Gubbi words unless otherwise indicated)

Notes on Pronunciation:

1) Generally, the first syllable is accented, although there are exceptions.

2) "a" is pronounced either like "u" in "mud" or "a" in 'father".

   "e" is either like the "e" in "yet" or the "ai" in "mail".

   "i" is like the "i" in "it" or the "ee" in "feel".

   "o" is like the "o" in "got" or the "oa" in "boat".

   "u" is like the "oo" in "foot" or the "oo" in "boot".

   "ai" has the sound of "eye".

3) dh: Watson says, "This consonant may be nearly pronounced by attempting to sound the initial letter in the English word jam without touching the palate with the tongue, thus converting it from a palatal to a dental. (The) articulation of this consonant was so characteristic of Aboriginal utterance that the late Mr. W.E. Parry-Okeden called it 'The Shibboleth of the Aborigines'."

Ariro!	Exclamation of surprise or wonder or grief, according to vocal inflection
Arum!	(As "Ariro!")
baiyaba	fighting ground
Balkuin	male marital class name
Balkuingan	female marital class name
bangwal	fern root (blechnumserralatum)
Barang	male marital class name
Baranggan	female marital class name
barpul	Wakka name for Queensland nut (macadamia ternifolia)
barrum	Queensland nut
Bigi	the sun (Yugara word, widely used in south-east Queensland)
binang	female genital
birra	the sky
birral	God (lit. "in the sky" – perhaps the result of early mission work)
bondaban	bull-roarer, a ceremonial noise-making instrument
Bulla	two
bulla-bira	chain lightning
bulla bulla	four
bulla kalim	three
bunbithin	suck
Bunda	male marital class name
Bundagan	female marital class name
Buran	wind
buruda	forest oak tree (Yugara language)

bu-ul	man who has passed the major man-making ceremony
dai-arli	tailer fish (corrupted by whites to "tailer")
degga	white man (Dhandai language)
dhagun	earth
dhakkin	rainbow; spirit of the rainbow
dhan	man (so called by the Undanbi)
dhandai	no (Dhandai language)
dhilla	bag of woven hair, grass or reeds
dhugai	white man (lit. "ghost", Yugara language)
dhuluru	early
dhun	penis; male genital
dhundharin	male beneficent spirit (Watson gives as "junjarin", the only 'j' in his list of Gubbi words)
dhur	major man-making ceremony (lit. "circle"); also called "bu-ul"
Dhuroin	male marital class name
Dhuroingan	female marital class name
Dibing	fly; mosquito; any small-winged creature
Dibing	white-flowered tea-tree, or paper-bark
dimmangali	sacred or tabu (Yugara word widely used in south-east Queensland)
dinda	peewee
Diraiyirki	morning star
E-e-e-e-e-e-e!	expression of approval or regret, according to vocal inflection
gilla	native bee; its honey
gimpi	stinging tree (also its bark and the cloth made by pounding the bark)

girraman	flying fox or fruit bat
Gogindi!	exclamation of surprise or wonder
gubbi	no; not; nothing; nowhere
guligba	vine with white under leaves, used for various medicinal purposes (mentioned by Gaiarbau)
guluwa	moonlight
gurwindha	number greater than four (many)
gutji	ground or grass goanna
idh	a dog call
kakka	platform of inverted wattle-tree used in initiation ceremonies
kakkar	spiny ant-eater; echidna
kalim	one
kambo	cobra or teredo (marine borer, an edible grub)
kin-bumbe	duel; a fight over a woman
kindelkindle	another name for the Queensland nut
kira	fire
kiraba	camp (lit. "place of the fire")
kirami	camp (lit. "place of the fire")
kivar	young man. (also called "kippa")
kivar-yangga	ceremony initiating boys to manhood
koala	native bear (also "goala")
kui	loud call to attract attention (pronounced "cooee")
kundir	magic quartz crystal (also "gundir")
kuruman	large adult male kangaroo
kurumbul	magpie
kutdhin	red clay

kuwir	stone curlew
magum	blue water-lily; its edible root (nymphoea gigantea)
mairwar	platypus (Wakka language)
makaron	evil spirit (name given to white man by the Gubbi people)
manngur	doctor (Gaiarbau says this Gubbi word means "He's got something!")
maroochy	black swan (from "murukutji" – lit. "red nose"- a Yugara word widely used in the region. TheGubbi word "kuluin" was also used.)
mei	Moreton Bay chestnut (castanospermumAustrale)
merbung	net for catching kangaroos
midyim	an edible green-spotted, sweet berry
minkom	black crystal used in magic (Gaiarbau says this crystal was used for evil purposes)
moi	white man (Wakka language)
mugara	thunder (Yugara language)
mula	fishing net
mullu	red-bellied black snake
mumba	thunder
murunmurun	game played by bouncing a specially-shaped stick along the ground. (The Wakka name for this game was "ngoi ngoi".)
muthar	spider
nara	hello (See "n'gara")
naruman	kick
nerida	blossom
n'gara	hello (See "nara")

ngita	easy pace
nguin	charcoal; black
nguin	boy
nguruin	emu
nguruingan	summertime; time of heat (One cannot help wondering if this season was so named because it was connected in some way with the female emu.)
nulla mumu	anus (lit. "hole in the buttocks")
pikki	palm tree (The flower-sheath, also called "pikki" was used as a water-container.)
purru	ball
purrupurru	ball game
talobilla	dolphin (Yugara language)
tilgonda	collared sparrow-hawk
wa!	No, no! By no means!
wabbalkan	small bull-roarer (Yugara language)
wakka	no (Wakka language)
wallaidhau	winter (lit. "time of intense cold")
Wapa	name given by coastal Aborigines to inland dwellers, by reason of the latter's slow and gentle speech in contrast with the quick emphatic speech of the former. (The inland Aborigines called those on the coast "Bidhali".)
warawara	game of cat's cradle
warawara	fence (so called because early "dog-leg" fences resembled the figures in that game)
winnam	breadfruit or pandanus tree
wundu	testes

wuruma	sea eagle (red with white head)
yau	yes
yau-ai	yes
yeraman	horse (an introduced word)
yeran	beard
yingu-yingu	soldier crab
yugara	no (Yugara language)
yugari	shellfish (still used in the region for the "pippy")
yugum	no (Yugum language)
yurra	vine used as a rope for climbing trees

Aborigines Mentioned in the Text Who Have Historical Reality

Name	People
Bomarigo	Dhundubari
Bongari (Bongaree)	Around Sydney
Bogi	Yugumbir
Korbenbob	Yugumbir
Maltagara (Multuggerah)	Yuggera
Meredeo	Yugumbir
Nganku	Dhundubari (called "Doctor" by Uniacke)
Yuonmandi (Uwenmundi)	Kombobura
Yelyelbah	Dhundubari

Escaped Convicts Mentioned in the Text

Aboriginal Name	**English Name**
Boraltju	John Baker
Daramboi (Durramboi)	James Davis
Moilu	John Graham
Wandi	David Bracewell

Please accept my apologies for any inaccuracies this book may contain.

I am 95 years old now, and this book was written when there was very little information online. Most was gained from books available at the time, and while I have attempted to update that information as best I can, errors will no doubt remain.

I hope that, despite these inaccuracies, I have been able to depict in some way the confusion the indigenous peoples of South-East Queensland felt at the time of white settlement in the area, and the atrocities they faced at the hands of these "invaders".

If I have been able to do that, then I have achieved what I set out to do.